The Essential
J. Frank Dobie

Edited and with an Introduction by
STEVEN L. DAVIS

TEXAS A&M UNIVERSITY PRESS ⊚ COLLEGE STATION

Library of Congress Cataloging-in-Publication Data

Names: Dobie, J. Frank (James Frank), 1888–1964 author. | Davis,
    Steven L. editor, writer of introduction
Title: The essential J. Frank Dobie / J. Frank Dobie ; edited and
    with an Introduction by Steven L. Davis.
Description: First. | College Station : Texas A&M University Press
    2019. | Series: Wittliff Collections literary series.
Identifiers: LCCN 2019021683 | ISBN 9781623498016 (cloth) | ISBN
    9781623498023 (ebook)
Classification: LCC PS3507.O1833 A6 2019 | DDC 818/.5209—dc23
LC record available at https://lccn.loc.gov/2019021683

For Bill & Sally Wittliff

Contents

Part 6. Wild and Free

Part 7. Europe Amid Two World Wars

Part 8. Texas Needs Brains

Part 9. Life and Literature of the Southwest

The Essential
J. Frank Dobie

Introduction

Why an Essential Dobie?

CORMAC McCARTHY, hailed as one of the world's greatest writers, is the one who finally turned me on to what an excellent writer J. Frank Dobie could be. Even though I'd published a biography on Dobie that tried to explain how he achieved his "liberated mind,"[*] I'd never really come to terms with him as a writer. I'd blithely absorbed too many anti-Dobie prejudices. Most notable among them came via Larry McMurtry, who scorched the freshly dead Dobie in a 1968 essay and then returned in 1981 to kick more dirt over his grave, judging Dobie's output "a congealed mass of virtually undifferentiated anecdotage: endlessly repetitious, thematically empty, structureless, and carelessly written."

McMurtry was joined by literary critics opining that Dobie's success had been mostly an accident, due more to "his cleverness as a self-promoter" than any innate literary talent. A *Texas Monthly* editor derided Dobie's books as "bedtime stories for boys in junior high." A flock of academics began excoriating Dobie as a racist, completely disregarding his courageous battles for civil rights that began as far back as the 1920s and ultimately led to his firing from UT-Austin after he called for integrating the university in the 1940s.

---

[*] *J. Frank Dobie: A Liberated Mind*, 2009.

Within twenty years of Dobie's death, his literary reputation had become, in the words of one scholar, "a heap of rusted,
abandoned scrap metal." When I took my own master's degree in
English in the 1990s—and, like J. Frank Dobie, I concluded there
was no profit in continuing on for a PhD—nothing was less stylish
in academia than J. Frank Dobie.

The truth is that literary scholars are as subject to the whims
of fashion as any pimple-faced teenager mobbing the latest pop
music sensation. This fact is amply demonstrated by the maze
of trendy literary theories that have swept through academia
in recent decades, each supplanting the next in momentary
appeal, and each, incidentally, requiring ideological contortions
that carry all the charm of one of Stalin's five-year-plans—and
demanding much the same regurgitation of prescribed dogma.

Happily for Dobie, he hasn't had to rely on English professors to keep his work alive. Instead, a steady group of readers,
sustaining itself generation after generation, has found its way to
Dobie's books, keeping his flame burning.

Along with the readers have been the writers. Larry McMurtry's
criticisms of Dobie notwithstanding, McMurtry has perhaps
borrowed more heavily from Dobie than any novelist, particularly
in crafting his masterwork, *Lonesome Dove*. Beyond McMurtry,
dozens of other significant writers from Texas and the West have
profited by consulting Dobie. Bud Shrake's *Blessed McGill*, also
considered one of the finest southwestern novels, has at its heart
a search for the Lost Tayopa Mine, which Shrake developed from
Dobie's account collected in these pages.

These novelists recognized that Dobie captured priceless
social history—and he did so at a time when most historians
accounted for the past by analyzing the military exploits of a few
"great men." Dobie was less interested in violence and battles
than he was in the far more complex and interesting questions of
how human beings manage to live among one another. In this view
of history, he was far ahead of his time, as he was in so many other
ways.

Dobie also had matchless personal adventures that later
writers could only dream of. He rode on rough trails through

open country, traveling hundreds of miles "without seeing a pane of window glass or going through a pasture gate." He joined searchers who'd staked their lives on finding fabled lost treasures. He met and heard the stories of Old West legends such as Charles Goodnight, who at age ninety-one thought enough of Dobie to send him a buffalo roast for Christmas. Dobie helped rescue the Longhorn and bighorn sheep from extinction in Texas, he helped inspire Big Bend National Park and Padre Island National Seashore, he slipped across the Spanish border to visit Basque villagers at the end of World War I, he dodged German VI bombs in England during World War II, he traveled throughout defeated Nazi Germany and toured Hitler's Chancellery (since demolished), and then came back to Texas to take on governors, senators, university regents—anyone who was an enemy to intellectual freedom or denied equal opportunities to others. He ended up being investigated by J. Edgar Hoover's FBI, feted by Lyndon Johnson's White House, and, ultimately, presented with the Presidential Medal of Freedom, the nation's highest civilian honor, just four days before he died in 1964.

In assessing the scope of Dobie's writing from today's perspective, it's easy enough to see that he was an eloquent witness to the end of ancient pastoral lifeways as they were being relentlessly crushed by an aggressive technological blitzkrieg. Dobie's sympathetic yet perceptive observations of the natural world, along with his criticisms of the machine age, seem to me as appropriate as ever. The machine age, for all its dominance, has never answered the questions Dobie raises.

While working on my biography of Dobie, I'd often come across passages of his that struck me as really fine writing—sentences and paragraphs that carried a powerful clarity of expression. Such prose was clearly indicative of a consciously sophisticated writer. I began to save some of these and share them with family and friends, all of us exclaiming on their merit.

But these were just isolated episodes, because I was reading Dobie in those days mostly to mine biographical data. Still, as I finished work on that book, I sensed there was more to Dobie's writing than I had tapped into.

Over the next few years I occasionally stumbled across other Dobie writings that seemed to me to sparkle with vitality. I also found myself attending the annual "Dobie Dichos" gatherings at the historic ghost town of Oakville, Texas, not far from where Dobie was born. Here, on an outdoor stage underneath the live oaks, writers and storytellers present Dobie's work to capacity crowds, year after year. The brainchild of Bill Sibley, himself a talented wordsmith, along with the dynamic Mary Margaret Campbell, "Dobie Dichos" is part of the annual George West Storyfest. For me, it was eye-opening to see how Dobie's writing continues to delight audiences.

Gradually, my respect and appreciation for Dobie as a writer was growing. And then I stumbled into the connection between Cormac McCarthy and J. Frank Dobie that changed everything.

The Wittliff Collections, where I work as the southwestern literature curator, was founded by Bill and Sally Wittliff with a gift of J. Frank Dobie materials. (Bill was a protégé of Dobie's and he in turn sparked my own interest in Dobie.) The Wittliff has grown and flourished over the years and now holds the archives of many other leading writers from the region, including Cormac McCarthy—winner of the Pulitzer Prize, National Book Award, and lauded as a genius by literary scholars around the world.

McCarthy is known to spend a decade or more composing his novels. At the Wittliff, I spent an afternoon examining McCarthy's research files for his novel, *The Crossing*. It is no secret that McCarthy, like other novelists of the Southwest, has borrowed extensively from Dobie. In McCarthy's archive I found a Dobie article about Babícora, William Randolph Hearst's sprawling, controversial ranch in Chihuahua that was twice the size of Texas's King Ranch. Dobie had visited Babícora in the 1930s, and his article became one of the very few firsthand reports on the ranch ever published.

McCarthy made exacting pencil marks in the margins of Dobie's story, and he relied on it substantially. He developed characters based on real-life people in Dobie's article, particularly that of Lupe Quijada, a college-educated Yaqui Indian who managed a section of the ranch. McCarthy's portrait of Quijada is so faithful to Dobie's that he even retained the man's original name in the novel.

Most notably—to my eyes—some of McCarthy's descriptions in *The Crossing* are nearly identical to Dobie's original language. For example, Dobie commented on the vaqueros who work at the ranch: "They were called mascarias—white-faces, mascaria being the Mexican name for white-faced cattle—the Babícora breed. They were also taunted as agringados—gringo lovers."

Cormac McCarthy, in *The Crossing*, writes: "They were called mascareñas for the whitefaced cattle bred on the Babícora and they were called agringados because they worked for the white man."

Here is the question I asked myself while comparing the two passages: "Why would one of the world's greatest writers feel compelled to borrow, nearly word for word, the writing of a man so often condemned as a half talent at best?" Also, not to insult McCarthy, but Dobie's passage strikes me as the more flavorful of the two.

That's when everything I'd been learning about Dobie came together. Sure, he was often too casual in his prose, but his writing could also be magnificent. Many times, however, this brilliance was concealed by his relish of meandering detail—a holdover from the oral storytelling tradition he'd grown up with. Once you prune away the brushy overgrowth, Dobie's writing often shines with a ripe, luminous beauty.

This book, then, is the result of that realization. I have read through Dobie's work again—this time with a literary eye—to select the most vital and enduring of his works, writings that speak to our time as much as they spoke to his.

I looked mainly for stories that only Dobie could tell—those enriched by his unique personal experiences and adventures. I also scouted for his key pieces on the natural world, social justice, and other areas where he best applied his formidable perceptions. Some of these writings come from his previously published books. Others have never before appeared in book form. Still others, drawn from the Dobie Papers at the Wittliff Collections, are published here for the very first time.

The most difficult part of assembling this was having to leave so many notable pieces out—including the Babícora article, which just missed the final cut. I also had to exclude Dobie classics like "Juan Oso: Bear Nights in Mexico" along with his account of Charles Goodnight's lead steer, "Old Blue," and much more, such as his famous essay, "Divided We Stand," which defended labor's right to strike during World War II and exposed the giant corporations that had quietly cooperated with Hitler. Some of those old political battles, while fascinating in the heat of the moment, are more temporal than eternal. For that reason, such works—while an important part of Dobie's biography—are only sparingly included in this volume.

In addition to being an *Essential Dobie*, this is an "Edited Dobie." In this regard, I've followed the methods employed by his wife, Bertha, who edited his work with an eye to economy and structure. Most often, I've simply deleted unnecessary words and reined in Dobie's desire to bushwhack up thicket-choked side trails. I've also reordered sentences or paragraphs here and there. I've also condensed some pieces, not necessarily because they needed it but so that I could also fit other works into this volume. In some cases, I've stitched together his separate writings, usually from his newspaper columns or magazine articles, to create new stand-alone pieces. (See "Story Credits" at the end of this book for a complete list of all original sources.) On extremely rare occasions I've added a word or two to supply a fresh hinge. I've also changed a small handful of words[*] to reflect more contemporary understandings.

---

[*] In Dobie's time, "Mexican" was the standard usage among Anglo-Americans for people of Mexican ancestry, no matter which side of the border they lived on. Américo Paredes has written eloquently on the problems with the word "Mexican" as spoken by Anglo Texans: "In Spanish mexicano has a full and prideful sound. The mouth opens on the full vowels and the voice acquires a certain dignity in saying mexicano." (See *George Washington Gómez: A Mexicotexan Novel*, 118.) I feel certain that Dobie would agree, and I've substituted "Mexicano" for "Mexican" when appropriate.

❖   ◎   ❖

While I've brushed some of the dust from his prose, this is Puro Dobie, distilled to his essence. My hope is that these stories will interest and delight you as much as they have me. I also hope that the quality of writings collected here will help all of us arrive at a more balanced judgment of Dobie's literary merit—which in the end is far greater than he's previously been given credit for.

Bertha Dobie once observed, "I should say that in Frank, pig, charging bull, and mule together make a half, and that the other half is humanity at its very finest." Plenty of people have criticized Dobie's less exalted qualities, myself among them. This book chooses to focus on the best half of Dobie—and I agree with Bertha that it represents "humanity at its very finest."

As the following works will indicate, the spirit of Dobie is as alive as ever. May you be nourished by it.

PART 1

Coyote Wisdom

Many times I have thought that the greatest happiness possible is to become civilized, to know the pageant of the past, to love the beautiful, to have just ideas of values and proportions, and then, retaining animal spirits and appetites, to live in a wilderness.—JFD

This, I Believe

In 1952, Dobie recorded a segment for "This, I Believe,"* a popular radio show hosted by journalist Edward R. Murrow. I've collected some of Dobie's other quotes and threaded them into the best of his original remarks, creating this expanded version of what Dobie believes.—SD

W E BELIEVE IN what we value most. I believe only free minds ever created anything beautiful.

The world's salvation will not be through more atomic bombs and warfare. It will be through clear thinking. The best thoughts and ideas of the human race are preserved in books. In books are kept the things that lead to richer living.

I feel no resentment so strongly as that against forces which make men and women afraid to speak out forthrightly. I am as much against forced literary swallowings as I am against prohibitions on free tasting, chewing, and digestion. I rate censors, particularly those of church and state, as low as I rate character assassins; they often run together.

The noblest satisfaction I have is in witnessing the progress of suppressed individuals and people. I am for human justice and decency. I know that keeping one's fellow human, no matter what color, down in ignorance is evil and undemocratic, and that such injustice results in evil to the oppressors as well as the oppressed.

I make no pretense to having rid myself of all prejudices, but

---

*The original text for Dobie's essay is online at https://thisibelieve.org/essay/16498/.

at times when I have discovered myself freed from certain prejudices, I have felt rare exhilaration.

An ignorant person attaches too much importance to the
chatter of small voices around him. The pursuit of happiness
is a natural right, but nature does not guarantee wisdom to the
pursuer. It is better to have a just sense of values unsatisfied than
to have a cheap sense of values fulfilled. No person who is even
half mature can be happy without having developed and enjoyed
resources within themselves.

There has never been a civilization without contemplation,
and for a hundred years every advance of scientific technology
has been to destroy rather than encourage contemplation. There
are no substitutes for nobility, beauty, and wisdom. The great
majority of people in this country have by now been trained not
only to accept but to clamor for new gadgets and new models of
old ones. Comparatively few want new ideas. Yet not three in a
million will be any happier inside of themselves possessing new
television sets.

Machine civilization has yet to demonstrate whether it can
create a culture that gives graciousness, depth, and tolerance
to human life. If culture amounted only to electric refrigerators,
it would make no difference who makes our songs or our laws
either.

I believe in a Supreme Power, unknowable and impersonal
that manifests itself in all living things. Yet I have no desire to
enter into the presence of any man-inspired All-Superior. I don't
have any more reverence for Christ than for Socrates or Shakespeare. I believe in questionings, doubtings, searchings, skepti-
cism, and I discredit credulity or blind faith. I see no virtue in
being meek. If the meek are going to inherit the earth they still
have a long way to go, though the weak could be a metaphor for
worms and insects, whom I expect to be the last survivors on
earth.

I am sustained by a belief in evolution—in which goodness
and wisdom and righteousness are evolving, with geological
slowness, out of the irrational. To believe that Garden of Eden

perfection lies further ahead—instead of further behind—gives me hope and somewhat explains existence.

The progress of humankind is based on questioning the commonly accepted. I'd rather starve and be independent than thrive on conformity. The noblest minds and natures of human history have thought and sung, lived and died, trying to budge the status quo.

When I was young I began associating all I could with old people to learn from them, to garner their experiences, their knowledge, their narratives and sometimes wisdom. I enjoyed their fellowship, sucked up life from it. For the same reasons I find myself now seeking younger people.

If during a decade a man does not change his mind on some things and develop new points of view, it is a pretty good sign that his mind is petrified and need no longer be accounted among the living.

Great literature transcends its native land, but none that I know of ignores its soil. You can buy objects of art, but you can't import culture. True culture harmonizes people to their own environments, and people who have it are not ashamed of their native speech; they are not aliens in their own homes.

Not all hard truths are beautiful, but beauty is truth. I have never heard a sermon as spiritual as, "Waters on a starry night are beautiful and free." No hymn lifts my heart higher than the morning call of the bobwhite or the long fluting cry of sandhill cranes out of the sky at dusk. I have never smelled incense in a church as refining to the spirit as a spring breeze laden with aroma from a field of wildflowers.

Beauty and intellectual freedom and justice are constant sustainers to my mind and spirit.

I have come to value liberated mind as the supreme good of life on earth.

How My Life Took Its Turn

The Brush Country between the Nueces River and the Rio Grande in South Texas, where I was born, is, as age goes in America, an old land, many a dry gully marking the rut made by a Spanish cart and many a title of ownership issued by the king of Spain. Mostly it is still a ranch country, arid and covered with thorned brush and prickly pear. This brush hides old, old secrets. A land that is not plowed up or cemented over and that maintains from one generation to another a pastoral outlook keeps its traditions.—JFD

ON OUR RANCH, out three miles from the house, is an ancient site known as Fort Ramirez. People say that Fort Ramirez used to be a Spanish mission. Maybe some padre did baptize wild Indians there; certainly it was the fortified stronghold of a Spanish ranchero.* According to the tradition of the country, the Ramirez people were very rich, and, of course, as there were no banks, they kept their gold and silver buried. So when they were massacred by Indians, they left their wealth for some stranger to find. Long before I was born men were digging for it; they are still digging.

For thirty years a half uncle of mine, Ed Dubose, tried to unearth it, and I suppose it was he who first introduced me to the tales and hopes and adventures of *Coronado's Children*. He

---

*See "The Buried Gold at Fort Ramirez" later in this book for more on the history of this early settlement.

and his associates had maps to silver bullion buried by ruins, on the edge of lakes, in mottes, stretching all the way from San Jacinto battlefield to the ancient church in Santa Fe. They had other charts to lost Spanish mines scattered from the lonesome hills of the San Saba to the Yaqui-guarded canyons of Sonora.

I heard the tales in snatches, and had it not been for the circumstances that arose years later they would probably have lain among many other dead memories. Furthermore, not until I was a mature man did I come to look upon the men who told the tales and participated in them, together with the ground on which they acted and to which they belonged, as being the most vital part of the narratives.

After my army service in World War I, I went back to my old job as instructor in the University of Texas. Long before this I had ascertained that the love of literature and the ability to impart that love bore no relation whatsoever to the advancement of English teachers in the "scholarly" colleges and universities of America. I'd been overseas and learned a lot. Life at the university seemed pretty tame, but that wasn't the worst. My wife and I were doing worse than starving to death on a government claim. My salary was meager, as all University of Texas salaries were at the time, but I was at the bottom of the ladder with very little prospect of getting higher up until I got a PhD degree, and I did not intend to get one.

Uncle Jim Dobie had been after me several times to go back into the cow business. He was willing to back me. One day along in the spring of 1920 he came to Austin and asked me once more why I didn't go to work for him. He owned 56,000 acres in La Salle County and leased land in La Salle, McMullen, Duval, and Webb Counties, altogether a big spread. He had a ranch down in Mexico. He had business interests in San Antonio and elsewhere. He said he wanted a kind of segundo to go around and look after his affairs. I agreed to go with him.

When spring came I resigned my job at the University of Texas and we moved to San Antonio. By this time the cattle market had begun to falter. Instead of traipsing over the country looking after varied affairs, I was managing the Olmos ranch in La Salle County, straddling the Nueces River. I had never been entirely weaned from ranch life, and I knew that I had just about reached paradise.

One of the ranch hands was named Santos Cortez. He had killed a man "on the other side" during the revolution and got to this side—the Rio Grande dividing the sides, of course. He was a good pastor (goat-herder), an indifferent vaquero, a skilled hunter, often assigned to furnish camp with venison and javelina meat, and a lover of talk. Sometimes at night he would come to my room in the ranch house to converse.

He wearied, he told me, of talk confined to the sore back of a certain horse, the low water in a certain tank, the distance a certain vaquero had run in the black chaparral out in the San Casimiro pasture before he got a glimpse of the outlaw steer he was trailing, the dry weather that had been and seemed likely to continue, and other such workaday matters. He craved conversation on higher things. Santos was a kind of freethinker and not at all orthodox in religion. "El padre tiene huevos como yo" was one of his heresies. But he believed in ghosts. That's where the intellect of a sophisticate comes in. I myself accept without reservation the ghost in Hamlet but reject the Holy Ghost as a metaphysical superstition.

One night after we had branched off on higher subjects, Santos told me of two remarkable experiences he could vouch for on a neighboring ranch. One was his own, the other a friend's. This friend was riding by the site of a long abandoned jacal one night when all of a sudden he felt the arms of a skeleton around him and realized that a ghost had dropped down from a tree under which he passed and was mounted behind him. His horse screamed in fright and broke into a run that the rider did nothing to hinder. It was about three miles to the ranch, and that skeleton clung all the way and then at the gate released its hold and disappeared.

"This did not pass with me," Santos said, "but I know it is true. I am going to tell you something that did pass with me. I have never told another. You are next to God with me, and will not laugh." When Santos became earnest in this way, there were always tears in his voice and in his eyes, too.

"Bueno. That was a lonesome camp where I kept the goats. At night only the coyotes talked, and they did not talk to me. The pastor dog slept with the goats, and I did not have even him for company.

"One night after I had been sound asleep for a while, I awoke drawing my breath in quick pants, like this. There was un bulto— a bulk—on my chest so heavy that it was smothering me. I always kept my rifle at my side. I tried to reach for it but could not move a finger. It was like I was tied down with a wet rawhide rope. Tight, man, tight! I could not raise my body to pitch the bulto off. I tried to yell. I had no breath to make a sound, and my mouth it was dry like lime. Look, my tongue would not moisten my lips. I was pinned back flat so that I could not bend my neck to see the bulto there in the dark. Pues, what could I do?"

"Then I remembered how it is said that thoughts of good will drive away the evil. I began to think of the good God and of the Holy Virgin. I thought hard, and in a little bit of while there was no bulto weighing down on me. I did not hear it run off. I did not see it. It vanished, and I was free. When daylight came and I looked for tracks, I could not find any. It is a thing I cannot explain, nor you either, though you are well instructed and have been a master in a big school. These things are not of the earth."

"They are not of the earth even when you see them. One night I was with two other men crossing the Arroyo San Casimiro at the Paso de la Gallina. And there right above the palo verde tree in which the lone gallina (chicken) used to roost, we saw a light so bright that it made my eyes go blind. Maybe it was twelve feet high, like a ball. It stayed there a little bit and then slowly, slowly it floated on down the creek. One man, thinking it would lead to gold, wanted to follow it, but it had not called my name. We stood still. It got a little dimmer, and then it just vanished, like a match that ceases to burn."

In the course of time Santos told me many other things. During the year I spent on Los Olmos ranch, while Santos talked, while Uncle Jim Dobie and other cowmen talked or stayed silent, while the coyotes sang their songs, and the sandhill cranes honked their lonely music, I seemed to be seeing a great painting of something I'd known all my life. I seemed to be listening to a great epic of something that had been commonplace in my youth but now took on meanings.

I was familiar with John A. Lomax's *Cowboy Songs and Other Frontier Ballads*. Indeed, I knew John Lomax himself very well. One day it came to me that I would collect and tell the legendary tales of Texas as Lomax had collected the old-time songs and ballads of Texas and the frontier. I thought that the stories of the range were as interesting as the songs. I considered that if they could be put down so as to show the background out of which they have come, they might have high value.

If it had not been for Uncle Jim and Los Olmos, if it hadn't been for Santos Cortez, the tale-teller, I don't know in what direction I might have gone. It was certainly lucky for me that I left the university in 1920 and learned something.

Uncle Jim went broke. The sharp decline of cattle prices beginning in 1920 broke cattlemen as the 1929 plummet broke stockholders. He and I agreed that I should go back to my old job at the University of Texas. There I helped reorganize the Texas Folklore Society, became editor of its publications, and have, since that time, been gathering, sorting, and setting down the lore of Texas and the Southwest. My academic work has been erratic and disrupted; the other has not.

I soon became as much interested in the history and legends of the Longhorn and mustang as in the traditions of old Sublett's gold in the Guadalupe Mountains. The coyote, the rattlesnake, the mesquite tree and the headless horseman of the Nueces are as interesting to me as the forty-nine jack loads of Spanish silver buried on the Colorado River just a few miles above Austin, where I live.

If people are to enjoy their own lives, they must be aware of the significances of their own environments. The mesquite is, objectively, as good and as beautiful as the Grecian acanthus. It is a great deal better for people who live in the mesquite country.

We in the Southwest shall be civilized when the roadrunner as well as the nightingale has connotations. Above all, I want to capture with their flavor, their metaphor, and their very genius the people who rode mustangs, trailed Longhorns, stuck Spanish daggers (yucca spines) in their flesh to cure rattlesnake bites, and who yet hunt for the Lost Bowie Mine on the San Saba and prospect for Breyfogle's gold in Death Valley.

For me, the best talk in the world is made up of anecdotes, pictures of highly individualistic characters, tales with "some relish of the saltness of time" in them. Consequently, I avoid as much as possible academicians with their eternal shop talk and drawing-room ornaments. I have sought the company of Mexicano goat-herders, dreamers with an eye for characters and a zest for hunting, trail drivers and people who know how to cook frijoles in a black iron pot. I belong to the soil myself, and the people of it are my people. I have certainly met many interesting talkers among them—and if they are interesting I don't care what else they are. We hear each other gladly.

Voice of the Coyote

In the year 1921 I began setting down some things I heard about Señor Coyote, but a full quarter of a century before that, while I was listening to the crickets behind the baseboards against the rock walls of our ranch home in Live Oak County, Texas, and to my mother's sweet voice, the coyote was talking to me. I did not at the time know that he was talking to me, but he was.—JFD

SYMPATHY FOR WILD ANIMALS has not been a strong element in the traditional American way of life. "I was wrathy to kill a bear," David Crockett said, and that is essentially all one learns about bears from the mightiest of frontier bear hunters—except that he killed a hundred and five in one season and immediately thereafter got elected to the Tennessee legislature on his reputation.

How familiar the iterated remark: "I thought I might see something and so took [or taken] along my gun."—as if no enjoyment or other good could come from seeing a wild animal without killing it. Buffalo Bill derived his name from the fact that he excelled in killing buffaloes, not from knowing anything about them except as targets or from conveying any interest in them as part of nature.

In *The Texan Ranger*, published in London, 1866, Captain Flack, fresh from the sporting fields of the Southwest, describes the game of slaughtering thus: The men of one community lined up against those of another to see which group could kill the most game during a day's shooting. A squirrel and a rabbit counted one point each, a wild turkey five points, a deer ten points. The number of points scored in the particular contest described by Captain Flack totaled 3,470.

These are not instances of eccentricity but of the representative American way, until only yesterday, of looking at wild animals. Often while reading the chronicles of frontiersmen one does come upon an interesting observation concerning wildlife, but it is likely to be prefaced by some such statement as, "I didn't have a gun, and so I thought I might as well see what happened."

The majority of country dwellers in western America today would consider it necessary to apologize for *not* killing a coyote they happened to see doing something unusual. This traditional killer attitude is a part of the traditional exploitation of the land. A few early farmers conserved the soil—George Washington was one—but they were stray oddities. A few pioneers had naturalistic interests, but any revelation of such interests branded the holder of them as being peculiar or even undemocratic. The mass rule then, as now, was: Conform and be dull.

❖ ◎ ❖

In 1846 a young Englishman named George Frederick Ruxton landed at Veracruz, equipped himself with pack mules, rode to Mexico City, then up through "the Republic" to El Paso, across New Mexico into Colorado, where he spent the winter, and thence back to "civilization," which seemed to him "flat and stale" on the Missouri River. He carried home a chronicle that remains one of the most delightful and illuminating books of travel that North America has occasioned—*Adventures in Mexico and the Rocky Mountains.*

In Colorado, as Ruxton tells in the book, he made acquaintance with a large gray wolf. He had just shot two antelope. Why more than one was necessary for a meal for him and his guide, he does not say. Anyhow, the bounty left for the wolf attached him to the provider. For days he followed Ruxton. At camp every evening, he would "squat down quietly at a little distance." Sometimes Ruxton saw his eyes gleaming in the light of the campfire. After the men had rolled up in their blankets, the lobo would "help himself to anything lying about." In the morning, as soon as the men broke camp, the lobo, in Ruxton's words, "took possession and quickly ate up the remains of supper and some little extras I always took care to leave him: Then he would trot after us, and if we halted for a short time to adjust the mule-packs or water the animals, he sat down quietly until we resumed our march. But when I killed an antelope and was in the act of butchering it, he gravely looked on, or loped round and round, licking his jaws in a state of evident self-gratulation. I had him twenty times a day within reach of my rifle, but we became such old friends that I never dreamed of molesting him."

No American contemporary of Ruxton's on the frontier would have resisted killing that wolf. He would have said that he was killing it because the wolf killed; he would have said that the wolf was cruel, sneaking, cowardly. Actually, he would have killed it because he was "wrathy to kill." It did not strike Ruxton that the wolf was cruel—at least not more cruel than man. It struck Ruxton that the wolf was interesting; he had toward it the sympathy that comes from civilized perspective.

I confess to a sympathy for the coyote that has grown until it lives in the deepest part of my nature. Yet sympathy is not enough for any study of natural history, any more than good intentions are enough for the executive of a powerful nation. I am not a naturalist or a biologist, but I have, I think, examined about all the scientific knowledge in print concerning the coyote. Seeking to make the observations of out-of-doors men my own, I have found a few such men who seem to me to know more about coyotes than most scientific writers. The garnered experiences, always freely given, of many men in the field have, in a way, offset the limitations of my own experiences.

The biography of any individual, unless of an absolute recluse, is full of the interplay between him and other persons. The coyote was never a recluse. The impact on him by wandering tribes, by civilizations that built pyramids in the Valley of Teotihuacán and perished, and then by inheritors of European cultures exploiting and adapting themselves to pristine lands, has been marked. The life history of the coyote consists not only of objective facts about the animal as an animal but of the picturesque and emphatic reality of his own impact on human beings. Like the dog, the horse, and the fox of Europe, the coyote cannot be disassociated from man and remain whole.

The important debates are not concerning animal behavior but concerning the animal's proper ecological and economic place in man's world. Most of the land in which the coyote is most at home never will be thickly settled or intensively cultivated. Nature has said so. One can drive fifteen hundred miles from Brownsville at the mouth of the Rio Grande to San Diego, California, and be out of sight of range country only for short distances. One can drive two thousand miles from Oklahoma City to Seattle and with only minor skips be in grazing lands and mountains all the way. All these spaces of plains, brush, hills, mountains, and woods are favorable to and are favored by native wildlife. To what extent should the coyote be allowed to continue here, also in Canada, Alaska, and on south into Central America?

Human values, intellectual and spiritual, are not invariably coincident with economic values. Every national park, zoological garden, and natural history museum in the land attests to this truth as respects wildlife. Tourists do not go west primarily to lodge in hotels and tourist courts. If chambers of commerce in western states that strive for tourist money had imagination, they would arrange hearing places for those who would like to hear coyote voices. They would both lure and educate tourists.

As Tolstoy said, there are questions "put only in order that they may remain forever questions." Putting on the spectacles of science in expectation of finding the answer to everything looked at signifies inner blindness. All of the ecological, biological, and other logical studies that public bureaus and private enterprise may forward still will not bring those "authentic tidings of invisible things" that the lifted voice of the coyote brings in the early evening while lightning bugs soften the darkness under the trees, or that the voice of some other belonger to the rhythms of the earth brings in a simple tale of Brother Coyote.

❖ ◎ ❖

It is late afternoon on a small ranch down in the Brush Country of Texas. The center of activities is between a quadrangle of rail corrals and a wooden windmill over a hand-dug, rock-curbed well. The main doer in the activities is the owner of the ranch; four or five Mexicano men help him. Before daylight tomorrow morning they will be riding. They have just butchered a beef—which to them never meant a calf or a yearling, but a grown steer. Dark of hue and strong with a gamelike aroma, quarters of the beef hang from crossbeams of the windmill tower. A tightly stretched rope is hung with strips of meat which two or three days of sunshine and dry wind will cure into jerky. The hide, hair side down, is laid across the corral fence. The big paunch and the guts—but not the ones the Mexicanos will cook into menudo—have been dragged out into mesquite bushes not far away. One—two—three—six buzzards are already circling overhead, very slowly, and more are sweeping in. Darkness will come before they and their gathering fellows can feast, and within a short time after dark there will be nothing left for them to feast on.

Off from the corrals maybe four hundred yards are two houses. The women from these houses are already stewing meat and grinding corn to make tamales. In a fine grove of live oaks, up the hill in the opposite direction, is the rock house in which the rancher and his family live. About dark as they sit at a supper of fried steak with hot biscuits and brown gravy, the rancher says, "Well, we'll have singing tonight."

The speaker was my father. The particular beef-killing day I am remembering was forty-odd years ago. Fresh meat and singing went together in the same place for forty or fifty years before that; they still go together. After a group of vaqueros—as Mexicano cowboys in the border country are called—fill up on fresh beef in the evening, they are going to sing, and if they have been freshly brought together for a cow hunt, they will sing more. When the coyotes smell meat after dark, they also are going to sing.

"Well, we'll have singing tonight." We did not have to wait. High-wailing and long-drawn-out, the notes of the native versos came over the night air. Perhaps they were about Gregorio Cortez on his little brown horse, perhaps about the young vaquero who did not come back with his comrades from the trail to Kansas, perhaps about the mulberry-blue bull with the goring horns. Whatever the theme, the wild notes seemed to go up to the stars. As they reached their highest pitch, a chorus of coyote voices joined them. When, at the end of the first ballad, the human voices dimmed into silence, the coyote voices grew higher; then all but one howler ceased. We heard a laugh, and one lusty vaquero yelled out, "Cantad, amigos!"—"Sing, friends!" The friends responded with renewed gusto.

For a time the antiphonies challenged and cheered each other, now converging, now alternately lapsing. The vaquero singing, on high notes especially, could hardly be distinguished from the coyote singing. Mexicano vaqueros are Indian in blood, inheritance, and instinct. Anybody who has listened long and intimately to the cries of coyotes seemed to express remembrance of something lost before time began must recognize those identical cries in the chants of the Plains Indians and the homemade songs of Mexicanos. English-speakers living with the coyote seldom refer to his voice as "singing"—to them it is "yelping," "howling," "barking," but to the vaquero people it is nearly always cantando.

❖   ◎   ❖

For all his littleness and all the abuse heaped on him—abuse that long ago became a convention among English-speaking people—the coyote has aroused the imaginations of people associated with him more than the biggest and most powerful bulls of the biggest herds ever have. And it is the voice of the coyote, more than all else, that has had this effect.

The sound belongs to the night characteristically, but not exclusively. Coyotes do not at all confine their voicings to the mating season. They are heard all the year round, but perhaps more in the fall and early winter. They are comparatively quiet at pupping time. Hunger no more than sex urge seems to motivate their music. I am positive that they sing for pleasure and out of sociable feelings as well as, sometime, from feelings of loneliness.

"Prairie tenor," some call *Canis latrans*. He does not bark like a dog, but he barks. He yelps as well as wails. Often his falsetto yips, coming fast like machine-gun fire, make him comical and familiar. Then he is the Laughing Philosopher of the Plains, cheering the bored and amusing the witty. Where he is unhounded by man—civilized man filled with lust to kill and with morbid righteousness against any other animal that kills—he goes about delighting in all the plays along his Broadway.

As the Zuñi Indians tell it, when he sees the blackbirds dancing, he is beside himself with joy; when he hears the ravens laugh, he sticks his tail up and laughs out of sheer sympathy. Sometimes his voice is as idle as the cricket's chirp; now it fills a valley like mist, carrying whoever listens to "old, unhappy, far-off things" and to the elemental tragedy of life.

Down in Guatemala the gente say that the coyote talks to fences and they let him through. When barbed wire came, the coyote could not at first make himself understood, but before long the barbed wire fences understood also and let him through.

According to Comanche legend, certain tribesmen long ago learned the coyote language through a boy who, while little and lost, was adopted by a family of coyotes. He learned to talk with them before hunters saw him run into a den, smoked him out, and brought him back to his family. A few Comanches can still understand what coyotes say.

The coyote, it seems, cannot speak English. He speaks many Indian languages fluently—for he is fluent beyond all other four-footed creatures of the Western Hemisphere. He also speaks Mexican-Spanish; pure Castilian, not at all; and only now and then a word of what some call the American language. The English-American speakers have never taught him any language but that of lead, steel, and strychnine.

❖   ◎   ❖

Long before white men appeared, the coyote's range extended from roughly the Pacific to the Mississippi, from British Columbia to southern Mexico. Coyote had become well accommodated to the human species of his habitat. The aborigines owned nothing that he bothered, and their religious regard for him was a protection against molestation.

About 1870 Stephen Powers found coyotes "thick about every mountain ranchería" of the California Indians: "They often chased the dogs into the village itself." An old hunter told him that he had seen "Indian dogs more than once turn on a coyote and drive it off a few rods, when it would fall on its back, turn up its legs, and commence playing with them."

As these regions were appropriated by the white man and as the white man's chickens, sheep, and other live property took the places of native fowl and quadrupeds, the coyote accepted the substitute flesh with alacrity and gusto. He himself was anything but accepted. In addition to being poisoned and otherwise destroyed as a menace, he was hounded for sport and shot at by everybody on general principles.

By the time Richard F. Burton reached Utah in 1860, the coyote was rapidly learning to observe civilized man from the highest bluff. A present-day hunter with hounds observes that the coyote no longer lingers to stare at a man in curiosity as he once lingered. He is "satisfied with a brief glance over the shoulder."

Today he tries to see without being seen. He has learned to lie down in water so as to appear a half-sunken log, to hide in a straw sack in an open field, to camouflage himself in immobility in the scantiest vegetation, rising up "out of nowhere" to break away when man comes threateningly near.

Coyotes are the arch-predators on sheep. But sheep are the arch-predators on the soil of arid and semi-arid ranges. Wherever they are concentrated on ranges without sufficient moisture to maintain a turf under their deep-biting teeth and cutting hoofs, they destroy plant life. Unless long-term public good wins over short-term private gain and ignorance, vast ranges, already greatly depleted, will at no distant date be as barren as the sheep-created deserts of Spain.

No tendency among human beings is more common than to blame others for what the blamers themselves do. The principal charges against the coyote are that he destroys too many valuable animals. This is simply not true.

Wherever jackrabbits are plentiful and coyotes exist, this prolific hare of the West affords the coyotes' principal non-vegetable food supply. A dozen or so jackrabbits will eat as much vegetation as a sheep, a fifth of what a cow eats; a horde of them will in a few nights denude a green field with the thoroughness of grasshoppers.

I know the Brush Country of southern Texas well. The truth is that where the most quail thrive, the most coyotes also thrive. There may be an individual calf killer now and then, but coyotes do much more good than harm over the whole plains area.

The chief biologist of the US Park Service says, "Throughout the ages the coyote has helped to weed out the unfit and keep survivors alert. Largely due to it and other predators, the deer, the antelope, and other hoofed animals have evolved into swift, graceful, efficient animals. Were it not for the coyote, they would not only overpopulate and overeat their ranges, but would doubtless become lazy and have cirrhosis of the liver."

❖ ◎ ❖

The fang and claw conception of life in the wild has been over-emphasized by a society devoted to propagating the philosophy of greed under the guise of free enterprise. In truth, the coyote continually shows his instinct for cooperation.

Coyotes habitually relay each other in chasing the jackrabbit. Going downhill, a coyote can gain, but uphill and on level ground the jackrabbit has the advantage. If it did not circle, it could probably run away from nearly any coyote, but pursued animals often circle. Thus, two or three coyotes working together can take turns cutting across circles and making stands. Coyotes are also known to cooperate in driving jackrabbit into barbed wire fences. They work both sides of a fence together so that if the chased rabbit gets through, it is picked up by the chaser's partner.

It is not uncommon for a coyote, the female especially, whose immature offspring is being chased by hounds to spring in behind the pup, zigzag back and forth across the trail and linger until the hounds get close enough to follow her. If they follow—and only the best-trained hounds resist such a temptation to switch—she will strike out in a direction contrary to that taken by her young one.

In the Frio County brush of South Texas, hunters came to know well a pair of coyotes they named Jim Ferguson and Ma Ferguson. If the dogs started Jim Ferguson and got hot after him, he would circle into Ma Ferguson's vicinity, and before long the dogs would be after her. If they started Ma, sometimes with a half-grown pup, she would be relieved in time by Jim. They afforded sport to hunters for four or five years, and so far as is known, neither of this pair was ever hounded down. As among people, it is the exceptional coyotes who have biographies.

When I consider how unsmart man is on the average, I never consider it a compliment to a horse or a dog to say that he's as smart as a human being. Still, it would be silly to consider the coyote as an "intellectual being." But no other wild animal of historic times has shown itself so adaptable to change.

The higher the intelligence of any species, the more variations in behavior among its individuals. The degree of their uniformity is in ratio to their stupidity. Sheeplike people fear any divergence from the walled trails in which they walk up and down. They come to believe, often passionately, that the walls are sacred and that anybody who jumps over or points out a new trail is antisocial, subversive, at best "a crackpot."

Coyotes probably are not so intelligent as the most sheeplike human beings, but on their own level of intelligence they often exhibit extraordinarily individualistic conduct.

A friend told me of watching a coyote come down to the Rio Grande, step into the edge of the water and grab a piece of willow four or five feet long that had been cut and peeled by beavers, and trot away into the brush with it. Why? I don't know.

If I were walking along the edge of water in the Rio Grande and saw a piece of barked willow all light and white, I'd pick it up and carry it along with me. Why? I don't know.

❖ ◎ ❖

Sheep of the West are far more destructive than any coyote. Metaphorically, the sheep eat up all the animals that prey on them—coyotes, wildcats, and eagles especially. On some sheep ranges, wholesale poisoning and trapping have destroyed nearly all potential predators. The surface of the earth does not offer a more sterile-appearing sight than some dry-land pastures of America with nothing but sheep trails across their grassless grounds.

The free enterprisers of these ranges, many of them public owned, want no government interference; they ask only that the government maintain trappers, subsidies on mutton and wool, and tariffs against any competitive importations.

The coyote far enough advanced to put two and two together can seldom add two more and arrive at six. Oren L. Robinson, of the Jackson Hole country, was once following a trapped coyote dragging a trap chain with a three-pronged grapple hook on the free end of it. The hook kept catching in small bushes, jerking the coyote back. Finally, the coyote picked it up in his mouth and carried it some distance. This behavior may be unduplicated in trapping history. It is certainly unusual. Before long the coyote stepped on the chain, thus jerking a prong of the hook into his mouth. Right there he stopped, absolutely baffled, and gave up.

In October 1946, A. B. Bynum, in charge of government trapping in the Uvalde, Texas, district, turned in the scalps of 522 coyotes slaughtered in one month by the cyanide trap gun. He set the guns daily himself, his wife helping him run the lines. Perhaps fifty coyotes that died got away in the brush, he says, so that they could not be counted.

This number broke all records of coyote destruction by individual trappers in America. The record could not have been made except in the Brush Country of South Texas, which contains the main concentration of coyotes left on the continent. It could not have been made except by use of the cyanide gun, called the "coyote-getter."

An explosive cartridge, attachable to the upper end of a steel peg, contains a charge of sodium cyanide and is hooded by a soft, absorbent, usually wool or rabbit, fur. At the place where the gun is to be set, the peg is driven into the ground and the hood is smeared with a fetid scent alluring to canines, also to a lesser degree other species, including skunks and occasional sheep and cattle. The cartridge explodes only when an upward pull on the small bulb-shaped covering releases a spring. On exploding, it shoots the cyanide through the soft covering directly into the mouth of the pulling coyote. Almost instantly, the poison ruins all the vital organs of the animal. Within five minutes it is dead, usually not more than seventy-five steps from the machine.

What thorough destruction of the coyote would mean to nature is suggested by the following account. Coyotes had been very destructive on a sheep range in the Big Horn Mountains of Wyoming. Denning high up in the rimrocks, they multiplied despite rifles, traps, strychnine, and cyanide guns. They killed and buffaloed the sheep dogs. Then at the end of World War II "the Federal pest control service came to the rescue with a magic powder called thallium. White, odorless, and tasteless, thallium is so deadly that handlers must wear masks when they inoculate bait. So far, Mr. Coyote has been unable to detect thallium. It leaves no occasional survivor to learn. Hawks, crows, and even the noisy magpies disappeared after the thallium campaign"— also, no doubt, other birds, along with skunks, foxes, badgers, and occasional carnivores.

Government poisoners, along with state poisoners, are keeping the public fooled on how much other wildlife they kill while using deadly poisons on the coyote. They say they are protecting the quail, or some other valuable commodity—but in fact they are protecting their jobs while destroying the balance of nature to benefit a select few.

❧   ◉   ❧

The Brush Country of Texas lies south of a line running west from San Antonio to about Del Rio on the Rio Grande. Except at the western tip of this line, there are almost no sheep in the Brush Country. The few flocks of Spanish goats are protected by shepherds and dogs. The Brush Country runs down into the lower valley of the Rio Grande, irrigated and thickly populated, where coyotes refresh themselves on orange juice.

It includes the million-acre King Ranch and other estates of feudal latitudes. It includes also many small ranches, many cultivated fields bordered by brush pasture, many oil fields with derricks and pumps pricking the brush. Sweeping northeast up the coast of the Gulf of Mexico, it takes in the sand-bar islands, on which coyotes follow the tides to pick up the wash of the sea.

Amid an infinitude of mesquites bearing succulent beans, thorned bushes furnishing berries, prickly pear purple in season with tunas, and an abundance of jackrabbits, cottontails, wood rats, armadillos, ground squirrels, and other flesh, no coyote of the Brush Country need ever starve—except when the terrible drought comes. Even then, there are mesquite beans for a long season.

When the chapotes (Mexican persimmons) ripen, some fall to the ground; others remain in easy reach on the soft-leaved, thorn-less bushes. Coons, hustling themselves high up, knock many down—and the coyotes gormandize on them with as little effort as Elijah exerted to take the bread and flesh brought by ravens.

In the opinion of some range men, coyote depredation on deer in the Brush Country is increasing; that is what men in the business of trapping want them to think. The trapping of them here is certainly on the increase.

Cattle people are generally conservative in the manner of the old-time English squire. The King Ranch may import bull snakes to swallow rattlesnakes and hire a biologist to ration the diet between skunks and armadillos, but lots of the ranchers— including some of the oil millionaires who sink their excess profits in land and live in Houston with their income tax lawyers—tend toward the George West point of view.

On his big ranch in Live Oak Country, Mr. George West always had big steers and plenty of deer, and he never arranged hunting parties in order to influence politicians. One time an eager young man met him in San Antonio.

"Mr. West," he said, "you wouldn't mind if I went down to your ranch for a little deer hunt, would you?"

"Oh," Mr. West said, "you can't see any deer down there nowadays for the brush. People shoot at deer in the brush and scare my steers, and then the steers run all the tallow off themselves. No, I can't let you hunt deer."

"But Mr. West," the eager young man went on, "I just want to get out on your famous ranch. I won't shoot at the deer. I'll shoot the coyotes."

"No," said Mr. West, "I've got to protect the coyotes to keep the jackrabbits down. If those jack rabbits were left alone to breed, they'd eat up all the grass."

"Well," the eager young man brightened, "I'll just shoot jackrabbits. That would be fine sport and useful too."

"No," Mr. West replied gravely, "we've got to have the jackrabbits to feed the coyotes."

The young man had by now lost his eager look.

"Maybe you've heard of the balance of nature," Mr. George West concluded.

❖ ◎ ❖

If I could, I would go to bed every night with coyote voices in my ears and with them greet the gray light of every dawn. When I remember their derision of campfires, their salutes to the rising moon, their kinship cries to the stars and silences, I am ten thousand times more grateful to them than I am to the makers of blaring radios and ringing telephones that index the high standard of American living.

PART 2

On the Trail with a Storyteller

"Where do you get your stories?" people sometimes ask me. I look for them, lay for them, listen for them, hunt them, trail them down, swap for them, beg, borrow, and steal them, and value above rubies the person who gives me a good one.—JFD

Across the Bolsón de Mapimí: Echoes of the Comanche War Trail

The great Comanche War Trail was worn deep by the hoofs of countless travelers over generations of time and was lined with the whited bones of horses. In Texas it has been plowed up, tramped over, cemented under. Trains and automobiles annually carry across it thousands of English-speaking people who are not aware that it ever existed.

But across the Bolsón de Mapimí and the land fringing upon it the raiders who beat out the Comanche Trail ride vividly in memory.—JFD

NORTHERN COAHUILA is a better grazing country than that we had set out from. Here a majority of the haciendas, many of them owned by Texans, Englishmen, and other foreigners, are fenced. A severe drought had been and still was on the country; had our animals not been desert-bred they could not have persisted. It was not feasible to carry rations of grain to last more than two or three days, and it was difficult to buy corn at the few habitations. Of grass there were only the roots and a few dead spikes protected by thorned brush.

One late afternoon while we were crossing an American hacienda partly watered by wells and windmills and known as Ojo Apache, I saw three men with axes chopping in a wide expanse of sotol. More than a hundred cattle were loosely bunched around them to eat the food that was being unlocked. Sotol is a species of low-growing yucca, the leaves saw-toothed. Out of it is distilled a fiery liquor also called sotol. Apache Indians used to eat the roasted hearts of it; some Mexicans still do on occasion. These hearts, from which the tough, serrated leaves spring out like the scales of the artichoke, will nourish stock, but they are so well defended that no animal can get to them unless the plant is chopped open.

My guide, Inocencio, observed the feeding. "Like hope," he said, "it will not fatten but it will maintain."

We approached a squat, thin-waisted man, his skin as dry and weathered as his sandal-exposed toes. I greeted him and asked, "How are you?"

"Pues, señor," he answered, "the whole caballada is trotted down."

He could have said nothing to express more fully the badness of things.

"Look about you," he said, accompanying every word with pantomimic gesture. "Plant and animal are alike withered, dying. No rain to make grass for nearly two years. We people still have corn and frijoles to eat, but how can we sprout a green leaf when nature suffers so?"

Noticing a large, very fat red steer among the poor cattle, I asked how the animal came to be in such prime condition.

"That ox," the sotol-chopper answered, "appears to have some secret of sustaining himself that he will not make known to the other cattle. Every morning he comes up to where they are chewing like slaves in order to keep their skeletons standing up. He comes alone from God knows where and salutes them like some hidalgo that will give only his cane to a peon to shake."

The speaker moved his hands to indicate the steer's inscrutable sapience. "He takes a little sotol to be polite and never says one word, not one word, as to how he keeps so fat."

"Yet the other cattle appear not to be jealous of him," I remarked.

He lowered his voice. "No, they are not políticos."

❖ ◎ ❖

For days that stretched into weeks we rode. After twisting up cañons lined with cedar, traversing arid and unstocked mesas merely patched with grass, and threading passes over mountains fringed with pine and piñon, we left all fence lines and came by degrees out on that vast and vaguely defined desert known as the Bolsón de Mapimí, on some old maps called Tierra de Muerte—Land of Death.

This is the southernmost portion of the Chihuahuan Desert, ranging below the Big Bend of Texas from the Río Bravo southward through western Coahuila and into neighboring Chihuahua and Durango, skirting Zacatecas and San Luis Potosí.

Maddeningly monotonous except to one who can "read infinity in a grain of sand," the Bolsón de Mapimí is an immense, seemingly barren land—yet productive of a fantastic life. It stretches out an irregular elevated basin hemmed around by low naked mountains that infringe up and crumple it and are always in sight. These shed the sparse rainfall into arroyos that are bone dry a few hours after a rain and sink into the parched solitude. It is as if a vast ocean had been petrified to remain forever silent.

A traveler through this region is fortunate to reach water of any kind once a day and he must tack his course to do that. The patches of coarse, wire-like sabaneta grass or the equally tough toboso or the fibrous chino are always far from any watering. Generally, we camped with no water except that carried in canteens. Occasionally we stopped at a lone ranchería of poverty.

The nights grew freezing cold; the days remained blazing hot. The sun flooded the immense vacuity of sky, the intense light blinding against the ashen soil. The powdered alkaline dust raised by the feet of our horses was swept into the nostrils of both man and beast.

And so we rode. It was as if I had never known any other land, any other life. The foothills were covered with black rock, which appeared to have been spewed out of a furnace. Now and then we came to sand dunes on which grew gray switch mesquite and gray chamiso, their roots affording fuel.

Far away sometimes a valley appears green; that green is an expanse of the ocotillo, each stalk studded with thorns protecting its miniature stemless leaves. All one afternoon I rode through a plain of big palmas, yuccas aflutter with thousands and tens of thousands of silent migratory bluebirds.

Moving seemingly as slow as the desert terrapin, day after day, through the gray and immense solitude of the Bolsón de Mapimí, a man grows to feel that no human drama ever was enacted, ever could be enacted, on such an unrelieved and empty stage.

Yet here also human history has written itself. Somehow, the long, lone cry of a Bolsón coyote in the night suggests human destinies as eloquently as the broken arches of the Coliseum ever spoke to Byron. By day the omnilucent glare of the sun palpitates an Iliad of vanished races, vanished centuries, and vanished ways of human life.

Under that sun long, long ago the conquistadores rode north this way to gather Indian slaves for their mines. They rode back, and behind them came the Comanches, beating out their great War Trail.

West of the Pecos in Texas, on the two great paralleling cordilleras of Mexico and over the broken plateau that lies between them, it usually rains in the summer, the average rainfall varying greatly according to the lay of the land. By September the grass is ripe and the holes are full of water. And so to old people in northern Mexico the September moon is still "the moon of the Comanches," though the Comanches themselves called it "the Mexican moon," for it was under this moon that they annually swooped down.

Astride half-wild horses captured from the mustang herds of the plains or from the caballadas of Mexican ranches raided the season before, they rode on stirrupless pads of sheepskin or buffalo hide, their bits and bridle reins alike of rawhide.

Their arms were mostly bows and arrows, the bows of Osage orange, the arrows of vara dulce, palo duro, or other tough growth. The arrows were carried in a quiver of wildcat hide slung from the shoulder. Each warrior was provided with a lance of ashwood and a chimal, or shield, of dried buffalo bull hide. Some of them carried Bowie knives or machetes from Mexico. Here and there one was armed with an old blunderbuss escopeta.

In the time of the Comanche moon they rode down the Comanche War Trail, which from their range on the Llano

Estacado to the depths of the Bolsón de Mapimí half a thousand miles southward stretched as plain as a chalk mark.

Once across the Río Bravo, these Cossacks of the desert scattered, some to push up the Río Conchos to the very walls of Chihuahua City; some to harass the ranches of faraway Durango; some to veer east and raid haciendas in Coahuila, where—in the region of Saltillo at least—cattle went unbranded for years because there were no horses on which to work them. The Comanches raided even into the states of Zacatecas, San Luis Potosí, and Aguas Calientes. Boys, girls, young women, and horses were their object—the children to be raised as true Comanches, the young women to serve as squaws, and horses—never enough horses— to ride, the symbol of power and glory and riches of all the Plains Indians.

Before the bitter *nortes* of winter blew down, the Comanche Trail was again vivid with life northward bound. On some of the captured horses were the lashed captives. About the belts of the captors that drove them dangled scalps taken from the kinsmen of the captives. The dust from the hoofs of horses rose in clouds. Behind them rolled clouds of smoke from grass fires set to impede pursuers. Now and then bands deflected from the trail to shun avengers.

Against this ravaging the central government did nothing. Far removed from the center where politicians lied and generals fought to possess the spoils of office, haciendas and ranches comprising an empire were by a few hundred naked Comanches kept shuddering with terror.

The only remedio was a bounty on scalps. The governor of Chihuahua stipulated that 100 pesos would be paid for the scalps of warriors and 50 pesos for squaws. Then into the Bolsón and the sierras rode James Kirker and John Joel Glanton and other scalp hunters, some of them from Texas. A scalp was a scalp to them, and when their perfidy in murdering innocent natives for the bounty was discovered, they had to flee.

In New Mexico, the bounty was on ears instead of scalps,

and in the Governor's Palace at Santa Fé were "windows of glass and festoons of Indian ears." When the Englishman George Ruxton reached Chihuahua City in 1846, he saw "dangling over the portals" of the cathedral "the grim scalps of one hundred and seventy Apaches who had lately been treacherously and inhumanely butchered by the Indian hunters in the pay of the state."

Twenty-eight years later August Santleben, noted freighter of the Chihuahua Trail, saw on the plaza in front of the cathedral a processions of conquerors, accompanied by bands of music, displaying scalps on poles.

For half a century the price of scalps rose and fell, and not all the raiders who rode down the War Trail lived to ride back.

❖   ◎   ❖

In southern Mexico the folk remember Cortés and Cuauhtémoc and La Malinche as of yesterday; in northern Mexico they remember the raiding Lipanes, Apaches, and Comanches as of last night.

One time in the Sierra Madre of Sonora a mestizo whispered to me in front of a cave: "Look at those bundles of shucks. Geronimo and his Apaches left them there." He seemed to feel that Geronimo might be lurking behind us.

In Coahuila, Chihuahua, Nuevo León, and Durango I have many times had pointed out to me a corral in which horses were guarded against the Comanches, a spring that the Apaches used as a rendezvous, a pass through which they swept their captives and horses, or some other feature commemorative of the invaders.

"He will make a fine man if the Apaches do not bind him to a cactus," is a saying still heard, reminiscent of the time when the "tigers of the desert" stripped Mexicans and bound them naked against thorns.

While the raiders rode their wild ways along the Comanche Trail, gigantic Mexican carts beat out another trail across the Bolsón de Mapimí. It became known to history as the Chihuahua Trail.

Their wooden wheels seven feet in diameter, screeching on wooden axles except when "greased" with succulent pads of the nopal, the mighty carretas lumbered along from the mining camps of Parral, through Chihuahua City, across the Bolsón, across the Río Bravo, through San Antonio, and on to Indianola on the Mexican Gulf—a distance of over 1,200 miles.

Not an ounce of metal in their ponderous frames, every timber was held in place by rawhide or peg. They carried silver, in bullion and in minted pesos, beans, salt, cotton, horseshoes, hides. The Mexican bulls, yoked by horns almost as ponderous as the cart axles, pulled their loads across the 90 waterless miles from Julimes to Chupadera—a mere "suck spring"—and then on 60 more waterless miles to the Paso de la Mula.

In time mighty freight wagons, each drawn by ten and twelve Mexican mules and driven by Mexican freighters, supplanted the ox carts on the trail, but not in the country. And the Comanches still rode. The wagons trailed in trains, camping two or three times between waterings, at every stop going into the corral formation which makes of wagons a fort. In the darkness before dawn the caporal would blow his whistle and each of the more than a hundred mules enclosed in the corral would go to his proper wagon. Within half an hour the train would be moving.

And then the wagons went the way of the carretas, and the Comanche Trail and the Chihuahua Trail became but traces in history, and the Bolsón de Mapimí became more silent and more deserted, emptier and vaster in its solitude than ever before.

The last stir of human life on the Bolsón de Mapimí was during the Mexican Revolution. In the early winter of 1913 old Don Luis Terrazas, his scores of descendants, and half a hundred other rich Chihuahuan families fled from Pancho Villa. They followed the Chihuahua Trail for the safety that lay north of the Rio Grande.

There were over 3,000 refugees. There were fine carriages drawn by fine mules with outriders. There were peon women carrying chickens and babies. There were single vaqueros and trains of wagons; there were ox carts and loose longhorned cows. There were disconnected strings of pack mules and burros.

Terrazas owned a large portion of the largest state in Mexico. He was the state. On the hegira he took 5,000 pesos in specie—so they say—and left 600,000 of it secreted in or under the pillars of his bank. But whatever the stuff in their cargoes, whether the pesos of Terrazas or the golden combs and jeweled earrings, no animal crossing the Bolsón de Mapimí carried anything more precious than a gourd of water.

Before the revolution these lands sustained hardy Mexican cattle that could go for days and even weeks without drinking, in seasons deriving what water they got from thorned prickly pear and the stalks and flowers of the varied yucca and agave growth, at other times walking four leagues from the rare watering places to the mountain rincones and low playas affording grass.

Here in this land a colt will follow its mother ten miles to water. It will never need shoes of iron, and it "belongs to the race that dies before tiring." It will carry a vaquero two or three days between drinks. Deer, antelopes, and certain other animals that thrive on the range do not drink water at all.

The animals, the gray brush, and the men who live here are all of one breed. A vaquero with the toothache will pour worm medicine into the cavity. If that does not "cure"—kill the nerve, he will have four men hold him down while a fifth inserts a red-hot wire end into the hole.

In 1917, Pancho Villa, retreating from Carranzistas, set out from the ancient mining town of Mapimí with 1,200 men. For four days neither the men nor their horses found water, for the sparse aguajes to the right and left were guarded by the enemy. The men singed prickly pear for their horses; they ate prickly pear themselves. But prickly pear is sparse where the Bolsón is worst. When Villa reached Los Jacales four days later he had only 900 men and many less than that number of horses. Had the men and horses alike not belonged to the desert, few indeed could have survived.

When a Pancho Villa gathers his "leathered ones" from the deserts and sierras of this North Country, the world may well shudder.

❖ ◎ ❖

At the Jaboncillos, where we watered our stock and filled can-teens, my guide Inocencio declared that although he had never traveled our trail to the Piedrita, he knew it must be "a little far," probably twenty-five miles. A man we saw tanning a deer hide declared, however, that it was really cerca, "near."

The next morning, after having ridden until nearly noon, we met a campesino. He stopped, according the custom of the country, on my left side, and, each of us reaching across his horse, shook hands.

"What is the news?" I asked.

"But no," he replied. "todo es pacífico."

Then in answer to the same question, I replied that where I came from "all was pacific" also.

He took me for a peddler and asked if I had in the pack any sugar, coffee, and thirty-thirty cartridges to sell. I gave him a cigarette and inquired about the distance to Piedrita.

"It is very near now," he said.

Along late in the afternoon, our horses and mule flagging from the heat, thirst, and the alkali dust, two peons driving a single burro loaded with sticks entered the trail ahead of us. As we overtook the pedestrians, the one on my side saluted in the old-fashioned way.

"How far is it, my friend," I asked, "to the Piedrita?"

"It is just over those hills and is muy cerquita," he said.

Hours later, when we at last arrived at the Piedrita, there was only enough light left in the sky to reveal the greenish scum on the pygmy hole of water that supplied the ranch, man and beast.

"Your leagues are long ones," I said to Inocencio.

"Si, señor," he replied, "son ligas de hombre—they are man-sized leagues."

❖ ◎ ❖

"Look at those tracks in the sky," Inocencio called to me one afternoon, at the same time gesturing toward some crows circling ahead of us. "They say there has been a kill at Chupadera del Indio. Perhaps we shall find a camp there."

The sun, throbbing out of a sky of brass, was still high; the end of the day's ride was still seemingly as far away as glasses tinkling with ice in some shaded room of cool air. The rough greasewood mesa crawled away under the glare of heat devils to naked mounds and gray and red.

"We go so slow," I said to Inocencio.

"Yes," he replied, "but, as you know, of more value a dropping of water that endures than a stream that dries up. Grain by grain the dove fills her craw."

On reaching the crest of a hill I saw coming along the trail a mule carrying a woman, behind her on foot a man with a guitar.

We all stopped for salutations. I asked the man where he was from. From Durango. I did not query as to why he was so very far from home. He was about forty years old and had a firm, unsmiling face. Clear across the left side showed a long, clean scar of other years. He was not afraid to look one in the eyes but he did not so look. He moved with the effortless alacrity of a cat. Both he and the woman were immaculately clean. She was maybe twenty years old, fresh and firm in physique, and about her there was something at once daring and modest.

After we had all drunk water out of my canteen and the man and I had smoked a cigarette each, I suggested a song. It took him some time to tune up. The young woman stood beside him, holding a metallic triangle which she kept time by striking it with a hardwood rod. From the moment he began picking his guitar she kept her eyes glued on his face. It was clear she worshipped his very breath.

The song was one of the several popular corridos about Pancho Villa. There were between thirty-five and forty verses—all about the "terror of the North," "the man who laughs and kills," "this Bonaparte of the sierras," shouting "We are born to die," "rude but great of heart," dynamiting bridges, burning caboose and passenger cars, now sacking Torreón, now in the town of Columbus leaving "as a little remembrance only sixteen dead gringos."

But alas for "pobre Pancho Villa." In Parral traitors and ingrates waylaid and murdered him.

Vuela, vuela, palomita,
párate en aquella orilla
avísales á los gringos
que murió Francisco Villa.
(Fly away, fly away, little dove,
But stop there just ahead,
And advise the gringos
That Villa at last is dead.)

❖ ◎ ❖

It was dark before we saw a light and knew that we were nearing La Joya—The Jewel—a lonely mud hut on the side of a naked hill at the base of which, however, there was a spring. We pulled saddles off against the wall of the house. The occupant, a poor renter, had his corn spread out on the bare ground in front of the adobe. He was glad to sell some, but at the request to let me have some fodder for our animals he flinched. What I saw was all he had on hand, he explained.

The renter invited us to share his house, but as it was occupied by his own family and consisted of a single room, I declined. The outside walls sheltered us from the wind. While Inocencio was watering the animals and I was trying to build a fire out of twigs, the woman of the house brought forth a stack of tortillas. I thought of one of those sayings about themselves the gente pobre have:

Where one can eat there is enough for two,
Where two can eat there is enough for three,
Where three can eat there is enough for four, etc.

Charles Goodnight
of Amplitude

In 1926, Dobie received permission to meet with ninety-year-old cattleman Charles Goodnight for a magazine story. Goodnight and his partner Oliver Loving blazed the Goodnight-Loving trail, and they became the historical inspirations for Larry McMurtry's Woodrow Call and Gus McCrae in Lonesome Dove. It was Loving who died on a trail drive after being wounded by Indian arrows, and it was Goodnight who brought his comrade's body back to Texas for burial. Woodrow Call [Goodnight] was played by Tommy Lee Jones in the classic television miniseries.

This story also mentions Goodnight's companion Bose Ikard, a former slave—who later served as the model for Joshua Deets in Lonesome Dove, played by Danny Glover. A quote of Goodnight's at the end of this story, ironically attesting to his "hell of a vision," was memorably adapted by screenwriter Bill Wittliff for the film version of Lonesome Dove.—SD

P EOPLE CALLED HIM Colonel Goodnight and still refer to him by that title. Born in 1836 in southern Illinois, he came to Texas in 1845 with his mother and stepfather. At the age of twenty he contracted, with a partner, to care for a herd of about four hundred cows on shares. The grass was all free.

During the Civil War he served as scout and ranger against Indians on the northwestern frontiers, becoming intimately acquainted with Plains country beyond all settlements. He had a compass inside his body, was never lost, day or night, alone or leading.

In 1866 he and Oliver Loving drove two thousand cattle of their own across ninety miles of desert from the headwaters of the Middle Concho to Horsehead Crossing on the Pecos and on to Fort Sumner, New Mexico, where contractors supplying government beef paid high prices. He trailed other herds west over the Goodnight-Loving Trail, now traced out on maps.

In 1876, he established the first ranch in the Panhandle of Texas, making the JA cattle on the Palo Duro perhaps the best-bred herd in the West. He blazed a trail to Dodge City, Kansas, his market. He roped a few buffalo calves, raised them, and developed the first controlled buffalo herd in the West. He led in maintaining law and order over a vast territory. In 1887, in the depth of a financial panic, Goodnight dissolved his partnership with John Adair and soon sold his own holdings, one hundred and forty thousand acres and twenty thousand cattle—at panic prices. After a disastrous plunge in Mexico mining, he settled down on the ranch, where I met him.

In response to a letter, he had replied that he would be "pleased to entertain" me any time I came. He had been interviewed and written about various times. He had himself written brief articles on handling a trail herd and other experiences. He was plainly not elated at my arrival, though courteous enough. He told me right off that he did not care a damn for any "publicity" that I or any other writer could give him. He was now ninety years old. His wife, married in 1870, had died the preceding spring. A woman of mature years was cooking and keeping house for him.

At supper I noticed on the table the biggest bottle of pepper sauce I have ever seen—red Mexican peppers in maybe two quarts of vinegar. He ate, without talking, as if he meant business, finished, pushed his chair back, said, "I never was a hand to dally around the table, excuse me," and left.

I stayed with him for three or four days, taking down voluminous notes. On the second morning he told me that his men were going to bring in and pen his buffalo herd. I wanted to ride with them.

"You'd be in the way and probably scare the buffaloes beyond control," he said.

He told me that if he felt dispirited and rode down into the buffalo pasture and looked at his buffaloes and the canyons, he always came back heartened and refreshed. The honesty of nature never failed him.

He made a good deal of the "cattalo," a cross between polled Angus cows and buffalo bulls. He became irritated when I asked if the cross could reproduce itself. It could not, consistently. An absolute master at breeding cattle, he had ideas on crossbreeding two species of animals that knowledge of biology would have dispelled. In Mexico he had heard of—not seen—a cross between a sheep and a hog. When I visited him he was keeping and feeding in a pen a sow and a ram, expecting a cross.

While he narrated experiences and observations to me, I sometimes had to prod for facts. Yet our chemistries mixed. At mention of "my old pardner Oliver Loving," his voice grew warm and tender. The Christmas following this visit he sent me by mail a fine buffalo roast. We remained in contact for the rest of his life. I developed a positive admiration for him as a man of large nature, wisdom, concern for other people, and a noble sense of values.

He told me about Old Blue, his lead steer on the great JA Ranch. Old Blue led beef herds from the Palo Duro Canyon to Dodge City and came back with the cowboys and the remuda. He was a camp pet. Many an outlaw steer roped in the breaks was necked to him to be led straight to the ranch corrals. Buffalo calves that Goodnight saved to start a buffalo herd with were necked to Old Blue for bringing in.

When I evidenced lively interest in Old Blue, Mr. Goodnight's spirits rose. While he would not give half of a damn for anything that anybody might write about Charlie Goodnight, he would "like to have Old Blue given his dues." Out of the rich stores of his memory he related instance after instance of the old Longhorn's behavior; he gave me a biographical sketch of him that he had written in doggerel verse.

Back in Austin, I wrote the story of Old Blue as best I could and sold it to a magazine published in New York. After I sent Mr. Goodnight the story as printed, he responded: "My eyes filled with tears when I read what you had written of my faithful old friend." Years later I put it in my book *The Longhorns*.

Another of his favorite characters was Old Bose Ikard, who had been born a slave in Mississippi and who for years rode with Goodnight on the long cattle trails and on ranges where Indians and white murderers and thieves made life dangerous.

Later H. B. (Tex) Willis of Dallas gave me an account of a trip he made, in 1919, with Charlie Goodnight in a car to Weatherford, where Bose was living. Tex said that as they approached Waco about four o'clock in the afternoon he asked Goodnight if he'd like to go by Sul Ross's place. Goodnight had been with Sul Ross in a fight with the Comanches when Cynthia Ann Parker was captured from them. She was the white mother of Quanah Parker, who became the most noted of Comanche chiefs. The dour Parker people to whom she was restored were utterly alien to her. She belonged to the Comanches, to her children, and to nomadic life on the plains. She died of grief.

Goodnight understood her tragedy. Sul Ross's subsequent vote-seeking and then governorship of Texas lessened him in Goodnight's eyes.

"Why in the hell," Goodnight snorted, "would I want to see anything connected with that old lying four-flusher named Sul Ross?"

He had known him in camp and had known him as politician. He had an instinctive dislike for people always eying the gallery and seeking "suffrages." He himself never had been afflicted with the itch for being noticed—that pimply outbreak on small natures who cannot abide with equanimity their own smallness.

Tex Willis said he showed more pleasure at meeting Bose Ikard than at meeting anybody else on the whole trip. He gave him a hundred-dollar bill and continued to send him money after that. After Bose Ikard died Goodnight had a granite marker placed over his grave attesting to his "splendid behavior."

It was close to six o'clock before he and Tex Willis got breakfast in Weatherford—mighty late for Goodnight. Word had got around town that the noted frontiersman was back on his old stomping grounds. Before they left the restaurant some important-appearing individual walked up to him boldly and said, "Mr. Charles Goodnight, I believe."

Goodnight never moved a muscle.

The enthusiastic greeter kept coming, holding out his hand. "My father used to be an Indian fighter," he continued.

With that, Charlie Goodnight rared back like a buffalo bull and, glaring right into the gladhander's eyes, growled: "God-damn poor recommendation, considering one Comanche warrior could drive all the sorry white people out of five counties."

❖ ◎ ❖

Goodnight had fought the Comanches himself. Also, while feeding beef to Quanah Parker's warriors on the Palo Duro, he had made a treaty with them. He respected their rights and respected them as human beings. They had once claimed all the country south of Red River and west of the Cross Timbers to the Rio Grande. They had, in Goodnight's words, "held for ages the land I and other white men controlled. By all laws of justice, it was theirs. We wanted it, fought for it, took it." He was a great friend to some of the Pueblo Indians. He rated natural men and nature above anything else.

At one time Goodnight partly owned and wholly controlled about 1,300,000 acres of land, some of it leased from individual owners, some of it fenced-in state land. Often over a hundred cowhands worked under him.

He forbade gambling and drinking on the ranches, demanded cleanness in person and camp. He encouraged his men to save money and invest it in cattle and horses, allowing their stock to graze on ranch property. He said he had not known of a genuine cowboy's having been tried for crime in the Panhandle. He did not rate outlaws as genuine cowboys. He recalled only two fights, merely fist fights, among his hired hands over a fifty-year period.

His wife of fifty-six years, Mary Ann Dyer Goodnight, knew all the men, nursed them when they were sick, sewed buttons on their clothes, now and then gave them a party, once in a while got a preacher to preach to them. Goodnight did not care to hear what he called "soul-sharpeners," was never "converted," felt no need of having his soul saved. Mrs. Goodnight cultivated flowers, brought books to the ranch, loaned them to whoever wanted to read.

As leader of the decent element, Charles Goodnight naturally became the fear of the bad element. When no legal power was at hand, he assumed it. The earliest settlement near the ranch was "Christian Colony," some twenty miles from headquarters. It was made up of well-meaning visionaries utterly incapacitated for pioneer life. One time a man with a wagon load of whiskey and another wagon loaded with dancing girls appeared in the Colony. He proposed to set up a saloon and dance hall. The colonists protested. The man laughed. The colonists sent for Goodnight. He came.

"Do you see that line of cottonwood trees?" Goodnight asked the promoter.

The man saw. He understood the uses to which cottonwood branches, plus ropes, were sometimes put.

"You have half a day to pack up and get out."

"I want only two hours," the man concluded.

Another time when district court was to be convened at Clarendon, the district judge was informed by a gang of outlaws who had ridden down from Mobeetie, bent on keeping the country lawless, that there would be no court. The judge reported to Goodnight, who "happened" to be in town.

"My outfit is here with me," replied Goodnight. "The guns are in the wagon. The men know how to use them. You can open your court and conduct it without trouble." Court was held—without trouble.

About this time Goodnight had his attention called to the fact that the nesters of Christian Colony (Clarendon) had children in need of schooling, that the parents were too poor to provide a school, and that there were no public school funds. He laid the matter before the Panhandle cowmen. Not a single one of them had a child to send, but they instructed Goodnight to prorate among them the expenses of employing a teacher, and for two years they thus financed the first school of the Panhandle.

The teacher was Tom Martingale, "a kind of roustabout and head of the cow thieves." But he was well educated and as smart as a steel trap. "We ought to hang the son-of-a-gun," said Good-night, "but let's put him to teaching school and keep him busy." The next year the Panhandle Cattle Raisers' Association made a brand inspector out of him, on the theory that a thief can catch a thief. He made a good inspector.

Goodnight said he could learn more about a man by camping out with him in Comanche country for ten days than by neigh-boring with him for ten years in a settlement. As he put it, "The purest metal comes out of the greatest heat." He found educated men more teachable, quicker learners, than ignorant men. He believed in educating young women, mothers of men to be. His wife was educated. They had no children. He built a combined church and schoolhouse at Goodnight when there were only six children within reach of it and hired a teacher for them. In 1898 he and his wife opened Goodnight Academy. Hundreds of young people were benefited by it, though it was hardly the equivalent of a modern high school.

His own schooling had ended when he was nine years old, but he read. He observed not only profit-making stock but all kinds of flora and fauna, and, above all, human beings. He reflected. He thought. As his own mind ripened, even while his energy ebbed away, he grew more interested in the development of intelligence and character than in the calving of his cows. Offshoots of wild plums he selected to plant along the Palo Duro bear fruit annually. At the end he was far from being wealthy.

Even while he was making big money, more for a partner than for himself, his reach was for something in life beyond money. I never forget his telling of coming back from Fort Sumner, New Mexico, across the desolate, waterless Pecos country, where not a single bird was sighted. He had a pack mule loaded with $6,000 in coin. He and his men were traveling mostly at night, "laying up," out of Indian sight, by day. They were short on food. Then on the desert, not far from Horsehead Crossing on the Pecos, they met a man with a wagon load of watermelons.

"Where he came from, where he was going, what he was doing alone in that wild country, I have never imagined," Good-night told, "but he was a godsend to us. As I rode along filled with watermelon we had bought, I thought, 'Here we have plenty of money. We can't eat money. We can't carry it with us when we leave this world. I believe I don't care much for money.' I have never since cared much for money."

A generous nature is generous with money—if he has any; often he has not. For years the widows of men who had kept the frontiers against the Comanches sent letters to Goodnight asking for help. They received it.

❖ ◎ ❖

One day while I was with him, we drove in my car a short distance from the house to the big pens. After we got out and looked around, he had difficulty sidling his thick body back into the car. While struggling, he said, "Old age hath its honors but sometimes it is damned inconvenient."

Another day I drove alone to the caprock rim of the Palo Duro and for the first time gazed on the pillars, hills, canyons, mesas, and slopes leading down to a small stream, miles away, twelve hundred feet below. When I returned and said something about the impression the fantastic sight had given me as I came upon it suddenly after crossing level land, his face brightened with remembrances.

At the age of ninety-one, early in 1927, he married a young woman who had cared for him in sickness and who typed letters as he dictated them. His correspondence was heavy. As a wedding gift I sent a pair of bronze bookends depicting an Indian on horseback, hands stretched out toward the sky, a replica of "The Appeal to the Great Spirit." These were trivial things. I did not select them in a spirit of irony but because I thought the Indian subject would appeal to Mr. Goodnight.

He wrote back: "If you had studied for a hundred years, you could not have found anything that would have pleased me more. If Providence permits, I hope to have some little Goodnights to hand them down to."

In October of 1928 he and his wife came to our house in Austin on their way south for a gathering of the Old-Time Trail Drivers of Texas at San Antonio. He had never been to the annual meeting.

Sixty-two years had passed since he blazed the Goodnight-Loving Trail on his first long cattle drive. He was now well stricken in years. His strong young wife evidenced respectful dedication to him. He told me she had had a miscarriage.

The trail drivers always met in the Gunter Hotel. Mr. Goodnight did not make a talk to the gathering, but greeted many men and was the center of curiosity and attention. For hours through two days he sat, wide and thick, on a long lounge in the big hotel lobby. Two or three times while I sat with him talking, a stranger came up to say, "This is Colonel Goodnight, I take it," or something like that.

His invariable reply was, "This is Charlie Goodnight." He had not been even a captain. He did not like complimentary titles implying a status contrary to fact. The present concern over personal "images" would have disgusted him. He preferred, I judge, Mister to Colonel.

He did not mind naming, to me at least, known cow thieves who had prospered—and even been "colonel-ed."

"No more night work for me," he said. "I've done my share of night work—and it wasn't after other people's cattle." In his adamantine code of honesty, thieves were among the primary enemies of society.

Some man said, "You have been a man of vision." "Yes," he retorted, "a hell of a vision."

"My life," he said to me on this last visit I had with him, "has been mostly a failure."

That self-depreciation did not keep him from feeling superior in a you-be-damned way to all hypocrites, liars, pretenders, leeches, and bootlickers, even when it was his own boots they tried to lick. I have never, however, known an authentic earthman who licked anybody's boots.

On December 12, 1929, he died in Phoenix, Arizona, where he had been eating buffalo meat sent from an animal of his own herd. He was buried in Goodnight, Texas, not far from the rim of the Palo Duro Canyon. I reserve severely use of the word great. Charles Goodnight approached greatness more nearly than any other cowman of history.

Searching for Lost Tayopa

Tayopa has been the longest sought-for, the most extensively hunted, and the most widely talked-of lost mine in North America. Barriers of tangled mountains and barrancas, or gorges, that cut as deep as the mountains are high, have so isolated the setting that it, like the lost mine itself, seems a story out of another world long vanished. Tayopa is of the buried past, yet it remains the perennial hope of men searching today and laying plans to search tomorrow.—JFD

MANY MEN, representing varied nations of the globe, have set out for Tayopa from many directions. Yet for me the one place from which it is oriented will always be the Cerro Miñaca. This hill rises on a plain overlooking the village of Miñaca some two hundred kilometers—as the railroad twists—west of Chihuahua City. It takes the tri-weekly train all day to get there, the terminus of rails. Beyond lie the Sierra Madre ranges, towering, barranca-cut, impassable except to footmen, airplanes, burros, and other hardy beasts.

The main trail—the camino real, the "royal road"—across this part of the Sierra Madre has been traveled since the time of the Spanish Conquest; doubtless, Indians traveled it long before the Spaniards came. It is still a camino real—a "royal road." No railway or modern highway has supplanted it and perhaps never can supplant it; it is less traveled now than it was two hundred years ago. On some stretches of it a man may ride one, two, or even three days without meeting a soul.

The trail crosses timbered mesas, the charred stumps of pine torches beside it telling how the running Tarahumaras have raced here in the night. It leads down into canyons along which these singular Indians live in smoked caves or in shelters of poles only a little more substantial than the nests of eagles, dress in breech-clouts, perform rites to "the diabolic root," peyote, and fade from view when a stranger approaches.

It winds under mountains on the sides of which, too steep for an ox to walk, the mestizo and the pure-blooded Indian alike plant corn by punching holes with a stick in the rock-littered soil, leaving the plants for nature to cultivate.

It enters silent forests in which gunless Pima Indians cut down great pine trees in order to kill a little squirrel. From the mountains overtopping Ocampo, snowclad in wintertime, it pitches down a mile in half a day's ride to the torrid level of oranges growing along the Mayo River and wild-cotton trees with thorn-studded trunks sticking out of its cliffs.

Then it corkscrews upward again into pine and spruce and the red-hued madroños flagged with the cocoons of the Mexican silkworm. It prongs off to pass the spot where bandits left a man buried one night with his head sticking out of the ground and returned next morning to find that lobos had guillotined it.

It passes many mounds of rocks, each supporting a cross, marking places where death has struck or where, on the crests, man and beast have since time immemorial been accustomed to halt for breath. And each time one of the faithful comes to such a marker he will make the sign of the cross and add another rock to the pile.

The trail goes through the territory of the now tribeless Ópata Indians, the women of which still weave baskets of the "Rattle-snake in the Grass" design and entwine into fiber ollos symbols secret to their people. It goes on into the varied lands of the Yaqui Indians of still unsubdued fierceness.

Whoever follows this trail westward from Miñaca will travel two hundred and fifty miles without seeing a pane of window glass or going through a pasture gate. He may pass the weekly— in flood season perhaps the monthly—mail, which goes only a part of the distance, carried on a little mule driven by a sandaled footman. Along the trail women comb their long black hair with combs made of cactus burr, boys at harvest-time stand on guard to frighten deer and bear out of corn patches, and old men sit up all night smoking javelinas to death in a rocky den.

Yet church bells have been tolling these people to pray for hundreds of years, though more than one agroupment of hovels where a church once stood now has nothing churchly left but an ancient bell, hung from a pole. Here and there, beyond the sound of any bell, the trail becomes a ladder of little round holes, knee-deep to a burro, that only the hoofs of centuries of climbing mules could have worn in the everlasting rock. The chief freight they carried was supplies into and silver out of the mines. Along these ways, conductas once bore cargoes of silver bars. "In those days," says one historian, "iron and steel were worth more than silver, which was often used to shoe mules with."

That was when Tayopa was in bonanza. Probably the King of Spain did not know it was in bonanza, though he and his ministers were as familiar with most of the paying mines of Mexico as the president of Standard Oil sitting in Wall Street is with a major oil field in Texas or Venezuela. Mining operations were a part of the public record, and the chronology of some of the great mines operating in Mexico today runs back with hardly a break to the times of Hernando Cortés.

If Tayopa, then, was as rich a mine as tradition credits it with having been, history should have something to say of it. History—published history—is silent. The absence of records does not, however, disprove the existence of Tayopa. It was located in the most remote part of New Spain. In the seventeenth century, as in the twentieth, there was such a thing as concealing profits. Tayopa seems, in short, to have been a kind of bootleg mine.

❖   ◎   ❖

When I met C. B. Ruggles in 1927, he had already spent six years looking for Tayopa. Before that he had just about run the gamut of outdoor occupations of the West. His father had been a government physician who practiced among the Indians of the Northwest and invested his savings in cattle. Ruggles had a smattering of both medicine and surgery, and had known Indians and the mountains all his life. He had ranched, trapped, hunted, mustanged, prospected, and guided parties into the Rocky Mountains before there were roads and trails. Above all, as I found, he was extraordinarily observant and one of the most interesting talkers as well as agreeable human beings I have ever met.

He told me of trails he had followed and of trail-less regions he had entered. He had gone into Mexico while the country was still lawless from the effects of years of revolution. He related experiences he had had: with an ambush of bandits whom he discovered before they discovered him, with a Tarahumara who stole his mules and played a homemade fiddle; with two Pimas who planted in his trail daggers of the maguey leaf tipped with rattlesnake venom that had been caught in a deer's liver; with distrustful natives who at one time set fire to a forest in which he was camped and at another time rolled boulders down a mountain to blockade a narrow pass in front of him; with a Yaqui who shot at him from a cliff a thousand feet over his head and missed; with javelina hogs that led him into a long abandoned mine tunnel that he for a time took to be Tayopa.

Yet, despite certain experiences, he had found the folk of the sierras friendly and hospitable. Always free with the medicines he carried in his pack, he had won the name of *el doctor* over a wide territory.

But he had not won Tayopa. And now Ruggles was setting out once more, and I was riding with him. From Chihuahua City a wooden coach, punctured by revolutionary bullets and guarded by a squad of soldiers, took us to Miñaca, the end of rails and roads. I climbed to the summit of Cerro de la Campana, which overshadows the village, and looked at the sun as it set. Ruggles had two little tough Mexican mules under the care of a man at Miñaca, and I bought two for myself. We engaged a mozo, who, according to the custom of the country, trotted on foot behind the pack animals. He had not been spoiled by shoes.

We meandered somewhat from the main trail, visiting the falls of Baseachic, higher than Niagara's, and going by Ocampo to see a merchant who had for years been giving calico to Tarahumaras in the vain hope of learning the source of certain ore they brought in for trade. We had been out nearly two weeks when we camped at La Quiparita, where we proposed to lay in a supply of meat and do some prospecting.

La Quiparita is in Pima country. It is marked by a group of ancient arrastres, wherein centuries ago Spaniards crushed ore from mines that nobody within memory has known the location of. Out of the once rock-paved floors of two or three of those old arrastres great pines now grow. Near them is good water. For miles and miles around, the land alternates between sloping mesas and pine-clad mountains and flats. Black grama and red bunch grass grow stirrup-high; every canyon holds water—and not a hoof-print of cow or horse indents the sod. We had been here six days, awakened every morning by the gobble of wild turkeys, and were preparing to spend our last night before moving on the next day, when our mozo sighted a traveler coming down the trail from the north.

He rode up to the camp. He had a good outfit, and he gave his name as Custard. He accepted the invitation to unsaddle almost before it was given. He was not a reserved man. His tongue had not had a chance at English for months. It soon came out that he was looking for Tayopa.

"I am not so much interested in the mine itself," he explained after supper, "as in the wealth supposed to be buried at Tayopa. I have a document concerning that wealth. I have a map to the location. You men are looking for the mine. I'm for pooling our knowledge and searching as partners, you to have the mine and I to have the treasure."

"We have made a contract," Ruggles agreed, with an assenting nod from myself.

Custard reached into his pocket and pulled out a long, heavy envelope. I thought I saw his hand shaking. Meantime Ruggles threw a fresh chunk of pitch pine on the fire—our only light. The air was chilly, but as Ruggles bent over I saw perspiration on his face. Custard held the envelope in his hand a full minute without opening it. Then he put it back into his pocket.

"Before I show the papers to you," he said, "you had better

know how I came by them. They are not originals, but they are true copies. They have a history."

The history, stripped of various geographical and biographical details, was this: A number of years back General Antonio Hernandez of Nogales was buying cattle in eastern Sonora. While he was in a poverty-stricken little pueblo called Guadalupe de Santa Ana, an old Indian woman whom the general chanced to meet asked him if he would deliver a letter to the priest in Guaymas, on the Gulf of California. General Hernandez told the old woman that he expected to be in Guaymas within a month or so and that he would then deliver the letter.

"It is a very important letter," she quavered. "Father Domingo made me promise to get it delivered. He was priest of this parish. He came here in 1887 and built our church. When he died he was an old man. He was a queer man. He was always walking about and looking, looking. He was very kind to me. He left me fifty pesos and all his belongings and this letter. I have had it for two years. You are the first traveler I have seen that I could trust with it. Many thanks and may the Virgin protect you in your journey and the Saints reward you."

As General Hernandez took the long envelope he saw that it was of inferior paper and that it was addressed and sealed. He put it in his inside coat pocket. After he left Guadalupe de Santa Ana, he spent several weeks trading for scattered bunches of cattle. When he finally reached Hermosillo, he decided not to go to Guaymas at all but to go north to Nogales, his home. He thought of the letter. He was now where the post office department functioned; he would stamp the letter and mail it.

When he removed the envelope from his pocket, he found it almost worn out and the mucilage all melted. He procured a fresh envelope and addressed it. While he was refolding the letter to place it inside the new envelope, his eye fell on the word TAYOPA.

He had heard of Tayopa all his life. It was human to examine further.

He scanned the map and read the document. Then he copied both, honorably mailing the originals to the priest at Guaymas.

General Hernandez is a good businessman. It was not until he had spent more than 6,000 pesos looking for Tayopa, mostly in Chihuahua, that he parted with his map and document and their history to a certain El Paso contractor with whom he had cordial business relations.

"And I," Custard concluded his explanation, "am scout for that contractor."

Again he reached into his pocket, and this time he spread the papers on the ground in the full light of the fire.

The map is boldly titled "Mapa del Camino de Tayopa" (Map of the Tayopa Road). It shows Tayopa to be in the Sierra Madre—certainly not a very specific location. It shows roads leading thither from two widely separated towns in western Chihuahua. It shows a great mesa called Mesa Campañero east of Tayopa and overlooking it. It represents Tayopa as being a group of "seventeen mines of good assay" in an oval valley in the center of which is the "Yglesia" (church).

The document itself is long, detailed, and formal. It consists of directions for getting down to Tayopa from the Mesa Campañero and a minute inventory of the riches stored and left at Tayopa by the Jesuits. It is dated February 17, 1646.

The directions into Tayopa from the mesa are precise:

First take the branch road on the left side of the Campañero ridge in the Sierra Madre. Thus traveling toward the west along the Arisciachi trail, you will turn down a very narrow and broken path that cuts off. Then you will come into a thicket of madroño trees very abundant in foliage. To the right side and far below will appear two hills or runt mountains (cerritos chapos) capped with red topueste dirt. From the madroños proceed 1200 varas on down and there on a canon slope you will find a clump of güérigo trees.

Here there appears to be no trail at all, but, keeping your course down on for a matter of 45 varas, you will pass under two notably thick güérigo trees that touch their tops with the top of a live oak. Hence the two cerritos chapos already mentioned form a kind of gateway by which to enter the Real of Tayopa. The slope between these cerritos is very steep and is for some distance thick with ocotillos, the torete prieto, the vino ramo, and other thorned growth. Descending more gradually now, you come to the border of the valley, where are the church and the pueblo, circumscribed by seventeen mines of good assay.

Two particulars in these papers seemed noteworthy. The full name of Tayopa was given as Guadalupe de Tayopa, and to get to this Guadalupe de Tayopa the Mesa Campañero was of pivotal importance. But where was that Mesa?

Ruggles had a theory that Sierra Obscura down the Río Mayo might be Mesa Campañero. We would follow the trail, then, to Sierra Obscura, look for two runty red-capped hills under it and watch, above all, for güérigo trees. What kind of trees were güérigo trees anyhow? The mozos had never heard of them.

❖　◎　❖

Custard had a trail of his own to follow, and so Ruggles and I set out. We came to the Sierra Obscura, an enormous mountain that drops from pines into the hot barrancas. While making our way up a rough canyon on one side of it, we arrived at a ranchito called El Tigre, belonging to Perfecto Garcia, a pure-bred descendant of an Ópata chief, though Mexicanized in ways and speech. It was near night and the great mountain was as dark as its name. Here we camped. Perfecto had all his cattle, forty or fifty head, in a pen. He kept them there every night, he said, to protect them from the lions, bears, and jaguars. His boy, without a gun, for the ranch did not possess arms of any kind, kept four fires burning about the pen all the night long.

After ten days of fruitless explorations we camped again at Perfecto Garcia's on our way out. The family was in great distress as well as excitement. Perfecto's brother had just come in horribly mutilated. He had been out with his dog hunting javelinas. The dog had bayed a big boar that refused to go into a cave. When the man rode up and saw the boar cutting the entrails out of the dog, he got down to attack with his machete, the only weapon he possessed. The vicious animal turned on him, and in a minute tusked his leg, his side, and his face, nearly cutting off his ear. It seemed that the javelina had the man down for good, when the wounded dog rallied and made a rescue. In the end, the dog died fighting; the boar got away, doubtless to die; and the man dragged in to the ranch.

Ruggles washed the wounds with carbolic soap and sewed and bandaged them up. Don Perfecto was in an expansive humor.

"Are you not hunting for mines?" he asked Ruggles.

"Yes."

"Do you have any documents to direct you?"

"Yes."

"I have one also. Let me show it to you." Then out of the niche built into the thick stone or adobe walls of so many Mexican houses, Perfecto took a roll of gamuza. He unrolled this buckskin and showed a worn parchment titled "Conocimiento de Tayopa," or, as we might say, "A Chart of Identification for Tayopa." He was glad to let us copy it. Exactly translated, the opening sentences run thus:

It is worthwhile to remember and never to forget that there is a famous mining camp of prodigious richness known to the antiguos by the name of Tayopa. Situated it is on the first flowings of the River Yaqui, on the downward slopes of the Sierra Madre, in the direction of the town of Yécora in the ancient province of Ostimuri. The smelters remain there not only with great deposits of ore of high assay but with considerable silver in bullion form, stored away just as the antiguos left it. During long years Ostimuri has been almost altogether depopulated.

From this point in the reading the parchment was so torn and rubbed that only a few unconnected words could be made out. Perfecto Garcia could not read the document himself, but he had had it read to him many times, he said.

"Where did you get this?" Ruggles asked.

"I will tell you," the ranchero, dignified by a consciousness of his lineage, replied. "It has been in my family for a very long while.

As the oldest son of my father, I inherited it from him. He and some other Ópata men took it from the Pima Indians. The Pimas had driven off my people's stock. My people followed and raided a ranchería of the Pimas. They sacked everything the Pimas had. This conocimiento was in an earthen pot in a cave. With it were also some bone tools, a silver buckle, three pieces of money, and a turquoise necklace. Nothing but the paper has come down. I do not know where the Pimas got it. You know all that I know."

Now the links were forging together. The district of Ostimuri at one time, I knew, comprised the southeastern part of Sonora, in which Yécora is located. Ruggles knew that directly west of Yécora lay a great mountain. Under and below this mountain lay Guadalupe de Santa Ana, where the old woman had given General Hernández the papers belonging to the dead priest. This Guadalupe de Santa Ana had the reputation of being a "nest of eagles," an "eagle" in this part of the Sierra Madre meaning a man tricky and murderous.

Yet if Tayopa was in Ostimuri, in the direction of Yécora, "on the first flowings of the River Yaqui, on the downward slopes of the Sierra Madre," then this big mountain west of Yécora should be the Mesa Campañero and Guadalupe de Santa Ana should be Guadalupe de Tayopa.

When we got to Yécora we created an excitement. We were the first foreigners the inhabitants had seen in two years. The Mesa Campañero? All gestures were toward the long pine-clad mountain to the west.

The trail from Yécora west skirts this mountain, looping northward so as to avoid the steep grades. On the eastern side of the Mesa the water drains into the Río Mayo; on the western side, into "the first flowings of the Rio Yaqui." The crest of the broad-topped mountain is perhaps five thousand feet above the gnarled floor of the basin wherein lies Guadalupe de Santa Ana. We resolved not to "cut for sign" but to work out the ancient road according to our map.

We spent two weeks tracing this road over the Mesa and down its western slope. We found living on the Mesa two families descended from Confederate soldiers who had left the United

States at the end of the Civil War swearing they would not submit to tyranny; their intermarried descendants spoke little English. Often we lost the old trace. On account of washes, we had to make wide detours. We had to work out the greater part of the route afoot. In one place we found a pavement of cobblestones. The trail came into a steep canyon called "Arroyo Hondo" and followed it downward, dropping from bench to bench. Of course it had never been used by vehicles. On some of the narrow shelves were holes that probably once supported a kind of scaffolding to widen the path.

The old "camino real" passed through more than one "thicket of madroño trees." As we proceeded on down, the long-crested and long-tailed urracas—Columbia jays—screamed and chattered at us like maniacs. Now and then we startled parrots.

Then we came to some immense trees, gnarled and old, the like of which none of us had seen before. They were near a seep of water, and it was well along in the afternoon when we reached them.

"We camp right here," exulted Ruggles. "I am going to find what these trees are. They were here before Columbus sailed. If they are not güérigos, I'll eat my hat."

He went off for the village of Santa Ana, an hour's ride distant. With him came back an old fellow named Juan, who claimed to be half French. This Juan said that everybody in the country knew the trees as güérigos, and that he made chairs of the wood. I bought one of the chairs the next day, but a pack mule broke it. I have since identified the tree as *Populus wislizeni*; it is rare, and old Juan said that in his region it grew only along two canyons coming down from the Mesa Campañero.

The route as we followed it down next morning ran between two "runt hills capped with red topueste dirt." It led into a kind of basin of rocky hills so rough and barren of soil that only thorns grow on them—just such a parched, bleak, barren, rocky, God-forsaken waste as marks the locality of many good mines.

Our map—the map that General Hernandez got from the old woman in Guadalupe—was indisputably made from the lay of the land. What would Guadalupe itself reveal?

As we rode into the irregular string of adobe houses built along the arroyo, we were conscious of a distinct hostility. This was the "nest of eagles." Inquiry brought us to the house of the comisario, the chief of the pueblo, Joaquín Flores.

He came out and greeted his visitors with three very blunt questions: "Where are you from? Where are you going? What do you want?"

If all the questions, especially the third one, were answered directly and truthfully, the reception would probably be still less cordial. Ruggles was parrying words when the wife of the comisario came out wringing her hands and crying, "Succor in the name of the Little Mother of the Holy Child!"

"What is the matter?" Ruggles asked. We were still on our horses, as we had not been asked to dismount.

"Our son is dying with the fever of influenza," Joaquín Flores stoically replied. "Our whole village is cursed with the disease."

"Have you a doctor?" Ruggles well knew that the question was superfluous. Then he added, "Let me see your son."

He was led inside. Presently he came out, unpacked the mule that carried his medicines, and selected a bottle of fever drops. The effect of the drug and of cold water that the parents were prevailed upon to allow the patient was immediate.

Joaquín became an entirely different man. "Unload your saddles and your packs under my roof," he said. "I have corn in abundance and wood. Here is your house. I am at your orders. All I have is yours."

He commanded a feast. He gave a dance in our honor that very night. The next day he placed a cabin at our disposal. He would not think of letting us go until our beasts had recovered and he had guided us to a choice game region near his ranch out in the mountains.

Within three days' time Ruggles had doctored fifty people, some of them brought in from as far as twenty miles away. For instance, a girl was brought in with face so swollen from poison ivy that she could open neither eyes nor mouth. With solutions of soda and potassium permanganate Ruggles cured her. Her father and brother offered themselves "as slaves" in payment. They had nothing with which to pay, they said.

Ruggles never took pay for his medical services.

In such an atmosphere of gratitude and trust it was easy to broach the vital subject—mines—and, when the siege of patients relented somewhat, to prospect openly. Every inhabitant of Guadalupe seemed to know what we had been trying to find out, and every person could show evidences of ancient workings and tell their names: El Refugio, El Santo Niño, El Apache, La Barbayeña, La Bronzuda, Los Dukes Nombres, the whole circle of seventeen mines—"of good assay," we hoped.

We found the ruins of vasos (smelters). We found five enormous slag piles, into which natives yet "gopher" for slugs of silver—for the old system of smelting was notoriously wasteful. We picked up pieces of tools, locks, and other objects evidently of Spanish usage.

Meantime, the Guadalupe men were unlocking their "word hoards" to add to the evidence. If there is any one thing that the men of Guadalupe excel in, it is in telling tales. In the summertime they shift their positions with the crawling shade and talk. In the wintertime they squat in the sunshine and talk. The nights were made for talking, they say. Their women, like the women of their Indian ancestors, do all the work.

After we had been in Guadalupe de Santa Ana long enough to know most of the men by name, we heard their stories. Don Joaquín Flores told of an iron door his mother and aunt had glimpsed during a rainstorm, which was later swallowed up by the earth. "Some say there is a great treasure in the tunnel," Don Joaquín said. "Some say the treasure is under the church. I do not know where it is."

"I have lived here all my life. In my time I have seen many searchers for mines and lost treasures come into these mountains. Some of them never went out."

One evening I stepped up to the hut of old Apolonio Daniel.

"Oiga! Listen!" he began as soon as I was securely inside. "One time I opened up a vein in that ancient Refugio Mine and took out eleven quinientos pounds [a quiniento is five hundred] of ore. It was good ore, but I had reason not to continue working it. Someone else that I could not see was working also in that mine. I kept hearing the sounds of hammer and pick other than my own. I thought at first that the sounds might be echoes of my work. So I stopped. But the other sounds kept on. The poor fellow making them was away down there in the ground. He could stop only for a few minutes in the middle of the day. He seemed to get no rest at all. Sometimes I could hear him crying out, 'Tor-ti-11as, tor-ti-11as, tor-ti-11 -as,' as if he were hungry as well as tired. Then he would beg for water, 'Agua, agua, agua.' Often I could hear him gasp out with each blow of his heavy pick, 'Ah-uhh, ah-uhh, ah-uhh.' There are strange things in these tunnels of the ancients."

And the Guadalupe folk had not only a great many tales about mines and treasures pertaining to their village but also written directions for finding Tayopa. The rich man of the town gave us a derrotero (chart). Drunken old Enrique Daniel sold the second for ten pesos. Francisco Beltran, the village saddler and chairmaker, bestowed the third. All the derroteros were heirlooms, and all of them corroborated the documents that Ruggles already possessed.

We sent word to Custard that we had found Tayopa. He arrived some time later while Ruggles and I were still trying to obtain fair samples of ore from the old tunnels, most of them caved in. We had found ore, but so far none in payable quantities. Custard understood that as a matter of prudence he would have to secure an official concession before bringing into the sunlight such a vast treasure as his waybill called for.

We told Custard of a recent episode in Tayopa history: A few months before our arrival, as was narrated to us with iterated detail, a "rich Arabe"—and an "Arabe" may be a Jew, an Assyrian, or of some other nationality—arrived from the west with a concession signed by General Plutarco Elias Calles, then president of the Republic of Mexico, a guard of forty soldiers, and several laborers. His concession, which he showed with ostentation, called on the authorities of Guadalupe de Santa Ana to allow him to excavate under the church or anywhere around it.

The mayor and all the citizens were angry at such desecration, but with the military order and the forty soldiers in front of them they could do nothing but yield. Not a hand of the village, though, could the "Arabe" hire to dig.

His men dug holes through the church floor and brought up skeletons—"nothing more." The people sat around on the ridges watching. The diggers struck a rock shelf underlying the church, but this they did not penetrate. Around the church they put down holes that we saw, yet unfilled. Then they left.

Custard was sure that the treasure must be under the rock that the "Arabe's" forces did not penetrate; yet he had the fate of other previous seekers to consider. A common Guadalupe story is about an Italian man who claimed to be a historian interested in writing a true record of the Indians and their relations with the Spaniards. Somehow he won the confidence of the natives and secured their permission to build a one-roomed adobe cabin fifty feet north of the church.

Before long, he was discovered digging a tunnel leading toward the foundation of the church. The mayor called the men of the village together, got a handful of small sticks of uneven length, and directed each man to draw one. The four men drawing the four shortest sticks were delegated to "escort" the Italian historian forth.

"And you know," concluded one of the "eagles" who told the story, "we never found a scrap of paper on his body."

The man's cabin was razed to the ground. A year later two well-equipped Italians came to Guadalupe to make inquiry concerning their compatriot. "He has left the country," was the only answer they received. They found it fitting to leave the country also.

Custard understood that getting to that treasure was a business that would have to wait and would require more than an official concession. Besides the keen need for diplomacy among the eagles, we would need to clean out and explore the old tunnels—heavy work that would require capital. We estimated that merely to denounce—survey and lay legal claim to—the far-spread pertenencias of land enclosing the scattered workings would take a year and more money than either of us had. My own small interest I turned over to Ruggles, fully realizing that I was still in debt to him. From a company of lawyers and engineers in El Paso, he raised enough capital to make denouncements and do more assay work. But the rich vein has not yet been struck.

❖   ◉   ❖

Nothing is ever settled until it is settled right—and nothing is ever settled right until it is settled in my way. Facts are stubborn things, but theories are stubborner. When a man becomes thoroughly convinced that a lost mine is in a certain area, nothing can unfix the idea. If the mine were found by somebody else in another area, he would merely say that it must be another mine and not the lost mine he was looking for at all. People are going to go on looking for Tayopa in many places.

One time I was riding in the Sierra Madre a long, long way from where Ruggles and I located Tayopa. I was riding for something better than gold or silver; I was riding for the elation of being free and having plenty of room. One evening—or late afternoon, as some people call it—we came to good water and made camp. Before long three men rode up and camped not far off. I was glad to have their company, for I knew I'd learn something about the country and its traditions from them. Soon we were all cooking at the same fire. They had some fresh roasting ears that, roasted in the shuck in hot ashes, were the juiciest and most toothsome corn I have ever tasted.

These men were of the peasant but not peon class, just and kindhearted and gracious. I noticed a blowing horn that one of them had. It was very long, and on it was carved in bold, crude lettering, Viva Díos (Long Live God). The sun was going down through a gap in the mountains, and just as a great boulder beside the trail crossing fell into shadow, the owner of the horn mounted the boulder and began to blow. His blasts made, it seemed to me, the trees tremble, and echoes answered back from far away.

"Can you hear it?" the blower asked of his companions.

"No," one answered.

"Not yet," replied the other.

The man went on blowing and blasting. I shifted my position

for the comfort of my ears. The horn blower's two companions were shifting around, cupping their ears, bending this way and that way, standing silent with open hands raised near their ears, seemingly searching for some sound as delicate as the last, low, solitary chirp of a cricket in late fall. The blowing and listening went on until dark. The men, who said nothing, were quite serious, though now and then they smiled at some attempted levity on my part. Eventually this levity gave way to a consuming curiosity. I waited until after supper to ask questions.

"We are trying to find the echo of Tayopa," the horn blower said. "Tayopa is in a canyon maybe not far from this place. The conductor of the mule train that carried the silver out from Tayopa was a forefather of mine long passed away. When he reached this crossing, he always blew his horn to announce his arrival. The sound would echo; then that echo would echo. The place where this third echo was made was Tayopa—perhaps a certain crevice in the rock, perhaps a tunnel mouth—who knows? The third echo would not come as such, but sounded as clear as the original blast, only shriller. This is a tradition with us. We know we are near Tayopa, but we cannot find it, and we are hoping this horn will tell us."

The next morning, I left rather early. As I mounted my mule, the good man mounted the boulder again, a smile on his face and Viva Díos in his hand. I heard its blasts a good while after a turn in the trail shut out all view.

The Last of the
Mountain Men

It was thirty-five years ago that El Paso began being for me the best story town in the world. In 1928 I was stopping there a few days on my way into Mexico to look for the Lost Tayopa Mine—or the story of it, which is probably better than the mine itself. It happened that the American National Livestock Association was in convention. I learned that Ben Lilly had been brought down to make a talk on predatory animals to the cowmen.—JFD

I HAD FREQUENTLY heard of Ben Lilly, this Nestor of the Mountains. He had been hunting all his life and he knew more about the wild animals than any other man in the mountains. His stamina was legendary. President Theodore Roosevelt, after a much-publicized bear hunt with Ben Lilly in 1907, had proclaimed, "I never met any other man so indifferent to fatigue and hardship."

Lilly was said to hate all restrictions, which were constrictions to him. He kept a little money in two or three banks. If he had occasion to write a check, he would not use a printed check but instead would write on a piece of bark, a piece of brown wrapping paper, or something like that—and the bank always made it good.

The one book that he read—and he knew it well—was the Bible. He was so religious that if his dogs treed a panther on

Saturday night, he and they would keep it in the tree until Monday morning before he would shoot it. Once he lost track of the days, however, and on bringing a panther hide to town was much chagrined to learn that he had killed and skinned the animal on the Holy Sabbath.

What most people consider ordinary comforts, he regarded as debilitating luxuries. He never wore a coat or overcoat in the winter, but did wear three or four wool shirts, which he changed by pulling off the one next to his undershirt and putting it over the one that had been outside. He held that the elements will cleanse any garment exposed to them.

According to one story, his wife, Mary, finally told her husband that if he ever left on another hunt, she hoped he would keep on going. One day toward the end of the year 1901, he transferred all of his property except five dollars to her, called his three children together, kissed them goodbye, very affectionately kissed Mary goodbye also, took his dogs and headed for the Tensas River in northeastern Louisiana.

He had been born with a talent for hunting, he said, "and if we are not faithful to our talents, we lose them."

He would leave camp to be gone a week or a month with his dogs, taking nothing but a sack of corn meal, some salt and a frying pan. He could find water to mix with the meal to make bread, and there was no danger of his running short of game meat for himself and his pack. Even in cold weather he would sleep with nothing but leaves and pine needles, and the dogs huddled close to him to keep him warm.

When I saw Lilly in El Paso, he was over seventy years old— stumpily built, with a complexion that glowed like that assigned to Santa Claus. He had one of the cleanest, mildest pair of eyes I ever looked into. His voice was so soft and his whole expression so innocent that anybody listening to him and looking at him for the first time would never suspect the stubbornness he kept in reserve.

He talked for an hour on bears and panthers and enjoyed himself immensely, although he admitted that this was his first public speech of any consequence except for a talk to a Sunday school class. Everything he said reflected a minute familiarity with animal ways and spaces beyond man-made trails.

After it was over I got with him and introduced myself, saying, "I have heard of you many times, Mr. Lilly."

"Yes," he replied, "my reputation is bigger than I am. It is like my shadow when I stand in front of the sun in late evening."

I persuaded him to keep talking. He was as full of philosophy as an egg is of meat. Every once in a while I would remark that Emerson or Henry David Thoreau or some other thinker had recorded an idea similar to one he had just expressed. These were all foreign names to him, but as they agreed with him, he thought they were mighty smart men, and he thought I was mighty smart, too, for being able to quote them.

The old man kept telling about the black bears he had killed in the canebrakes of Louisiana, the grizzlies he had tracked to their doom in New Mexico and Arizona, and the big ones he had got down in Mexico. Finally, I asked him how many bears he had killed.

"That's a secret I am keeping for my book," he said.

At this time, *Trader Horn* was one of the most popular books in America, and when I told Mr. Lilly that his experiences and philosophy would make as good a book as the one about Trader Horn, he was delighted, though he had not heard of Horn before this. I meant what I said. Then I let him know that I was a writer. He seemed to become more interested in me and said that he had something he would show me, and suggested that we go over to the old Shelton Hotel, where he had a room.

I was staying there also. The Shelton was wonderfully made, with about half a dozen levels to each floor, and with halls as full of turns as a trail down one of the Sierra Madre mountainsides. When we got into the lobby, he walked over to the desk and said something to the clerk. The clerk worked the combination on the lock of the door to a steel vault just back of the desk, opened the ponderous door, and reached into a cavern that had hid fortunes in gold and silver smuggled across the Río Bravo in revolutionary times, and pulled out a sack that had at one time been white and held forty-eight pounds of XXXX flour. A knot was tied in the open end.

Mr. Lilly took the flour sack, indicated that I was to follow him, and led the way upstairs, along various lanes, or halls, over the up-and-down levels and stopped finally at the door to his room. We went inside and he locked the door. Then he opened the flour sack and pulled out a manuscript of perhaps twenty-five typewritten pages. "You can read it," he said, handing it to me. These were the first words he had spoken since his request of the hotel clerk.

I took the manuscript, saw the title, "What I Know about Bears," felt for a chair, and read, utterly absorbed, until I had reached the end. It proved to be one of the most fascinating pieces of natural history and outdoors lore that I have ever read. It was full of concrete, firsthand observations. He could tell the sex and age of any bear he trailed, and he would not trail it long before he knew where it had been and what it had been doing and where it was going and with what purpose. His manuscript was not written in a style that any publisher would approve of, but I soon learned that Mr. Lilly did not intend for anybody to change a syllable of it. He had had a schoolteacher in a New Mexico mining camp type it, he explained, and in his mild way he was incensed that she had made several changes in his punctuation.

By the time I had finished reading "What I Know about Bears," it was good dark. Mr. Lilly said that if I would come back next evening I could read the second chapter. I asked him to eat supper with me. He declined. He did not want so much as a cup of coffee. He never drank coffee or tea, much less any kind of spiritous liquor. I learned later that he did not like to eat in a dining room. "I just can't do it," he'd say. He would take his food out on a bench or to a log so as to escape being shut up inside at a formal table.

He let me know that he was not sleeping on the hotel bed but was spreading some of the bedclothes on the floor and sleeping there. He complained of the "rancid" air. "Every man and woman ought to get out and be alone with the elements a while every day, even if for only five minutes," he said.

"When I am around babies," he went on, I always tote them out on my arm in the evening and let them look at the stars and feel the wind. They sleep better for that. The would sleep better still if they had their pallets on the ground. I always sleep better on the ground. Something agreeable to my system seeps into it from the ground."

Late the next afternoon we got together again. He retrieved the flour sack out of the vault, got on the right trail to his room, and we were locked inside it once more. The title of the second chapter was "What I Know about Panthers." I had in the pocket of my coat a copy of the *El Paso Herald* and a *Saturday Evening Post*.

While I was taking a preliminary glance at the manuscript, but before I had entered upon the joy of reading it, I thought of the newspaper and magazine, and, pulling them out, said, "Mr. Lilly, perhaps you would like to read something in these while I am reading what you have written."

"No, I thank you," he replied. "I find this very interesting."

I looked at him. He was deeply immersed in his own manuscript on "What I Know about Bears."

In addition to many natural history observations, the chapter on panthers contained several stories of attacks on human beings. I was regretful that there was not a third—or a thirtieth—chapter to read.

That meeting in El Paso was the last, as it was the first, I had with Ben Lilly. As I was to learn, not long after he returned to the mountains from El Paso, he took pneumonia. He recovered but gradually declined.

For several years I kept hoping, yet hardly expecting, that his book would be printed and placed on the market. Then I learned that he had lost his mind and was being cared for by a rancher. He lived to be almost eighty years old. He died December 17, 1936, and his last words were, "I'll be better off." His shadow went on lengthening.

A decade later out in the Gila National Forest, the dearest hunting range of his long life, a bronze plaque was erected to his memory. In bas-relief his head is flanked on one side by the head of a bear and, on the other, by the head of a mountain lion.

The loss of his manuscripts seemed wrong to his memory, and to the knowledge he had gained. I wanted to make use of them. I made a trip into New Mexico trailing—without success— those chapters on "What I Know about Bears" and "What I Know about Panthers."

In 1940, I wrote an article on him, emphasizing the lost manuscripts, and sent copies of it to the El Paso and two New Mexico papers. Dr. L. A. Jessen, a dentist in Bayard, New Mexico, wrote to me: "Somewhere I have two articles by Ben Lilly, one on bears and one on lions, both in his fine hand, written with pencil on cheap tablet papers." I responded, asking to be allowed to copy them. Other men and women wrote to me about Mr. Lilly, but I heard no more from Dr. Jessen.

One August day, toward three months after his note, I stepped into Dr. Jessen's office.

"I haven't been able to locate them," were his first words. One of the articles he had loaned to somebody whose name was forgotten. The other was "probably" in a storeroom, in fragments. This storeroom was of adobe with a dirt floor. Lime, spilled from three or four sacks, was mixed with the papers and miscellaneous junk. Dr. Jessen's boys had gone through the papers more than once looking for old stamps, their energy evidently outrunning their sense of orderliness.

The first leaf of Ben Lilly's penciled tablet that I found was numbered 32. Most of the leaves turned up separately. By the time I found the last leaf of the tablet, number 89, only four were missing. It was sundown and I could no longer breathe the lime-dusted air. I told the Jessen boys that I would be back in two or three days and would pay a quarter apiece for the missing leaves. They had them when I got back.

At the GOS ranch headquarters, where Lilly had once lived, a cowboy helped me to excavate the bed of a disused wagon, under a brush shed, about a hundred yards from Lilly's cabin. It was more than a foot deep in gunny sacks and straw, with empty patent medicine bottles and papers mixed in. I saved all the papers and found among them a letter from W. H. McFadden of Ponca City, Oklahoma, thanking Mr. Lilly for a diary. I wrote to Mr. McFadden, who sent me a carbon copy of the diary.

Had Mister Ben Lilly written his book, I would have never begun mine, which became *The Ben Lilly Legend*.

Now, thirty-five years after my one encounter with Ben Lilly, I still see his clear, serene eyes, as limpid as childhood's. The "power of harmony" had given them open assurance, and in one way they seemed to hide nothing. Certainly they reflected nothing of design on other human beings. Yet in a strange way they seemed to shadow personal matters never to be revealed. He took a certain pride in being eccentric. Teddy Roosevelt summed up Ben Lilly as "a religious fanatic." Fanatic he was, but about hunting, not religion. The demon that possessed him was of the woods and the mountains, not of theology. His life was a sermon without words. He had been born too late to share the "perfection of primitiveness," but he belonged to the outdoors as essentially as the bears themselves.

On the Trail of the Panther

At this time I was writing considerably for the Country Gentleman magazine—hunting stories, legendary tales, historical sketches of the Old West and Southwest. My trip into New Mexico had been after a panther story to put in the magazine. Joe and Dub Evans had caught lots of the creatures and they were mighty free with their stories about them as we at around the fire every night.—JFD

EIGHTY-FIVE MILES by automobile from Magdalena, New Mexico, across the winter-browned Plains of San Agustín, then to the road's end in the Black Range, and we were at the Evans brothers' Slash Ranch at Beaverhead. Twenty miles with pack mules over a trail of Datil National Forest, and we were at the Horse Camp on the Middle Prong of the Gila River, near Apache leader Geronimo's birthplace—and perhaps the best mountain lion country left in the United States.

Formerly, the panther ranged over entire North America, but a lion country nowadays must be inaccessible. The forks of the Gila, with their intersecting canyons, are as rough as any malpais, "bad country." Here are volcanic mountains covered with pine, spruce, and fir and fringed with manzanita and stubborn shinnery. Here are slopes and plains dotted with alligator junipers and sweet-nut-bearing piñons. Here are wide mesas of grama grass, and moating the mesas are rocky canyons that cut down a sheer thousand feet.

A lion country must also be prolific of lion food. The lion's staff of life is deer meat. He likes turkeys, and there are plenty of turkeys in the Mogollons. He licks his chops over antelope and beaver, both of which survive in numbers along the Gila. Frequently, other food being scarce, he kills calves and yearlings, but seldom does he bother cattle in the Datil National Forest.

He grows fatter on colts and mules than on anything else, but horse raising is pretty much an obsolete business now. All he asks is venison, and anywhere on the upper forks of the Gila venison may be had for the asking. Every day we rode I saw forty or fifty deer.

But even in the best lion country rigid requirements are necessary for catching a lion: trained hunters, trained dogs, and, generally, persistence and endurance. Lions are shy and wily creatures. Men who have hunted them a lifetime and have killed scores of them have told me that they never saw one until after he had been jumped by dogs.

The Evans brothers, Dub and Joe, are certainly experienced hunters. Seventy-five years ago their grandfather was ranching and hunting in southwest Texas. Nearly fifty years ago their father pushed into the Davis Mountains, on the western edge of Texas, where the lion and the Apache had for ages held possession.

By the time Joe and Dub were ten years old they were running *ladino* ("wild") Longhorns and following the hounds. In a single year they helped catch fifteen lions out of the canyon on which the Evans home ranch was established—Panther Canyon, it is called. Altogether they have caught hundreds of lions. In the few years they have ranched in New Mexico they have caught thirty-three. They're what the Mexicanos call *hombres del campo*—"men of the camp."

As for their dogs, there is not a better pack in Texas and New Mexico. The family of hounds of which they are the latest generation has been with the Evans men for thirty-nine years. When a year old, the original pair of pups, Belle and Brownie, began hunting lion and bear and soon developed into remarkable dogs. By line breeding, with an occasional cross with bloodhound and Redbone hound, the characteristics of old Brownie and Belle have been strictly preserved.

The original names pass down from generation to generation. Today the leader of the pack is Brownie, mighty of foot and mouth and muscle, as confident of himself in the field as Admiral Nelson at the Battle of Trafalgar. As good and more energetic is Belle, beautifully spotted and amiable of disposition. Then there are Short Brownie, Little Brownie, Francis, Trumm, and Lee Wilson.

The older dogs never notice the tracks of deer, coons, coyotes, foxes, and the like. They will take a wildcat's track, but are easily called off it. The only animals they really hunt—and, once they have struck the trail of, follow despite hell and high water—are lions and bears. Our hunt was at a time when most bears have gone to sleep for the winter.

The moon was yet shining, the thermometer was at zero, and the dogs were comfortably filled with the flesh of a slaughtered mare when we struck out across Black Mountain the first day of our hunt. About noon, as we were riding down in the very bottom of a deep canyon, the dogs opened up, but the trail soon proved old. After much searching Dub Evans made out two lion tracks, one of a full-grown lion going down the canyon, the other of a young lion going up; neither track fresh enough to follow.

We went on, the dogs smelling at the foot of trees and nosing along the base of boulders and palisades. The lion likes to walk on a narrow bench under bluffs. He likes to cross rough saddles, or dips, between highlands. He likes to prowl the length of narrow hogbacks that look down into chasms on either side. He likes to meander along projections and indentations of a naked rimrock, following the ragged edge sometimes for miles.

Brownie and Belle and their followers knew all this. They never failed to examine any log so fallen that there was space between it and the ground. The lion likes to walk under such logs, bow up his back, and rub it like a cat. If a twig bent over the trail, the dogs sniffed it, for the lion often leaves the scent of his body or tail on weeds and bushes.

We topped out of Brother West Canyon and followed the trail over a malpais ridge.

"Over yonder is the canyon of Indian Creek," Dub said.

Beyond the blue vacancy I saw a line of cliffs. Suddenly the dogs stiffened their tails, stretched out their heads, worked their noses, let out a long and peculiar bay, and were gone.

"They have smelled a kill!" said Joe.

We followed at hot speed. Presently we came upon the dogs tearing at barren deer bones over which no lion would ever again lick his "thankful chops." The ribs were still red with dried blood, but they had been picked several days before.

The kill was under a gnarled juniper tree on a shelf of rocks overlooking the junction of Indian and the Middle Prong of the Gila. The bark of the juniper was scratched with lion claws.

Spread out below us, like the ruins of some incomprehensible and fantastic mammoth, was a skeleton world over which the hounds of the elements had gnawed and snarled for dizzy eons. The dried and scattered ribs of the skeleton were cones of rock, red and yellow and gray. The twisted and broken legs were ridges of wrecked boulders. The grave of the skeleton was walled in with cliffs that only an eagle could surmount. If it was not the Grand Canyon, it was a grand canyon. On the point of an escarpment I saw a blotch of red. It was possible to work one's way out to it. The blotch proved to be a bone of the lion-killed deer.

"The raven we just saw put it there, I guess," said Dub. "Always watch for ravens. They locate the kills every time."

We had trailed a lion either to or from the kill, we did not know which. It was entirely possible that we had back trailed. Certainly it was an old track to an old kill. Yet we had little doubt that a lion was within finding distance. During the night he might, out of idle curiosity, pass the abandoned kill. We would come back in the morning.

Dawn found us, Indian file, rimming out of the deep canyon in which we were camped.

As we topped out onto a mesa the dogs took an east-by-north course instead of our intended east-by-south direction. Luck, destiny, providence, something might be directing them. We were outward-bound, bound to get a lion. Yet we did not strike even an old trail that day. We cut for sign over some of the ground we had traversed the day before, but the dogs were too intelligent to take up again a trail they had worked on and abandoned.

The next day bore the same lack of luck and the next and the next. We scouted east and west, north and south. It snowed, rained a little, and the southern slopes melted. It snowed again, and the northern slopes were as slick and hard as glass. We slid down those slopes into warm, deep canyons and somehow wound and climbed out of them.

Often we were afoot leading our horses. I discovered that by grasping the tail of the horse in front of me as we plodded upward I could get my wind and my footing with much less heaviness.

Those mountain horses climb like Rocky Mountain sheep and are as fearless as rock squirrels. They went up desolate steeps that would literally pen in to death and starvation a trainload of plains horses. I would not have traded my mount, Insect, for the finest stabled steed in Newport.

One day we saw an eagle maneuvering to catch a fawn. Another day we let the dogs tree a wildcat. On the iciest, shadiest, roughest slope in Catron County we found where a huge black bear had spent a week not long before. Flocks of piñon jays jeered at us. Tassel-eared squirrels played bo-peep from the branches of great pines. We saw more deer than cattle, mule deer and white-tails both. Often we looked eagerly at ravens, but the fact that ravens locate a panther kill does not mean that every raven denotes one.

Up at four o'clock in the morning. Before dawn a hot and meaty breakfast, saddles, and the clear bugling of a hunting horn. Some raisins and nuts in the pocket to munch on for lunch. Hours and hours of riding and hoping and looking. Such was the order of the day for three, four, five, six days. On one of those days, Sunday, it was snowing, and we rested ourselves and the dogs. The Evans boys don't hunt on Sunday anyhow.

And the shadows of evening always found us back at the Horse Camp, ravenous, tired, every fiber in the body yearning for hot food and a roaring fire.

How much hot beefsteak one man can eat I do not know, but had a weigher been present at the Horse Camp any night we were there, he might have found out. Plenty of meat, plenty of tobacco, gallons of coffee, forests of pitch pine to burn, a snug cabin, company immensely congenial, grain for horses and mare meat for the dogs—what better camp could a man ask for?

The winter nights in New Mexico are long, long nights, and the talk often turned to panthers. How lions kill, how they cover their kills, their strength, their size, their disposition to travel, their scream, their fear of man, their ferocity, their playfulness, their patience, their markers—every phase of lion nature we discussed and yarned over.

We must have talked more about panther kills than about any other feature of the great cat. The lion is more prodigal of meat than any other predatory animal. Sometimes he slays merely for exercise or nothing more than a drink of blood from the jugular of his victim. At the same time, in the care of his meat he is probably the most intelligent and meticulous animal in the world. He likes his meat fresh and clean.

As soon as he makes a kill, he removes the entrails from his prey. Unlike the wolf, he begins eating on the foreparts of an animal. If the place at which he has slain a buck or other game does not suit him, he carries it to a proper location. Then he carefully covers it with leaves and twigs.

And so the nights passed, with talking on many things really, but never long off the subject of lions and lion dogs and lion hunts. On the morning of the seventh day we were down in House Log Canyon. About ten o'clock Brownie let out a bellow, Belle sent up a cry, and the other dogs turned loose a varied and stirring noise that sent the blood tingling to the roots of our hair.

"Lion sign and no fooling," said Dub as I rode up to where he had already dismounted at the root of a pine. The dogs were slowly working away up the canyon.

"I've been telling you about lion markers," Dub went on. "Here they are."

What we were looking at were parallel scrapes on the ground about eight inches long, at the base of them a little mound of pine needles. They had evidently been made by the lion with his claws hooded. Only males make them. As the lion rakes back toward his body, a marker always indicates in what direction he is going, whether any tracks are visible or not. The markers remain for weeks after tracks have vanished.

For an hour or more we worked up the canyon, so slowly that most of the time we were on foot, trying to help the dogs with the trail.

"Look here," called Dub, who had followed the dogs to a bench fifty feet above our heads.

He had found another marker made in gravel against the bluff.

The trail finally climbed out of the canyon and struck across a lava mesa. It came to a kind of barren place with not a twig or a blade of grass to hold the lion smell. It took us an hour to go less than half a mile.

When we struck the southern slope, where the snow had all melted and run over the tracks, we were absolutely stalled. We were a day too late, and the day's work was about over. People don't hunt mountain lions at night as they do coons.

On the trail into camp, Dub told me a remarkable story about lion markers. A year or more ago a government hunter in the Middle Gila country got on the trail of two lions, a male and a female. He followed them for two days, camping out both nights without food. On the third day he caught the female lion; then, seeing nothing of the male, he went on.

Two weeks later while riding after cattle Dub struck a fresh kill made by a male lion. He knew the lion was a male from the markers right at the kill. It was in the country the government man had hunted over.

Dub went to the ranch, got his dogs, and was at the kill early next morning. He had no trouble in striking a good trail, but the lion was not lying up to digest food. He was roving, day as well as night.

Over Black Mountain and down into the canyon country, Dub followed the trail at a good gait all day long. And every little distance he found a lion marker. He is sure that he found a hundred markers, all made in one day's time. The lion was putting out sign for his mate. He was searching the country for her.

Late in the evening the dogs jumped him, and even after he

was jumped he made a marker—a very, very unusual act. After Dub killed him he cut him open. There was not a bit of food inside him. He had been too despondent to eat.

When the morning of the eighth day dawned, the world was white with fresh snow.

Hardly a quarter of a mile from the camp the dogs opened up on a hot trail. Joe and Dub called them off without even looking at the trail. What the dogs said to them was "wildcat."

Well, the day closed, the magazines of our saddle guns were as full of cartridges and our hands were as empty as they had been for a week. We were thoroughly disgusted with the Middle Fork and all its eastern tributaries. The lions might be on the other side of Gila. They were not on our side, for certain. They might be ten miles away, and ten miles of canyons that include the Gila River in the Mogollon Mountains is as far as two hundred on pavement.

Our plan was to leave very early the next morning without packs, but carrying on our saddles a ration of grain for the horses, some mare meat for the dogs, and coffee, bread, and meat for ourselves. We would cross the Gila and let luck direct us.

It must have been about two o'clock when we struck a fresh kill. It was a ten-point white-tailed buck. One forequarter was gone and the tongue eaten out.

There were two or three markers under the trees about it.

"We've got a check and all we have to do is cash it," I yelled.

"Wait," said Dub.

"Just wait," said Joe.

It happened that the kill was on a mountainside where very little snow had fallen, but there were plenty of rocks and timber. Before we had time to do anything the dogs were coursing off at a lively rate. If a lion has smeared blood, the contents of a deer's entrails, or other fresh animal matter on his paws, he leaves a trail that can for many hours be scented at a long run. The way our dogs were making tracks indicated that they were on an outgoing trail made by lion feet well smeared.

Still, there is only one sure way to know whether dogs are going with tracks or are back trailing. That is to see the tracks.

The blindness of dogs to tracks is as remarkable as their acuteness in smelling them.

We followed them, now galloping, now pausing, looking all the while for tracks. When we came to where the dogs had crossed a gulch in the bottom of which was sand, the tracks were plain. We were back trailing.

There was nothing to do but call the dogs off and return to the kill for a fresh start. Quickly the eager dogs found another track that we made sure was outgoing.

It went down into a rough country of tumbled boulders. The dogs came to bluffs over which they had to be lifted. Even if a lion were jumped there, he stood a good chance of getting away. With night about to close down it was folly to trail farther.

"It's only about a mile from here to a spring in Little Bear Canyon," said Dub. "I packed some deer hunters into that place a month ago. A quarter of a mile above the spring I saw a cave. We'll spend the night there."

Dogs, horses, and men were all glad when we struck the soft bottom of Little Bear. At the camp we found a side of deer ribs that the hunters had left and that a month of cold weather had not injured.

When I fed the dogs I noticed for the first time that their noses were bloody raw. No wonder! Those noses had been, without letup, grazing over malpais rocks by the tens of thousands and poking under acres of snow, snuffing, snuffing for lion sight. Galley slaves never worked harder than those dogs worked for us. They were used to sleeping out, but when we found a place for them in one corner of the long cave before which we built two fires, they were very grateful. The pleasure in seeing them warm was about the only pleasure I realized that night.

With the first light we saddled. A short hour's ride and we were at the kill. The lion had been there during the night, although it was apparent that he had not eaten more meat than he could well carry. He might be lying down within a hundred yards, or he might be off at some distance. We took his trail at a gallop. It made for the rough canyon we had quitted the evening before.

As the dogs struck the canyon rim they all at once hushed,

apparently nonplussed. Dub and Joe were down on their knees, working like dogs themselves.

It took ten minutes to discover that the lion had leaped from the rim into a juniper tree that grew out of the canyon wall, had climbed out on a limb of the tree, and then dropped off under the rimrock. A lion does not often play fox tricks.

As the dogs with a joyful bound again took off, we remained on top where we could hear and see and come as near being with the dogs as we could be anywhere.

They followed down the canyon under the rimrock on our side, crossed, and began working back up the canyon on the other side. Above them towered an uneven wall of rock that could be scaled only at intervals.

Brownie was at least two hundred yards out from the canyon rim on a smooth mesa. Between him and the canyon was growth of scattered cedar.

"Look! Look!"

It was the first time I had seen Dub excited.

"I caught a glimpse of a panther in that cedar. I'll swear I did."

Nobody else saw a panther in the cedar, but what we all saw a minute later was a long, tawny form gliding through the grass away from the canyon of barking dogs and toward silent Brownie.

With the corner of my eye I saw Belle about to climb out. The tawny form was gliding, drifting, moving like an effortless ghost straight toward Brownie. And Brownie had sensed the panther. He turned and was coming in a long run back toward the canyon and the lion.

In mid-prairie they met.

It is a mystery of nature why such a powerful and lethal fighter as the mountain lion will run from a dog. But run he will invariably.

The lion wheeled like a released bowstring. I would not attempt to say how high or how far he jumped. As he whirled and leaped the slant morning sun showed his breast dazzling white.

When he reached the canyon rim he was at the climax of his speed and he never checked a second but spread himself flat like a flying squirrel for the awful leap. It was a hundred and twenty-five or a hundred and fifty feet to the first bench below, but the space was not altogether clear. Some rocky spires jagged up part of the way.

With outstretched paws the lion caught one spire, swinging himself a quarter around and slightly breaking his fall. A second rock he barely scraped.

While he was making that leap I do not think that one of us drew breath. By the time he hit, Brownie and Belle on the rim above were simply having fits.

It was a lucky thing that the younger dogs had not topped out. One of them must have seen the lion leap. In a minute's time they were in full blast behind him. The race could not last much longer now. With long tail straight up over his back, the lion was doing his best but was plainly flagging.

Directly he came to a series of rocks that ran out at right angles to the main canyon wall and sloped sharply up. He ran out on them, leaping over a little gap that the dogs could negotiate. On a pillar-like abutment he halted. Far above him Brownie and Belle, who had kept up with the race, hung their heads over and cried. Below him the other dogs gave the cry of conquerors. He was bayed.

When we got down to him he was still panting hard. He lashed his tail and opened his mouth and spit. He seemed to consider trying another desperate leap. He was game and noble game, the noblest and the most beautiful predatory animal on the American continent. As a bullet found its mark I felt, momentarily, mean and ignoble. I shall never forget him. That last bit of chase, that leap, the fervor of the dogs, the tawny bundle of cornered killer up there on the pillar of rock were worth all the ten days of grueling work we had put in.

When the lion's body fell to the ground and we examined it, we found that all the claws of his right paw had been pulled out by the clasp he gave the rock that checked his fall. One claw on the left paw was out. But he did not have a bone broken.

He measured eight feet and six inches from tip to tip.

PART 3

Open Range Tales

Any tale belongs to whoever can best tell it.—JFD

Snowdrift: The Hunt for Montana's Last Wolf

On a trip to Montana in the 1940s, Dobie encountered Bob Kennon, one of the hunters who'd tracked the famous wolf, Snowdrift, during the 1920s. Kennon talked about Snowdrift as Dobie took notes in longhand. "How casual the chances for good stories seem," Dobie observed later. He considered this tale "one of the best I've written on any subject."

Today a trading post in the town of Stanford, Montana, claims to have Snowdrift's body on display.—SD

S NOWDRIFT, THEY CALLED HIM, but it was not the heightened grayness of his coat that made him famous. Whiteness is unfavorable to a wolf for the same reason that on Indian-threatened frontiers no man wanted to ride a white horse. White makes too clear a target at night.

Night was when Snowdrift operated mostly, night and dusk and dawn. For the comparatively few men who ever saw him, one glimpse was enough to identify him. The handicap seemed to sharpen his intelligence; it illuminated his achievements.

Ranchers knew him for 300 miles around. His most familiar beat was over a wide front in Montana between the Belt Mountains and the Bear Paws. It took him through the Highwood Mountains and across the Missouri River, which he swam whether it was high or low, churning with ice or clear. In the frozen dead of winter he walked across it. To go the length of his range, he had to cross two railroad tracks, the rights-of-way of which were fenced with sheep- or wolf-proof wire.

He would find a low place and dig under or use a culvert, but never used the same place twice. There were other wolf-proof fences he had to pass through. He was known to cover 125 miles in 24 hours. When he was bound for far places, he traveled in a long, sweeping trot that approached a lope, and it was tireless. He had longer legs than nearly any other wolf. Not once, but again and again, he made a kill fifty miles from where he had made one the preceding night.

As a young wolf, he had been caught in a trap and lost a claw from his left front foot. The missing toe made his track distinct, and tracks always make a record for those who can read.

He began depredating on cattle about 1917 and during the next thirteen years killed perhaps 1,500 head, two a week being a conservative average. During the years of his killing, between 150 and 200 other wolves, counting pups, were cleaned out of his territory; indeed, it was absolutely exterminated of wolves. Only Snowdrift remained as Montana's last wolf.

Rewards up to $500 were offered for Snowdrift's scalp. Dozens of trappers from Montana, other states, and Canada tried for the reward and the reputation that getting him would bring. Ranchmen in his wide and shifting range habitually carried rifles, hoping for a shot at him.

The individuals who sighted him at anything like close range were almost invariably not looking for him and were as much taken by surprise as he was. He always seemed to know when a man was on his trail. Then he took to the mountains, coming down only for beef.

Sportsmen from as far away as New Jersey came with their hounds to hunt him down. When they got a firsthand view of the millions of acres of canyons, peaks, and ridges that made up most of Snowdrift's range, they usually lost their dream of swift execution. He turned on a pack of five Russian hounds that had run themselves down after him and killed the isolated leader. The other hounds made for their far-behind master. The idea of running Snowdrift with hounds died.

Yet he bore none of the scars that usually mark fighting

leaders. He did not want to lead a pack. So far as known, he did not once gang up with other wolves to run a deer or antelope into a snowbank for capture. He relied on his lone self. He wanted liberty above all else, and he knew that he could maintain it only in loneliness, without obligations to, attachments to, or connections with any other individual of his kind, be she winsome or be he ever so cunning.

During all the years of his hunted life no man ever saw Snowdrift with another wolf. Always he ranged alone. Yet he was no celibate. Early in 1923 Barney Brannon, noted hunter of predatory animals, learned by sign that Snowdrift had mated with a female known as Cripple Foot. Barney turned his attention to her, hoping to intercept Snowdrift. He knew that she would pup in about two months, and at the end of that period he became convinced that she had a den along Dead Man's Coulee in the Little Belt Mountains. For two weeks he rode hills and cuts, lay under snowbanks, crouched behind rocks, trying to see Cripple Foot or her trail. Then one night snow fell and the next morning Barney struck the track he was looking for. He followed its twistings for five miles before coming to a craftily concealed hole in rocks under fallen logs.

When he dismounted to inspect the hole, he left his rifle in the saddle scabbard. As he leaned over, Cripple Foot charged to the mouth of the opening. He kicked in dirt and stones to drive her back. She came on and he hit her on the mouth with a big rock. As she backed down, he stuffed his chaps and coat into the hole to bottle her up. He always carried a short-handled shovel on his saddle. With it he dug a hole straight down to the tunnel. As soon as it was made, Cripple Foot tried to come up but was killed with one shot. Barney got two pups and was about to leave when he heard a whimper in another compartment of the den. There he found four others. The den was on a conspicuous mound. Cripple Foot had been using the pile of logs over it as a lookout, well concealed, for spying over the country before leaving to hunt.

At this very time, as it was later learned, Snowdrift was in the Bear Paws, away north of the Missouri River. He was never known to enter a den.

A Biological Survey man kept a pet female wolf that had lured many a male to death. One winter she came into heat in Snowdrift's range. The trapper chained her out and ringed the ground around her with traps. If Snowdrift sensed her, he went the other way.

Like other males of the canine family, he left his "sign" on bushes and revisited them to see if a female had responded. Many traps were set at these "markers" of his—traps smoked over burning sagebrush, dipped in sagebrush tea, rubbed with beef tallow, handled only with smoked gloves. Never was he known to come to a bush or tree where a trap had been set.

Once, a wolf caught in a trap chained to a clog dragged it quite a distance before it hung up. Snowdrift came along, followed the drag only a few steps, then circled around the trapped wolf, near enough for his senses to tell him all that he wanted to know. He kept far enough away to be safe from machinations that might be allied to the man-trapped animal.

No man who followed Snowdrift ever figured him out well enough to "take roundance" on him. One of his followers was Bob Kennon, packer, cowboy, forest ranger, trapper, friend of the artist Charlie Russell. One winter while I was in Great Falls, Montana, on Charlie Russell's trail, I fell in with Bob Kennon and from him learned the main parts of this history.

Bob Kennon joined hunter Barney Brannon and they began a long quest to kill Snowdrift. They wore sheepskins over their shoes to hold in the human scent. They boiled sage and soaked their boots in the tea. They smeared cow manure over their boots and tried in other ways to make their trails smell only of the range. Barney Brannon found some enormous hoofs slipped from a steer's skeleton. He fastened them on the bottoms of his shoes so that his tracks looked like cow tracks, and thus followed Snowdrift to study his habits and learn his ways. He thought that if Snowdrift doubled back, as he sometimes doubled, he would be thrown off his guard. He never was. A wolf is likely to use a certain beat over and over if he is sure that a man is not after him. After Snowdrift had marked a route, a long time had to pass before he considered it safe. He had plenty of room and he knew every feature of it.

He would not approach a place, particularly a pass, that his senses told him had been touched by man. His intuition often seemed keener than his keen senses. Maybe two or three days after he had passed a certain way he would sneak back to it, only from one side or the other, to see if a man were tracking him. He took toward all men the advice that Jim Bridger gave the Indians: "When you see sign, look out; when you don't see any sign at all, look out sharper than ever."

Once men rolled up the wire of about a mile of fence that he was used to going through. Old posts left in the ground continued to mark the line. Until the end of his life, Snowdrift always went around that mile-long scar; he was never known to cross it again. Something had been there; men had come and done something. He did not understand exactly what, but he understood the deadliness of men.

In 1922 government surveyors worked for several weeks on Baldy Mountain in the Highwoods. This mountain had been one of Snowdrift's resorts. It was three years before he came nearer than three miles to the pegs the surveyors had driven down, the trees they had blazed, the lines through the underbrush they had cut.

When the fall roundups, lasting a month or so, were on, Snowdrift altogether avoided the range they were working. He was not daring, but discreet.

It is wolf nature to follow the tracks of another wolf. When Snowdrift came upon tracks, he instead crossed them at right angles or veered away, changing his own course if necessary. Constantly and unceasingly he did all he could to avoid calling attention to himself.

Coming to a small branch of water, he would hunt a narrow place—or go directly to it, for he seemed to have a memory of every feature of the land—and jump it, so as to not make plain tracks in the mud. He never crossed twice at the same place. To defecate, he walked out into brush, made his deposit unobtrusively, and circled back to his route.

Wolves have a great amount of curiosity, but Snowdrift never allowed curiosity to get the better of his judgment. Once Bob Kennon and Barney Brannon tried the flag trick on him. They tied a piece of red cloth to a green bush in a place he was almost certain to pass. He, as tracks told, passed some distance to one side but made no investigation. Two other wolves that investigated stepped into traps.

It is the nature of wolves to gnaw on old bones, chew on the tips of cow and buffalo horns lying on the ground. Bob and Barney collected bones of cattle that had died on the range and piled them into a conspicuous mound on an open flat. The bone pile attracted the attention of a number of wolves. One would circle around it, at first staying maybe a quarter of a mile away, gradually over a period of nights drawing nearer and nearer, though few would get too near. One night four young crossbreeds, half wolf and half dog, got close enough to be caught in the maze of traps. Snowdrift saw the bone pile all right but never swerved from his direction, more than a quarter of a mile away, to investigate it. He ignored mounds of rocks—an often-used decoy—in the same way.

The wiliest of wolves succumb eventually to curiosity concerning a scent or to its magnetic power. Barney Brannon dug holes, sprinkled the bottoms with his most potent scent lures, fixed traps over the holes and covered them with leaves, twigs, and dry horse manure. Some smart wolf might try to dig under the trap to get to the smell and catch a paw in the steel jaws. Snowdrift would run from any such scent as if it were as dangerous as a man shooting at him.

In winter Barney would shoot a rabbit with a .22, bend his ears back, where they remained frozen stiff, as if the rabbit were asleep, and place the body in snow near a tuft of grass. A coyote or a green lobo might be fooled, but Snowdrift disdained investigating any such falsity.

Trappers put out dummy baits, balls of cow or horse tallow, getting wolves used to them before inserting strychnine in similar balls. Snowdrift was never known to notice such a bait, though his tracks passed right over it.

No king of the Middle Ages with an official taster was more distrusting of food set before him and no connoisseur of wines could be choosier than Snowdrift was of his meat. He killed on high ground. He killed only when he was hungry, never wantonly, and he habitually selected his fare. If he had a craving for strong meat, he did not hesitate to bring down a cow or a steer weighing a thousand pounds. He could top a herd as accurately as a stockyards butcher. After his prime was passed, he generally took younger animals, but never a cull. If fat meat was available, he had it. He preferred killing far out on the range, but he ate from cattle on feed, near human habitations, and took his toll from farmers as well as from big ranchmen. There were farmers in the Judith Basin who almost nightly for years hung lighted lanterns in their cow lots to ward off the light-fearing bandit.

His method—the wolf method—was to find an animal out from a bunch, run at it, cut its hamstring and eat either the hindquarters or the vitals. After he had taken his fill of meat, he was through with the carcass. He did not return for a second meal as most young wolves and many grown ones do. Some wolves will approach an old carcass apparently only for a delicious whiff; some will chew like a coyote on a piece of dried hide. Snowdrift was a patrician. He would not approach to smell and would not touch in any way any carcass but a fresh one of his own killing.

As soon as he ate, Snowdrift left the telltale carcass for some hiding place he had in mind, there to rest. But he wouldn't rest long. He seemed to require as little sleep as Napoleon. Moving or in hiding, he kept alert. For months at a time there was not a day when some man was not on his trail. He knew that he was hunted. Year in and year out, he lived on the dodge.

One summer morning while Bob Kennon was packing salt on mules, to be distributed over the range, he left his rifle in camp. That was the morning he sighted Snowdrift lying down beside a knoll of rocks on a ridge, a long way off. Bob turned back for camp, released the mules, and put the rifle in his scabbard. Of course Snowdrift had disappeared long before he returned to the resting place. Bob trailed him all day without finding where he stopped again. He did find a kill the wolf had made not far from where he was sighted.

Trappers on high points sometimes caught glimpses of Snowdrift through field glasses, generally far off. He would walk slow, stop, sit on his haunches and look around in all directions. If all was clear, he might pick out a spot whence he could see and there lie down and put his ear to the ground to listen.

He liked to travel ridges, against rocky bluffs, in brush, but up where he could look out. He never followed a trail or road. In daytime he would hardly cross an open draw, where a man on horseback could get a run at him. He had been chased by cowboys and once by a car. He always seemed to know the features of the land ahead of him for a long distance. He would not run blindly into unfavorable ground. Although his habitual posture was upstanding, he could crawl on his belly to keep hidden. He would go a mile out of his way to get on a high point with a clear view in all directions. Here he would lie down in sagebrush, unseen but seeing.

He had favorite lying-up places, scattered over the country, but would never go directly to one of them. He would go to some point, look long at the place where he wished to hide, and then, if it seemed safe, go to it. When he got there, he would not lie down under a bush where he had lain before.

As he grew heavy-footed from age, the long delayed shot of finality was almost inevitable. It came one spring morning in 1930 from a rancher out looking through his cattle. Snowdrift was eating from the carcass of a fat calf when he heard, too late, the hoof beats of the rancher's horse. The years had no doubt deadened his hearing. He had to run across a little open flat and was about two hundred yards off when the bullet overtook him. He was so old that all his hairs had turned white. His back teeth were gone and the front ones were worn down. His left hind leg bore the scar of a bullet that another range man had fired in 1926.

When the rancher brought the carcass into the town of Stanford, it created the kind of sensation that the exhibition of Billy the Kid's head would have made in Santa Fe in the 1880s. The wolf looked as big as a weaned calf. He measured six feet from nose to tail-tip. The shape of his head made some people say that he was part dog, but this could not be proved. His intelligence had been that of a wolf. Despite all the meat he had consumed, he was gaunt. During a six-week period of the preceding winter he had killed ten head of registered Herefords.

Ranchers who paid the reward had Snowdrift mounted. But tradition more than a visible carcass has kept alive the wisest, the cunningest, and the most noted wolf that ever ranged west of the Dakotas. No hunter ever out-witted him. Old age and chance combined to end his life.

The Dream That Saved Wilbarger

One cold night soon after he came to Texas, Bigfoot Wallace was sitting in the warm cabin of a settler down the Colorado River when a man wearing a strange-looking fur cap entered, stood bent over the fire a few minutes, and then removed his headgear to warm his head better. At sight of the raw-looking, hairless scalp thus exposed, Bigfoot Wallace broke the social code against asking questions.

"My friend," he ventured, "excuse me, but what is the matter with your head?"

"I have been scalped by the Indians," the stranger replied.

Josiah Wilbarger wore a cap or hat, even at the dinner table, from the predawn hour of rising until bedtime, when he put on a nightcap. The story of his scalping and of the dream that saved his life is still told by descendants of early settlers and may be read in reminiscences of those times.—JFD

I N 1830, Josiah Wilbarger, lately from Missouri, located on a headright survey along the Colorado River about ten miles above the crossing of the Camino Real—the royal road, as the Spaniards called it—between San Antonio and Nacogdoches. His nearest neighbor was thirty miles or so down the river. Two years later his friend Reuben Hornsby moved into a double-log cabin up the river, nine miles below the present city of Austin, with his wife Sarah and eight children. Although separated by several miles, the families were close neighbors. The names Wilbarger Creek and Hornsby's Bend fix permanently the locations of these two outposts of colonization.

Sarah Hornsby was a little, black-haired, black-eyed woman of pure Scottish blood. She sang Highland ballads, read the Bible to her children, and taught them to read the box of books she had hauled in an ox wagon all the way to Texas from Mississippi. One time when all the men were gone from her home in Hornsby's Bend she dressed in man's clothes and showed herself armed with a rifle in order to scare off lurking Indians. Another time while her husband was away she sent two of her boys at milking time to bring in the cows from the wild rye that stretched out from the house like a field of wheat. From the window, gun in hand—for there was never a relaxed minute at this habitation—she watched them. Then, powerless to give aid, she saw Indians raise up with a yell behind the boys, but the boys got into the house unharmed. Another time she saw Indians kill two young men hoeing in the field; then after dark she and her young sons buried them. In time she would bury one of her own sons and another youth who were fishing in the river when Indians killed them.

Early in August, 1833, Wilbarger went up to the Hornsbys' to join a party of men scouting for headrights. The Hornsby home had already become a kind of land's-end headquarters. After spending the night, Wilbarger, in company with four men named Christian, Haynie, Standifer, and Strother, set out to explore to the northwest. On Walnut Creek they sighted a lone Indian, who ran and escaped into the cedar hills.

After the chase the party turned homeward. Near Pecan Spring, as the place was later named, they halted to noon. Wilbarger, Christian, and Strother unsaddled their horses and hobbled them to graze; the other two men staked theirs with the saddles on, merely removing the bridles.

While the men were eating, Indians sneaked up in the brush and fired on them. Some of the Indians had only bows and arrows. The white men got behind trees that were small, and returned the fire, but soon Strother received a mortal wound and a ball broke

Christian's thigh. Wilbarger, with an arrow through the calf of a leg and a flesh wound in his hip, dragged Christian behind a tree. About this time an arrow went into his other leg.

Haynie and Standifer now made for their saddled horses. As they mounted, Wilbarger started running toward them, calling on them to wait. They saw him pitch headlong to the ground. Then they saw "fifty Indians" rushing for his scalp. They got away and reached the Hornsby house in safety.

There they told how they had seen the Indians scalping their dead comrades and heard them yelling the blood yell. For the present, all the men agreed, the dead would have to care for the dead. The Indians were in such force and had met with such success that they might well be expected to attack the Hornsby outpost. A rider was sent below to carry the tidings to the Wilbarger home and to summon help.

At last, as evening fell, the house was still. Sarah Hornsby fell asleep. About midnight she jumped awake from a vision as sharply defined as the peaks of clouds under sheet lightning. She shook her husband, speaking so loud that the men in the other room of the house heard.

"Wilbarger is not dead," she cried. "I saw him in a dream. He sits under a large post oak tree, naked, covered with blood from wounds, scalped. But he is not dead. I saw him plainly."

Reuben Hornsby tried to pacify his wife by going over the details she had plainly heard from the two survivors. He laid the dream to overwrought nerves. She quieted down and went back to sleep.

But about three o'clock she sprang from the bed, more excited and intense this time than before. "I saw him again," she cried. Her husband could not pacify her now. She threw a dress on, lit a candle, aroused all the men.

"As sure as there is a God," she repeated, "Josiah Wilbarger is alive. He is alive out there, all alone under a large post oak tree. His only covering is the blood from his own wounds. He is scalped, but he lives, suffering tortures, hoping and waiting for help."

"But"—started to explain once more one of the men who had left Wilbarger.

"But me no buts," Sarah Hornsby went on with rising voice. "I saw him as plainly as I now see you safe and sound in front of me. If you are not cowards, go at once or he will die."

"I'll say it again as I have already said it many times," the escaped man now got his word in. "I saw Wilbarger shot down. I saw at least fifty Indians around his body. They were even then lifting his scalp. They never leave a victim breathing."

"I don't care what you saw," Sarah Hornsby retorted. "Maybe you were too busy running to see anything straight. Anyhow, I have had the last look. I know that Wilbarger is alive. Go. Go at once."

There was no arguing, but Reuben Hornsby now pointed out that if he and the other men left before the expected recruits arrived from below, she and the children would be in grave danger.

"Never mind me," his wife flared. "I and my children can take to the elbow bushes and lie hid. Go, I tell you, to poor Wilbarger."

Against such resoluteness Reuben Hornsby and the other men could not now stand. Still, they refused to leave until daylight, by which time the recruits from below were expected. Sarah Hornsby made coffee, cooked breakfast. Daylight comes early in August. With it came the expected reinforcements. Then the searching party prepared to ride.

"Take these three sheets," Sarah Hornsby called. "Two to bury Christian and Strother in. One to wrap around Wilbarger. You will have to bring him home on a litter. He cannot ride a horse."

The last sentence of her prophecy alone proved erroneous. The men went to the campsite where the Indians had attacked the day before. They shrouded the bodies of Christian and Strother, from whom all clothing had been stripped. After much search, late in the afternoon, they sighted a red-hued figure under a big post oak tree. An advance rider, mistaking him for an Indian, called out, "Here they are, boys!"

At this, the figure rose up, saying, "Don't shoot. It's Wilbarger."

His body was caked with blood. The only particle of clothing left to him by the Indians was a sock. This he had torn from his foot, swollen from the leg wound, to cover his peeled skull.

With the sheet wrapped around him he was placed in Hornsby's saddle, the lightweighted Hornsby riding behind and holding the wounded man in his arms. Very slowly the horsemen filed toward the cabin in the river bend, six miles away.

There they found all in readiness for the rescued man: a bed, warm water to cleanse the wounds, poultices of wheat bread— a bread too scarce to eat—and bear's oil to dress the scalpless head.

"I knew you would bring him," Sarah Hornsby said.

❖　◉　❖

Wilbarger's own story made Sarah Hornsby's dreams seem even more remarkable. The shot that knocked him to the ground had gone into his neck from the rear and come out at his chin. It only creased—temporarily paralyzed—him, he said. He did not feel pain; he could not move a muscle; yet he was conscious. He knew when an Indian cut his scalp around with a knife and jerked it off. He did not flinch; there was no pain to flinch from. The only sensation he experienced was a sound as of distant thunder. He knew when the Indians were stripping off his clothes. They had cut the throats of the other two men; the sight of the bullet hole under his chin perhaps made them think that act unnecessary with him.

There was a lapse of time during which Wilbarger knew nothing. The sun was in the western sky when he recovered consciousness and felt pain and knew that he was alone and could move. Dried blood was all over him, and he was still bleeding. He felt a thirst that was agony. He tried to stand up and walk but could not. The directions of the compass were perfectly clear to him. He knew where the camp waterhole was. He dragged himself to it. He drank and lay down in the water. He lay there until he was almost numb with cold. Then he crawled out on dry ground, to be warmed by the sloping rays of the August sun.

Green blowflies were buzzing around his head. It does not take the eggs they lay long to hatch into flesh-eating worms. His wounds had ceased to bleed. He was again consumed with thirst. When he had drunk again, sharp hunger came upon him. His constitution was crying for nourishment to rebuild what his body had lost. He crawled to some bushes and ate a few snails that he found. He drank more water. He felt the maggots in the naked flesh of his head.

About nightfall he determined to crawl to the Hornsby house. But he had gone only about a quarter of a mile before, utterly exhausted, he halted under a large post oak tree. There in semi-consciousness he rested until roused by a cold wind on his naked head. The only sounds that came to his ears were the pulsing of the crickets, the hoot of an owl, and the long, long wail of a wolf. The dying moon came up.

Then, as he lay under the tree, he saw suddenly, distinctly, without warning, the figure of his sister Margaret Clifton. He saw her; yet she, he well knew, was living in Missouri, near Saint Louis, more than eight hundred miles away. It was not until many weeks had passed that he learned she had died the day before he was wounded and even at the hour of his vision was spending her first night in the grave.

Standing near him, the sister said, her voice calm and restful, "Brother Josiah, you are too weak to go any farther by yourself. Remain here under this tree and friends will come to take care of you before the setting of another sun."

When she had spoken thus, she began to move away in the direction of Hornsby's house. Such was Wilbarger's state of mind, and so vivid was the visitant's form and so clear were her words that he did not question her reality. As the vision vanished, he raised himself and with an imploring gesture called after her, "Margaret, my sister Margaret, stay with me until they come! Margaret!"

But the air was empty.

Josiah Wilbarger recovered, though the skin never grew entirely over his skull bone. He lived for eleven years, leading an active life, until an accidental blow on the exposed skull hastened death. No one who knew him or Mrs. Hornsby ever doubted the veracity of either in their accounts of the dream— or spirit—visitations. Wilbarger told his story long before he heard of his sister Margaret's death. As near as could be figured out, Mrs. Hornsby's first vision of the wounded man occurred shortly after Wilbarger heard his sister's voice and called out after her vanishing form.

Sancho, the Tamale-Loving Longhorn

Writers come to have an extraordinary fondness for certain characters, and I have told the story of Sancho to many audiences. He is my favorite among the many cows that enter into my book, The Longhorns. I first heard Sancho's story from John Rigby of Beeville, who I judged had made up a good deal of it. I myself did some constructive work on Sancho over the years.—JFD

I N THE MESQUITE and whitebrush country southward from San Antonio, a man named Kerr had a little ranch on Esperanza Creek. He owned several cow ponies and maybe forty cows and their offspring. His dog guarded a small flock of goats, bringing them about sundown to a brush corral near the house, where Kerr's wife barred them inside. Three or four acres of land, fenced in with brush and poles, grew corn, frijoles, watermelons, and calabazas—except when a drought was on. A hand-dug well equipped with a pulley wheel, rope, and bucket furnished water for the establishment.

Kerr's wife was a partridge-built Mexicana named María. They had no children. She was thrifty and cheerful, always making pets of animals. She usually milked three or four cows and made the soft cheese called asadero out of goat's milk.

Late in the winter of 1877, Kerr while riding along San Miguel Creek found one of his cows dead in a boghole. Beside the cow was a scrawny, mud-plastered, black-and-white paint bull calf less than a week old. It was too weak to trot; perhaps other cattle had saved it from the coyotes. Kerr pitched his rope over its head, drew it up across the saddle in front of him, carried it home, and turned it over to María.

She had raised many dogie calves, also colts captured from mustang mares. The first thing she did now was to pour milk from a bottle down the orphan's throat. With warm water she washed the caked mud off its body. But hand raising a calf is no end of trouble. The next day Kerr rode around until he found a thrifty cow with a calf not over ten days old. He drove them to a pen. By tying her head up close to a post and hobbling her hind legs, Kerr and María forced her to let the orphan suckle. After being tied up twice daily for a month, she finally adopted the orphan as a twin to her own offspring.

Spring weeds, especially the tallow weed, came up plentifully, and the guajillo brush put out in full leaf. When the mother cow came in about sundown and her two calves bolted through an open gate, it was a cheering sight to see them wiggle their tails while they guzzled milk.

The dogie was a vigorous little brute, and before long he was getting more milk than the mother's own calf. María called him Sancho, or "Pet." She grew especially fond of him and would give him the shucks wrapped around tamales to hold them together while they are being steam-boiled. Then she began treating him to whole tamales, made of ground corn rolled around a core of chopped-up meat. Sancho seemed to like the meat as well as the corn. As everybody who has eaten them knows, true Mexican tamales are well seasoned with pepper. Sancho seemed to like the seasoning.

In southern Texas the little chiltipiquín peppers, red when ripe, grow wild in low, shaded places. Cattle never eat them, leaving them for the wild turkeys, mockingbirds, and blue quail to pick off. In the early fall wild turkeys used to gorge on them so avidly that their flesh became too peppery for most people to eat. The tamale diet gave Sancho not only a taste but a passion for the little red pepper growing under trees and bushes along Esperanza Creek. In fact, he became a kind of chiltipiquín addict. He would hunt for the peppers.

The tamales also gave him a tooth for corn in the ear. The summer after he became a yearling he began breaking through the brush fence that enclosed Kerr's corn patch. A forked stick had to be tied around his neck to prevent his getting through the fence.

He was branded and turned into a steer, but he was as strong as any young bull. Like many other pets, he was something of a nuisance. When he could not steal corn or was not humored with tamales, he was enormously contented with grass, mixed in the summertime with the sweet mesquite beans. Now and then María gave him a lump of the brown piloncillo sugar, from Mexico, that all the border country used.

Every night Sancho came to the ranch pen to sleep. His bed ground was near a certain mesquite tree just outside the gate. He spent hours every summer day in the shade of this mesquite. When it rained and other cattle drifted off, hunting fresh pasturage, Sancho stayed at home and drank at the well. He was strictly domestic.

In the spring of 1880 Sancho was three years old, white of horn, and as blocky in shape as any long-legged Texas Longhorn steer ever grew. Kerr's ranch lay in a vast unfenced range grazed by the Shiner brothers, with headquarters on the Frio River. That spring they had a contract to deliver three herds of steers, each to number twenty-five hundred head, in Wyoming. Kerr helped the Shiners gather cattle, and along with other ranchers he sold them what steers he had.

One day in late march the Shiner men road branded Sancho 7Z and put him in the first herd headed north. The other herds were to follow two or three days apart.

It was late afternoon before the herd got its final "trimming" and was "shaped up" for the long drive. It was watered and eased out on a prairie slope to bed down. But Sancho had no disposition to lie down—there. He wanted to go back to that mesquite just outside the pen gate at the Kerr place on the Esperanza where he had without variation slept every night since he had been weaned. Perhaps his appetite called for an evening tamale.

He stood and roamed about on the south side of the herd. A dozen times during the night the men on guard had to drive him back. As reliefs were changed, word passed to keep an eye on that paint steer on the lower side.

When the herd started on the next morning, Sancho was at the tail end of it, often stopping and looking back. It took constant attention from one of the drag drivers to keep him moving. By the time the second night arrived, every hand in the outfit knew Sancho by name and sight—the stubbornest and gentlest steer of the lot. About dark one of them pitched a loop over his horns and staked him to a bush. This saved bothering with his persistent efforts to walk off.

Daily when the herd was halted to graze, spreading out like a fan, the other steers eating their way northward, Sancho invariably pointed himself south. In his lazy way he grabbed many a mouthful of grass while the herd was moving. Finally, in some brush up on the Llano, after ten days of trailing, he dodged into freedom.

The next day one of the point men with the second Shiner herd saw a big paint steer walking south, rode out, read the 7Z road brand on his left side, rounded him in, and set him traveling north again.

Sancho became the chief drag animal of this herd, too. Somewhere north of the Colorado there was a run one night, and when morning came Sancho was missing. The other steers had held together; probably Sancho had not run at all. But he was picked up again, by the third Shiner herd coming on behind.

He took his accustomed place in the drag and continued to require special driving. He picked up in weight. He chewed his cud peacefully and slept soundly, but whenever he looked southward, which was often, he raised his head as if memory and expectation were stirring. The boys were all personally acquainted with him, and every night one of them would stake him. He never lunged against the rope as a wild cow brute would.

One day the cattle balked and milled at a full-flowing river. "Rope old Sancho and lead him in," the boss ordered, "and we'll point the other cattle after him." Sancho led like a horse. The herd followed. As soon as he was released, he dropped back to the rear. After this, however, he was always led to the front when there was high water to cross.

The rains came right that spring, and grass came early. By the time the slow-traveling Shiner herds got into No Man's Land, beyond the Red River, they were putting on tallow every day and the sand-hill plums were turning ripe. Pausing now and then to pick a little of the fruit, Sancho's driver saw the pet steer following his example. Learning to eat chiltipiquíns on the Esperanza had made him experimental in foods.

Meantime, the cattle were trailing, trailing, every day and Sunday too, in the direction of the North Star. For five hundred miles across Texas, counting the windings to find water and keep out of the breaks, they had come. After getting into the Indian Territory, they snailed on across the Wichita, the South Canadian, the North Canadian, and the Cimarron. On into Kansas they trailed and across the Arkansas, around Dodge City, cowboy capital of the world, out of Kansas into Nebraska, over the wide, wide Platte, past the roaring cow town of Ogallala, up the North Platte, under the Black Hills, and then against the Big Horn Mountains. For two thousand miles, making ten or twelve miles a day, the Shiner herds trailed.

When, finally, after listening for months, day and night, to the slow song of their motion, the Longhorns reached their new home in Wyoming. Sancho was still halting every now and then to sniff southward for a whiff of the Mexican Gulf. The farther he got away from home, the less he seemed to like the change. He had never felt frost in September before. The Mexican peppers back home on the Esperanza were red ripe now.

The new outfit received the cattle and branded CR on their long sides before turning them loose on the new range. And now the Shiner men turned south, taking their saddle horses and chuck wagons—and leaving Sancho behind. They made good time, but by the time they turned the remuda loose on the Frio River, a blue norther was flapping their slickers. After the "Cowboys' Christmas Ball" most of them settled down for a few weeks of winter sleep.

Spring comes early down on the Esperanza. The mesquites

were all in new leaf with that green so fresh and tender that the color seems to emanate into the sky. Bluebonnets, pale pink Mexican primroses, and red phlox would soon sprinkle every open flat and draw. The prickly pear was ready to be studded with waxy blossoms and the white brush to be heavy with its own perfume. The windmill grass—rooster's foot, as the vaqueros call it—was crowding the tallow weed out in places. It was time for the spring cow hunt and the putting up of herds for the annual drive north. The Shiners were at work.

A cowboy named John Rigby was riding close to Kerr's cabin on Esperanza Creek. "I looked across a pear flat and saw something that made me rub my eyes," Rigby said.

He looked to his companion, Joe Shiner. "Do you see what I see?" Rigby asked.

"Yes, but before I say, I'm going to read the brand," Shiner answered.

They rode over. "You can hang me for a horse thief," Rigby said. "If it wasn't that Sancho paint steer, four-years-old now, the Shiner 7Z road brand and the Wyoming CR range brand both showing on him as plain as boxcar letters."

The men rode on down to Kerr's.

"Yes," Kerr told them. "Old Sancho got in about six weeks ago. His hoofs were worn mighty nigh down to the hair, but he wasn't lame. I thought María was going out of her senses, she was so glad to see him. She actually hugged him and she cried and then she begun feeding him hot tamales. She's made a batch of them nearly every day since, just to pet that steer. When she's not feeding him tamales, she's giving him piloncillo."

Sancho was slicking off and seemed mighty contented. He was coming up every night and sleeping at the gate, María said. She was nervous over the prospect of losing her pet, but Joe Shiner said that if the steer loved his home enough to walk back to it all the way from Wyoming, he wasn't going to drive him off again.

As far as I can find out, Old Sancho lived right there on the Esperanza, now and then getting a tamale, tickling his palate with chili peppers in season, and generally staying fat on mesquite grass, until he died a natural death.

PART 4

The Southwestern Tempo

What is the spirit, the tempo, the rhythm of this plot of earth to which we belong and as writers endeavor to express? Often it seems that the essential spirit has been run over and killed. But nature is as inexorable, as passionless, and as patient in revenge as she is in fidelity to "the heart that loves her." In the long run, she cannot be betrayed by man; in the long run, man can betray only himself by not harmonizing with her.—JFD

Earth Rhythms and
the Southwestern Tempo

Mary Austin wrote the book, The American Rhythm, in which she said no poet would be authentic until the rhythms of the land entered into him. I know that the right tempo for the land of the intense sun is under shade.—JFD

O N MY WAY TO ENGLAND, I flew over the ocean without seeing it, and realized again the distinction between transportation and travel. The other passengers inside the clipper plane played cards or chess, read magazines and books, and talked above the roar of the propellers as the fog of clouds cut off all vision.

In the days to come, when air travel is as common as automobile travel, I doubt that people will experience novel and pleasurable sensations from being in the air. Like other kinds of transit, airplanes will be valued chiefly for transporting a person from where he is to where he wants to go. No amount of advertising will make air travel capable of transporting a person outside of himself. And that is the only kind of traveling worth calling by name.

Riding a mule, accompanied by another mule carrying bed and grub, through the mountains of Mexico is my idea of travel. If I start out as John Doe, streak across space for 3,000 miles, and land as the same John Doe, having dragged John Doe's body and personality all the way with me, what is the use of setting out?

The sensation of speed does not at all depend on actual rapidity of movement. One time in a wagon—the wagons having no springs—behind a pair of runaway mules that were pulling a load of mesquite across a roadless, gully-cut, bush-studded stretch of pasture land, I received as lively a sense of motion as any human being could ask for. Any cowboy that socks the spurs into his horse and tears out across a flat after a thicket-hunting steer gets a far keener sense of motion than he could get in a fighter plane leveling out at 350 miles per hour.

Man may achieve super-doubly-super planes that rocket into space clear beyond the point where the law of gravity operates, but the rider of that plane will never experience the sense of motion that a rider on a good horse burning the breeze lickety-brindle, hellety-spit, the wind tearing at his hat and streaming out the beautiful mane and tail of his horse, enjoys.

One winter evening long ago, when I was a boy, a wagon drawn by two horses approached our house at a tempo in harmony with the coming of dusk. In those times the sight of any arriving human being was an event.

The driver proved to be Mr. Dan Shipp of the Shipp ranch, 10,000 acres stretching from the Nueces River to the east fence of our ranch. While he and Papa were unhitching the horses, to be fed and then turned into the little horse pasture, I saw in the wagon seven mesquite posts. Each had been hewed with an axe to a flat surface on one side at one end, and incised with a number: 7, 8, and on to 13. Mr. Shipp was setting mileposts alongside the public road running from Dinero on the Nueces River to Ramireña thirteen miles west.

I knew this road well. I rode horseback once or twice a week to get our mail at Dinero, usually without meeting a soul. I knew certain places where deer would often cross the road. I knew two glades where quail were plentiful. I knew an opening in the brush where I nooned once in a wagon and let the horses graze. I knew where I was almost sure to see a paisano running down the road, though I might see one anywhere. If it had rained, I could expect a certain caliche hill covered with ceniza bushes to be turned by their sudden flowers from ashen gray to almost solid lavender.

I knew where sandy loam gave way to gravelly soil and where juajillo thrived. I knew where the redbirds, migrating from the north, were thickest in wintertime. Certain mesquite trees and certain live oaks along the road were personalities to me and were cherished as friends.

Mr. Shipp had spent the day coming west from Dinero, setting posts. He had measured the circumference of a front wagon wheel and had wrapped a piece of rawhide around the rim at a spoke to which a white rag was tied. Rawhide wears out very slowly. As his team pulled the wagon along on the road at a slow walk, he counted the revolutions of the wheel. When enough had been made to cover 5,280 linear feet, he said "Whoa!," got down, dug a posthole, and planted a post with the correct mile number facing the road. At some spots he would have to cut a bush or prickly pear away to clear the ground, though if he saw a clear place nearby, he could dig there. He had come to our house to eat supper and spend the night before going on early next morning to put down the remaining mileposts.

That was when a mile was a mile. People who watch horse and relay races may have some conception of a mile, but in an age when an airplane circuits the earth, no traveler can have much conception of a mile. He doesn't "travel" either; he is merely transported.

❖　◎　❖

The tempo of the Southwest is seen in the rhythms of its folklore, most of which deals with country things and ways, with nature and animals and people. Southwestern folklore has grown out of a continuing way of life. There is plenty to say against the rigid conservatism of the Old South, but it is from settled ways of life—the Old South ways, the old rancher ways, the old Mexican ways, the old Indian ways—that folklore of charm and imagination comes. Ghosts do not haunt one-night camps.

The folklore of this region has not been woven by people of worldly success. The only mines that amount to anything in folklore are lost forever. The only money that figures in it is buried deeper than oil drillers ever bored. The hunters and tellers of lost mines are the hopefuls, with time to spare. Southwestern tales of the much persecuted coyote have not come from the owners of sheep, but from unpropertied Indians and Mexicans. These people have lingered with the grass, the rocks, the thorned shrubs, and the chirping crickets. They have had time to fancy and imagine and have felt a kinship for their fellow creatures of the earth.

Genuine range people—among whom are not included oil millionaires who have bought ranches and hire somebody else to run them while they themselves operate in air-conditioned office buildings—have a limitless capacity for reserving their energy.

Their tempo has been so betrayed by Hollywood and Western, or "action," fiction that only the initiated know the truth. In this fiction, cowboys almost never walk the easy way that belongs to them and to cattle that have just watered. Instead of stepping through doors, they jump out of windows with six-shooters blazing.

In the 1920s while Zane Grey was manufacturing Westerns at a jet-propelled rate, I spent a few days in the camp of Dr. A. V. Kidder, archaeologist. He was excavating the ruins of Pecos Indian villages in New Mexico. Sometime before that, he related, he was, while working in an Arizona canyon, awakened one night by what sounded like the clatter-wheels of hell—yelling, shooting, shod horse hoofs running across rock, whips popping, lariats hitting against leather. He slipped on shoes and stepped out of his tent. The moon was full. Just as he emerged, a cowboy dashed up and stopped. Kidder recognized him as a pick-and-shovel excavator who had been in his pay a short time back.

"My goodness, John," he asked, "what is going on here?"

"A damned fool named Zane Grey has hired us to make local color," the cowboy replied, "and we are doing our best to make it."

In every motion picture I have ever seen showing a herd of cattle they are kept moving at such a rate that no spectator can read their brands. Sitting through one of these pictures, a person who didn't know better would think that a trail herd of cattle bound for Montana from South Texas ran up the trail all day and stampeded sky-westward and crooked-eastward every night.

Actually, they walked maybe ten miles a day, grazing a considerable part of the time and taking a long time to water out. Slow motion with stock is natural to stock people. The songs sung around herds on their bed-grounds were in tempo as slow and monotonous and doleful as camp meeting tunes designed to draw sinners into the mourners' bench.

> *It's a whoop and a yea and a driving the*
> *dogies*
> *For camp is far away*
> *It's a whoop and a yea, get along my*
> *little dogies,*
> *for Wyoming may be your new home.*

If you listen to talk by men of the range tradition you will hear more about "moseying around" than about moving "like a bat out of hell." The good storyteller likes to linger in the shade, and his best stories have a lingering quality.

> *Oh beat the drum slowly and play the fife lowly*
> *Oh, it was a long and lonesome go*
> *As our herd rolled on to (New) Mexico.*

All cowboy songs sung to cattle were long and lonesome in tune. A man loping or trotting could not keep the tune. It was timed to a slow walk and was meant to quieten all hearers.

Andy Adams tells of an old Texas Longhorn that always got up from his bed and stretched out his neck when at night he heard the long drawn-out notes of "Jesus Lover of My Soul." Many a cowboy had seen cattle quieted down by the slow sad sounds of "Bury Me Not" as well as by "Lie Down, Little Dogies."

Old-time ranchers went by sun time, not railroad time; they went by what country Mexicanos call "el tiempo de Dios"—God's time, not "el tiempo oficial."

Men have invented an atomic bomber, but no man can ever absorb its speed into his own body. Human energy pulses with desire to rise higher and travel faster; hence, the thirst for strong drink and swift movement, but the tempo of all earthborn is the tempo of the earth itself. A raging hurricane may lash a sliver of it, a volcano may spew up some inside matter, but the tempo of the earth sustaining its bipedal nurslings is of growing grass, ripening corn, and drifting leaves.

We behold expanses of glaring electric lights. We become fascinated and terrorized by torrents of headlights rushing along speedways in the night, but the light that burns under the stars with the tempo of mother earth is that of a lone campfire.

A long time ago I was a boy riding with my parents in a hack on a dirt road west of the Nueces River. For hours we had not met a single traveler or seen a human habitation. Darkness came, and then away down the slope we saw a little fire, no bigger than the fluttering blaze of a match. It was beautiful and in the emptiness all around it was a mystery. Slowly, as we approached, it grew a little larger. It was beside the road, on Agua Dulce Creek. My father stopped the horses to speak. A lone camper was cooking supper in a skillet beside a coffee pot. He asked us to get out and have something. With thanks and a good night, we drove on. I have smelled a mesquite fire in darkness before I saw it and felt a harmony. The tempo of earth people

> *Rolled round in earth's diurnal course*
> *With rocks, and stones, and trees,*[*]

has seemed to me more pronounced in mature, even fading, cow-men than in springy cowboys out for a high-heeled time.

---

* From "A Slumber Did My Spirit Seal," by William Wordsworth

The Mesquite

The mesquite seems to me the most characteristic tree or brush that we have in the Southwest. Its name comes to us from the Aztec, and its association with the land and the peoples of this region is dateless. The mesquite is as native as rattlesnakes and mockingbirds, as distinctive as northers, and as blended into life of the land as cornbread and tortillas. Humans and other animals have been making use of it for untold generations; they are still making use of it.—JFD

THERE IS AN OLD SAYING, "The mesquite knows." It knows when winter is over and will not be caught putting out leaves before the last frost has passed. Generally, the mesquite does know.

"When the mesquite begins to bud, it's time to put out the tomato plants," is one old-time garden direction. Again, "plant cotton when the mesquite leafs." Even if the mesquite occasionally—very occasionally—makes a mistake, its general reputation has never been confused with that of the redbud, which, because it so often puts out buds that get nipped by frost, was in the Cherokee tongue called "liar."

Mesquite is something intensely native, something that belongs, something akin to folks with roots in the soil. It holds all the memories of the soil itself.

The first written account of the mesquite is in Cabeza de Vaca's narrative of his journey after being cast on Texas soil in 1528 and spending eight years among the Indians. Of one tribe, he describes a "great celebration" that involved a feast of *mesquiquez*. The Indians would dig a hole in the earth, fill it with mesquite bean pods, and mash them with a wooden club. They would add water and dirt to "sweeten" the juice and neutralize the bitterness. The Indians, he said, got very big bellies from the feast.

In the 1850s, James G. Bell, who kept a diary of a trip he made to California with a herd of Texas cattle, found the Pima Indians on the Gila River utilizing the mesquite in much the same way. The poorer Mexicans of Mexico and occasionally of the border country on this side of the international line still use it as a food staple. They crush the beans on a metate, in the way corn is crushed, working the hard seeds and the strings out. Then they sometimes mix the brown cane sugar called piloncillo with the mass. The meal, dried, will not deteriorate. It is made into bread; it can also be mixed with water and made into atole, a kind of mush.

Often I get homesick for the smell of burning mesquite wood. Many a time in the brush country I have smelled out a jacal, hidden by darkness or the lay of the land, by the aroma of mesquite smoke going up its chimney. The flavor that mesquite gives to broiling meat certainly surpasses in virtue any other wood that I know.

The Comanches are said to have favored mesquite wood for fuel because, while making a hot fire, it gives off comparatively little smoke—always a telltale sign of campers. Live oak coals will last longer than those of mesquite, but are not nearly so aromatic. When old Bigfoot Wallace wanted to describe eyes as being especially bright, he said they "glowed like mesquite coals."

"To find shade under a mesquite tree is like dipping water with a sieve," wrote an early day traveler. The shade certainly is speckled, but on a hot day of burning sun it may be very grateful both to man and beast. The small pinnate leaves prevent evaporation; no large-leafed tree can exist without abundant water. In Death Valley and on the deserts of Sonora, the leaves of the mesquite are much slenderer and shorter than on the mesquite growing under the fairly abundant rainfall of Central Texas.

Old-time belief had it that the roots of big mesquite trees go to water and that the place to dig a well is beside a mesquite tree.

The roots are unbelievably long. Along washes I have seen them exposed for forty feet and I have read of longer roots. Ranch children use these roots for whips and quirts. Also, the roots make as good toothbrushes as twigs of hackberry and anacua.

Not many thorns are harder than the mesquite's—as many an automobile driver has discovered when cutting across country and having his tires punctured. Mesquite thorns have served frontier people as pins. They have stove-up many a good cow horse, too. They will not decay in the flesh as will prickly pear thorns. Jabbed deep into muscle or joint, they emanate a kind of poison that makes the wounded person feel momentarily faint. It is these thorns that make the cowboy of the Southwest ride with leather toe-fenders, protect his legs and thighs with leather leggins, wear a jacket of heavy duck, ride in gauntleted gloves, and regard his felt hat as a kind of military helmet.

As for remedies provided by the mesquite—through bean, leaf, root, branch, and bark—they are many. Like the name of the mesquite itself, most of the remedies are Indian, though many have been taken over by Mexicanos from whom English-speaking people of the Southwest in turn borrowed. I know of a man who, out on the frontier in the 1880s, had such a severe case of dysentery that his life was in jeopardy. Tea made of mesquite root restored him. Tea of the bark is said to be excellent for the same malady.

The root boiled in water is also recommended for nervousness and the colic and as a balm for flesh wounds. The Yuma Indians use an infusion of the leaves for venereal diseases. For headaches, the Yaqui Indians mash the leaves to a pulp, mix with water and urine, and bind the poultice around the forehead. On a hot day one may often notice a vaquero—or Mexicano laborer of any kind—wearing mesquite leaves under his hat. This may be para dolores de cabeza (headache), but more than likely it is simply to keep his head cool and prevent his getting soleado, a sunstroke. The fluid extracted from the leaves, which is called alcool, is used in Chihuahua as an eye lotion. The sap is just as good for the same purpose.

Between the Nueces River and the Rio Grande, women can yet be found who, in order to make clothes especially white, will put a handful of mesquite leaves, tied up in a cloth, in a wash pot and let them boil with the clothes. The same woman will assure you that the white inside the mesquite bark will cure dyspepsia.

Various attempts, without appreciable success, have been made to commercialize the translucent, amber-colored gum exuded in large quantities by old mesquite trees. Its properties resemble those of gum arabic. Dissolved in water, it is used as a gargle for sore throat and is swallowed as a relief for dysentery. A preparation of the gum has been dispensed by a drug company in the United States as an emollient for inflammation of the mucous membranes. The gum in a pure state is chewed by Mexicanos for toothache. The gum makes a glue, and the Apache Indians long ago put it to good use as a coating to make baskets watertight.

The Lipan and Apache Indians, and perhaps other tribes as well, made bows of mesquite wood, reinforcing the wood by wrapping it with hide thongs. When the patriot Morelos in 1810 armed his troops with machetes and rawhide reatas to fight for Mexican liberty against Spain, he constructed the first Mexican cannon out of a mesquite log. It was split, the inside hollowed out, and then the halves were fitted back together and bound round and round with green rawhide. This rawhide preserved the cannon barrel so well that it is yet to be seen in the National Museum at Mexico City.

The posts of the first barbed wire fences in Texas were mesquite, and some of them have not rotted away yet. The first paving in the city of San Antonio, around 1880, was of Alamo Plaza, and the paving consisted of mesquite blocks cut into hexagons. As long as it didn't rain, they made a good pavement, but when the ground became soaked, whole areas of them would squish up.

Though the trunks and limbs of mesquite trees are neither long nor straight enough to furnish building lumber, the interior woodwork of various old Catholic churches and ranch houses of the Southwest is of mesquite. A few cabinetmakers are educating the public to appreciate the beauty of finished mesquite wood. The grain is not surpassed by that of walnut, rosewood, or mahogany. The color varies from marbled yellow to a smoldering blood red, and it takes a superb polish.

Only the outer parts of large trunks, however, can be expected to yield first class slabs. Under the force of winds, the heart of the standing timber "shakes," or cracks, badly. (Mesquite is emphatically not a forest tree. It is correctly classed as brush.) Mesquite furniture is as beautiful in texture as any redwood, but it is likely to remain high-priced because workable wood is scarce and probably never will be plentiful even in a region covered with mesquite trees.

Nearly all beans that produce new mesquite plants have been swallowed by animals. In other words, mesquite spreads not by root projection or self-sowing but through the stomachs of animals. The mesquite bean grows in a long pod not unlike that of some varieties of snap beans. In dry weather, beans will last a long time for the benefit of hungry stock. It is from the juicy bean pod, rich in protein, that animals get nourishment. Few of the hard seeds are masticated. During drought, cattle browse on the leaves and pick up and pull off the ripe beans. "Bitter mesquite and poor folks' children are plentiful," is an old border saying.

Horses do better than cattle on the beans. Fiber from the beans and leaves may, however, wad up in an animal's stomach with disastrous results. In the old days, before corn was procurable, ranch people would gather up mesquite beans and store them for horse feed. They would keep for years. Mexican freighters used to carry sacks of them to feed their oxen.

More than a hundred years ago, oxen driven from far down in Mexico to salt deposits east of El Paso were fed mesquite beans by their drivers. You can still see the long, irregular lines of mesquites that were planted in this manner. In New Mexico, too, more than one old roadway is lined with mesquites. It is said that between Ponca City and Elgin, in Oklahoma, lines of mesquite trees show where Texas cattle were driven after they had been unloaded in the old Indian Territory.

In recent generations, the mesquite has marched upon a

conquest of its own good earth with an aggressiveness scarcely matched by any foreign invader. When white men overgrazed the country and grass became scarce, stock ate every mesquite bean found—and then dropped the seed where the rootlets could, on germination, get into the ground.

Grass will grow underneath a single mesquite, but when mesquites make a thicket, the grazing area diminishes to the vanishing point. Today the mesquite's thorned branches cover tens of millions of acres. The white man sowed with overgrazing; he is now reaping thickets of mesquites that are sterilizing an empire of land into nonproductivity.

Ranchers are battling to reclaim their land from the usurping mesquite, using kerosene and ten-ton roller tractors that are as formidable in appearance as any German war tank. The machine age is bound to curb the mesquite. But there should be no disposition to annihilate it.

Dwellers of this region knew and used and lived with the mesquite for centuries before the land was overrun by invaders from Europe and then gashed in a frenzy of exploitation. The human natives resisted long, always retreating, and then were broken and silent. Many of the nonhuman natives have met a similar fate.

Yet the mesquite has a power of adaption that in the animal kingdom of the Southwest is equaled only by the coyote. Following the will of nature, it has not retreated but now advances as conqueror over the titled domain of the conquerors. Is there nothing that can stop it? Even as individual trees are destroyed, other mesquite will steal up behind its destroyers.

Hard things have been said about the mesquite, but to many of us born and reared in the Brush Country, the mesquite is as graceful and lovely as any tree in the world. When, in the spring, trees and bushes put on their delicately green, transparent leaves and the mild sun shines on them, they are more beautiful than any peach orchard, to which they have often been compared. The green seems to float through the young sunlight into the sky. Then the mesquite is itself a poem.

Primroses burn their yellow fires
Where grass and roadway meet;
Feathered and tasseled like a queen,
Is every old mesquite.

I ask for no better monument over my grave than a good mesquite tree, its roots down deep like those of people who belong to the soil, its hardy branches, leaves, and fruit holding memories of the soil since the time when thorned men began to walk on it and remember.

What Every
Curandera Knows

The medicinal plants of Mexico include over fourteen hundred specimens, hundreds of them also common to the southwestern part of the United States. It is hard to find a bush, weed, or tree that a man or woman of Indian blood does not know some human use for.—JFD

WANDERING THROUGH the market in Oaxaca, always a drama of life, vivid with color and variegated with wares, I came upon the booth I was looking for. Spread out within, hanging above, and crammed everywhere about it were a multi-hued, multi-odored assortment of herbs, nearly all of them dried. Also present were frog and lizard carcasses, snake skins, rat bones, sea shells, and a hodgepodge of other medical material.

This was the apothecary, the pharmacopoeia of the native folk of the region. Its duplicate is to be found in the public market of every city and sizeable town of Mexico. Its stock of goods has changed but little since the time of Cortés. Many of these same herbs could also be gathered from the Mexican botánicas of San Antonio.

With permission I examined certain specimens, asking questions about the use of this and that. Then, with many thanks, I started away.

"But, señor," the stalwart proprietress asked, "will you not buy?

"Why should I when nothing ails me?

"Come back," she called. "Here is what you need!" She was laughing as she elevated in one hand a paper sack of unknown ingredients.

"Why do I need it? For what does it serve?"

"The señoritas—with this, you could not keep them away!"

❖　◉　❖

The herb woman, or curandera, to be found prescribing cures in every community is probably little changed from her antecedent of preconquest times. In her, science and superstition are inextricably mixed. She does not know modern medical facts common to any hospital nurse. But she is not a pretender. She is ripe with experience; she has a great deal of common sense. Above all, she knows her herbs.

It is well known that a large percent of the standardized drugs on the markets of the civilized world have been taken from folk pharmacopoeia. The Spanish conquistadors who encountered chocolate, vanilla, corn, cotton, potatoes, beans, squashes, pumpkins, peanuts, rubber, various dyes and fibers, and other foods and materials now common everywhere were amazed at the herbal remedies they found among the Indians. From them they early learned the medical uses of quinine, cascara sagrada, cocaine, and ipecac.

Although the secrets of the laboratory have in the popular mind displaced those once supposed to be held by the Indians, the Natives had—and yet have—an intimate knowledge of plant life. Many Indians do not concern themselves primarily with the beauty of flowers, as does the poet and gardener, nor with the ornamental features of shrubbery, as do nearly all city dwellers. Instead they want to know what a plant can do for them.

The Mexican Indian appreciates the fact that the barrel cactus, viznaga, will give him drink in the midst of the desert and that the barbed ocotillo of lava lands makes a good fence when planted close together in rows, but it would never occur to him to construct a rock garden to set off these botanical specimens.

His practical way of looking at nature gave him foods, colors, fiber, clothing, shelter—and medicines. How did he in the beginning come to this knowledge of medicines? Nobody can say absolutely, but certainly he came by some of it through watching animals.

At several places in Texas and many in Mexico one who does not have time to go out and gather it may purchase dried huaco, a plant used against rattlesnake bites. Indians, according to a very old tradition, discovered the supposed virtues of this plant by watching the paisano eating some of it after he had been bitten by a rattler.

The process of building up an immunity through inoculation was certainly not scientifically understood at the time, but science does not laugh at beginnings.

Medicine men of the Kickapoo tribe, now located in northern Mexico, following the method of their forefathers, long ago inoculated against rattlesnake poison. They would kill a rattler without angering it and then extract the fangs and the poison-filled sacs attached thereto. A shaman inserted a fang into the arm of a child and then squeezed the poison sac. If the arm swelled too much, he lacerated it and pressed a goat's horn, the little end cut off into the hollow, over the wound. Then he sucked out some of the poison through the horn. Both arms and both legs of the child were thus inoculated, and, because of this immunity, it was believed that rattlesnakes would avoid them.

Many a folk remedy going back through the ages was probably arrived as an accident. How a warm brew of greasewood leaves soothes bruised, aching feet I well know—soothes them better than mere warm water, but how some desert-treading Indian centuries ago happened upon that balm I cannot imagine.

To touch on the medicinal uses of urine is to embark on an ocean of lore involving many forms of folklore and religion. A remedy "as handy as a shirt pocket," every vaquero knows, especially when dealing with eye infections. I've seen a vaquero just before mounting his horse in the morning urinate into his hand and then rub the urine into his eye. It must have done some good to somebody, temporarily at least. The best that any doctor can do is temporary.

The Mexican countryman takes for his toothbrush the root or stem of a tubular plant called blood-of-the-dragon. It is a better brush than the sometimes substituted chewed-up end of a hackberry twig.

Some of the common remedios may have been arrived at by simple instinct. A natural dog—I know nothing about parlor poodles—will when his insides have suffered a revolution turn from fatty or cooked foods and eat grass. Just eat grass.

Certain highly seasoned Mexican foods are calculated to produce such revolution in the digestive organs that remedies for settling and healing the stomach must be available. Stomach cures are innumerable in Mexico. There must be scores of herb teas good "por el estómago." Certainly every region has one handy. None is better than tea of the manzanillo, a camomile. It is recommended to anybody after a bait of the great national dish called mole, consisting of forty-nine kinds of seasonings mashed and boiled and mixed so as to entirely kill the taste of any meat they enswathe.

No remedy taken over by Anglo-American settlers from Mexicanos or from Indians of the Southwest is better known than prickly pear poultice for bruises, cuts, wounds, thorn pricks, etc. It was as good for horses as for man. A leaf, or "pad," is taken from the nopal, then lightly roasted, the thorns thus being singed off the outside and the inside vegetable flesh softened and warmed. Then the leaf, which is sometimes a half inch thick, is split open and applied to the wound, flesh side in. The emollient effect is almost immediate.

One time in the early days the noted adventurer Bigfoot Wallace had a man severely wounded by Comanches. He applied prickly pear to the wound, but the injury was so grave Bigfoot thought it best to carry the man to a frontier army post for treatment. A few days later he returned to the post to see how the wounded man was progressing. He found him worse. The post surgeon had disdained the prickly pear poultice treatment.

Bigfoot took possession of the man at once, removed him to his own camp, renewed the nopal treatments, and soon had him entirely well. The fact that one can't buy prickly pear in a drug store or requisition it in a hospital is not proof that it may not be as effective as some lotion with a French name.

Of course many of the remedies prescribed by curanderas and tribal medicine men are sheer witches' brews—a yellow-hued plant for the yellow jaundice, a red leaf of any sort to counteract the vomiting of red blood. Animals are also harvested on this same principle.

In the western Sierra Madre of Mexico the marvelously, astoundingly beautiful imperial woodpecker yet survives—sparsely.* His wild cries and his steam riveter pecking on hard wood can be heard fully a mile away. The day I heard a pair of these imperials and then half an hour later saw them will always remain for me my Era of Discovery. The reason why this wonderful, this magnificent bird is sought, killed, and eaten by Indians and mixed-bloods of the Sierra Madre as a cure for deafness must be because he is the opposite of silence. On the same principle his flesh would be even better for blindness.

No aboriginal herb doctor ever acquired definite understanding of nerve centers, blood circulation, germ actions, toxic poisons, etc. All "primitive" peoples, their herbalists included, believe in an easy transference of properties from one form of matter to another. Thus at least one tribe of Plains Indians, not cannibalistic, ate the palms of their slain enemies in order to acquire their cunning. Thus some of the ancient Mexicans rubbed deer tallow into their own joints in order to absorb the deer's fleetness.

In parts of Mexico one may occasionally see a coyote's skull tied around the neck of a goat. The coyote is very, very cunning, and he eats goats. This cunning, seated in the skull, will be translated to the goat if he associates intimately with the skull; then, as a result, he will be able to outwit the coyote.

---

*The last confirmed sighting was in 1956, and the species is now considered extinct.

Some archaeologists have suggested that Aztec priests through their practice of sacrificing multitudes of human beings acquired a remarkable knowledge of the human anatomy. Through examination of exhumed skeletons it is known that the Aztecs and Mayans both were masters of the difficult art of trepanning— opening the skull to relieve brain pressure. To perform the operation they used a crude circular saw of stone. They excelled also in bloodletting, using delicately filed, keen-edged obsidian knives for the venesections.

Headaches called sometimes for a combination of medicine and surgery. In the tropics, banana leaves, so cool and fresh, are still applied to the temples for headache. In the arid north country, leaves of the mesquite or willow pressed into a sombrero and then pulled down over the head are supposed to be alleviative. Carvings on architectural ruins of the Aztecs show a man with porcupine quills sticking in his forehead—presumably not through his skull. The quills made an opening for the stubborn headache, which refused to surrender to cool leaves, to get out through.

Modern Mexico is changing fast, and it is increasingly utilizing science for health. Yet the herbs and remedios of ancient civilizations remain ever present, as whoever goes to the marketplace can readily see.

The Madstone Cure

Until the researches of Louis Pasteur led, in 1885, to successful inoculation against rabies, there was no sure way to prevent a person infected with the rabies virus from succumbing to hydrophobia. Of course, not every infected person succumbed. Just about 80 to 85 percent of human beings are naturally immune to the virus. But even with that knowledge, mighty few people bitten by a rabid or potentially rabid animal want to risk not being immune.—JFD

T HE MADSTONE, in a way, is a symbol of humankind's enduring credulity, which never turns loose of one phantom without grabbing on to another. For many people on the frontier in pre-Pasteur days, the one hope of being saved from the horrible malady of rabies was to get a madstone. Since the vast majority of those exposed could not go mad because of their natural immunity, the madstone got credit for saving them. It took years for Pasteur's science to supplant the theory and application of madstones.

The power to suck poison from the flesh and absorb it that believers ascribed to the madstone was, for them, the same magic ascribed to the bezoar stones in ancient Persia and Greece. The "stones," originating in animals' guts, were said to be an antidote against any poison. The most valued and historic madstones of recent times in the United States came from the stomachs of ruminants.

As a boy, I found a "stone" that had been carried by a fat cow butchered on our ranch. In shape it was a flattened ball, maybe two inches in diameter. A smooth, speckled-gray, permeable covering of calcium enclosed a compact mass of material that looked like hairs and moss fiber.

People who claim to know the most about madstones say the best ones come out of the stomachs of white deer. No stone out of a cow could have the virtue of one out of a deer. The deer that had a stone was not always white, but whiteness in a carrier always gave the stone more drawing power.

The way the stone was used was to moisten it with milk—water could not be trusted—and apply it to a wound. If it did not adhere, the person being treated was presumed not to have the virus. To do any good, it had to stick to the flesh for a long time, drawing the poison out of the wound and absorbing it into its own porous substance. Then it would be put into a vessel of hot milk, and the milk would turn green from the poison being released from the madstone. Some let the milk boil and considered the thumping of the madstone on the bottom of the vessel a good sign. Its pores having been cleansed, it would be applied again to the wound until it no longer adhered.

It was supposed to be effective in drawing out snake venom, but victims of snake bite were seldom within reach of a madstone when bitten and could not wait to get to one and had to resort to whiskey or some other remedy.

It was generally considered that a person infected with rabies could not go mad for at least two weeks. Even in the horse age there was time for a victim to ride hundreds of miles to a madstone. A dispatch from the *Galveston Daily News* of May 3, 1879, reads: "A man in town yesterday from the Pan Handle said he had been bitten by a mad dog and had ridden 350 miles in four days and nights, coming to a mad stone [here]. The stone stuck nine times."

Agnes Morley Cleaveland, in her excellent book on ranch life, *No Life for a Lady*, tells of "a haggard-looking man on a haggard-looking horse" riding up to her ranch, out from Magdalena, New Mexico, jerking off his hat, showing her two red marks next to the hairline on his forehead, and announcing, "A hybie-phobie skunk bit me. They say there's a madstone in Socorro! If I can git to it in time! I've been on this horse twenty hours already. He can't make it on."

He drank a cup of coffee, slept two hours while competent Miss Agnes rustled up the remuda and saddled him a fresh horse. Then he rode on. Returning a few days later, he jubilantly described how the milk-soaked madstone had "pulled" the poison out of his head.

An heired sword could not be divided, but an heired madstone could. Collin McKinney of Kentucky settled in Texas in time to sign the Declaration of Independence from Mexico, after which he served in the Congress of the Republic and had Collin County named after him, along with the city of McKinney. McKinney's friend, Ben Milam, thought enough of McKinney to present him with a third of a madstone, "about the size of a goose egg."

Before McKinney died he cut his portion of the madstone into enough parts for each of his children to have a precious piece of it. A son in Collin County in 1875 had a portion only about half an inch square, but it was still drawing poison out of flesh bitten by rabid animals. This McKinney son claimed that in forty-seven years the stone had saved 400 persons from hydrophobia and had failed to work on only two. One of them was already having convulsions when the stone was applied to his wound; the other had so many whiskers on his chin, where the bite had been made, that the stone could not adhere. Presumably the man of whiskers preferred hydrophobia to shaving; not long after the madstone failed to draw out the poison through his whiskers, he went into the horrible convulsions of hydrophobia.

I have never heard of an owner or a madstone who charged outrageously for the use of it. In 1875, one W. M. James of Fannin County was bitten on the leg by a mad dog loose on the streets of Sherman. He rode at once to the McKinney farm in Collin County. The madstone was applied. It adhered to the wound and at once began drawing. For thirty-one hours, during which time it dropped off four times and was four times relieved of its surfeit of poison by being soaked in hot milk, it sucked poison out of the leg until not a tincture remained. The shrines of Guadalupe in Mexico and of Lourdes in France never did better. McKinney charged Mr.

James only $3.00 for taking care of him and his horse for three days and letting the madstone cure him besides.

People used to city life with all its mechanical and scientific devices for the body's health and comfort must employ the transporting power of imagination to realize the utter helplessness of a human being away out in the country bitten by a mad animal or a poisonous snake—and also the wish to be helpful by someone possessing a madstone. The remedies that doctors before Pasteur had for hydrophobia were no more valid scientifically than the madstone treatment.

Praying for Rain

When a few years ago Governor Allan Shivers of Texas proclaimed a day for prayers to break the drought, I wondered why he as a very astute real estate trader did not corner—for a song—a big block of fertile land west of the Pecos, take along a colony of believers, and lead them in prayer to God to change the climate. The climate of the Sahara or of the North Pole is as susceptible to prayers as the climate of Texas.—JFD

WHAT LONG AGO CAME to be called "cattle country" is a land of not only little but varying rainfall. Land averaging twenty inches a year may get less than ten inches one year and thirty the next. Lots of cattle country averages no more than fifteen inches. Some good soil in desert spaces may be irrigated to grow feed, but the water comes from precipitation somewhere.

Owners of ranches purchased with money from oil, gas, factories, city business, and the like are not among the drought-marked. Air-conditioning may erase the mark on town dwellers in arid regions, but air-conditioning does not make grass grow.

Flying cloud seeders, Hopi Indians ceremonially dancing for rain while holding rattlesnakes between their teeth, Christians kneeling to pray for rain, all have proved no more effective than setting up a rain gauge in the Sahara Desert would be.

My father was a praying man. Every night he held family prayers, reading first, by light from a kerosene lamp, a chapter in the Bible and then kneeling down to pray aloud, all other members of the family kneeling also. But though the grass usually needed it, I never heard Papa pray for rain.

Knowledge of scientific facts spreads, but feelings contrary to knowledge linger. Still, people don't believe in heavenly appeals for rain as much as they used to. One time after several people gathered to pray for rain, somebody started a discussion over the power of prayer on the weather. A ranchman who would never have been called a chatterbox said: "I don't mind praying, but I can tell you right now it won't do a damned bit of good as long as this dry wind stays in the west."

At another prayer-for-rain meeting, five young men who did not approve of the preacher's stand on prohibition entered wearing rain slickers. They sat down on the front bench. The preacher was outraged. When he heard tittering, his outrage mounted. He ordered the slicker-wearers to leave. One said, "We just came prepared for the rain."

The late Captain William M. Molesworth, who ranched up the Nueces River, used to tell of a neighbor named Chappy Moore, noted for prolonged and chatty prayers to the Lord. The more people there were at a table and the hungrier they were, the longer Chappy Moore's blessing. One day he rode up the Molesworths' just in time for dinner. The host, knowing his intimacy with God, did not fail to call on him to ask the blessing.

"Oh, Lord," Chappy Moore began, "while I think of it, I sent Juan out into the Vara Dulce pasture this morning to bring in a cow with a wormy calf. When I saw them two days ago, I was in a buggy and couldn't doctor the calf. That's a terribly brushy pasture, and a little water is left in a tank where she ranges. I guess she'll bog down pretty soon unless you see that Juan finds her. You can count her ribs, she's that ga'nt, and her hocks knock together when she walks. I'm afraid she drank last night and is hid out in the brush now. I'd appreciate it, Oh Lord, if you'd take the trouble to direct Juan to this cow. She's a brindle with the left horn kinda drooped. If Juan don't doctor that calf, the screwworms will kill it.

"Now we thank you for the plentiful and tasty repast the good sister of this household has provided. Bless her and may all who eat of her cooking be properly thankful. Thou hast given us many things to be thankful for, Oh Lord, but I'll tell you that nobody is thankful for the drought you are visiting upon the people of this land and their cattle and horses and other livestock. A lot of the cattle are past suffering. They are dying. Water is playing out in every direction. The wind won't blow. The windmills can't pump enough water to supply the roadrunner birds. We humbly call upon you to end this drought and send us rain. When I say rain, I mean rain. One of your little drizzle-drazzles won't fool us. It's time to get a soaker. We need a fence-lifter and a gully-washer. We want to see the ground covered with green. Amen."

Drought, like other soul-searing experiences, tempers a human being, brings him to accept what is.

In dry weather all signs fail, people say. "The only sure sign is an old Indian sign," my mother used to say—"black all around and pouring down in the middle." The only proven prophecy in drought is that every dry spell ends with a rain.

When it finally comes, people—men more than women—will walk out into it, bareheaded, in shirt sleeves, arms stretched out, eyes shut, head thrown back, mouth open, soaking in the wonderful rain. They will walk around in an uplift of thankfulness. If they don't live by a creek, they will—unless on the flat plains—go to where they can see the water flowing.

Within three days what looked like dead roots will be sprouting, green blades will be shooting up around the wooden stools of bunch grass. If wet weather holds on a little while, millions of grass and weed seeds hidden in and on the dirt will be coming up. Some seeds of plant life belonging to arid lands always keep themselves in reserve. I have seen a desert on which seed had not sprouted for nine years turn into bloom.

When it rains, animals understand that grass is coming. Understanding by instinct is sometimes more beautiful than understanding through reasoning powers. Horses out in the pasture will dash about as playfully as if they were colts. Calves will chase away from the cows. Deer and other wild animals are likewise quickened.

All the lightning that I have in all my life seen flash and race, whether in sheets or forked lines, has been beautiful. All the thunder, near or distant, earthshaking or a low mumble, has been music to my ears. Rain may not accompany thunder and lightning, but it is promised. Coming together, they give life one of its climaxes.

No journey from any Main Street to Fifth Avenue in New York, from any province in equatorial Africa to Parisian Champs Elysees can mean more to an eager traveler than the change felt by a man of drought-perished soil when rains at last fall upon it.

The Campfire

"We sat down with the greatest philosopher on earth—the fire." Dobie had that sentence, adapted from Frederic Remington, carved into the mesquite mantelpiece above his fireplace. That mantelpiece is at Dobie's old country place, Paisano—now home to a prestigious writer-in-residence program that has nurtured many of the state's top writers for over fifty years.—SD

I LIKE THE CAMPFIRE when it is blazing, and I like the last dim glow of its embers. I like talk by it and I like silence beside it. It makes company more companionable, and it makes solitude richer. I remember certain campfires as I remember certain faces, certain friends, certain experiences that make human sympathies glow.

The earliest specific campfire I recall was late in the year 1897. I was toward three months beyond my ninth birthday. My Uncle Jim Dobie had contracted to buy around 415 head of stock cattle and he took me along with a wagon and several vaqueros to receive the cattle and drive them to our ranch, between two and three days' travel by cloven hoofs to the south. Before we got to the ranch a cold, wet norther hit us. Everybody got shivering wet, and we "made camps" in a thicket of heavy brush and trees.

In those days in that part of the world, many things were home-made. Mexicanos on the ranches lived in jacales thatched over with bear grass. Some of the men wore rawhide chivarros (leggings, now often called chaps), the hair turned in. When rawhide gets thoroughly wet, it becomes as limp as a wet dishrag. When it dries, it sets as stiff as a board. One young man with us who wore rawhide leggings went to drying them by the campfire. The rain had quit falling, and we were all feeling mighty cheerful from the warmth and glow of blazing mesquite wood. I guess this vaquero didn't pay much attention to the drying process. He was quite loquacious, and after we had filled up on hot bread out of a Dutch oven, a pot of frijoles with plenty of bacon in it that had been brought along already cooked, and sorghum molasses, the young vaquero noticed his leggings. They were as dry and stiff as a pair of stovepipes. He stood them up in front of him, and there in a theater of earth and firelight extemporized a kind of play. He talked to them and had them talk back to him. Everybody was laughing. I have no recollection whatsoever of anything that was said. I only remember the bright fire, its wonderful warmth after the cold and wet, and the colloquy between fire-flushed vaquero and fire-hardened rawhide leggings standing up empty in front of him.

Many years later, over a considerable period of time, I made various pack trips, mostly alone except for a mozo, across the Sierra Madre and winding around through the mountains of western Mexico. I can look back on myself at certain campfires on those trips as another man.

After riding all day in the cold, without seeing a human being or a fence, he makes camp behind a windbreak of trees. A creek of clear water flanks it on one side, and a glade of matted mesquite grass on the other. After watering and hobbling their horses and pack mules, the man and his mozo build a fire, wash hands, faces, roast a side of fat venison ribs and eat most of them. The mozo rolls into his pallet. The man puts fresh wood on the coals and sits down where the warmth comes steady and there is no smoke. He fills his pipe and smokes it, looking into the fire.

He is comfortable inside and out. The sound of the wind, only moderately high, in the branches adds to his feeling of being an unstriving master of Time, and of being in place—without ambition to turn the place into capital gain.

The coyotes, smelling the cooked meat and serenading the cold moon, talk to him also. They seem to go with the fire.

The man's mind tracks back to many things—to love, to his

childhood hearth, to action, to illuminations out of literature, to good companions. Thoughts come to him on subjects far remote from the life he is leading, yet nothing seems remote to the light and the warmth of the fire. He spreads his hands before it, not because they are cold but out of geniality. He remembers with understanding the ancient Persians who worshipped fire. He feels thankful to the Unknown for wood and the mystery of its burning.

He gets up to put on more wood and stands with back to the blaze. He looks out to the shadows rising and falling on a tree trunk by which his pallet has been spread. The silent play of shadows from the fire, silent except for now and then a hardly perceptible pop, when a coal cracks, makes his mind more active without marring serenity. The activity is comfortable in the way of the sound of his horse cropping grass just beyond the tree is.

He turns back to the fire. He has known good company, good talk, but none better than this. Yet recalling good talk by other fires, he wishes a certain person, maybe two or three certain persons, were here now, perhaps to talk, perhaps to be silent, certainly to be genial with the fire. At the same time, he is glad to be alone. The whole man is composed of many parts.

He has time and again been burned by fire. He has seen fire released from the air consume cities and has traveled over a nation devastated by it. He has seen it annihilate a family's all in less time than it takes to be born. He knows nothing more awful than fire can be. But he is so in harmony with the little campfire that he seems to himself to be a part of it, as he is a part, a mere particle, of the elements—the elements that according to the ancients consisted of earth, air, water, and fire.

Many hunters nowadays lodge in hotels and tourist camps in the vicinity of hunting grounds. They get their nightly hot baths, sit in chairs at a table and order from banal menus, and may kill just as much as if they were camping out. But to my taste, they miss more than half the pleasure and recreation that belongs with a hunt. I remember one campfire in the desert of Sonora, against the Gulf of California, where I sat on the vertebra of a whale that had been dragged out of the surf by Indians. Old King Cole had not a more comfortable chair. Another camp—in desert country of Chihuahua—where we had a hard time boiling coffee with nothing but stems of weeds for fuel, while the unremitting wind blew too much sand to make sitting on the ground bearable, makes in memory a brighter lodging than any room in any New York hotel where I have lodged. Mere comfort without geniality is never memorable.

Many times I have fallen into remembering a before-daylight visit a long time ago with Mexicano hands at the Abras Ranch out from Cotulla. Beside their bunk cabin they had for kitchen and dining room an unroofed corral of tightly wedged mesquite pickets. They were sitting on chunks of wood or standing about the fire in this kitchen-corral drinking coffee when I drove up. I guess the coyotes had been listening to the car. As soon as I stopped and went to the fire, they opened up.

After the first few low words of greeting nobody was saying anything. The day before I had been hunting on the Olmos Ranch, twenty-five miles or so down the Nueces River. While riding horseback, I had come upon a patch of greasewood (gobernador) on a ridge out from the river on the south side. I like to smell greasewood, especially after a rain and especially the incense from its burning. I had broken off three or four leafy sprigs and put them in a pocket of the ducking jacket I wore. Now, beside the fire, I pulled the sprigs out and pitched them on coals. They are rich in oil, and they burned brightly, the strong, pungent odor pervading the air.

One of the Mexicanos silent there was old Jacinto de los Santos, which name literally translated means Hyacinth of the Saints. He looked no more like a hyacinth than I look sweet sixteen. He was puro Indio in blood. His features were solemn and sad, and when he spoke, the words seemed to come from deep down in his strong frame. He was more fence-builder and tanker than vaquero; he could have told you how many strands of barbed wire were stapled to posts fencing in 40 or 50 big pastures; he was as much of the campo as any keen-scented wild thing that ranged it. He and two of his boys, both superb vaqueros, squatted by while the burning greasewood scented the air.

"You have been to Los Olmos?" Jacinto de los Santos stated. There is where we had come to know each other years back.

"Yes."

"The gobernador grows on the long ridge across the river from the Olmos ranch house," one of the boys said.

"Yes," Jacinto nodded solemnly, "and there is another patch north of La Mota." Then followed minute directions to this other patch, not far from the relics of a sheep pen that began falling down before the stage from San Antonio to Laredo quit running. Presumably no other greasewood grew in an area of several hundred thousand acres of land in that country.

I am sitting alone in the cold dawning by my campfire; I have old Jacinto de los Santos for company. He was honest and kind, but if there be a company of saints in some ethereal region of the universe I doubt his being with them. He ceased to be here on earth long ago. My imagination is limited, and I can't imagine any place of disembodied spirits where Jacinto de los Santos would be as much in place as at a ranch campfire before daylight in a vast land where he knew every trail, every fence gap, every particular patch of greasewood, ceniza, coma, palo verde, and dozens of other thorned species belonging to the arid soil in which he was rooted. If I can't have as company one who belongs to the ground on which a campfire flickers, the fire itself is sufficient to make me feel ample.

PART 5

The Brush Country

"The Brush Country of Texas is my querencia."—JFD

A Plot of Earth

I was born and reared on a ranch in the Brush Country of southern Texas. It has thorned me, parched me, repelled me, and after long years of absence it still holds me; my roots go into it deeper than ever mesquite sent its roots for moisture. Like the mountains, the Brush Country casts a spell not of charm but of power.—JFD

ON THE TWENTY-SIXTH DAY of September, 1888, I was born in a three-room whitewashed rock house on the ranch of my parents in southern Live Oak County, Texas, in the Brush Country west of the Nueces River.

Ramireña Creek and Long Hollow coursed through the ranch. My father owned the land before he and my mother were married. They added to it and added to the house while rearing six children, I being the oldest. As ranches went at the beginning of the 20th century, it was small, approximately seven thousand acres.

A little while ago as one of six heirs I signed a piece of paper passing ownership of the inheritance to alien hands. Not one of the six men who bought it has any idea of living upon it. They are oil men, not ranchers; they bought it as a hunting place and as an investment. It has become a piece of property and little more.

Time with its unending changes may see another human being on this plot of earth with roots into it as deep as mine, but not soon, I think. Before long I shall become a clod of earth. Until then, no matter who holds title to the ground, my roots into it will be ineradicable.

In a way I feel that for a piece of money I have betrayed the soil that nurtured me, though the purchasers, with means and with modern ideas of conservation, will probably do more to restore it than my family did. As a matter of fact, we did absolutely nothing to restore it. For nearly thirty years it has been leased to individuals concerned, through circumstances and inherited attitudes, only with wringing a season-by-season profit from it.

After 1906 we were absentee owners. In that year my family moved to the town of Beeville, twenty-seven horse miles over a weary road to the east, where we used to trade. That fall I left for college, never to reside again in the region. Nevertheless, for years after I left, I spent summers on the ranch, and have never ceased returning to it with eagerness.

I never recollect the ranch as being what is called romantic. I was not a good roper or a good rider, and never shot a six-shooter until I got into the army during World War I, but from the vaqueros and my father I learned to soothe wild or restless cattle with my voice. Sometimes in a way I seemed to become one of them.

It has been a place where I belonged both in imagination and in reality, a place on which I felt free in the way that one can feel only on his own piece of earth. It has said more to me than any person I have known or any writer I have read, though only through association with fine minds and spirits have I come to realize its sayings.

It is not a rich land. Caliche hills and thorned brush make a section of it forbidding. The remainder is sandyish. Yet sweep of hills and valleys, wooded Ramireña Creek, and live oak trees scattered singly and clustered into groves make the ranch gracious. One of the live oaks has the largest spread in all that part of Texas. Chiltipiquines, the little round, red Mexican peppers, grow wild under it. It is near what used to be called Alligator Waterhole; alligators lived there before I was born.

In a seasonable spring all the land is beautiful with growing grass, fresh leaves on the trees and brush, wine-burnished hollyhocks and baby-blue-eyes in the valleys, Mexican primroses, pink phlox and Indian paintbrushes on the slopes, splashes of bluebonnets, and scores of other kinds of wild flowers everywhere.

I did not know it at the time, but I began listening to this piece of land talk while I was the merest child. The jackdaws—grackles, as called now—that nested in the oaks about our house and lost young ones that we children rescued; the calves sucking their mothers and playing about them out in the pasture; the bob-whites' cheerio to morning, the bullbats' zoom at twilight; the sandhill cranes fluting their long, lone cries on a winter evening; the coyotes serenading from every side after dark; my horse Buck pointing his ears when I walked into the pen; the green on the mesquites in early spring so tender that it emanated into the sky; the mustang grapevines draping trees along Ramireña Creek; the stillness of day and night broken by windmills lifting rods that lifted water; the south wind galloping in the treetops; the locusts in the mulberry tree, the panting of over-ridden and over-driven horses accentuating the heat of summer; the rhythm of wood-cutting in cold weather; the rhythm of a saddle's squeak in the night: these the land gave me. Its natural rhythms and the eternal silence entered into me.

❖   ◉   ❖

I do not wish to go back there to live. The summers are scorching; for nine months of the year the air is enervating. Clouds drift up from the Gulf of Mexico, barely fifty miles away and not more than a hundred feet lower, but they seldom drop rain. One can waste his heart out there vainly hoping for rain, and during the frequent drouths the unyielding land is a desolation.

If I were wealthy, I should buy the ranch, modernize the house, and live there during the hunting season with books, typewriter, some pictures and mesquite furniture beside the fireplace in the room where I was born. The fire in that fireplace would talk to me as no fire in any other fireplace can talk.

The richest days of my life have not been spent on this ranch, not at all. The hymn-singing we had on Sundays at home gives me a depressed feeling to this day. I was afraid of God, prayed Him to help me find a lost pocketknife, and found out that we did not have much in common. In time the personal God of my forefathers became for me as mythical as Jupiter and not nearly so plausible as Venus. Itinerant preachers were favored in our home above all other company. They specialized in eating fried chicken, potato salad, and lemon pie, long blessings at the table, longer prayers in the evening.

But no play world could have been happier than ours. With pegs, twine, and sticks we built big pastures and stocked them with spools from my mother's sewing machine, which became our play horses. We used tips of cattle horns sawed off for cattle, oak galls for sheep, and dried snail shells for goats. We made long trains of flat, rectangular sardine cans to haul the stock from one ranch to another. For wagon and team we snared green lizards with a horsetail hair and hitched them to a sardine can or—better, because lighter to pull—a matchbox. When it rained enough to make the creek run, we made waterwheels with my father's help and had a fine time with them while the water lasted.

Our ranch house, the main part of which still stands, is in an extensive grove of live oaks on a kind of plateau overlooking the valley of Long Hollow. The house had a paling fence around it, and in the yard were more flowers than any other ranch in that part of Texas had. The garden, very prolific, was where vegetables grew. They and the flowers were irrigated from a cypress cistern and a supplementary dirt tank into which a windmill, just back of the kitchen, pumped water. The yard was bare of grass, in the pioneer tradition that guarded against snakes. Now and then a rattlesnake was killed in it.

My mother had some sort of help a good part of the time but often none. With or without help, she was too busy cooking, sewing, raising children, and keeping house to garden. My father tended the flowers as well as the vegetables. He set out orange trees, which never bore. He laid out a croquet ground in the shade of oaks. He could do anything from repairing a windmill to making a coffin for a Mexican child that died on the ranch and lining it with the bleached domestic my mother kept on hand. He was patron for some Mexicanos who did not live on the ranch, sometimes going security for them at the store where they bought food and other supplies—though we were often in debt ourselves. He hoped his eldest son would choose a career better than ranching—that of a clean-collared banker perhaps. He paid 8 and 10 percent interest to his banker and liked him.

Back of the house was a rock smokehouse, long ago crumbled down, for the rock was caliche, not true stone. Every winter my father, aided by local Mexicanos, killed hogs and cut them up for curing. Occasionally he killed a calf. The meat he butchered was all the meat we had. It was ample. The Mexicanos cut the long, strong-fibered leaves of bear grass (a yucca), heated them lightly over a fire to make them more pliable, and then used them to tie the hams, shoulders, and side bacon to poles across the smoke-house. The meats were cured by smoke from a fire of corncobs kept smoldering for days on the dirt floor. We had no hickory, needed none.

Hams and bacon were nothing to us children compared to the bladders of the slain hogs and cattle. They were the only balloons we knew. No child could ask for better. The way we made a blad-der expand was to warm it slowly by a fire, gradually blowing air into it through the quill of a turkey feather, until the walls became so thin that it would have floated away had it not been restrained. At last, yielding to temptation, somebody gave it a pommel and it burst with a wonderful sound. Nobody wanted to part with his balloon, but nobody could resist that grand explosion.

Beyond the smokehouse was a big stable combined with corn-crib, hayloft, and rooms for tools, saddles, and buggies. Along the near end of it grew a row of pomegranates, so hardy that after fifty years and through the recent drought that killed many oaks, one still exists. Near them a stout mustang grapevine twined up into the Coon Tree, an oak out of which a chicken-stealing coon had been shot. High up across its branches, we children had a platform—the "house in the Coon Tree," we called it—to which we ascended by the grapevine and on which we spent golden hours reading books or playing and in season drinking (without ice, of course) pomegranateade.

The cattle pens were on down the hill from the ranch house, about two hundred yards away. The well there was one of the oldest in the country, hand-dug and rock-curbed, about fifty feet deep, amid magnificent oaks. When the wind did not blow during the dog days of August and the big cypress cistern ran empty, water for stock had to be hauled up by pulley. One end of the rope was tied to a large wooden bucket, the other end to the horn of a saddle. Then I used to ride Old Baldy back and forth, back and forth, hour after hour, over a fifty-foot stretch, drawing water. I can see my father standing on a wide plank over the well curb and hear his hearty "Whoa!" as the bucket came up and he reached to pour the water into a long cypress trough.

Water from the well was cool and delicious, but the cattle could not get half enough. At night they would stand outside the pens where the troughs were, bawling the most distressful bawls that a cow can make. If the pen gates were left open, the cattle would fight each other over the smell of the damp cypress troughs. I have heard them bawling all night long and all day long for water.

No ranch person, no cowboy can accept "Home on the Range" as an authentic range composition. That line idealizing the range as a land where "the skies are not cloudy all day" stamps the song as not belonging.

No cattle ever died on our ranch for want of water, but they died on Tol McNeill's ranch west of us, and on the Chapa ranch up about the head of Ramireña Creek, where my father frequently bought steers. They died on other ranches. Men driving herds through the country frequently held them overnight in our pens. If a thirsty herd came when there was no water, it made too much noise for peaceful sleep. After my mother moved to Beeville, I heard her express thankfulness that she would never again have to listen to the bawl of thirsty cattle.

It was thirst in summer and hunger in winter for drought-starved cattle. The only reserve of the land is prickly pear cactus. It is made up of about 10 percent fiber and 90 percent water and defends itself by an armor of thorns. Before the portable pear burner—a flame-thrower fed by gasoline or kerosene and air pump—enabled one man to singe the thorns off enough pear to feed a hundred cows, ranch people fed a few of the poorest by chopping the pear down, dragging it to a fire in the open, holding it on the end of a green pole over the flames, and then pitching it to the slobbering animals.

My father and Uncle Jim Dobie, the big speculator and operator of the family, had gone into partnership in the summer of 1898 and bought several thousand cows. They leased the Dewees ranch on the San Antonio River and stocked it. During the winter that followed the cows died like sheep.

This cow venture so nearly broke my father that he decided to farm. About six lumber cabins were built for Mexicano families along Ramireña Creek, and the men plowed up several hundred acres of open sand hills that never should have been disturbed and that within a few years were turned back to the field mice and the ground squirrels and the hunting hawks. The Mexicanos grew enough corn and beans to live on, shooting rabbits and trapping quail to supplement the fare, but neither they nor the landlord made money out of four-cent cotton.

When we were running cattle, the sharecroppers quit the fields to work for four bits a day. On rainy days they braided horse-hair ropes and shelled corn. They were better vaqueros than they were farmers. It was a torture to me that I was not allowed to quit school and ride with them for nothing a day.

One of them, Genardo del Bosque, entered my life. He is still living, old and blind, on a little piece of land in San Patricio County that my father had taken in on a note and that my mother deeded to Genardo for a small sum. As long as she lived, he brought her a turkey every Christmas and received his "Christmas" in return. From the time the family moved to town he looked after the ranch. He is little, wiry, quick, with a Spanish sense of irony and a reddish complexion. His people once had land in Texas. His wife Emelia learned to read English in the school in which my mother taught at Lagarto before either was married. He was the best trailer I have ever known. His intelligence, energy, cow sense, and responsibility would have made him a first-class manager of a big outfit.

I and my brother Elrich felt freer with him than we felt with our father and, after the family moved to town, delighted in staying on the ranch with him during summer vacations. He ruined an eye running in brush after a Rio Grande steer of enormous horns that had jumped out of our corral.

Genardo del Bosque "had a mano" (a hand.) When a horse threw me on my back across a ridge, injuring a vertebra that still gets sore sometimes, he rubbed the pain down sufficiently for me to ride to town in a buggy. After the ranch was leased he did not remain on it long under the new employer, but he did not want to leave. "Yo tengo raices aqui" (I have roots here), he said.

My book *The Mustangs* is dedicated to him. In him and in what he represents, as well as in the land to which we both belong, *yo tengo raices*.

❖ ◎ ❖

Our schoolhouse, on a patch of open land against black brush and guajillo hills to the west, overlooked live oak slopes to the south and east. One day a flock of wild turkeys that came feeding near the schoolhouse while we were inside disrupted study. Another day just as we children burst out of the building to go home a big buck jumped a pasture fence in front of us. One evening while John Dobie and I were walking to his home from school, a coyote followed us. Ours was still wild country, we children thought.

Of several Mexicano families living in the area only one sent children to school and, as I recall, they went only one year. They belonged to Feliciano Garcia, who worked for us and lived on our ranch. Neither Pancho nor his sister could speak English, and the teacher had no time for special instruction. They were ostracized by the English-speaking children both in the schoolroom and on the playground. The progress of Mexican Americans in the Southwest and the progress of English-speaking whites in civilized attitudes toward them is one of the improvements in life I have seen.

My father organized a Sunday school that met in the second schoolhouse. About a mile up Long Hollow, on our ranch also, were the camp meeting grounds, where, at the time watermelons ripened, two preachers and a dozen or more families camped for ten days annually and were "revived."

One of the preachers was a horse trader. At the Lagarto store, which was about six miles from our ranch, I bought a Spanish pony, still saddled, from him for twenty-five dollars. I was not more than fourteen, but I had the money. When he took the saddle off, a raw "setfast" showed on the horse's back. I said I did not want the horse. The preacher said, "You've already bought him." That was a fact. However, he let me withdraw from the trade, probably because my father was a member of his church. In teaching me never to buy a horse covered up, he gave me more than any sermon of his ever gave.

We got our mail at Lagarto and I rode horseback to get it on Saturdays. The coming of the *Youth's Companion* was a red-letter day. I might gallop all the way home in order to read at once "Land's End" or some other serialized story I'd been waiting to continue. During the Spanish-American War I read the semiweekly newspaper from the saddle while riding slowly. The newspaper account of Queen Victoria's death made me sense the end of a great drama.

So far as book education is concerned, the only specific pieces of learning I can recall from ranch schooling are how to spell the word irksome, on which I was turned down in a spelling match, and knowledge that a branch of science called physical geography existed.

Literary associations, aside from textbooks, included a paperback novel titled *With Leavenworth Down on the Rio Grande*. A boy named Irving Watson brought it to school, and I read it clandestinely behind my desk. It was one of those "blood and thunder" novels that my mother positively forbade. No book pertaining to the Wild West ever entered our home, not even *The Log of a Cowboy*, although it had a sort of connection with our family in that the author, Andy Adams, was my Uncle Frank Byler's friend.

Tennyson's *Idylls of the King* put me into a world where for months wan lights flickered on plains farther away than Troy. I had read of the music of the spheres, and one starlit Sunday night while I was riding home on horseback alone after all-day church service, the other members of the family traveling in a hack, I heard what I took to be the music of the spheres. After that I would go out at night to listen to it until I discovered that the sound was made by a variety of katydid. Nevertheless, a certain pulsation of night has continued to seem to come down from the stars rather than up from the earth.

❖ ◎ ❖

The one romantic feature of our ranch was what we called Fort Ramirez. It never was a fort, but it was a fortified ranch house built by the Ramirez family around the turn of the eighteenth century and abandoned a few years later after a catastrophic Indian attack. Not within the memory of the oldest resident of the country had the fort been inhabited.

Some of the rock walls were still standing when I was a boy, and a person on top of them had a grand view of the S-winding Ramireña Creek. Granjeno bushes grown from seeds planted by birds that lit on the old picket corrals still outlined them. A patriarch named Gorgonio who lived about half a mile away and with several parientes (kinsmen) farmed a considerable field on shares used to tell of lights flickering about the ruins at night, also of chains making a terrifying noise.

People said that a fortune in Mexican gold or silver was buried there. Almost every year strangers asked permission to dig on the premises. Many holes were dug without permission, some in the night. Digging under the walls contributed to their downfall. Some of the holes in and out from the structure were big enough to bury a wagon and team in.

Uncle Ed Dubose, my mother's half brother, had a hope for digging up treasure and a faith in divining rods and fortune-tellers not shared in the least by either of my parents. But one time he came with such a plausible legend, together with a map along with specific directions from a fortune-teller in Victoria, Texas, about where to dig, that my father agreed to help. He and Uncle Ed and several ranch hands spent three days sinking a big hole. Fort Ramirez contributed to my book *Coronado's Children*, which is made up of hidden treasures and lost mines.

❖ ◎ ❖

The first thing the recent purchasers of the ranch did after taking possession was to tear down the corrals and burn up the pickets.

They were the oldest old-timey corrals in that part of the country. Now they are where Fort Ramirez has gone.

No matter what is discontinued, the land remains. A thousand years, ten thousand years hence, the Dobie ranch will be where it was before the Ramirez grant took in a portion of its pristine acreage. It will have other names, be divided, and then be absorbed. The land will always be grazing land, for neither soil nor climate will permit it to be anything else. It is possible that an oil field will temporarily mutilate it.

The time may come when people passing over it will speak a tongue that no one now living down in the Brush Country could understand. The thought of times in which I shall not participate disturbs me no more than thought of times in which I did not participate.

Nevertheless, when I consider the break now made with that plot of land on Long Hollow and Ramireña Creek—a measure of ground to which I am more closely akin than to any other on earth, not excluding the lovely creekside here in Austin that has been home to me for a quarter century—I feel that the end of something has come.

The Buried Gold
at Fort Ramirez

*Fort Ramirez—or, more properly, Rancho de la Oja de Agua Ramireño—
belongs to the Nueces country. As a boy I knew it well, for its remains
were situated on our ranch. Frequently I rode by it, and sometimes with
legs stiff in leather chivarras climbed its walls, there to gaze long at
the serpentine winding of Ramireña Creek below and the oak-fringed
hills beyond. Often I listened to tales by Mexicanos and ranch people
concerning it.—JFD*

T HE WALLS THAT I USED to stand on are all down now;
treasure hunters are responsible for that, and insensate
workmen for a pipeline company recently hauled away
most of the rocks. In another generation Fort Ramirez will hardly
be more than a name, and treasure hunters may even debate on
what hill to sink their holes. Let it be recorded that it is the hill
in the southeast corner of what is known as the Primm Pasture
overlooking Ramireña Creek to the north and Ramirez Hollow to
the west.

Built sometime in the late 1700s or early 1800s by Don José
Antonio Ramirez and his son, Don José Victoriano Ramirez, the
ancient landmark was undoubtedly the first of any permanence
to be erected within the confines of what is now Live Oak County.
The Ramirezes filed for a Spanish land grant for eight leagues of
grazing land (about 35,000 acres). The family cleared land for
fields, built a tanyard, erected corrals and ranch houses, made
other improvements, and were living in peaceable possession of

the estate. In 1812, as a result of Mexico's revolt against Spain, all troops were withdrawn from the frontier country in Texas. This released hordes of Indians to prey on the few scattered rancheros—including apparently the Ramirez people.

No official documents explain what happened to them, but an old neighbor of ours, Tol McNeill, shared what he knew with me.

McNeill had settled on the Ramireña a few miles above the Ramirez stronghold in the 1860s, and in time the talk was that he had dug up $40,000 of the money buried on the property. When I was a boy, he used to be pointed out as a man who had killed several others. His right arm terminated in a stub about halfway between wrist and elbow, and the name "Mocho," which this defect won him among the Mexicanos, was about as widely used to his back as "Old Man Tol." Despite its absence, he could roll Bull Durham cigarettes as facilely as anybody, and during his years of activity he was an expert roper both on horseback and in the pen, where he cast the loop with his foot.

His cattle were about the wildest in the whole Brush Country. He believed in "natural water," but the water holes on the creek always went dry in the hottest part of the summer and at the same time his two or three little tin windmills quit pumping; then some of his cattle would die of thirst, but the wilder ones survived on prickly pear. A cow that had to be supplied with water by a gasoline pump and couldn't "chaw" it out of prickly pear wasn't worthy of an old-time Texan cowman anyhow.

Tol McNeill never owed anything on his land or stock, never bought on credit, and he did not have to raise many cattle in order to keep himself and family supplied with such necessities as Bull Durham, frijoles, salt pork, kerosene oil, calico, and a good buggy.

When "Old Man Tol" was converted at a camp meeting, his conversion was counted as about the greatest victory for the Lord that the Ramireña country had ever witnessed. It was not long, however, before he "backslid" and was "cussing" as vigorously as ever.

As a boy I often wanted to ask him about Fort Ramirez and the buried treasure, but it was not until a year or so before his death that I mustered up sufficient courage when I encountered him at a meeting of trail drivers in San Antonio in 1927.

"About that old Ramirez Mission down there on your pa's land, I'll tell you all I know," he said. "When I first saw it, the walls were all standing and everything about it was good except the roof. They say it was one of a line of Spanish missions that extended all the way from Corpus Christi to San Antonio.

"Well, along after the Civil War brother Pate and I heard of an old Mexican woman who was said to know all about the Ramirez Mission. People were talking about the treasure buried there and some were already digging. We were interested and we went to see this woman. She lived on Captain Kenedy's Lapara ranch down on the coast. She was old, old, maybe ninety or a hundred years old.

"Yes, she said she'd been at the Ramirez before it was abandoned. That was when she was a little girl, hardly more'n big enough to carry water from the creek. One day she was just starting up the hill with an olla of water on her head, she told us, when a vaquero galloped up and yelled for her to get on behind him, that the Indians were coming. He had sighted them at the big Ramirez waterhole, which, you know, is only a mile or so above the old Ramirez house, and about the time he saw them they took after him. I guess he figgered there were too many Indians for the people at the Ramirez ranch to stand off. Anyway, he stopped just long enough for the girl to jump behind him. She rode astraddle, hanging on to him, until they crossed the Lagarto. Afterward they went down the country till they got to the Casa Blanca. It was deserted and half destroyed. The Indians had started their raid at Corpus and come on up the country sweeping clean everything in front of them. They killed every soul on Ramireña Creek.

"Well, after telling us all this, the old woman claimed she didn't know a thing about the money in the Ramirez house, but she said the dueño was muy rico. She said also that somewhere between the Casa Blanca and the Ramireña the Indians had wiped out a wagon train hauling some pretty valuable freight.

"I guess it must of been about a year after picking up all this ancient history that I was running wild horses over south of the

Picachos on Lagarto Creek. I was going lickety-split hell-bent for breakfast trying to head off a gotch-eared brown stallion and his bunch when all of a sudden I ran into a lot of human bones. I stopped right there to examine them. There was heads and arms and legs scattered all about. They were as white as bones can bleach. That night I told Oliver Dix about what I had seen and we rode back next day to take another look at the bones. He had been in the country longer'n I had and he just knew those bones were remains of the Mexican freighters who'd been killed by the Indians on their big clean-up.

"Of course digging has always been going on at the Ramirez Mission itself. It was along in the early 'Seventies, I guess, that I hitched my bridle reins to a granjeno bush one day and stepped into the main room of the Ramirez building. Right there on the ground were pieces of a jarro [an earthen pot] that had been dug out of one corner. The print of some of the coins was still fresh and plain on the caked earth sticking to pieces of the jarro. I don't know how much was found. If the Ramirez outfit didn't put all their money in one place, some of it is still there to find. I know damned well I never got any of it."

❖ ◎ ❖

East of the Ramirez ruins is a big field. The Mexicanos who cultivated this field lived in a jacal near the creek, and at night they were always seeing mysterious lights flickering and flitting between the rock walls and the creek, but never around the fort itself. Many people have held that a tunnel once ran from the fort to the creek; the lights indicated treasure hid in the tunnel. Several shafts have been sunk in attempts to probe the tunnel, but none has succeeded.

One man on our place, Antonio de la Fuente, used to tell how as a child he came with his parents to the Ramireña. They had a little money, and, as land was then very cheap and as the fort was still in tolerable condition, all that it needed to make it habitable being a thatch of bear grass, they considered buying it. One day while they were approaching it to examine it more closely, a white panther leaped out; then when they got inside, Antonio saw many curious coins on the walls and dirt floor. But he and his parents were afraid to touch the coins, and of course the idea of purchasing the place was abandoned. The white panther was the soul of the dead dueño of the treasure there to watch it.

One time a man from over about Runge, seventy miles to the northeast of us, drove up to our ranch in a buckboard. He asked permission to dig at the fort, and the permission was readily granted. He had a man with him who claimed to have been digging at the south wall some ten years before when all of a sudden, just as he was sure his telache had struck the lid of the chest, he heard an unearthly yell and the rattle of trace chains behind him. It was night. He had enough presence of mind to kick a few clods back into the hole, which was small one; but he was so frightened that he left in a run and had never been back. I went along on horseback to guide the treasure hunters to the fort. When the men got there they appeared to be strangers to it. They moved very little dirt.

Not long after this we ourselves had an experience in digging, led by my mother's half brother, my Uncle Ed Dubose. He had met earlier with a Mexicano sage who gave him "the true facts" about Fort Ramirez. He must look for the treasure in "a secret cave," or cell, hard by. Uncle Ed had a partner, Stonewall Jackson Wright. They possessed a "gold monkey"—a mineral rod—and this instrument they took to the fort with great ceremony. It oscillated toward the west and made two locations. After excavation proved futile at both places, Stonewall Jackson Wright quit, but Uncle Ed kept on. Fort Ramirez "just looked too good" to abandon.

The next step was to consult a noted fortune-teller at Victoria. The seer described Fort Ramirez satisfactorily and said that for $500 he could and would locate a buried chest of money near it. The agreement was made and one night Uncle Ed drove the man to the fort. The fortune-teller went immediately to the north corner and, walking thence east a few paces, planted his foot down, and said: "Here it is. Dig a round hole here ten feet in diameter."

When the two got back to Wade's Switch about daylight, the

man demanded his $500. Uncle Ed told him that he would have to wait until the money was dug up and offered to allow him to be present at the ceremony, but he refused to stay. He declared that unless he was paid his fee at once, "spirits would move the box," and it would be useless to try to find it.

He was not paid at once, and despite the threats of malignant spirits, Uncle Ed somehow persuaded my father to help him dig.

I believe that my father had as little superstition and was as little given to extravagant fancies as any man I have ever known, yet there is something about the lure of buried treasure that will cause almost any man to "make one trial." It happened that work was slack about this time, and so one morning with a wagon loaded with tools, bedding, chuck, a lantern, a gun or two, and three Mexicano laborers, we all set out for Fort Ramirez. A big hole was to be dug and it was to be guarded until completed.

When the diggers got down six or seven feet, they came upon some loose soil that was quite different in color and substance from the contiguous earth. It appeared to be "the filling" of some old hole. Hopes became feverish, but after about a barrel of the extraneous earth had been removed it petered out. At the depth of twelve feet the men quit digging. Evidently the spirits had moved the box.

❖   ◉   ❖

I saw the old digging site the other day. On four or five acres of ground around it are many other holes, some freshly dug.

All I regret now is that the stones of Ramirez Fort have been carried away. I should like to stand on them once more in April and gaze across the winding Ramireña upon the oak-fringed hills beyond. Yet the hills could hardly be so lush with buffalo clover—as we used to call the bluebonnet—and red bunch grass so soft and lovely, as they are in the eyes of memory.

I Remember Buck

All the old-time range men of validity whom I have known remembered horses with affection and respect as a part of the best of themselves. After their knees begin to stiffen, most men realize that they have been disappointed in themselves, in other people, in achievement, in love, in whatever they expected out of life, but a man who has had a good horse in his life will remember him as a certitude, like a calm mother, a lovely lake, or a gracious tree, amid all the flickering vanishments. I remember Buck.—JFD

H E WAS RAISED on our ranch and was about half Spanish. He was a bright bay with a blaze in his face and stockings on his forefeet. He could hardly have weighed when fat over 850 pounds and was about fourteen hands high. A Mexicano broke him when he was three years old, but I don't think he pitched much. From then on nobody but me rode him, even after I left for college. He had a fine barrel and chest and was very fast for short distances but did not have the endurance of some other horses, straight Spanish, in our remuda. What he lacked in toughness, he made up in intelligence, especially cow sense, loyalty, understanding, and generosity.

As a colt he had been bitten by a rattlesnake on the right fore ankle just above the hoof; a hard, hairless scab marked the place as long as he lived. He traveled through the world listening for the warning rattle. A kind of weed in the Southwest bears seed that when ripe rattle in their pods a good deal like the sound made by a rattlesnake. Many a time when my spur or stirrup set these seeds a-rattling, Buck's suddenness in jumping all but left me seated in the air.

I don't recall his smelling rattlesnakes, but he could smell afar off the rotten flesh of a yearling or any other cow afflicted with screwworms. He understood that I was hunting these animals in order to drive them to a pen and doctor them. In hot weather they take refuge in high weeds and thick brush. When he smelled one, he would point to it with his ears and turn toward it. A dog trained for hunting out wormy cases could not have been more helpful.

Once a sullen cow that had been roped raked him in the breast with the tip of a sharp horn. After that experience, he was wariness personified around anything roped, but he never, like some horses that have been hooked, shied away from an animal he was after. He knew and loved his business too well for that. He did not love it when at the rate of less than a mile an hour he was driving the thirsty, hot, tired, slobbering drag end of a herd, animals stopping behind every bush or without any bush, turning aside the moment they were free of a driver. When sufficiently exasperated, Buck would go for a halting cow with mouth open and grab her just forward of the tail bone if she did not move on. Work like this may be humiliating to a gallant young cowboy and an eager cow horse; it is never pictured as a part of the romance of the range, but it is very necessary. It helps a cowboy to graduate into a cowman.

Buck had the rein to make the proverbial "turn on a two-bit piece and give back fifteen cents in change." One hot summer while we were gathering steers on leased grass about twelve miles from home, I galled his side with a tight cinch. I hated to keep on riding him with the galled side, but was obliged to on account of shortage in horses. As I saddled up in camp one day after dinner I left the cinch so loose that a hand might have been laid between it and Buck's belly. We had to ride about a mile before going through a wire gap into the pasture where some snaky steers ran. As we rode along, a vaquero called my attention to the loose cinch.

"I will tighten it when we get to the gap," I said.

"Cuidado. And don't forget," he said.

At the gap, which the man got down to open, I saw him look at me. I decided to wait until we struck something before tightening the girth. Two minutes later my father yelled and we saw a little bunch of steers high-tailing it through scattered mesquites for a thicket along a creek beyond. I forgot all about the cinch. Buck was easily the fastest horse ridden by the four or five men in our "cow crowd." He left like a cry of joy to get around the steers.

As we headed them, they turned to the left at a sharp angle, and Buck turned at an angle considerably sharper. Sometimes he turned so quickly that the tapadero of my stirrup raked the ground on the inside of the turn. This time when he doubled back, running full speed, the loose saddle naturally turned on him. As my left hip hit the ground I saw stars. One foot was still in the stirrup and the saddle was under Buck's belly.

I suppose that I instinctively pulled on the reins, but I believe that Buck would have stopped had he not been bridled. His stop was instantaneous; he did not drag me on the ground at all. He had provocation to go on, too, for in coming over his side and back the spur on my right foot had raked him. He never needed spurs. I wore them on him just to be in fashion.

Sometimes in running through brush, Buck seemed to read my mind—or maybe I was reading his. He was better in the brush than I was. In brush work, man and horse must dodge, turn, go over bushes and pear and under limbs, absolutely in accord, rider yielding to the instinct and judgment of the horse as much as horse yields to his.

Buck did not have to be staked. If I left a drag rope on him, he would stay close to camp, at noon or through the night. He was no paragon. Many men have ridden and remembered hardier horses. He was not proud, but he carried himself in a trim manner. He did the best he could, willingly and generously, and he had a good heart. His chemistry mixed with mine. He was good company. I loved to hear him drink water, he was so hearty in swallowing, and then after he was full, to watch him lip the water's surface and drip big drops back into it.

Sometimes after we had watered and, passing on, come to good grass near shade, I'd unsaddle and turn him loose to graze.

Then I'd lie down on the saddle and, while the blanket dried, listen to his energetic cropping and watch the buzzards sail and the Gulf clouds float. Buck would blow out his breath once in a while, presumably to clear his nostrils but also, it seemed, to express contentment.

He never asked me to stop, unless to stale, and never, like some gentle saddle horses, interrupted his step to grab a mouthful of grass, but if I stopped with slackened rein to watch cattle, or maybe just to gaze over the flow of hills to the horizon, he'd reach down and begin cutting grass. He knew that was all right with me, though a person's seat on a grazing horse is not nearly so comfortable as on one with upright head. Occasionally I washed the sweat off his back and favored him in other ways, but nobody in our part of the country pampered cow horses with sugar or other delicacy.

All the rose-lipped maidens and all the light-foot lads with whom I ran in the riding days of boyhood and youth have receded until they have little meaning. They never had much in comparison with numerous people I have known since. Buck, however, always in association with the plot of earth over which I rode him, increases in meaning. To remember him is a joy and a tonic.

PART 6

Wild and Free

Naturalists of today, however steadily they may gaze on the wild life of America, can get only broken peeps at what was once a vast pageant. The testimony of early observers suggests habits and movements of the wild that civilization has curbed forever.—JFD

Cedar Fever

I have been here two weeks [outside of Alpine, Texas]. It took me a week to recover sufficiently from the hellish hay fever that Austin cedars give me at this time of year to have a head clear enough to work.—JFD, January 1939

For a month, while I had hay fever, I was merely a log—the worst curse on earth to a man who knows what it is to feel life.—JFD, March 1942

We have made arrangements to go to Port Isabel for a month or more. There I'll be out of the accursed cedar pollen.—JFD, December 1944

I am always in fine health, but would run across the world to get out of the cedars when they pollinate. I guess cedars prevent me from feeling any real affection for the land in this part of the state.—JFD, December 1946

DOBIE OFFERS TO CUT MALE CEDARS
J. Frank Dobie, nationally recognized writer and member of the English faculty at the University of Texas, who is at present exiled from this city by the male cedars whose pollen has caused him to suffer annually from hay fever, has said he "will be glad to cut down, free of charge, all the male cedars that the owners may desire cut."

– *Austin Statesman*, January 25, 1928

From Dobie's letter to the *Statesman*:

It is not true that I have left Austin permanently on account of hay fever engendered by cedar pollen. It is true, however, that if I continue for a year or two more to suffer from it as intensely as I have suffered from it this season, I shall leave. No sane and independent person can look forward with equanimity to living permanently in a place where for six weeks or two months out of each year he must endure the tortures of the damned and be so drained of vitality that for weeks afterward he feels like a cast-off dish rag.

Yet those weeks of torture and that aftermath of debility— to a certain extent, perhaps permanently—are suffered by hundreds of Austin citizens each year. Doctors of the city say that the numbers of sufferers are increasing. Certainly, though, some of the town boosters may, ostrich-like, stick their heads in the sand and refuse to see or hear, Austin is acquiring the kind of reputation over Texas for hay fever that New Orleans once bore over the US for yellow fever.

Yellow fever was found to be preventable. Hay fever is also preventable. When the city of Austin pays as much attention to the physical—and therefore moral and mental—welfare of its citizens as it does to mudholes in its streets, the intensity of hay fever within its limits will be appreciably diminished.

The air carries cedar pollen for miles, but the pollen is densest and most malevolent near the male cedars that grow the pollen.

If the city of Austin would compel the cutting down of all male cedars within its limits, the suffering of many citizens would be considerably alleviated and not so many new victims would be added each year.

Any wood chopper can tell a male cedar from a female. If a mistake is made and an occasional female cedar is cut down, the country will not lose much.

I intend to remain away from Austin until "the season" is over. As soon as I return I shall be glad to cut down all cedars in Austin that the owners may desire cut.

An ordinance compelling the destruction of male cedars would be as logical as the ordinance prohibiting pigsties within the corporate limits.

Of course, we must all have our jokes about hay fever. Mercutio jested well on his grave-wound. But only a fool or an ignoramus will treat with levity the maddening and constitution-destroying hay fever engendered by the virulent and accursed pollen of male cedars in and around Austin.

The Beginnings of
Big Bend National Park

In December 1930, State Representative R. M Wagstaff of Abilene came across Dobie's essay, "The Texan Part of Texas," in Nature magazine. "In his story," Wagstaff recalled, "Dobie expressed regret that none of the state's public lands had been set aside for park purposes." Wagstaff decided to try to save land in the Big Bend for a state park. He gained support of locals and negotiated land titles. In 1933 he introduced legislation to establish "Texas Canyons State Park." The bill was signed into law in October 1933. Ten years later, out of the lands Wagstaff and others working with him preserved, Big Bend National Park was created. Years later, Wagstaff credited Dobie's story in Nature for inspiring him to act. Here is the relevant portion of Dobie's article.—SD

T O DISCOVER THE CHARACTER that differentiates Texas from other sections a visitor must feel Texas northers, see bluebonnets in the spring and smell greasewood after a rain, gaze at stars that look as near and bright from a flat Texas prairie as if seen from the summit of Mount Whitney, and observe a thousand other natural phenomena.

When Texas entered the Union it reserved the right to control its own public lands; as a result it is the only state in the Union in which the federal government has not directed the distribution of the public domain.

The land—where has it gone?

Vast areas were patented to homesteaders. Other vast areas have been sold, mostly for grazing, to the highest bidders. Millions of acres were granted as subsidy to railroads; millions were issued in scrip. Another vast portion, much of it not reckoned as tillable, was set aside for the University of Texas and the common schools. The finding of oil on some of the grazing land owned by the University of Texas has made that institution wealthy.

And now the public domain, except for scattered sections, has all been distributed. Texans of cultivated minds are lamenting with increasing regret that none of the beautiful hill country, none of the deep forest land, none of the coastal marshes, none of the wild Big Bend country, none of the cool Davis Mountains, none of the deep and mighty canyons of the Plains—not one acre of the multiplied millions—was set aside for parks and public enjoyment.

The proverbially "wise forefathers" of Texas did not reserve even enough land to maintain a herd of the all but extinct Texas Longhorns . . .

The Longhorn's Dying Bellow

After the arrival of railroads and the end of the open range, ranchers turned to fat, docile cattle breeds. Longhorns began to disappear, and by the 1920s they were scarcer than buffalo. Dobie's extensive efforts to save the Longhorn made him "the single most important person involved in the Longhorn preservation movement."* It was this article, published in The Cattlemen, in 1926, that galvanized many ranchers to join him in the cause. —SD

W ILL C. BARNES, an old-time cowman of Arizona and New Mexico, now in the US Forest Service, has recently established a herd of Longhorn cattle in the Wichita National Forest of Oklahoma. His idea is to preserve the breed, just as the buffalo has been preserved, from extinction.

It is high time that some such step is made, though it is exceedingly doubtful if even a few cows and bulls as lanky and tough as the genuine Texas Longhorns of fifty years ago can be found. Twenty-five years ago such specimens were becoming scarce. However, some Mexican ranches of South Texas and across the Rio Grande still grew them.

If relics of the old breed yet exist, their whereabouts should be made known. The Longhorn belongs to no other region as it

---

*T. J. Barragy, *Gathering Texas Gold: J. Frank Dobie and the Men Who Saved the Longhorns*, 2002.

does to the old Texas ranges. He was peculiarly adapted to the time and the country. The Longhorns ran wild like the mustangs and held their own against any creature the wilds produced. His legs were long and his sinews were tough. Thousands of them had no owners, and hardly a drop of high-grade blood infiltrated into the countless herds. He needed no breeding up—he was better off without the fine blood. If water dried up or grass failed, he could walk to where there was grass and water. His constitution was such that he could go for days without any water at all, and in the pinch of necessity he could thrive on brush and prickly pear.

In the 1860s, trails opened up, stretching a thousand, two thousand miles from the breeding grounds of southern Texas. Among all cattle of the world only the Longhorn could have traveled those trails as they did—sometimes for days without water, sometimes on long forced drives to escape Indians, and at the end of months of such driving arriving at their destination in better flesh than when they set out.

He stands alone. He came from Texas and belongs to Texas— and now the national government is trying to preserve his kind. All honor to Will C. Barnes and his enterprise! May he fully succeed in it.

But it is an outrage on history that some stretch of the old Longhorn range between the Nueces and the Rio Grande in Texas is not set apart by the state as a refuge for a few lingering specimens of the great breed that once roamed there supreme. Let the border country on both sides of the Rio Grande be combed and if a nucleus can be found, let it be nourished on tunas and chaparral against extinction.

It will not be necessary to build a tourist road into that range. If a tourist feels compelled to get into it, let him put on leather leggins and a ducking jacket. When he gets there he will see nothing but brush and hear nothing but the cracking of brush. If he is wise though, when he hears that crack of limbs down in some thickety hollow, he may guess that down there an old dun cow has been hiding a calf with coarse brown hairs around its ears or that an old brindle bull has there left his mark on a stalk of prickly pear that sprouted in the last century.

The Longhorn, almost as much as the lone star, is the emblem of Texas. It is for the Texas cowmen to give the word, and the State of Texas will take steps to preserve this symbol of her contribution to the West's life and prosperity.

Stompedes

De longibus cornibus quod ille non cognivit, inutile est allis cognoscere.
(What he does not know about Longhorns is not worth knowing.)
—From an honorary degree presented to Dobie by Cambridge University.

S TOMPEDE WAS THE OLD TEXIAN WORD, and no other cattle known to history had such a disposition to stampede as the Longhorns. Their extraordinary wildness made them nervous, constantly expectant, habitually alert, and gave them keenness of senses to detect objects that even the most nature-sensitive of outdoors men were obtuse to.

Like the cattle and much else pertaining to ranching, the word came from the Spanish, estampida. Greek herdsmen called the same thing "panic terror." An old-timer's definition, not in the dictionary, was: "It's one jump to their feet and another jump to hell."

The worst stampedes were in the night, attended by the unknown inherent in destiny-weaving darkness. Range men dreaded them not so much because of danger as because of the likelihood of losing cattle, the time entailed in getting the stampeders back together, and the injury to the cattle themselves.

The most terrifying and the most common cause of stampedes was thunder and lightning. "It don't storm now like it used to," you'll hear old-timers say. People—ranch men included—don't live out in the weather as they used to. "I was gone nine months and seventeen days and had slept under shelter only once in the whole time," an old trail man concluded his narrative.

Maybe you, in your steam-heated apartment or your snug cottage, sometimes wonder what the wild-crying geese flying through the night might tell, if they could speak, of the elements. Ask the men who went up the trail in '67—if you can find one—and who, in the seventies and eighties, without tents, often without slickers, "circle-herded, trail-herded, night-herded and cross-herded too," following the Longhorns from where the Gulf breeze blows with salty freshness on and on up a slow trail that endlessly pointed to the North Star, and then who, when they got back home from the long drive, read sign and guarded a range stretching houseless and fenceless from moonrise beyond all sunsets. Ask them. They know as much of the elements as the honking geese or the wolf hounded out of his den.

Some of them can tell things of stampedes in electric storms that seem as foreign to this world of lights, warmth, and comfortable shelters as the craters in the moon.

It was a June night of the year 1884, on the Cimarron. The air was hot, stifling, absolutely still. It had been thus all day. Now the sky became overcast, and dull sheet lightning began to blink along the horizon to the west. Two men rode around twenty-five hundred big steers, as wild and sinewy as ever came out of the chaparral down by the Rio Grande. About two hundred yards away was camp, though the fire of cow chips had died and not a spark revealed the nine sleeping forms in their pallets near the chuck wagon. Near each sleeping man stood a horse—his night horse, the clearest-footed and surest-sighted of his mount—saddled and tied. Somewhere out in the darkness the horse wrangler kept drowsy guard over the remuda.

The cattle and the night were so quiet that the two herders stopped now and then on their rounds to listen. They could not help expecting something. The air grew warmer and more stifling as the lightning flashes approached and dim thunder began to rumble up. The men could still skylight the cattle.

Presently a dun steer that had been in the lead of the herd from the beginning and had been named "Old Buck" awoke, lifted his head slowly, rose to his knees, and looked around. Evidently he did not trust the looks of things, but, being long experienced in life, he wasn't startled, and he said nothing. He got on his feet, raising his nose to smell, and gazed toward the approaching storm. The two men on guard sang as gently as they could the songs they had sung over and over to soothe the cattle down and prevent any sudden sound from breaking in and frightening them.

But Old Buck had no idea of going back to bed. He seemed to be expecting something—something as sudden as a telegram can be. Another steer got up, stood still, expectant; then others and others arose until the whole herd was on its feet, motionless. The songs were louder now, unrelenting, pleading.

The night grew blacker, the lightning brighter, the humidity of the air more intense. And then, almost at once, on every tip of the five thousand horns of the waiting steers, appeared a ball of dull phosphorescent light—the fox fire, St. Elmo's fire, will-o'-the-wisp of the folklore of the world. In the intervals of utter blackness the two guards on the lone prairie could see nothing but those eerie balls illuminating the tips of mighty antlers.

The ghostly balls of fire on horns must have looked as strange to the steers as to the men. The steers began to move at a walk, their motion becoming circular, the riders around them preventing any decided movement away from the bed ground. At first the walk was slow; soon it became faster. And then out of blackness came a great flash of zigzag lightning forking down over the seething mass of animals, so close that darting tongues of flame seemed almost to lick their backs. At the same time a mighty clap, a roar, a crash of thunder shook heaven and earth, reverberating and doubling.

Its answer was the thunder of ten thousand pounding hoofs that popped and clicked, while horn clacked against horn. The stampede started with the swiftness of the lightning's leap.

The cowboys arrived from camp just in time to join the pursuit. The gigantic thunderbolt had knocked out the sluice gates of the sky. The water poured down in sheets and barrels. It rained blue snakes, pitchforks, and bob-tailed heifer yearlings all at once. One minute it was darker than the dead end of a crooked tunnel a mile deep under a mountain. Then the prairie was a sea of blue and yellow light dazzling to all eyes.

No matter. Hang with the cattle. Trust your horse. Follow those balls of fire tossing in the void of blackness, too dim to illumine even the horn tips they play upon, sometimes darting across to dance with each other, again fading out altogether. When the lightning won't light, run by ear. When the lightning blinds and the thunder drowns all other sound, keep on riding hell for leather. To get around them and circle the leaders, you must run wilder and madder than the horror-lashed cattle themselves.

It would probably have been better had the two night herders not been recruited. The object was to swing the leaders around into the tail end of the herd, thus turning it into a mill. A single man who knew how could do this better than a bedlam of riders. Then gradually the whole mass would be wound into a self-stopping ball, the momentum dying down like that of a spent top.

One of the two night herders with this stampede on the Cimarron was Robert T. Hill, who in later years became a mining and oil geologist renowned over the United States and Mexico.

"Before long," he says, "I found myself and another rider chasing a small bunch of cattle, close upon their heels. Never before nor since has thunder sounded to me so loud as on that run or have lightning crashes come so rapidly and so near.

"At a crash that was the climax my horse stopped dead in his tracks, almost throwing me over the saddle horn. The lightning showed that he was planted hardly a foot from the edge of a steep-cliffed chasm. A little off to one side, the horse of John Gifford, the other rider, was sinking on his knees, John himself slumping limp in his saddle. Just beyond him lay Old Buck, the mighty lead steer, killed by the bolt of lightning that had knocked John Gifford unconscious. The rest of our bunch of cattle were down under the cliff, some of them dead, some squirming."

When morning came, clear and calm, not a man was in sight of the cook, all of whose provisions had been drenched and who could not begin to start a fire with the soaking-wet cow chips. The twenty-five hundred steers that had been trailed and guarded a thousand miles from southern Texas toward the market at Dodge

City were scattered to the four winds. Before noon, though, men by ones and twos began driving in bunches from different directions. Hours later the last man was in. Meantime, the wrangler was supplying fresh mounts and the boss, going at a long lope, was leading all hands, except two or three on herd, to comb the country. The men could eat later on, and a trail hand was supposed to get his sleep in the winter.

❖ ◎ ❖

Many more deaths undoubtedly came to cowboys from lightning than from stampedes themselves. In fact, the memories of living men and authentic records alike are notably deficient in instances of cowboys' being trampled to death under stampedes. Dick Withers disposed of the matter thus:

"We had a stampede in the Territory. My horse fell, and I thought the steers would run over me. But I soon learned that stampeding cattle will not run over a man when he is down underfoot. They will run all around a fellow, but I have yet to hear of a man being run over by them."

Ab Blocker says the night can't get too black for cattle to split and go around a man in front of them. He "never heard of a cowboy's being run over in a stampede." On the other hand, not many men who knew cattle would have willingly got down in front of a stampede on a dark night to test out the splitting.

❖ ◎ ❖

It was a saying that if you could drive a herd for two weeks without a stampede, the danger was over. It certainly was diminished. The change from familiar to strange surroundings and from sleeping in free isolation to being bedded down with a horde of other animals guarded by the most fearsome enemy of cow liberty that the primitive cattle knew—man—was naturally conducive to nervousness and panic. On their home range, cattle are familiar with every bush, gully, and stone. Driven into a territory where nothing is familiar, they are apprehensive. After some days of trailing, however, change becomes routine.

It became a belief with various trail men—despite the contrary experiences of others—that after a herd crossed the Arkansas River it would not stampede again.

A stampede might start from anything—but not, as has often been said, "from nothing." Most of the unknown causes probably lay within the realm of smell, from which civilized man, generation by generation, becomes increasingly estranged. A breeze suddenly springing up after dark carried the odor of a strange man cooking for another outfit to a herd of steers that had been driven for three months by a crew without a bobble. They ran as if to make up for lost opportunities.

The whiff of an Indian started many a run. Beef-hungry Indians not infrequently tried to stampede herds, so as to get a chance at scattered animals. One of their favorite ruses was to burn a sack of buffalo hair on the windward side of a herd. A stampede that lasted all night was started by the "war whoop" of a bull that smelled the blood of a yearling just butchered for camp. A panther smelled some fresh beef hanging close to a chuck wagon. Trying to get to it, he was sensed by the cattle—and the powder house blew up.

Obvious trivialities started more stampedes than anything else except storms: A stray dog sneaking up and smelling around a sleeping animal on the edge of the herd, a bunch of wild hogs rooting into the bed grounds, the cough of a cow, a human sneeze, the snapping of a twig, the sinking of a circling horse's foot in a prairie dog hole.

It was suddenness of a sound or movement rather than its unfamiliarity that made the drags wake up and forget all about sore feet. A polecat would come sashaying along in its nonchalant way into the edge of a herd; some steer, awake and investigative, would begin following the hopping creature. Then, noticing the approaching monster, the little hair ball would stop, pat its forefeet against the ground, and go to jerking its tail with comical swiftness. Mr. Steer had never seen this performance before— and it was "so sudden." He would wheel and snort, having no intention of starting a stampede, but a moment later he was part of the panic terror he had caused. Like people, cattle are at their best when separated from the mob.

Here was a great herd, any antlered creature of which would have chased the biggest lobo of North America and, if able to catch him, would have gored him to death, yet the sharp smell of a coyote pup coming unexpectedly at a certain steer might startle him and the startlement be instantly translated into mob panic.

The fact that oftentimes the cause could not be sensed by men, could in no way be accounted for, and that the run seemed to be contrary to all known principles of cow psychology, gave to it something of dark mystery. It would be bright moonlight. A cowboy, halted in his rounds, perhaps smoking a pipe cigarette, would be looking at a great herd of steers bedding down comfortably and spaciously on the rich grass of a bald open prairie, every animal absolutely quiet, some with heads north, some south, some east, some west. They had been eased to the bed grounds, after a light day's travel, full of grass and water, contented. Then, in one instant, every animal would be plunging in mad flight, all in one direction.

Such a stampede was unusual; it was the exception. It was one of the profound mysteries of nature that made cowboys mystics and fatalists under their rough-and-ready exterior. Many of them held that cattle dreamed and saw ghosts. Some cowboys went strong on premonitions. This one "felt a quiver in his spine" when he went on guard and "just knew" the stampede was coming. That one "felt the air charged with tenseness." Another "grew cold with a chill" not out of the night air. An Arizona waddie, who had learned about spirits from an Apache medicine man, said: "When cattle has got these stompede devils in 'em, anybody can tell it. As soon as the sun goes down, their eyes begin to burn like bull's-eye lanterns. And when you ride in among 'em you can just feel that crazy, locoed spirit." Cowboys not superstitious about anything else were often superstitious about stampedes.

❖ ◎ ❖

The worst stampede I was ever in, in my limited experience, was with about a thousand head of steer yearlings on the Nueces River. We had spent the hours from before daylight until slap dark on a July day—fifteen hours at least—making fifteen miles through a country of lanes and thickets. We put the dogies to bed that night in the only place we could put them, though it was not at all to be chosen—a patch of open space with a fence on one side, the bluffs of the river on the other, and a ranch house not two hundred yards away on a third side. The country out and around was a thicket of thorns cut up with barbed wire and gullies. Camp was made close to the house. The night was dark and muggy.

About nine o'clock one of the ranch boys clicked an iron latch on the yard gate. I heard it—as plain as if a six-shooter had been clicked in my ear. The yearlings heard it too. They ran to gullies; some of them piled over the bluff; they kept running intermittently all night long. After we got them home and spread them out in the pastures, a hundred or two of them would for weeks get together every few nights and run to Jericho, tearing down fences and cutting themselves up. Just the click of a gate latch.

Wild and Free

No one who conceives him as only a potential servant to man can apprehend the mustang. The true conceiver must be a true lover of freedom—a person who yearns to extend freedom to all life. The aesthetic value of the mustang topped all other values so far as humans are concerned.

If I have idealized the horse, I have not overestimated its importance in social history. The more machinery man gets, the more machined he is. When the traveler got off a horse and into a machine, the tempo of his mind as well as of his locomotion was changed. All my nature is against machinery and for the horse.

As a determinant in social economy, the horse is utterly of the past. Yet even at this late date a saddle seems to me a more natural seat than a parlor chair.—JFD

T HE SIGHT OF WILD horses streaming across the prairies made even the most hardened of professional mustangers regret putting an end to their liberty. When the mustang stood trembling with fear before his captor, bruised from falls by the restrictive rope, made submissive by choking, clogs, cuts, and starvation, he had lost what made him so beautiful and free. One out of every three mustangs captured in southwest Texas was expected to die before they were tamed. The process of breaking often broke the spirits of the other two.

The mustang was essentially a prairie animal, like the antelope, and like it would not go into a wooded bottom or a canyon except for water and shelter. Under the pursuit of man he took to the brush and to the roughest mountains, adapting himself like the coyote, but his nature was for prairies—the place for free running, free playing, free tossing of head and mane, free vision. He relied on motion for the maintenance of liberty.

One early morning on the south plains of Texas, a surveying party saw a great troop of mustangs galloping toward them fully two miles away. Not a tree or a swag broke the grassed level, but from pure wantonness of vitality the oncoming line, following the leaders, deflected here and there into a sinuous curve. Coming nearer, the phalanx charged straight. A hundred and fifty yards away, it halted, with a front of about a hundred horses. Heads tossing high, nostrils dilated, the wild and free stood in arrested animation. The bright light of the rising sun brought out details of prominent eye, tapered nose, rounded breast, and slender legs on small feet. It glistened on sleek hairs of bay and sorrel, brown and grullo, roan, dun, and gray, with here and there black, white, and paint. Now with loud snorts, they wheeled and dashed away like a flight of sportive blackbirds, adding symmetry of speed to symmetry of form, contour of individual blending with contour of earth-skimming mass.

Only by blotting out the present can one now see those wild horses of the prairies. They have gone with the winds of vanished years. They carried away a life and a spirit that no pastoral prosperity could in coming times re-present.

Mustangs never migrated from north to south and back like the buffaloes. Nor did they migrate sporadically in the manner of squirrels, wolves, and some other quadrupeds. They did not drift before winter winds as Longhorn cattle on the open range sometimes drifted. Had they habitually kept together in vast droves, depletion of grass would have made constant change of grazing grounds necessary. Droughts and scarcity of grass from excess horse population caused irregular shifting. If rain fell on a restricted area, mustangs from far away would find the fresh grass. Perhaps the movement of bands near it communicated what they had sensed to other bands. With a continent over which to roam, every band of mustangs habitually kept to a range seldom more than twenty miles across.

While out of view, they often smelled travelers and their

horses and came pell-mell to investigate. If they could see but not smell strangers, they were not satisfied until they had circled into their odor. "Their playfulness rather than their fears seemed to be excited by our appearance," one early explorer wrote. "We often saw them more than a mile distant leaping and curvetting, involved by a cloud of dust, which they seemed to delight in raising." They were free to satisfy curiosity. Occasionally one horse—"the spy"—came alone from a band to inspect strangers and snort the signal for flight.

The snort was often startling, audible hundreds of yards away. In cowboy language, the mustang had "rollers in his nose." Mexican soldiers on the road from Laredo to San Antonio managed to rope a slow, pregnant mare out of a band of mustangs and brought her to the evening camp. "She made so much noise snorting" that nobody could sleep until she was released.

The keen sense of smell in feral horses was among their pronounced qualities. Careful mustangers avoided altering their odor by a change of clothes, especially of underwear, while following a band of wild horses and trying to get them used to their presence. A tamer who changed clothes while breaking a captured mustang would have to do everything over again. A Texas rancher whom I knew rode a primitive-natured horse that was gentle for him but for nobody else. One day after saddling the horse, he drew on a pair of new leggins before mounting. The horse would not allow him near until he had removed the foreign-smelling leather.

If Indians on a horse-raiding expedition killed and ate a horse, they washed themselves thoroughly in sand or in mud and water before approaching the enemy's camp. The horses were so sensitive to the smell of blood and fat of their own kind that they would not allow a man bearing it to come near them.

An old range man of the Texas Brush Country told me that he once had a Spanish horse that often gave notice of a rattlesnake smelled many yards away. Frontiersmen claimed that mustangs were alarmed by the smell of Indians. Indians took warning from mustang behavior in the vicinity of white men. Actually, horses used to the odor of either white man or Indian were alarmed by that of the other.

Many a pioneer Texan relied on his horses to give warning

against Indians. A few frontiersmen with the help of friendly Indians trained horses to fear Indian odor. One family on the Sabinal River was awakened repeatedly at night over a period of years by a horse that would run up on the porch and paw and neigh at the smell of Indians.

It was not solely to detect enemies and water, to trail dim scents and locate far-off oases of grass that the nostrils of the mustang worked. When spring opened and the south wind blew over new grass and nectared flowers, he inhaled the air with a gusto and exhaled it in elated whinneyings that plainly bespoke enjoyment of the earth's fragrance.

The mustang's eyes were as alert as his nostrils. The only way to approach a band that had been hunted was against the wind and under cover. Any rider who sighted a lookout mustang silhouetted on high ground two or three miles away knew that he had been seen. Indians claimed that if a man crept up a ridge to look through grass or bushes at wild horses in the valley below, a sentinel would detect his presence. Even antelopes took warning from mustang behavior.

One need not have observed mustangs to know that they were sociable; sociability is a characteristic of the species. In my mind's eye I see Snip and Snap, a pair of bays, standing side by side, head to tail, each switching flies and gnats from his own rump and his comrade's face. I see Canelo, a meek red roan, freshly unsaddled, approach the remuda, whence his devoted friend, a broad-hipped dun as yellow as ripe corn, steps forth nickering low to greet him. Then after they have affectionately rubbed noses and said something no man will ever know, I see the two grazing in a harmonious contentment that memory makes a benediction. I see a narrow-chested, nervous little bay Spanish pony named Cardinal, after being released into the horse pasture, shortening his drink to trail down his fellows. He trots with nose to ground, smelling tracks, smelling dung. He nickers now and then, but there is no response. Nor does any horse notice him when he approaches the bunch, but fulfillment of his desire to be with his kind sets him at ease.

A solitary mustang seemed always to be seeking company.

Now and then one took up with buffaloes. The chronicler of Long's expedition made this entry in August, 1820: "A few wild horses had been observed in the course of the day, and towards evening one was seen following the party, but keeping at a distance. At night, after our horses had been staked near the camp, we perceived him still lingering about, and at length approaching the tent so close that we had hopes of capturing him alive. We stationed a man with a noose rope in the top of a cottonwood tree, under which we tied a few of our horses, but this plan did not succeed.

"On the following morning, one of our hunters discovered the horse standing asleep under the shade of a tree, shot him, and hastened to camp with the intelligence. We had all suffered so severely from hunger, that we ate greedily of this unaccustomed food. Yet we felt a little regret at killing a beautiful animal who had followed us and then lingered with a sort of confidence about our camp."

A man-driven caballada was sometimes joined by a lone stallion. One morning in 1884 a bright chestnut stallion with head thrown up and "long mane and tail floating out in the air like liquid gold" dashed into a herd of 500 Spanish mares and colts and a few stallions trailing north from southern Texas across the Indian Territory. He whipped four stallions and virtually took control of the herd before cowboys roped, threw, deprided, and then cast him out.

The habit an occasional ranch horse has of re-depositing his dung at a certain spot is a relic of earlier times. To riders across the plains in early days, mounds of freshly topped manure were the main mustang sign. Washington Irving was too elegant to mention the crudity in his account of mustangs, but Henry Leavitt Ellsworth, who accompanied him, noted "pyramids of manure often 2 or 3 feet high." Zebulon Pike, ahead of Irving, saw "ground covered with horse dung for miles around." Campers on New Mexico plains west of the buffalo range burned wild horse dung instead of the usual "prairie coal." Stallions were the main accumulators. A stallion's addition to his private "pyramid" was a notice to other stallions that he had been there. He looked and smelled for notices left by other stallions.

Only the sense of being part of a place gives natural horse or natural man contentment. A range mare drops her colt year after year in the same place. Old-timers of South Texas who had driven horses far north and east used to tell of mares that in the spring came back to their stomping grounds to foal. One fall a rancher named Adams near San Antonio sold a little fifteen-year-old red roan mare to a vaquero to ride to his home in San Luis Potosí, Mexico, 600 miles southward, not a fence or a bridge between. The next April the mare came pacing up to the gate in front of the Adams ranch house and asked to be let in. The other horses, some her own offspring, greeted her with demonstrations of affection. A week later she brought her colt. According to a letter received from the vaquero, the mare had been about three months making the trip home.

The power of Spanish horses, both mustang and tamed, to go without water has been exaggerated. Their thirst-resisting power was, nevertheless, remarkable. One dry June my friend Rocky Reagan of the Brush Country took all the stock, except seven or eight ladino horses that could not be caught or shot, out of a 4,000-acre pasture in which the dirt tanks, the only source of water, had gone dry. After September rains, he rode into the pasture and found horse tracks; he saw where the left-behind horses had pawed down the trunks of prickly pear and chewed the fiber for water. Two or three of the horses had perished, but the others were in good condition. During droughts on the open range, some mustangs not only chewed prickly pear but broke through the defenses of the Spanish dagger to eat the flowering stalk. Many cattle of Spanish blood have survived droughts on water from cactus, but the mouths of horses are generally too tender to overcome the spines.

Over the greater part of North America, the only formidable natural enemies met by the Spanish horses, aside from flies, mosquitoes, and screwworms, were the panther and the lobo. All horses are afraid of bears, but grizzlies in California, where they were most numerous, killed few horses. Living on the prairies, the wild horses were comparatively free of insect pests.

Wolves in packs followed the buffalo herds, cutting off and

bringing down stragglers. They sometimes attacked mustangs also, but horse flesh was never their main diet. After cattle took the place of buffaloes, they continued to prey more on cattle than on horses. The defense of a solitary horse against them was limited. A band upon being threatened formed a circle, heads out, colts in the center. Running away meant exposure of the hindmost to the enemy. They did not run. Safety lay not only in numbers but in standing. A mustang in a threatened bunch would grab an over-bold wolf with his teeth and beat him to death with his front feet. Sometimes the mustang chased the wolf, seized it by the back, tossed it into the air, and then stamped it to death.

The panther lives now mostly in broken country, but he was once common in brush and timber contiguous to mustang-inhabited prairies. His natural prey is deer, but once he has eaten horse meat, especially colt, he rates it above any other flesh. In 1926, I was on the Rio Grande with a rancher who that year raised only three or four colts from 400 Spanish mares pasturing on mesa range in Mexico. The others had been devoured by panthers.

This rancher, Asa Jones, has seen many a mare with a clawed face, indicating that she had tried to protect her colt and been slapped back. One of his stallions came in with nose bitten off. Few men have seen the attacks, which are mostly at night, but claw marks indicate that the panther either leaps directly for the head or springs on the back of its victim and, digging hind claws in for a purchase, bites into neck and throat. Some mustang stallions were no doubt aggressive toward panthers.

Years ago now, John E. Hearn, a trapper in the brush on the Texas border, rode an old dun horse—a coyote dun, with line down his back—that had been brought across the Rio Grande and left by tequila smugglers. One day while trailing a panther dragging a steel trap, Hearn cornered the animal in a large clump of prickly pear, shot it dead from the saddle, and then got down and pulled the carcass out onto open ground with the intention of loading it on Old Dun to take in for skinning. Dun was thoroughly gentle, but when led up, he let out a squeal louder than a panther scream and the next instant was pawing, kicking, and biting the carcass. Hearn blindfolded him, but he would not allow himself to be loaded with a panther. Hearn rode to a ranch for help. When he returned to the carcass, Old Dun tried to seize it in his mouth like a bulldog.

Victor Lieb, of Houston, told me that while he was mining in the Sierra Madre of Chihuahua before the Madero revolution of 1910, he became the friend of a little ranchero who owned a stallion named Chinaco. He was a blood red—the color of the uniform worn by Don Porfirio's rurales (mounted police), known as chinacos. Black points and short coupling bespoke his Arab-Barb origin. His neck and face bore scars from clawings by a panther that had leaped on him while he was a colt.

Chinaco had other encounters with the león—mostly, after he was grown, of his own seeking. His owner said that if a man were riding him when he smelled a fresh track, the only thing to do was to dismount, remove saddle and bridle, and turn him loose. He was too powerful to manage in a frenzy of hate.

He had all the bottom that generations of toughness could transmit, and he was also a family pet, very gentle with children. His owner would not sell him.

But the ranchero owed a note to Don Luis Terrazas, whose haciendas covered millions of acres and who dominated thousands of peons. Now it was either pay the note or enter into a peonage extendable even unto the third and fourth generations.

Victor Lieb paid the note for the man. The next day Chinaco was led to Lieb's camp. He would not accept the horse to keep— only for riding while he remained in the region.

One early morning he rode out after venison. He was on a short stretch of softish mountain trail when Chinaco began to sniff and grow excited. Examining the ground, Victor Lieb saw a fresh panther track. Chinaco was already straining. Lieb removed saddle and bridle, turned him loose, and followed afoot. He could not see how the fight started, but when he got around the mountain he saw Chinaco rushing with extended head upon the dead panther's body, grabbing it by the neck shaking it, flinging it to the ground and striking it with both forefeet at once. After he was satisfied with his conquest, Chinaco showed great pride. He had received no wound. Without even a hackamore, he bore Victor Lieb bareback to where saddle and bridle had been left.

Even in rough, panther-infested country where the mustang made his last stand, it was man—not panther—that proved to be the mustang's fatal enemy.

The Paisano, Our
Fellow Countryman

Born and reared in Southwest Texas, I was grown before I knew that the roadrunner had any other name than paisano—which name I intend to keep on using, because it expresses a quality that is to me fundamental. The bird and I are fellow natives of the country.—JFD

THE COMMON NAME for the Spanish-speaking areas of northern Mexico and the American Southwest is paisano, which means countryman, also fellow countryman. One of the early English-speaking chroniclers of the border heard the bird called corre camino, literally, (he) runs the road; hence, roadrunner.

Perhaps no other native bird of North America, excepting the eagle and the turkey, which the Aztecs had domesticated, has been so closely associated with the native races of this continent. It appears in the mythology, songs, and legends of many Indian tribes—and it has gained fame in our time as a killer of rattlesnakes.

Paisano is sometimes said to be a corruption of faisan—pheasant—which some early Spaniards considered the bird. Yet the paisano belongs to the cuckoo, not the pheasant, family. Descriptions always emphasize the paisano's running ability, the long tail that serves as a brake, the plumage on his lustrous-feathered head, comical antics, and insectivorous appetite. A good deal of the time, he seems to say *crut, crut, crut*, rolling and trilling and twirling the *r* sound with such mastery that people swear Spanish has become his native tongue.

The bird has a great deal of curiosity and is easily domesticated if taken young. One will hop into the open door of a house and stand there a long time, looking this way and that. Perhaps he has an idea that some shade-loving creature suited to his diet is in the house. He will come up to a camp to investigate in the same way.

Sometimes he falls in behind a traveler and follows them. I never tire of watching one of these birds dart down a trail or road, suddenly throw on the brakes by hoisting his tail, stand for a minute dead still except for panting and cocking his head to one side and then to the other, and then suddenly streak out again.

He enjoys a dust bath. He can stand terrific heat, but on hot days he likes to pause in the shade, even though it be nothing but the shadow of a three-inch mesquite fence post.

Though essentially a ground bird, he can volplane for long distances down a hill or a mountain. Frequently one will fly up into a tree to get a wide view. His speed, like nearly everything else connected with him, has been greatly exaggerated. Any good horse can outrun one on a considerable stretch. Yet running down a path ahead of a buggy or a horseman, the roadrunner often seems to enjoy the exercise as much as a pup enjoys chasing a chicken or a calf. While speeding, he stretches out almost flat.

The very track of the roadrunner has among some of the Pueblo Indians of New Mexico given the bird significance and protection. This track shows two toes pointed forward and two backward, and Indians duplicate it on the ground all about the tent of one of their dead so as to mislead evil spirits seeking the course taken by the departed soul. Again, an Indian mother will tie the bright feathers of a roadrunner on the cradleboard so as to confuse evil spirits that would trouble her child's mind. Here the feathers signify the track, which not only points two ways but is four directioned like the Cross.

Certain of the Plains Indians hung the whole skin of the roadrunner—to them the medicine bird—over a lodge door to keep out henchmen of the Bad God. Before setting out on an expedition, a warrior would attach one or more paisano feathers to his person. At least one tribe of California Indians used the feathers for adorning their headdress—probably with symbolic intent also.

The rattlesnake-killing power of the paisano long ago entered into folklore. This is established beyond all doubt, although scientists have been slow to admit the fact.

For many years I have hoped to come upon a paisano-rattlesnake combat—but the witnessing of such a phenomenon depends so much on chance that only a few individuals among many who spend their lives out of doors happen upon the scene at the right time. I have questioned scores of hombres del campo—men of range and countryside—about paisano-rattlesnake fights, and I have the testimony of several whose word cannot be doubted.

Sometimes the paisano is described as giving a "war dance" about the rattler to confuse and infuriate him. Wild turkeys are said to make attacks, occasionally, on rattlesnakes in much the same manner.

One informant, Bob Dowe, of Eagle Pass, a strong-bodied and strong-minded man who had a great deal of experience on ranches on both sides of the Rio Grande, told me that he once saw a paisano kill a rattlesnake about three and a half feet long. The fight was in a cow pen. With wings extended and dragging in the dust, the bird would run at the snake, aiming at its head. The snake struck blindly, several times hitting the paisano's wings, without effect, of course. Finally, the bird pecked a hole in the snake's head and punctured the brain. It ate the brain but nothing else.

One of the most familiar facts regarding the paisano among the public is the story about the bird's corralling a rattlesnake with cactus joints. I am not prepared to deny that paisanos ever do this. The bird is certainly more interesting for this commonly believed story—as related in several books and also told to me by several informants. The act would be no more of a strain on nature than the building of a web by a spider to entrap a fly. Snakes, rattlesnakes included, eat rats. All kinds of rats in all parts of the Southwest build about their nests a defense of thorns against snakes and other enemies. The paisano is a very clever animal and likely understands that rattlesnakes can't go like a shadow through an armor of thorns.

In Mexico City, I heard an account of this behavior from E. V. Anaya, a practitioner of international law. He was reared on a hacienda in Sonora, where he was associated with Ópata Indians. He told me about seeing a paisano—called a churella in that part of the country—kill a rattlesnake by building a corral of cholla cactus.

"I was out gathering pitayas," he said. The pitaya, or pitahaya, is a cactus fruit. "It was in the month of May—the month of pitayas. I was just a boy, about 1908. I was with an Ópata Indian.

"Just as we got to the top of a mesa, the Indian very cautiously beckoned me to come nearer. Then when I was close to him, he whispered, "See the churella.""

"Churella," I replied. "What of it?" The bird is so common in that country that little attention is usually paid to it.

"This one is killing a rattlesnake," the Indian spoke softly. "Let us watch."

"We crept up silently, until we were within twelve or fifteen yards of the churella. A rattlesnake lay coiled on the ground, out in a little open space, apparently asleep. The churella had already gathered a great many joints of the cholla cactus and had outlined a corral around the snake."

While Anaya spoke, I judged that if a roadrunner were going to use any kind of cactus to corral or torment a rattlesnake with, cholla joints would surely be best suited to that purpose. Each joint is so spined that if one single thorn takes hold of an object and the object moves the least bit, another and then several other thorns will dig in. Instead of throwing off the cholla joint, movement causes the one thorn in the flesh to act as a lever for giving more thorns entrance. The Papago Indians used to dispose of their dead by laying the body on open ground and then heaping cholla over it—a thorough protection against all beasts of prey.

Anaya continued, recalling the scene he had witnessed. "The churella was working swiftly. Cholla was growing all around us and the joints were lying everywhere on the ground. The bird would carry a joint in its long beak without getting pricked. He built the little corral up, laying one joint on top of another, until it was maybe four inches high. Then he dropped a joint right on top of the sleeping snake. The snake moved, and when he did, the spines found the opening under his scales. The snake became frantic and went to slashing against the corral. That made it more frantic. Then the churella attacked it on the head and had little trouble in killing it. The spines made it practically defenseless."

❖ ◉ ❖

Generally, in northern Mexico and among Mexicanos of the Southwest the bird means good luck. In times before the country was settled, they say, a lost person who followed a paisano came to a trail or road and followed it to human habitation. But local interpretations can vary.

A few years ago, I was riding a mule across the Sierra Madre in southern Mexico, near Oaxaca, twisting through Indian country. The cavalcade consisted of two gringos besides myself, two mozos (servants), and our pack mules loaded with bedding, grub, and personal belongings. One morning about ten o'clock we came to a spring at the foot of a mountain. While we and our beasts were drinking, three Indians walked up.

They did not speak Spanish and I knew not a word of their language, but somehow we got along sympathetically with each other. I guess we felt that we were paisanos. While I was consorting with them, the pack outfit went on and was immediately out of sight. After I had, with permission, taken a picture of them, I asked which of the three was the cacique (chief). The two end men pointed at the center man. I gave him a package of Mexican cigarettes. He opened it, took a cigarette himself and gave one to each of his companions. After we had all smoked together in silence for a while, I mounted my mule and headed up the trail.

The cacique followed at my heels, and I imagine he could have walked and trotted as far in a day in that high, rough country as any horse or mule. I judged that he was following to see that I reached my companions in safety. After we had climbed and twisted for maybe fifteen minutes, I saw a paisano come down the mountain from the right and cross the trail in front of me. The Indian picked up two or three rocks and chunked at the bird with intense earnestness, missing him, however.

I was surprised, and asked why he wanted to kill a bird that brought good luck. He said something in reply that I could not understand. Before long, I caught up with the outfit and the Indian disappeared.

Later, a scholar in Oaxaca, knowledgeable of the folklore of the region, explained to me why the Indian had thrown the rocks. "He was trying to avert bad luck for you. The Indians believe that if the paisano crosses the path of a human being from right to left, he will bring bad fortune, but if he crosses from left to right he brings good fortune. There are two ways to avert the bad fortune. One is to kill the bringer of it; the other is to make him cross back from left to right."

Yet in many places in Mexico the bird is regarded as benevolent without respect to the direction in which it may be traveling. "Look, patrón," I have had a mozo say to me in the morning, "look at that paisano over there. We'll have good traveling today."

A paisano that stays about the house is often cherished by Mexicans as much as the swallow building its nest under the shed roof—the swallow that always betokens good fortune. Among Mexicanos on the Texas border the paisano takes the place of the stork in bringing babies into the world.

❖ ◎ ❖

The only vicious folklore I know about the paisano is the ignorant idea that he is a primary enemy of quail.

Now that the urban hunter is envious of every quail, the paisano has been charged with eating quail eggs and killing and eating young quail—and the paisano is even being exterminated in many places on the assumption that this charge is true.

Studies by scientists and ornithologists have proven that the bulk of the paisano's diet is insects—mainly grasshoppers. The value of the roadrunner to the farmer as an insect destroyer is so obvious that it need not be dwelt upon.

Paisano also consume rats, mice, lizards, spiders, centipedes, scorpions—along with the occasional bit of snake. A University of California study found no quail in examining eighty-four road-runners' stomachs, but two small birds were found as well as a tiny cottontail rabbit. The small amount of vegetable matter consumed by the roadrunners appeared to consist of sour berries.

An occasional paisano surely does eat an occasional egg or an occasional little quail. What of it? If the matter is to be put on a purely utilitarian basis, there is no doubt that paisanos in the aggregate destroy more rats and snakes that would, if left alive, destroy more quail eggs and young in any given area than all the paisanos in that area destroy directly.

Nature balances itself far better than man can ever balance it. The most quail I have ever seen in my life were where I also saw the most paisanos.

And what if the paisano is now and then directly responsible for one less quail to shoot at? People who kill roadrunners are killing not only a creature useful to man and actually, in the long run, friendly to quail production, but destroying a form of life that makes the landscape more interesting. He is a poor sportsman whose only interest in wildlife is something to kill. How much more interesting and delightful is a country where a variety of wildlife abounds! If it were necessary to choose between ten quail and no paisanos, or nine quail and one paisano, not many people who have any capacity for being delighted by nature would hesitate to choose the latter.

People like the paisano. The bird brings good luck and cheerful thoughts, whether you believe in signs or not.

When one man in this bird's wide range meets another that he feels warm sympathy for, he may say, "We speak the same language." But, if there is great gusto in the correspondence of spirits, he will say, "Nosotros somos paisanos—we are fellow countrymen—we belong to the same soil." And we true paisanos of mankind include in our kinship the paisanos of birdkind.

It is good fortune to encounter any form of life that makes the spirit rise. That is what the paisano does.

PART 7

Europe Amid Two World Wars

I was destined, in a way, to learn something of the foreign. There was in me a vacancy that, for my work, must be filled with life abroad.—JFD

... From Two Letters to Bertha Dobie during World War I

Dobie volunteered for the army as soon as the United States entered the First World War. Commissioned as a lieutenant in the field artillery, he was kept stateside as a camp instructor during most of the war, much to his annoyance.

As was the habit throughout their lives, Dobie and his wife, Bertha, corresponded frequently when they were apart from each other, sometimes on a daily basis. Among the Dobie treasures Bill and Sally Wittliff preserved and donated to establish the Wittliff Collections at Texas State University are several letters written by Dobie to Bertha during the First World War. What follows are excerpts from two of them.—SD

Camp, Tuesday night [February 5, 1918]
My precious Burbie Wife:
How are you I wonder indeed. It has been a very busy day for me, and the high dusty wind has put in me a spirit cherished by the devil himself—but that feeling never extends itself to you. This evening an order came out that I feel especially malicious towards. All of us must henceforth take all the examinations that we can take; that is, all that come when we are not employed otherwise. I shall have to take one the day after tomorrow. If I were left to myself I could learn about ten times as much as I learn messing with other peoples' methods. Be that as it may, I must get to work. If I could though, I should like to get to sleep.

I send you three goodnight kisses. Distribute them properly. I love you with infinite solicitude and long to hear *how* you are.

FRANK

Note: At the time of the following letter, the women's suffrage movement had endured recent setbacks and Bertha was frustrated at the chauvinistic rhetoric coming from those who opposed granting women the vote. Dobie's letter expresses his own views on the matter. Throughout his life he remained a steadfast supporter of women's rights.—SD

Camp, Wednesday night [February 6, 1918]
My dear:

If anything were needed to prove that a woman has a soul, that she is *not* nothing, that she is plentifully endowed with esprit and spirit too, the manner in which you espouse a principle and despise grossness in the letter received this afternoon, would prove it. But no such proof were necessary.

I am sorry that you found that book. It disturbed you more than it was worth. The spirit has indeed been fretted by evil-doers.

One consolation there is: women after this war will have a far larger part in affairs. She has the voice now, though not the vote. She is depended on so tremendously that with a little more organization and can—and will—wrest from relenting—and not altogether grateless—man—her rights. I guess you know that my ideas coincide with yours, *entirely*, without reservation, in these matters.

Goodnight and I pray that all's well with you.

YOUR FRANK

A Day with the Basques

The army finally shipped Dobie to France in October 1918. Two weeks later the Armistice was signed. He wrote to Bertha, "God knows, Burbie, I want to go home to you, but it is bitter to have trained so much and to have come so far . . . and then to be failed of one single battery volley into the Hun ranks. . . . I think I should be ashamed when I get back, never having endured one hardship or fought one fight."

Dobie remained in France during the postwar occupation. He visited the Louvre, took in plays in Paris, and enrolled for courses in the Sorbonne. He soaked up the experiences and wrote to Bertha, "When I feel myself so happy here, so congenial, and then I think of the ashen and fruitless days I spent at American colleges and universities, I could cry."—SD

I T WAS THE SPRING of 1919. I had *permission*, and I meant to see the Basques. Ever since Pierre Loti's *Ramuntcho* acquainted me with the Basque smugglers I had wanted to be among those folk. I took the train from Paris to Biarritz. What Montmartre is to the real Paris, Biarritz is to the real Basque country. In normal times it is for professional resortists, principally English; in armistice times it was a designated leave area, infested by thousands of American soldiers and patrolled by scores of M.P.'s.

I liked the sea breaking in over the rocks at night, and I liked the urbane young French gentleman who pointed out to me the house up the coast where a Parisian journalist had once kept a real Turkish harem, and another house made notorious by the traitor Bolo Pasha. Yet Biarritz was not the Basque land I was seeking.

By noon of the next day I was at Hendaye on the border. Here were fewer M.P.'s and no Americans on leave. I found Pierre Loti's house. For a long while I watched the dun-colored oxen, as shaggy as their shaggy headdresses, pulling up the riverbank great-axled carts loaded with oranges and wine from Spain. Their drivers, dressed in slouch caps and faded sashes and armed with long poles, shouted and prodded. Half a millennium past, when all the lower Basque country was a part of the Kingdom of Navarre and Queen Margaret was writing into the *Heptaméron* her witty stories of carnality and cruelty, dun-colored oxen, prodded by be-sashed men, were lumbering in the same way into Hendaye with the golden fruitage of Spain. But even Hendaye has something of the cosmopolitan, something of the blasé air characteristic of a port of entry. I was not where I wanted to be.

Of course, in the uniform of a belligerent nation, I could have no passport into neutral Spain, though plenty of American AWOLs were in Madrid. I did not wish to go to Madrid, but did wish to get among the mountain Basques on the Spanish side. The American M.P. advised me not to go beyond the middle of the bridge; the Spanish guard ordered me not to touch Spanish soil.

"Do you think I could get into Spain above Saint-Jean-Pied-de-Port?" I asked of the M.P. major, who was down from Biarritz.

"Never," he snapped back.

"Are there any Americans there?"

"None at all."

That evening I was riding up the valley of the Nive River on the little branch railroad that terminates at Saint-Jean-Pied-de-Port.

"*Taisez-vous*; méfiez-vous; *les oreilles de les ennemis vous écoutent*," read the long familiar sign of warning, once stuck on every place in France where the eye of talking man might rest. The war was over, but the sign was still pasted in my compartment, and as I saw the sun setting on the mountain hills, all the significance of that warning of distrust seemed to me as far away as a playtime battle of boyhood.

Darkness came just as we were entering the mountains. The loquacity of the French family sharing my compartment suffered a twilight change. The light overhead burned dimly, and I began to hear the sound of dashing waters. I tried to peer out, but the night was too dark, and so I but listened to the water running alongside our not noisy train.

A while before midnight we came to Saint-Jean-Pied-de-Port. There was but one *voiture* at the station, and it was engaged. I knew not what hotel I should go to or which way the town lay. But I struck out in the direction taken by several other pedestrians and soon came up with a fellow singing a song, rather unsteadily, it is true, but with immense gusto. Yes, he would conduct me to the Hotel Central, and there *Monsieur l'Américain* should find lodging most excellent. Our street turned in all directions of the compass, but presently we were at the Hotel Central and the host was being roused with hearty knockings. But my guide was reluctant to take any pourboire: he had not put himself out any, as he was coming my way anyhow; it was a pleasure for him to conduct *l'Officier Américain*, and besides he was happy as he was. Nevertheless, since I insisted, he would take the coin in order to drink to my health, and so goodnight, and "may Monsieur find pleasant the land of the Basques."

When the window of my room was opened, I could still hear the rush of waters. The sound was as of a mill race beneath me. It so filled me with eagerness for the light of day that I could hardly go to sleep. What on earth is quite like coming into a place of beauty and adventure in the night time and expecting the revelations of the morning! The buoyancy of suspense, to wait for the dawn to uncurtain a strange land, is like having suddenly inherited a fortune but not yet knowing what the fortune is to be; is like having read *Romeo and Juliet* and then while you are young and in love waiting at the theater for the curtain to rise on Julia Marlowe in the balcony scene.

When the dawn did come, I looked out of my window. The world was too good to rush into. I would dally awhile with the anticipation, eat my breakfast like a gentleman of leisure, and then saunter forth full provided. My host was a thick heavy man only recently de-mobilized, who would like to know if I could tell when the peace would be signed, and who gave me full directions for reaching the border.

It was Palm Sunday, and across the Place du Marché, on which the hotel opened, I saw the people bearing their branches of green to the ancient church. On three sides of the village glistened the snowy peaks of the Pyrenees; on the fourth, battlemented, somber, and reposeful with age, loomed the citadel, once the grim protector of the capital of Navarre, for such St. Jean was; then the fortress whence marched the troops of Wellington into the Peninsula; now a military prison, subdued by the centuries into a kind of harmony with the shining mountains and peaceful valley.

When I had climbed the heights to inspect it, the only beings I saw were a woman and her child. She was looking for wood, she said, and it was "*tres difficile*" to find and "*tres cher*" to buy. "We are nearly all Basque here," she assured me, and she taught me the Basque expression for "good day." Though I remember having used the greeting on more than one occasion later, I have now entirely forgotten it.

For such a lapse of memory it seems there is distinguished precedent; indeed, the difficulty of the dialect is the subject matter of folklore and story. According to a legend of the country, the Devil, astonished that so few Basques were coming his way, determined to ascend and learn the language so that he better beguile them; he finally learned to say "good day" but by the time he had learned "good bye" he had forgotten the first phrase; then, in final desperation, he went back to hell, resolved to leave the Basques alone.

George Borrow must have suspected the Devil of breaking resolution; at any rate, he translated into Basque the Gospel of St. Luke. Evidently he got along with language better than the Devil.

I doubt if anywhere in Europe the ordinary dwelling houses are older than those of the Basque country; certainly none are confessedly older. Here many are dated, and on the front of the house you will see an inscription such as this:

"Bati par Arrochkoa Gorastequy et Gracieuse Bidegaina, 1675."

In front of one of these ancient houses, I found an old man and a boy playing what they told me was the game of *Le Berger et les Moutons*—Shepherd and Sheep. It was played with small stones on a rock with a network of intersecting lines cut into it, the object of the game being to get a certain number of sheep herded into position. There on this rock, generation after generation of boys and men had played this selfsame game of *Le Berger et les Moutons*. The edges of it were all rounded and smooth from the feel of those generations of fingers. The old man offered to teach me the game, but I went with the boy to see a dungeon, the concierge of which was a shrill old woman who stuttered out a story of Inquisition tortures there and showed in the stone floor a dim path that some long-lived prisoner had circled at the end of his chain.

Arneguy on the Spanish border was eight kilometers away, and up the Nive valley I struck out for it, afoot. All along the way I met peasants, some walking, some on bicycles, some on burros, all genial in their salutations. Many of them bore evergreens, and once two boys stopped and gave me sprigs from their branches. Sometimes the road led down close to the river bed; sometimes it was a hundred feet above. The valley is narrow, at places little more than a deep canyon, and the hillsides are tessellated off with rock fences into a crazy patchwork of mosaic. Now and then I could hear the tinkle of bells and could see the little flocks of sheep grazing.

The sun was out; beneath it the smoothly graded road was white; and ever beyond gleamed in their whiteness the snowy heads of the Spanish Pyrenees. I came to a spring and drank. I climbed high above the road and gathered curious snail shells and the first wildflowers of the season. I thought of how Stevenson had traveled with his donkey, and I dreamed of hiring one—another Modestine—for myself and tramping on and on through this fine world. To ride would have been confinement. I wanted to walk forever, to run. And before I knew it, I came to Arneguy, a mere handful of houses, where the upper Nive marks the Spanish border.

Here, past the friendly old Territorials who were guarding the French side, past the easygoing Spanish guards, who halted at my halting French but mellowed at my Mexican Spanish, I crossed into Spain. Presently I came upon a woodcutter, a Spanish Basque, who had spent all his years cutting wood alongside the road, and who could remember most of the people who passed his way in the last decade or two. Only one American, an engineering officer, he said, had in years, and never before had he met an American who could talk his language. He boasted of how much money he was making off the French with his wood cutting, and after a little gossip of this kind, I returned to the border, according to my promise to be back at the pass by noon.

I might have spared my pains for all the guard cared about how long I stayed across. When I applied to him for information that would lead me to a dinner, he pointed to one of the half-dozen houses on his side of the river and said: "*Señor*, there you will find excellent food, not elegant, but clean, very clean."

And so it was I remained in Spain. I was conducted into a long, low room with a long table in it at which two men were playing cards. They greeted me, and I soon learned that they were French Basques from Saint-Jean-Pied-de-Port come over to eat. One of them had a slow, ponderous voice and a hand that could have spanned the side of a burro. Before long more men filed in—there were about ten of us in all—and the table was set. I found myself seated between the big Basque, who took a kind of benevolent possession of me, and a sharp but genial-tongued Spaniard. When the latter found that I could talk his language a little, he loved me "like a very brither." His name was Juan.

One, two, three hours we ate, course after course, one a kind of sweet hominy bean, the name of which I wish I could remember. There was no lack of drinkables either, and here for the first time I learned what an ambrosial mixture is cognac and hot coffee. There were toasts in four tongues, French, Spanish, English, and Basque, and the climax was my repeating, syllable by syllable after Juan, three jaw-wrenching Basque words.

Before this, when I had toasted in French—no matter how bad—I provoked the jealousy of the Spanish side; when in Spanish, that of the French side; and when in English, which they with a kind of childlike glee would have me speak, I set myself apart. I was a kind of strange and unimpeachable arbiter come to these folk of a frontier isolation, and they treated me as if I were a princely guest. A merry table we were, and I can see now across from me a certain face nodding and shaking at every word spoken, the exact replica of the famous picture of "The Laughing Philosopher."

Heretofore, out of deference to my ignorance, my friends had refrained from speaking Basque to any extent. But now that the stranger had uttered a Basque word—though as a parrot—and that everybody had one of my USA Quartermaster cigarettes (which two or three who did not smoke put providently away for a rare gift to some smoking relative) the babble of tongues was loosened into an Euskarian sounding one that might have made George Borrow mumble in his grave.

Then it ceased. "*Amigo*," said Juan, "we want you to go with us to Val Carlos. It is but three kilometers from here. We shall walk there and back, and then I shall take you like that"—he snapped his fingers—"in my cart to St. Jean."

"But," I explained, "I have given my word to the guard to return immediately after dinner. You know I have no passport."

"We know the guard. We shall respond for you," he urged.

I wanted to go, but in my uniform I could not take chances of being detained. So I argued further: "It will be late when we return; the guard will be changed; I shall not be known."

"It makes nothing," he replied contemptuously, and then his voice fell into a kind of well-done stage whisper. "*Mira! Nosotros todos somos contrabandistas y podemos ir a donde queremos.* [We are all contrabandists and can go wherever we please.] If necessary, we can ford the river above. There is a trail across the mountains. We wish you to take back a happy souvenir of your day in Spain with your Basque friends."

The matter was settled. Forthwith we set out, having paid the ridiculously low price of five francs around for the dinner. But if I have given the impression thus far that all was harmony between the two houses of Basques represented, I have erred. A federation of spirits there was.

"We are *un petit morceau du peuple* like the Belgians," the old Frenchman had said to me, "and there are Basques in Spain who cannot speak Spanish and some old Basques on the French side who don't know how to speak French, but we all speak the Basque." But an international acquiescence there was not. At the entrance of each new course of the dinner almost, Juan would whisper with gathering pride into my ear: "Look, could you get food like this in France? No, and there they will rob you for what you do get." Or again: "Have you tasted any such red wine as this in France? I think not, and at the end you will see that we shall pay very little. In France they have nothing and they cheat you on that."

The road to Val Carlos led us on and higher, but the farther we got away from France, the rougher and muddier it became. I waded and picked my way alongside my burly French patron. "*Voila!*" he kept saying to me over and over with an inward satisfaction that is untranslatable. "*Voila ce chemin maudit de l'Espagne.* Did you ever walk in mud like this on the roads of France? Huh! Huh! Huh!" Deep out of the bowels of his being his irony arose: "You see well that you are in Spain now. You will take *un bon souvenir* of this country back *chez vous* on your boots, I think. These Spanish are with the Germans. They say nothing, but we know them. Your country gave them a good thrashing too once. *Vive l'Amérique!*"

We had not proceeded a great way before a young Spanish guard whom I had seen before overtook us. He was considerably excited over the prospect of my going into the village and declared that his lieutenant, who lived there, would intercept me. He seemed to think that it might be his own duty to halt me, but as he had no symbol of authority more powerful than an umbrella, I took no thought of him. Juan had the policy to ask him to drink a little *vin rouge*, but he peremptorily stated that he never drank. However, his vehemence soon died down, and in a little while he himself invited us into a kind of roadhouse for cheese and refreshment.

In this house I met a curious old Basque. He had been a *pastor*—a sheep herder—in California once but had returned from America twenty years ago. All the English he could remember seemed to be "damn, hello," and with this iterated phrase he made me warmly welcome, shaking my hand long and, after I had been seated, coming over to the table and patting me on the back. At Arneguy I had met another Spanish Basque who also had been a shepherd in California, but he spoke English quite well—and proudly. And I heard of several Basques being in America, all in California herding sheep, an occupation common to the whole Pyrenees country.

When we got to Val Carlos, I went into a little store to buy a handkerchief; I had no change smaller than a fifty franc note, and the sharp-faced old proprietor would not change it. "Nevertheless," said he, "you will take the handkerchief as a *recuerdo* of your visit to Spain." The wife, though, of this gallant tradesman was hardly so generous. My friends seemed to be thirsty again, I ordered something to drink; she charged me so that she had no difficulty in finding enough change to return for my fifty francs.

Eduardo, Juan's bosom companion, called her "*una ladrona vieja*"—an old hag robber—and the words were about to run high. Juan secured the peace and we all departed; the Spaniards highly incensed, my old French patron wonderfully pleased and plethoric with words on Spanish honesty, and I sufficiently diverted. The event was one of humiliation for Juan, and the shame of it remained with him all the remainder of the day.

It was now near sunset, and I was eleven kilometers from my hotel and baggage. However, as I had daylight to catch my train, I was in no hurry to get back. "Juan," I said, "it will be dark before we can reach Arneguy. I have no fear now of being halted by the guards, but you have told me that there is a pass a little way above here. I wish to experience it. Let us take that route back to St. Jean."

"Good," he agreed. "It is warm enough, and the señor is a man not to mind a little water."

He desired to take back with him a pair of new shoes for some *amigo* in France, some sugar, a little candy, and some cotton cloth. Having secured these articles, he, Eduardo, and I struck for the trail of the *contrabandistas*, the remainder of the party having by this time separated from us.

It was a good night for *contrabandistas*, misty and such as you may read about in Pierre Loti's novel. The old French Territorials were none too alert, doubtless feeling they deserved an easy time after the rigorous vigils of the long war. We experienced no difficulty in effecting the pass. The Nive was swift but not deep, and I took off my boots to cross—thus keeping on them the "*bon souvenir de l'Espagne*." The trail was rough, though, and long, and I wished that we had gone back by the high road.

Just at daybreak I left Saint-Jean-Pied-de-Port. Down the clean and vivid valley we went, in sight of the waters I had heard all the night I came up. And from that day to this, I have hardly ceased to regret that I did not spend all of my allotted time in a region so friendly, so beautiful, and so fraught with the possibilities of adventure.

Birds under Bombs: In
England during World War II

*I wanted to get as close to the war as I could. I have not wished Germans
slaughtered and sent to hell merely because I feared they would scorch
my part of the green earth. Much as I love the greenness of the earth, it is
not the limit of my inheritance. The Nazis have been out to exterminate
a civilization, with all its values and accumulations of what is beautiful
and noble. It had been my war ever since.—JFD*

I N 1943, Cambridge University invited me to become a visiting professor of American history, proclaiming they wanted
an explainer of America who had mud between his toes and
grass burs in his heels. So, on a September day, four years after
the Germans began their murder of humanity, I left my home in
Austin, Texas.

Even though I was too old to fight it was something to be
going in the direction of fighting men.

It was dark when I got to London, and because of the German
bombers the city was in a total blackout. The next morning, the
route to London station led through blocks of utter destruction
around St. Paul's Cathedral. I crowded onto a train filled with soldiers, carrying my portable typewriter and a cardboard suitcase.

We passed peaceful grazing cows. I glimpsed wood pigeons,
crested peewits, or plover, and a few partridges in the green
fields. We rolled past hedges, houses, and villages as war planes
flew overhead.

I had never been to England, but for the better part of my life I have been an eager reader of English literature. I once thought I could live forever on the supernal beauty of Shelley's "The Cloud" and his soaring lines "To a Skylark," on the rich melancholy of Keats's "Ode to a Nightingale," on Wordsworth's philosophy of nature—a philosophy that has illuminated for me the mesquite flats and oak-studded hills of Texas.

Shakespeare and a world of other inspiring things that English literature has bestowed on us is still the richest of heritages. But literature is not enough.

My living quarters at Cambridge were inside a three-storied hall constructed of ancient stones, flanking a courtyard of green grass and cobblestone walks. To get to my lodging I stepped through a massive archway, opened a door, and entered a large, high parlor, furnished very comfortably and with three large windows looking out onto the front court of the college. Yet coal was scarce and the room could not be heated against the damp chill.

That first afternoon I went to the police station, presented my passport, and received an identity card, such as every civilian in the British Isles carries. I went to another place and was issued food and clothing coupons. I learned that I would be granted a pint of jam or marmalade every four weeks; that every Monday morning I would receive an ounce of butter and a small amount of sugar.

People often said to me, "It is too bad you can't be here in peacetime. Then we could show you more gracious ways of living." Life would no doubt be more comfortable in peacetime, but it could never be so interesting. I thank God that comfort is not my chief god.

❖   ◎   ❖

At the university, I found about 200 RAF and Royal Navy "short course" cadets in one class and about twenty youthful civilians in another class. Their patronage of Hollywood cinemas made it possible for them to understand my accent.

In Texas, I had been used to announcing to a roomful of young barbarians that my knowledge of history consisted mainly of facts relating to the length of the horns of Longhorn steers, the music inherent in coyote howling, the way mother rattlesnakes swallow their young, the duels Jim Bowie fought with his Bowie knife, the cleverness of black bears in playing the accordion, the smell of coffee boiled over mesquite wood, the habits of ghosts in guarding Spanish treasure, the religious note in ballads about Jesse James and Sam Bass, the shade-hunting serenity and grass-chewing leisureliness of cowboys as opposed to the tone Hollywood gives them, and what, in general, Texas and the surrounding territory was like before, to quote Bigfoot Wallace, "bob wire played hell with it."

These Cambridge students gave me to understand that while the picturesque was entirely agreeable to them, they were faced, according to long traditions, with severe examinations on the political phases of history. They were hell bent on hearing my interpretations of the American Constitution—and of our entire political system.

I had not read the American Constitution since I was a boy and did not understand it then. A wise lecturer talks so strongly about what little he knows that no listener ever gets a chance to probe him beyond. I have never been wise. I had to bone like a freshman to keep up.

During my first weeks teaching at Cambridge, I realized that an American businessman would probably denounce the university system. Cambridge consciously aims *not* to apply the factory method of standardized mass production. Cambridge promotes the amenities of civilized society as well as the knowledge. The old Greek ideal of balance, a rounded individual with "the elements mixed," prevails. Correct English is as highly regarded for an economics course as for one on Shakespeare. Cambridge still thinks that education which leads to "the art of living" is as practical as a course in salesmanship.

In America, a powerful and persistent doctrine dictates that businessmen should run the government and also education, and that a poet is to be distrusted even in a minor government post. The stark passion for stark business in charge of government will have nothing to do with the thinking and imagining class.

Millionaire businessman William Randolph Hearst may buy art in wholesale lots, but somehow he has never melted the beautiful and the free into his own soul.

❖   ◉   ❖

I was soon invited to give a talk on Tom Paine at the town of Thetford, where this great revolutionist was born. It is the English sympathy for liberty that makes Thetford today very proud to claim Tom Paine as a fighter for freedom, even though he fought against England.

Some men from America's Eighth Air Force were present, there to join me in dedicating a plaque memorializing our fellow patriot. They had brought one of their planes, a B-17 Flying Fortress with the name TOM PAINE painted on its nose. On the grim steel beneath the name was one of Paine's piercing sentences: "TYRANNY, LIKE HELL, IS NOT EASILY CONQUERED."

The pilot invited me to inspect the bomber. As I climbed aboard, I could see that the ground crew had shoved keepsakes for Germany into the plane's racks. I thought of Paine's intellectual bravery. One of his first articles in the colonies had urged freedom for slaves. He also wrote against dueling and argued for more humane treatment of animals. In January 1776 his *Common Sense* appeared. What *Uncle Tom's Cabin* later did in awakening the North against the slave-holding South, Paine's *Common Sense* did to help inspire the colonies to revolt.

In the winter of 1776, Paine wrote another stirring pamphlet that was read to every corporal's guard under General Washington's command. "These are the times that try men's souls," the famous opening sentence of *The Crisis* goes. "The summer soldier and the sunshine patriot will, in this crisis, shrink from the service of their country; but he that stands by it now deserves the love and thanks of man and woman."

Crawling through the gigantic aircraft I met more of the crew, including the rear gunner, a sergeant who had already made eight shooting trips in this plane. The sergeant spoke of one mission on which he shot over a thousand rounds, and there was a gleam in his eye as he pointed out the crossline sight on the end of his gun.

Emerging from the TOM PAINE, I came to feel that the whole outfit would readily defend "The Rights of Man" til hell froze over.

Several nights later, I witnessed the climax of anti-aircraft action against the German raiders. The only way I can suggest the sound of these rocket guns is to call on all the "clatter wheels of hell," roaring and stampeding headlong into each other as their barrage filled the sky, cutting through enemy flares and searchlights and assorted aerial explosions. All the while, the clouds glowed orange, reflecting the blazing London buildings hit by German bombs.

About three hours after the raid was over, the night turned absolutely clear. The stars were not so bright as in Texas, but they spangled the whole welkin and seemed to me as "beautiful and fair" as Wordsworth's "waters on a starry night." I stood alone in Green Park in the heart of London. There were no passers-by, though it was only ten o'clock. Not a hundred yards away a searchlight was throwing its beam across the spaces. The great Hunter hunted low down in the east, and the North Star stood much higher than it stands at home.

Then far away, somewhat west of north, I saw the giant beam from the searchlight leading a silver plane across the sky over London. Other beams converged on the plane until there were eighteen or nineteen focused on it. It was so high up that I did not hear its motors. It was one of ours. A little way off the ruins of bombed walls had been turned into a soft dream by the shadows of night. And the airy sliver of brightness up there in the apex of the searchlight beams moved on softly as a feather wafts downward from an eagle in flight.

❖   ◎   ❖

When I came to England I knew that I would with my own ears hear nightingales, cuckoos, skylarks, thrushes, blackbirds and the chaffinch "on the orchard bough." I knew that I would see with my own eyes hosts of golden daffodils, the hawthorn hedge in bloom, the daisy that Burns plowed up, a violet by a moss-grown stone.

The English, high and low, rich and poor, educated and uneducated, all seem to love their lovely landscapes. Here nature is agreeable in a state of cultivation that only loving care, science, and rooted humanity can give it.

On the edge of a little village in the hills occupied by an American military outfit, I stayed at Orchard Lea. The house is set in a ramifying garden that runs into an orchard, which runs into a meadow of about fifty acres, joined by other meadows and fields. What constantly strikes an American is that so much countryside is preserved in a country so densely populated. In the yard, against the lane, is a magnificent beech tree that has been declared a national monument.

My host was a man past sixty-five years of age who served as infantry colonel in the last war. He manufactures ammunition now. His wife, a strong marshaler of affairs, works as hard with her vegetables, flowers, and chickens as any farmer. The colonel represents a type of Englishman by no means obsolete. He has never let his work in business atrophy the art of living. He reads for reasons other than to kill time. He has compiled a local history, and he draws, wood-carves, and has collected a fine library of natural history and sporting books. The walls of their home are lined with pictures of landscapes, animals both wild and domestic, birds, flowers, human nature, historical places. I thought of a certain ostentatious mansion in Texas, built by a rancher whose sole decorations in his ample den consist of multiplied enlargements of Kodak pictures of himself and his prize Hereford bulls.

In a US Army jeep provided for my benefit, the colonel and I rode into moorlands. We got out and walked and lingered. We started up two or three grouse and could hear them calling in every direction. We saw snipe flying and could hear them drumming on the descent. The lapwing was flying and calling its lonely cry. The "wandering voice" of a cuckoo went up a valley.

For fifteen minutes I watched and listened to a thrush sing without a stop. He sat on a small, down-hanging limb of a horse chestnut white with flowers. I like the old name "throstle" better than "thrush." As Wordsworth wrote, "And hark, how blithe the throstle sings!"

According to the last official count, or estimate, of the birds in Britain, there were close to a hundred million—ten million chaffinches, four million sparrows, with blackbirds, robins, and thrushes close runners-up. There must be more birds in England than in any other developed land of its size on earth. It isn't just that they find refuge and feed in the gardens of town and country and the hedges that divide the plots of land and in the woods, or that the land's productivity favors them as no other land. It isn't just that. There are hardly any birds, comparatively, in France. They were killed out long ago.

The English people cherish birds as creatures that add to the interest and charm of life. They cherish them and protect them also as economic destroyers of insects and rodents hostile to produce.

People talk and write about the soul of France and the spirit of Paris as easily as they sing about the sidewalks of New York. It is seldom suggested that London has a soul. People who know that their feet are on the ground are shy of mentioning souls. Yet I am dead certain that the love of the English for the "fair Earth" and for the growing and flying and running and crawling and standing things on it is enormously responsible for their fixed and unwavering character.

❖   ◎   ❖

I went to the American Cemetery not far from Cambridge. Thrice weekly taps blow over new graves and then the faraway bugle responds, making the finest earthly sound that a soldier being put back to earth could have.

This cemetery is on a gentle hill-slope, looking far away to the east and to the north. On two sides of it are tall woods famous for nightingale singing in the spring. On the other two sides are fields of skylarks through the fall—the "holy lark" that Chaucer, Shakespeare, Shelley, and so many other poets have been making to "shake the dew" from its "light wing" as it "at heaven's gate sings."

The sky above is a vast pathway for war planes. I counted hundreds of planes flashing in the sun on their way to German destruction. As I have known this spot only in wartime, they seem to me as much in place as the great flocks of rooks that stream from far places at evening to roost in the trees of the woods overlooking the cemetery.

On a late afternoon I went to hear nightingales sing in a tangle of hawthorn beside a stretch of tall woods. I was more eager to hear them than I have ever been to see Rome. They did not disappoint me, in the twilight and then into the darkness. What carrying power their voices have, seeming to envelop the whole air! A timber man tells me that last year a camp of foresters in Surrey were so kept awake by the all-night singing that they moved camp out into a field. It was the monasterial Edward the Confessor who grew so sick of the incessant singing of nightingales in the forest where he housed that he prayed heaven to silence them—whereupon they left and did not come back until after he had died.

I doubt if the nightingale song is any more beautiful than that of our southern mockingbird, which in the spring goes absolutely delirious with the joyful prickings of nature, often springing upward from its high, clear perch as if to race with the song itself and sometimes keeping up the singing the livelong night.

But is not mockingbird a flat, too literal, name? I wish we had adopted the Indian name, zenzontle, used by the Mexicanos for it, as we have adopted mesquite, coyote, huisache, and many other native names for native life.

I have a thousand times heard the bobwhite call clear over the mesquite grass at sunrise, the roadrunner go crut-crut-crut in the chaparral in the middle of the day, the bullbat zoom down over the prairie at twilight, the querulous little screech owl, who never knows how deliciously funny he is, complain in the gathering darkness, and the lonesome calls of the southbound sandhill cranes come out of the night. These and many other creatures that add to the song of the corner of the earth in which I have my roots are very dear to me, but often I miss the endowments, the lightings up, the translations of them into the stream of human destiny that only Bards of Passion and of Mirth can give.

Without such, the skylark would be a kind of naked ghost of what the enrichers from Homer's time have been making him. There is no civilization without art; there is no art without the beautiful; half of what is interesting and beautiful lies in accreted memories.

Here in the larches, the ashes, the oaks, the elms, the willows, and the shrubbery the birds seem always to be singing while the fleets of bombers and fighter planes roar toward destiny.

❖ ◎ ❖

On June 7, 1944, the afternoon after D-Day, I went down to the Cam River, where the soaring and ever-singing skylarks rose over Grantchester meadows just up from the river from ancient Cambridge town. Overhead, Allied planes on their way to France whizzed by; Mustangs, Lightnings, and others—all painted for the invasion. Thrushes sang on the boughs as swallows dipped over the mown lawns.

Cambridge's madrigal singers were giving their annual concert, which went ahead as scheduled even as the battle of destiny raged across the English channel. The singers were in boats, with their voices coming down the water and over the gardened lawns and up into the trees. Families of mallard ducks paid them little mind. The cawing rooks observing from the branches seemed to enjoy it, along with a thrush that turned himself loose not unlike a mockingbird. Overhead, every few minutes, new waves of planes flew past, and in a way they added to the harmony. The birds did not seem to notice them any more than nightingales are said to notice barrage guns.

❖ ◎ ❖

The Germans are in retreat across France but continue to attack Britain with their VI rockets, remote controlled flying bombs that look like pilotless planes. The British call them "doodlebugs." Hundreds of these are being fired at England every day. From miles away you can hear the buzzing drone these craft make. Then the sound goes silent in the final seconds, as their engines cease and the missiles begin plunging toward their targets. The next sound you hear is the explosion.

After you have heard these machines you can never mistake them for a living sound. When the explosion shakes the air, you may feel grateful that it passed you by, but you will not thank God that it blasted out the soul or the home of some other living being.

I have heard thousands of other planes, singly and in armadas of inexorable destiny. Although a machine can have no soul, I have become accustomed to regarding those machines of the sky as personifications of men, young men bright with life, mostly young men of my own blood and tongue. The living made them, the living guide them; they live to assert humanity's right to live free.

But this strange, lone machine in the sky that cannot veer or check until its swift clock has run down, moving without a hand to guide it and without a life to share its destruction, has a sound different from all other sky-cleavers you have ever heard. It is not even manned by a ghost, as was the specter-ship the Ancient Mariner saw. These "doodlebugs" are killing thousands, but I've heard people say they preferred the destruction of the Blitz during the Battle of Britain to this. As one old woman said, "It seemed so much more natural."

On a July night in London I barely slept. Throughout the long hours the drone of doodlebugs and their explosions could be heard across the city. In the hour before dawn, while I looked at moonlight's magic on walls bombed to ruins years ago in this long, long war, I decided I should go down to Kew Gardens in the morning.

It was a warm day and the clouds were low and thick. The Alert remained and as I left the center of London, I could hear the deadly drone of another incoming flying bomb overhead with its burden of destruction.

By the time I reached Kew Gardens along the River Thames, the All Clear had sounded. I walked through roses, grass, and trees, and came to a lake, beside which a tall, slender old man was feeding bread crumbs to a swarm of house sparrows. A chaffinch, dressed as gallantly as Little Lord Fauntleroy, was trying to get a crumb but was too genteel in his nature to become part of the mob. The old man pitched him something apart. He also fed a half-dozen half-grown mallard ducks and their mother, also a moor hen, in the water. Three middle-aged women in some sort of home-services uniform, each with a lunch wallet, watched him for a while. He told them the last time he had been in the gardens he was with his daughter, and a duck they had fed followed them along the gravel walks for half a mile. "It was on a Sunday and there were crowds," he said. "Now a hen will lose her head and get excited in traffic, but a duck keeps as calm as a cork when there ain't no wind, no current, and no fish in the water. That duck she just keep waddling at my heels."

After the three women went on, I spoke to the old man. He'd come out to Kew, he said, to get some peace. The night before a German doodlebug had exploded all the windows out of the house he lived in. I asked him if it had done much other destruction. He said he didn't know, that he didn't look for the place where it landed because he didn't want to add to human morbidity. He had been bombed out during the great blitz in 1940, but he had no thought of leaving London now. He was seventy-six years old and had a job—messenger in a government office.

While he spoke, the siren went again. Soon we could hear the buzzing noise of another flying bomb approaching. We both looked up into the sky but couldn't see it for the low clouds. He turned and looked down a path leading toward the garden lunchroom, continuing his conversation. "It was right here," he said, "that the duck began following me and my daughter. Did you ever see anything more independent than a duck waddling when she knows exactly where she wants to go?"

Now it was "cheerio" and each went his way. More doodlebugs sporadically strayed over. I went through the rock garden, where I found the heather always planted in such places. While I was walking on grass beside a bed of blooming dahlias, I could hear the noise of another flying bomb. I noticed two bumblebees in the dahlias. There was no sunshine, but they were making hay. The buzzing noise grew louder. I looked up through a break in the clouds and caught a distinct view of the doodlebug as it sailed over me. It was still going horizontally, droning that ashes-to-ashes-and-dust-to-dust buzz. The bumblebees took no notice of it. I decided that the bombs didn't seem destined to explode at Kew Gardens on this particular day.

About one o'clock I approached the lunchroom. I saw tables

on the lawn and people seated before them. Everybody had to get his own tray of food rations, cafeteria style, from inside. The youngest seemed more engaged in feeding the hordes of sparrows than in feeding themselves.

Just as I reached the entrance of the cafeteria, the noise of another bomb grew and an officious-looking man screeched out, "Take cover! Take cover!" He flattened against the building's wall. I looked at the people at the tables and saw that nobody paid the least attention to him. The flying bomb certainly did sound directly overhead. In a short time, the man, who looked as if he had not been sleeping much or eating much either, spoke again. "That one's going to London," he announced.

Again it was All Clear. There was no sunshine, but the ground was as warm as the air. I found a little opening of springy grass, surrounded by trees—an opening about big enough to stake two horses on. I could see in all directions from my pallet. I pulled my hat over my eyes and went to sleep. When I awoke a kestrel hawk was hanging in the air not far away.

I walked by a longish lake and saw three American soldiers trying to Kodak a pair of foreign-looking geese. I had saved half my luncheon bread for useful purposes. A bit of it brought the geese into proper position. Eight children and their mothers came up to enjoy the birds. I threw the last of my bread into a small pond nearby covered with water lilies. It was a joy to see a moor hen and her three little ones run over the big lily pads.

I went on down to the Thames River and walked up it, watching slow barges laden with coal, lumber, and other goods being towed by. The men on the barges and boats all seemed interested in the shore life, just as scattered spectators such as myself seemed interested in the river life.

I rode back to London on top of a bus. I saw fresh debris being carted down side streets, a pitiful pile of furniture beside one unit of demolished walls and homes. I saw people looking and talking, talking about the remote controlled flying bombs and their deadly work. Like Hitler's bombers during the Blitz that were going to conquer England by cowing the people, these would only fortify their souls. They will never destroy the character that the bomb-makers hate.

Meanwhile, the bumblebees in the dahlias, the wood pigeons so gentle in the gardens though they are always wild and wary elsewhere, the duck that follows a man and his daughter for half a mile, the children feeding birds, the barges on the water, the trees on the banks, the kestrel in the air, and the chaffinch in his gray coat on a bough: these will always be new, refreshing.

Across the Rhine
Travels in Postwar Germany

Dobie spent several months in Germany as a lecturer for the US Army. He considered writing a book of his observations about Germany, which would be something of a sequel to his A Texan in England. He'd compiled several newspaper columns along with a feature story in the National Geographic. Yet he concluded, "I have not learned enough" to justify an entire book.—SD

I T WAS DECEMBER of the first winter of peace when I headed for Germany from Paris. I am a civilian hired by the Army. I wear a uniform, am subject to numerous Army regulations, and have the simulated rank of a field officer. Like other civilians in zones presided over by the military, I am absolutely dependent on the Army for food, shelter, and transportation.

The run to Frankfurt was at night, and the train was mostly loaded with American soldiers who had been in Paris on leave. I was informed that I would have no sleeping berth for the overnight trip, on account of my having no real military rank—but that I could have a seat in a day coach.

I got onto the train early and saw that ranks from lieutenants to a brigadier were being bedded down. My compensation for sitting up in a compartment holding six was the company of five genuine soldiers. I considered the compensation adequate. My companions included a lanky Texas cavalryman who has not been on a horse since he left home. We spoke of the rights of

Negroes to good schooling, the vote, and a fair deal in labor and on trains and buses.

Every time the train stopped, armed guards would get off and patrol to see that no thief crawled into the baggage car. Dawn came as we were creeping across the Rhine on a temporary bridge alongside the dynamited ruins of the great bridge at Mainz, of which the Germans were once so proud.

From the station in Frankfurt we drove in a jeep through the destruction caused by Allied bombs. Not a single department store or any other large building was left undestroyed downtown. On the edge of the central business district, untouched by bombing and artillery fire, is the largest office building I have ever seen. The corridors are as long as the Rockefeller Center is high. This massive complex was formerly headquarters for the I. G. Farbenindustrie. It was spared by Allied bombers because the victorious army planners knew they would need office space when they occupied Germany. It is now Supreme Headquarters for the Allied European Forces. It is also the headquarters for the US occupation forces. In and around Frankfurt are stationed tens of thousands of troops, using thousands of motor vehicles, occupying acres of offices overlooking miles of devastation— and dominating hordes of Germans.

We made our way beside bleak fields to Höchst, a suburb with more I. G. Farbenindustrie offices. These heavy, dreary office buildings sprawl amid smokestacks and streets of houses, all untouched by war. This is the headquarters for the US Army's Information and Education division (I&E), which includes the army newspaper, radio, photographic services, carloads of paraphernalia, and tons of pamphlets.

I am assigned to this division and this is my base. I&E requires American soldiers to receive two hours of lecture and discussion each week. My main job is to give talks on the theme of Modern Citizenship, or The Necessity for Thinking.

I am more interested in seeing how I&E promotes democracy and denazification among the defeated Germans. The army gives a lot of credit to itself for its education program in the European theater. They have been increasingly encouraging Americans to "play ball" with German youth and try to democratize them through sports. Of their own accord, American soldiers teach baseball, like gum-chewing, to every people they encounter.

A mile away from I&E headquarters is a residential neighborhood, completely surrounded by rolls and walls of barbed wire. Military police guard the entrances day and night. The houses have been commandeered from German citizens. Only military personnel and accredited German laborers are permitted entrance. This area is known as "The Compound." It is where I will live.

Nearly all American officers and many enlisted men live in private houses requisitioned from Germans. The house I am assigned to has an apartment downstairs and another upstairs. A steam-heating furnace is in the cellar and the radiators heat 24 hours a day, making us the envy of shivering Germans. Two middle-aged German women provide domestic duties. One of them is the owner of this home. Upon being evicted from this house, she and her family had been quartered with another family outside the Compound. Every house in Germany, whether in village or city, is subject to taking its quota of the influx of displaced Germans, as well of the houseless who belong to the area. The burgomaster of every hamlet must find quarters for numbers allotted to his district.

For laundering our clothes and shining our shoes, we give our landlady PX candy and cookies. Like other household labor, she is paid by the Germans on order from the American Army. Along with other workers in the compound, she arrives at 8:30 in the morning and leaves about 5 pm.

This woman often asks me how long the Americans are going to stay. When I tell her I do not know, she says, "If I do not have my home back in one year, I will hang myself."

Across the street from the I&E offices is another vast I. G. Farbenindustrie structure. This is called the Casino, where a mixture of a thousand or more civilians and officers from many nations eat and drink every day. At the door an armed soldier stands constant guard to prevent unauthorized persons from taking advantage of the excellent dollar-a-day fare.

The waiters, as at other messes, are Polish or other DPs (displaced persons.) A cigarette or two is considered a fair tip for any service anywhere in Germany. The collector of ashtrays at a table where cigarette smokers have lingered is a highly favored individual. German men and children can be found hanging around outside any concentration of foreign servicemen and women—they are looking to pick up discarded cigarette stubs.

Few retail stores are in operation. A handful of trucks could haul away the bulk of goods for sale in all the stores in Frankfurt. There are no furniture stores operating, though a German agent can find a whole set of furniture if offered enough cigarettes. One manufacturer of hand luggage sold a new suitcase for four cartons of cigarettes. He said he would use them to get priority on meat at controlled prices.

We are in deep winter, yet there is no coal for civilian use. Fuel among the Germans of this area is far scarcer than clothes, food, and cigarettes. People in the streets keep an eye out for anything dropped from a passing Army truck. I saw a very respectably dressed man step off the sidewalk and pick up a bit of coal no bigger than my thumb and put it in a handbag.

A piece of coal, no matter how small; a cigarette stub, no matter how short; or a bit of horse manure, precious for fertilizing a kitchen garden, will disappear almost as soon as dropped on any German street.

Not all, but nearly all, motor vehicles are military operated. I have seen a good many horse-drawn wagons, hauling wood more than anything else. For miles out from the center of the city one may see civilians pushing prams or wheelbarrows loaded with wood gathered in the forest. Often the wood is little more than twigs. Bicycle riders carry in bundles of fuel from long distances.

Used to obeying orders and being regimented, the civilians do not hack down any tree they can find. They take only what the forest supervisors designate. Yet it is also common to see men climbing trees on ladders and sawing off branches to be used for fuel.

I find nothing to love in this country, though it is not time yet for the primroses to bloom. I suppose the primroses bloom here—as they do in England. But what a drama it is with the armies of four strange countries—none stranger than my own—occupying it, with hundreds of thousands of displaced persons from all the nations of Europe along with Germany's own millions, as incomprehensible as so many millions of sphinxes, milling its bombed cities, working its fields and everywhere seeming to be waiting for something that they themselves perhaps have not defined.

There have been so many shattered lives in Europe that there seems to be no political solution that will not entail great human suffering. Hitler had the right sow, but he had her by the wrong ear, when he wanted a united Europe. He wanted a Europe united under German lordship. Yet Europe will never be peaceful and prosperous until the diverse European states are united for mutual advancement.

And neither America nor any other considerable part of the earth can go its free way with Europe in chaos. We live in one world, and we are all as dependent on the welfare of Europe as the water level of the Pacific Ocean is dependent on the water level of the Atlantic Ocean.

❖ ◎ ❖

In the terribly devastated city of Darmstadt, about twenty miles south of Frankfurt, I stopped at public market tables on a square. A well-fed farm woman sat behind the best-stocked table. It was loaded with cheeses and eggs to sell—to be bought only with ration coupons, of course. As far as food goes, a farm family with two or three cows, a few chickens, and a few acres in wheat is now better off than the wealthiest urban manufacturer.

I spent five hours in a nearby camp holding German war prisoners. I went among the hospital wards, where the prisoners are under the care of German doctors who are also prisoners. The men in this camp are being screened for Nazi associations and are being discharged every day.

I saw that many of them had a book or two. I was curious as to what they were reading. *The Three Guardsmen* by Alexandre Dumas seems to be a favorite. I suppose that the censors can always admit old novels as being innocent of dangerous ideas. The American military government, however, has banned Spengler's *Decline of the West* and other books. I think that forbidding any book by anybody is a mistake. Censorship except for military security is always a curse.

The library at this camp serves thousands of soldiers. It consists of a few dozen paperback novels. Added to it a few days before I arrived was a collection of over a hundred books in English. These consist of such twaddle as Zane Grey's *Riders of the Purple Sage* along with old textbooks on radios and motor engines.

Several of the hospital prisoners I talked with wanted something "serious" to read—books of history, biography, philosophy. They do not have access to a single paragraph expressive of the democratic way of life to which their conquerors are supposed to be educating them. Yet these men are being released to citizenship.

Making war is so easy, making it successfully is very, very easy compared with filling the minds and spirits of human beings with noble thoughts, beautiful images, and the active desire to have good and justice prevail all over the world.

As I see it, there are only two things to do with the Germans: either kill them off or educate them. We are not going to transform the Germans solely through popular music, chewing gum, and baseball games.

❖   ◎   ❖

I drove with a major over the famous German autobahn to Heidelberg, about 75 miles away. Hitler made these autobahns for military use, and I saw hundreds of trucks, militarized civilian cars, jeeps, and command cars. The wide, straight "superhighway" is merely efficient, lacking in grace and in picturesqueness. In places the parkway between the double line of lanes was cemented over and converted into a runway for bombers and fighter planes. Retreating Germans blew up all the bridges. It will be a long time before some of them are rebuilt.

At intervals we passed army service stations. We stopped at a long Red Cross hut designed to furnish free coffee and doughnuts to users of the road. The autobahn, with endless road signs in English, in this part of Germany certainly gives one the impression that America is totally occupying the country.

At Heidelberg, I saw that the famous university town escaped all bombs. The rumor is that an understanding between the British and the Germans exempted both Oxford and Heidelberg from bombing. I'm told by the military that no such understanding existed. Probably war has not scarred Heidelberg because there were too many other important targets.

The stores here have more shoes and clothing than others in Germany. All such articles are, of course, severely rationed. I noticed more Germans lingering in front of the display windows of a big clothing store for American officers than anywhere else.

In the venerable University of Heidelberg, the Americans have built up the best library of English-language books to be found in the occupied countries. Though it is largely run by German help, no German student is allowed to read these books.

How are we to reeducate the Germans if we do not allow them to learn what we are thinking? Germans, intellectually starved, are hungry for reading matter out of the democracies. The most grateful German I met was a professor to whom I gave two pamphlets, one on democracy and one a summary of events in Washington.

The Army is spending many millions of dollars in a bumbling education program that reveals the stark fact that the US Army is not intimately interested in thought, in ideas, in education that means civilization beyond the merely physical. This Army is so little interested in current realities that it accords only its own censored newspaper to the hundreds of thousands of Americans in Germany under Army domination. There is no substitute for brains, whether in the realm of brass, increased cigarette rations, radio tunes, or other physical attempts to fill up vacancies in military skulls.

❖   ◎   ❖

Riding on railroads in Germany is more interesting than the highways. You see more of what has happened, of life going on. I'll never get used to the burned-out skeletons of trains on side tracks, still standing where they stood when they were machine-gunned by Allied planes during the war. Now and then we pass a rusting armored engine, or freight cars that have fallen onto their sides down embankments.

Allied bombers did an exceedingly thorough job on all railroad stations of any consequence. Most are ruined shells now. In these seatless caverns you see the anchorless populations sitting on their luggage, sometimes eating bread, often drowsing, nearly all of them listless, waiting for hours, sometimes for days, for a train. They must have permits to buy tickets unless they have a travel order.

On a daylight trip out of Frankfurt to the east, I rode a civilian train. One compartment in a third-class coach was reserved for Allied personnel such as myself. Germans scrambling to get on that train reminded me of moths clinging to the window screen in summertime. Some were even riding on top of coaches, though this is verboten. On the open platform in front of our compartment, eight or ten people occupied all the standing space during the entire journey.

Most Americans who travel any considerable distance by train in Germany ride the military trains, from which German civilians are excluded. These trains run at night, and are made up of chair coaches, and of sleeping cars for those who can rank a berth. They are divided into compartments, each with a lower and an upper bunk. Sometimes they have good reading lights, sometimes not. Sometimes there is a jar of drinking water and water in the lavatory reservoir, sometimes not. There are never comfortable pillows, for the Germans don't understand pillows.

❖ ◎ ❖

In Munich, at the fringe of the Alps, people swarm the downtown streets, putting in hours a day locating and bartering for some commonplace piece of food or household article. The central part of the city looks 90 percent destroyed, but miles of apartment homes on the outskirts shelter hordes of human beings. They jam into streetcars, three cars coupled together and driven by one motorman. GIs ride these cars for free. Hanging onto the steps is verboten, but they are as crowded as the inside of the cars.

I'm staying at the Excelsior Hotel, the only building on this downtown block that is not ruined. Large numbers of Germans pass it continually on their way to and from the charred husk of the central railroad station. As the passers-by know, the Excelsior is one of the few places in Munich, all of them American operated, where plenty of warm food, warming drinks, heat, fresh linen, hot water, soap, bathtubs, and other material comforts can be enjoyed. To the have-not Germans the Excelsior represents the all-having of their conquerors. Standing at its front windows, watching people walk by, I have caught more than a few looks of bitterness and resentment.

Curiosity led me to the Hofbrauhaus, the beer hall where Hitler founded the Nazi Party in 1920 and in which the Party members annually celebrated its founding until the British Royal Air Force stopped them. Today, in a restored portion of this supreme shrine to the Nazis, the American Red Cross gives out free doughnuts to GIs.

I found my way to an exhibition of paintings and I have never seen anywhere else so many gory representations of the beheading of John the Baptist, to say nothing of the endless iterations of Christ bleeding on the cross. After Dachau and much else of this war, Christ on the Cross looks pretty tame to me.

One night in the American Officers Red Cross club at Munich the band started playing "Lili Marlene." An American woman arose, came over to the club director, and objected to having this German song, so popular with the Nazi soldiers, played to Americans. Her objection reminded me of the patriots who, a day or two after Pearl Harbor, tried to cut down the cherry trees in Washington—because they came from Japan.

"Lili Marlene" is the one hauntingly beautiful melody that World War II produced. In dining rooms in Germany I often request the musicians play "Lili Marlene." Anything that is beautiful transcends man-made boundaries and belongs to humanity more than any nationality.

❖ ◎ ❖

Of all the criminal faces I have ever seen those of the Storm Troopers now imprisoned at Dachau are the most horrible.

Dachau, you will always remember, is where the Germans cremated their victims. I saw the ovens, the gas chambers, the iron hooks from which tortured bodies hung, the pits in which the hordes of human beings were shot, the kennels for the dogs trained and kept to bring down helpless victims.

I passed two or three hundred of the SS prisoners, in groups. They glared and with their eyes cursed. No chamber of horrors could cull more depravity and inhuman malice than those SS faces. I am not delicate, but I positively shudder now at the remembrance.

And these men were the flower and the fruit of Nazi philosophy! They were the darlings of the German army. I have read that after much screening about 150,000 of them are segregated from other prisoners. If they are ever turned loose in Germany, they will negate all the education that the Allies are capable of giving the German nation.

I confess to having had feelings of hatred at times, though life has been too bright and good and energy too precious to spend it in maintaining hatred. But the sight of these faces is enough to make any normal human being loathe all emotions of hatred. Yet for years hatred has been cultivated among Germans as a virtue.

You see representations of the Crucifixion everywhere in this part of Germany: in front of hundreds of houses; in wayside shrines, at forks of the road, and beside little bridges and old gates. And what good effect on the population has this bloody symbol ever had?

❖ ◎ ❖

After talking to soldiers of the Fifth Infantry at Augsburg, I went driving with two Texas officers. We jeeped for miles through farmlands, along canals. It is the time of year for fertilizing the soil. Men and women were spreading manure over the fields, and wagon-carried tanks were spraying the earth with manured water. I saw more cows hitched up to carts, wagons, and plows than I ever saw oxen in old-time Mexico. Neither these cows nor their ancestors have ever heard the clatter of a tractor.

We passed several small flocks of sheep on our rounds. When

a shepherd saw us nearing him, he would stand at attention and remove his cap. This deference was not to Americans, but to military uniforms. Perhaps it also was to the car. The Man on Horseback gave way a generation ago to the Man with a Motor, but peasants of Germany as well as of other European countries still live in the feudal age.

Later, I joined a lieutenant colonel who took me to a cooperative farm settlement established by the Nazis in 1933–1935. The date is on a granite monument opposite the schoolhouse in the center of the settlement, but the swastika signs have been chiseled off the granite.

We saw a good percentage of the population and spent an hour with one farmer and his family, talking and inspecting. The farmer and his wife had seven children. Two boys were killed in the war. Another is now a prisoner in Russia. The farm contains fifty acres, worked by the remaining family and four horses.

The farmer assured me with vehemence, without my bringing up the subject, that the Nazis had tried to eject him from the land for not joining their party. He had "just stayed on."

As I have watched the farmers in England and France and Germany fertilizing their plots of earth, it has seemed to me that through the long centuries of living on and by the soil they have developed a kind of unconscious fidelity to the soil that makes them also live for it. Absentee landlords never benefited a country, and the vast acreages in America owned by investment corporations and other money-makers, interested only in what profits they can get out of the soil and devoid of any feelings of loyalty to the earth itself, will some day present the bill of reckoning.

❖ ◎ ❖

Hitler called Nuremberg "the most German of all German cities." It certainly seemed to be the capital of Nazism. On the edge of town is the vast arena constructed so that Hitler could review division after division of his storm troopers, millions of men in all, drawn up in goose-stepping formation.

Nuremberg's bells ring no more. Its thriving war factories were destroyed by Allied bombs. Virtually all of the ancient Nuremberg center, once surrounded by deeply moated walls, is now absolute rubble. Not one house stands whole. The narrow, winding streets are still piled high with broken bricks and mortar a year after the city fell to America's Seventh Army. Strings of abandoned street-cars remain as ghosts, machine-gunned and fire-gutted. It took a hundred years of forced labor to build the mighty walls about the town; it took only a few nights of Allied bombing to demonstrate their utter obsoleteness.

The Nuremberg courthouse in which Hermann Goering and nineteen other German war criminals are now being tried is an island in this sea of devastation. It is also the most heavily guarded place I've seen in Germany. In front of the courthouse American soldiers, as polished in appearance and as precise in movement as the famous guards of Buckingham Palace, walk their posts. They stand in booths at every entrance. Beside the courthouse are machine-gun equipped tanks.

Inside, the American guards are in every passageway, wearing white helmets and carrying revolvers in white holsters attached to white belts. They allow no one to pass without credentials being examined and reexamined. In the courtroom a row of guards stands behind the two rows of seated prisoners. Other guards monitor the visitors' gallery and the press section. It takes time for a spectator to forget all the guards and pay attention to the tribunal, the prisoners, the attorneys—and the battalion of interpreters whose translations come into the adjustable ear-phones in four languages.

I have studied the faces of SS prisoners in the barbed-wire camp at Dachau. They are the most depraved, thug-featured faces I have ever beheld. The faces of the Nazi prisoners now on trial are no less horrible. If a face is an index to character—and the face is always an index, these are men hardened by brutality and crime.

Why did intelligent, decent Germans allow themselves to be ruled by these low-browed criminals, even brought to adore these criminals? It is astounding, incomprehensible.

In Nuremberg, Stefan Kupowski, minister of justice in Poland, is one of six men representing a nation in which the Germans had killed six million people. He brought me a heavy document that detailed Nazi crimes in Poland. Among the outrages: tens of thousands of human beings murdered at an extermination camp called Majdanek, their corpses turned into fertilizer.

Kupowski told me about a young Polish woman who, on being put into the witness stand recently, was asked what she knew about the fate of 2,000 Polish children at a concentration camp. She turned to the Nazi prisoners and gestured, "Perhaps they can tell you." This young Polish woman was pointed out to me. I saw on her arm the concentration number that the Nazis had branded there.

❖   ◉   ❖

Like most Americans in Germany, I wanted to get to Berlin. Taking the overnight army train from Frankfurt, I looked out the window at daylight and saw we were in a snow-covered forest country— mostly small timber. About two hours later I disembarked at the edge of Berlin. Then I got in an army truck and was driven into the city.

The main part of the sprawling, ruined capital is in the Soviet Zone. In no other urban center have I seen such a dearth of human activity. In front of the ancient Castle, right in the midst of what was once Berlin's busiest area, a woman and two men were pulling and pushing a cart loaded with freshly killed beef. They had the whole street to themselves.

Not one of the great hotels in which Berlin used to entertain the world is left. Nowhere in Berlin are there crowds of people walking the streets as one sees in Frankfurt and Munich. Instead, I saw small groups of women picking up rubble by hand, one piece of brick at a time, and loading the pieces in a truck.

The United States Zone of Berlin, the southwestern residential part of the city, embraces the least-damaged business area. The few shops that are open seem to have a limitless supply of bread and eyeglasses. The British Zone, which includes the Hitler-built Olympic stadium surrounded by hideous beer-hall-looking statues, has assumed a casual and well-managed appearance. The French, who can always be depended on for a fine gesture, have the Tricolor flying above the soaring Column of Victory built to celebrate their defeat seventy-five years ago.

I met two Germans who cried on my shoulder without any invitation about their reduced circumstances, yet neither had the slightest realization of the fact that they and their people have merely reaped what the Germans sowed. They demand sympathy for personal misfortunes that they in no way connect with whole-sale misery that Germany inflicted on tens of millions outside of Germany. They have no imagination.

What is the GI attitude towards the Germans? It is as diverse as human attitudes usually are toward anything. A battle-experienced sergeant told me that two fresh recruits from the US, both feeling pretty high, stopped him on the street and said, "Come on. Let's give some of these blankety Krauts hell. The way to treat 'em is to be rough with 'em, and we're going to be rough."

The sergeant didn't go with them. "I've seen all the roughness I want to see for a long time," he told me. "At one bridgehead in one day I saw my company of 185 men reduced to 78. These recruits seem to think that they have to be rough now to make up for the war they missed."

With an afternoon free, I procured a jeep, a German driver, and a German guide to see Berlin. This guide is twenty-four years old and was a fighter pilot in the Luftwaffe. He is plenty tame now and plenty intelligent. An only child, he lives with his parents, whose house was bombed. He said they are able to procure enough wood to keep from being cold, though sometimes they are not very warm.

We drove first through Grunewald, an enormous park, in which much wood was being cut. Later I saw the denudation of the Tiergarten in the heart of the city. This famous park is now more naked of trees than of statues that will not burn. It is pitted with shell and bomb holes, but I think it can grow fine trees again before commerce and prosperity rebuild the utter devastation around it.

My guide was more eager to show me Hitler's Chancellery than anything else. One can still walk through the gutted rooms of imitation marble that the Nazis erected for their Führer.

A Russian sentry at the entrance of the Chancellery spoke in a sharp hiss of German, demanding my guide's identification card. Once we were inside, the guide led me to where Hitler used to stand on the balcony to harangue the adoring crowds. He showed me a half dozen other places where Hitler was wont to sit or stand.

"Now," said the guide, with what seemed to me like reverence in his voice, "we come to the most important of all the rooms. Here was Hitler's desk. There by the fireplace Hitler held his most secret conferences. That door opens into his bedroom."

We advanced forward. The guide spoke somberly. "The bunker out the window there is over the bombproof shelter in which he took last refuge. Next to it you see Ribbentrop's house, then the house of Hitler's mistress, Eva Braun. They say that his body and hers were burned four meters from the bunker door. I don't know if this is true or not."

An Englishman and an American with cameras had joined us and wanted to take a picture of the bunker. "A Russian guard is inside," the guide said. "It is against orders to take his picture." The camera hounds advanced across the open litter toward the bunker for a nearer view. I went with them. A guard came out. The cameras were raised; the guard's stern shake of the head put them back in their cases.

After Hitler's bunker, we visited the most conspicuous monument in Berlin—the Victory Column erected to celebrate Germany's victory over France in 1870. On one side of it is another of the inevitable monstrous statues of Bismarck with helmet and sword. In villages and cities all over Germany, heroic-sized monuments of Bismarck dominate plazas and squares. And always you see Bismarck with an iron helmet on his head, an iron-hard expression on his face, a sword in his merciless fist.

I think it would be a pious idea to tear down a lot of these wearisome German war monuments. All countries have atrocious war monuments, including our own.

Near the Reichstag, which the Nazis burned in order to destroy the German Parliament, and overlooking the great avenue that cuts through the Tiergarten, the Russians have erected their

own war monument—a mighty soldier, with columns of inscrip-
tions on either side. At the soldier's feet and at the bases of the
columns are many fresh wreaths. A lone Russian soldier, fully
armed, stands guard.

I wonder how many years a Russian man of arms will stand
guard here in Berlin and how long the monument will last after
there are no more guards to protect it.

❖   ◎   ❖

Spring is arriving. The sun has been shining for three weeks now.
But the German land needs rain. Bees are in the fruit blossoms.
The bumble bee, that "yellow-breeched philosopher," stays closer
to the ground and has more self-sufficiency than anybody else I
have met in a long, long time. The blackbird singeth blithe, and
the chaffinch is on a thousand boughs. The slow oxen lead their
heavy masters up and down the rows, and the milkmaids without
audible sound are spreading manure where sugar beets will grow.

Considering how the Allies have had to make over the whole
political and educational systems of this country, besides regulat-
ing everything from hen eggs to freight trains, and considering
how all big plans require time, I have come to the conclusion that,
on the whole, we are doing fairly well in the business of occupying
Germany.

We can control the Germans; we can see to it that the Germans
are subjected to democratic ideas; but nobody can guarantee
what form the German mind will mold their ideas into.

German regimentation is not the answer. I have walked in
several pieces of forest planted by the Germans, who have proven
themselves extraordinarily efficient in growing timber. Nearly all
woods are delightful to me, but these German-planted, German-
cultivated forests seem like regimented nurseries; they have
nothing of the casualness of nature. These forests, no matter
how much timber they produce, have the tone of the autobahn,
constructed merely for efficiency.

The spring green carries me to mesquites at home and English
meadows. Apple and almond trees brighten the landscape with
blossoms. I realize now that a hundred years of labor by ten

million men with a million machines could not change the face of Germany as April suns and showers are changing it now.

I remember the first skylark I heard in Germany. I was at Nordholz, not far from the North Sea. I was walking across a piece of wasteland covered with a kind of salt grass. I heard a sound that I would have gladly listened to many times in England. I could not believe my ears. Then I saw a skylark rising while it trilled down the cascade of silver that so many English poets have made more lovely by their interpretations of it.

This skylark and its companions, for there were many larks rising, descending, skimming, and singing, seemed to me like aliens, there in Germany. They belong there, I know, as the grass and sky belong, but German song has not made the skylark and integral part of the German landscape as English song has made this lovely bird a part of the English landscape.

The sun is shining. Its warmth and light give hope, but the rays do not illuminate the future.

PART 8

Texas Needs Brains

While the profit-motivated are proclaiming themselves as sublime and are warring to suppress thought and intellect, prating on the Texas tradition becomes sawdusty.—JFD

Texas Needs Brains

N O TEXAN EVER FORGETS that his state is not only the largest in the Union but larger than all the New England states combined with New York, Pennsylvania, New Jersey, Delaware, Maryland, Virginia, and West Virginia.

It is, however, seldom compared to Siberia.

The territorial lines of Texas are man-made and the Texans, especially the native born, have never forgotten that they were once a nation unto themselves. Annually, Texas celebrates the independence she won over a hundred years ago, and constantly Texas denies the vote to the Negro.

Texas, with all of its acres and wealth from oil and beef, cotton and wheat, irrigated valleys of cantaloupes and citrus fruits, pine forests and lumber mills, shipping ports and banks, has not yet produced a poet, novelist, humanitarian, artist or thinker to be ranked as a great American.

Somehow, during the period of "manifest destiny," people of Texas, especially manifest males, began bragging on themselves as "rugged individualists." Texas has indeed produced plenty of highly flavored individualists—noted in these whirling days for their blindness to change and sympathy for corporations over people.

Some of the loudest shouters for "individuality" are flunkey-natured echoers of banality, just as some of the loudest advertisers of their own piety are the cheapest hypocrites. The only kind of "individualism" they recognized or desired was conformity with themselves—and their own prejudices.

Unless freedom of enterprise includes freedom of intellectual enterprise, that form of enterprise cannot sustain, much less extend, liberty. Liberty means liberty of mind as much as it means liberty to make a profit.

Texas needs less boasting on itself and more intelligent consideration. Texas bragging that goes no deeper than the imitation felt of a big hat is as short on thought as it is on originality—and the truth is, most Texas boasts are pure plagiarisms. People without imagination should never boast, unless they want to be taken for bores.

The fact is, Texas needs brains.

True Patriots and
Pappy O'Daniel

W. Lee "Pappy" O'Daniel* was a flour peddler who became a leading radio personality in Texas during the 1930s. Known as "Pass the Biscuits, Pappy," he perfected flatulent appeals to Texas pride while affecting homespun virtues. His popular appeal launched him into the governor's mansion and, later, the US Senate.

Dobie recognized O'Daniel as "a sleazy pious fraud," and he attacked O'Daniel several times in his newspaper columns and in speeches. In 1946, Pappy announced a $75,000 libel suit in response to Dobie's remarks. The case went nowhere, and eventually the majority of voters came to agree with Dobie. By the time O'Daniel left office in 1948, his senate colleagues openly shunned him and his approval rating in Texas had sunk to just 7 percent.—SD

S OME MEN NEVER develop mentally. Senator "Pappy" O'Daniel is one of them, though one might speculate on what effect army life would have had on him had he not been so successful in keeping out of it during the last war.

He has never shown an iota of knowledge or care concerning the grave crisis that liberty and civilization are facing. According to Sen. O'Daniel, the war is virtually over—despite the fact that we have as yet not taken one inch of the territory seized by

---

*The Coen Brothers' 2000 film, *O Brother, Where Art Thou?*, features a huckstering politician named Pappy O'Daniel, loosely based on the actual figure.

Japan. Despite the fact that the Germans are still deep in Russia. Despite the fact that the Germans and Italians are still undefeated in Africa. Despite the fact that the Germans go on with their rule of terror in the conquested countries where they have killed hundreds of thousands of citizens.

Sen. O'Daniel never discussed the war before he entered the senate, never appeared to recognize the fact that the lives and liberties of the whole world were at stake.

Explaining that he knew better than the military men how to conduct military affairs, Politician O'Daniel's first vote in the senate was against continuing the draft. And he hardly sees any reason for bringing the war into discussion now.

When Sen. O'Daniel went around the state a few weeks ago, repeating over and over, and pleasing many people by his prophecy that "there ain't gonna be no gas rationing," he showed about as much conception of what total war means as a four-year-old child just learning to pronounce its words plainly.

As governor, he prated for more than two years about his love for the aged, the poor, the mothers, and the children of Texas. Then, underground, he demonstrated that while he was the poor's elector he was the rich man's governor.

A man may be cunning, like a coyote, though ignorant. If he does not realize his ignorance on certain matters and is not willing to trust leaders who do know and then in addition uses power to block them, he is a dangerous man.

Alas, we are a long and bloody and terrible way yet from that blissful state in which biscuits form the only proper subject for the junior senator from Texas.

Only a Man with Eyes in
the Back of His Head . . .

At our mother's home in Beeville for Christmas, my brother Elrich gave me some advice. I always like to listen to Elrich. He told me to quit being critical of affairs of state and society and go back to cows, cow horses, bob wire, roadrunners, and a thousand other items in the tradition of Texas.

He might be right. I don't want to be personal, but a man's bound to think these days. I'm going to try to keep the dust out of my eyes, so that I can see the main target. I want to see whether the target is the good of mankind, the freedoms, or just greed.—JFD

SOMETHING OVER A hundred years ago Davy Crockett of Tennessee killed 105 bears in one season and the next summer got elected to congress on his reputation. Littler men have been elected for smaller reasons since.

Crockett looked wise but later confessed that he did not know any more about the judiciary than a hog knows about a sidesaddle. Because of his picturesqueness, he cut something of a swath in politics.

The national government was at that time, compared with the present, as simple as the setting up of a backwoods homestead. All a man had to do was to find a wife, squat on free land, build a cabin out of tree logs, kill his meat out of the woods, raise a little corn and a few pumpkins. It cost Crockett about $10 to furnish his cabin.

There was land fertile and free for everybody who wanted it.

The government had not yet begun its policy of subsidizing railroad companies with the 158 million acres of land—an area about the size of Texas—a wonderful catalyst for free enterprise among railroad magnates headquartered in Washington. The government had hardly begun its policy of protective tariffs that was the make the great manufacturing enterprises free to reach into the pockets of the poorest farmers.

The great American forests stood in their pristine nobility and waved their beautiful tops over tens of millions of acres of land as yet untouched by the free enterprisers who were to turn them into deserts, regardless of the effects on erosion, on floods, on soil owned by farmers, and without regard to national needs for timber in the next generation—without regard to anything but booming profits for the free enterprisers themselves.

So far as an ordinary citizen was concerned, there might almost have been no government. No foreign power threatened us. Although there was slavery, in a way the white citizens of America were nearly as free of control as were the great herds of mustang horses, descended from escaped Spanish stock, grazing on the free grass of coastal prairies and high plains.

The free grass and free soil were conducive to free enterprise. Then, about ten years before the century ended, there was no longer either free grass or free soil to speak of. The free mustangs that had tossed their heads so wild and beautiful on the free grass had been killed and roped off by men who wanted to use the grass. The mighty herds of buffaloes that once moved on the great sea of grass as primordially as the winds were all but annihilated.

Only a man with eyes in the back of his head could expect now to return to free grass and free soil normalcy.

While the century was approaching its end, a great drought caused widespread distress among settlers on western lands that had but recently been grazed by mustangs and buffaloes. Congress voted an appropriation to relieve the distressed. President Grover Cleveland vetoed the appropriation with the observation that it was the business of the people to support the government and not the business of the government to support the people.

The great corporations that had so long been beneficiaries of government enforced tariffs to "protect" the goods they manufactured piously agreed with the president.

Meanwhile, the country was striding in seven league boots to become what it is today—technically and mechanically the most highly developed and most abundantly supplied in the world. The man with the hoe, regarded from times immemorial as "brother to the ox," must follow the science of soils and cultivation if he is to reap profit from what he sows. The banker who used to do nothing but sit in his counting house a-counting out his money must now know how to obey and how to get around several volumes of tax laws, must be prepared to administer estates so complicated that they would stump a Philadelphia lawyer, and he is enough of an economist to look with contempt on political charlatans who try to laugh the science of economics out of existence.

We laugh at the alphabetical combinations that indicate government bureaucracies. I hold no brief for bureaucracy, but it seems to me that in the army there are as many alphabetical combinations representing technical operations as there are in the government. Think of how much more a crew of one of those Flying Fortresses must know and how much more they must coordinate than the driver of a Ford truck. Then think how much more there is to a truck than there was to an old-time cart in Davy Crockett's day.

We became a machine-geared, technical-scientific world quite a while ago. We accepted it for every part of life except for politics and government. We still favor a Davy Crockett who killed 105 bears in one season, and though he does not know the judiciary from Adam's off-ox, we will elect him to make laws that not even a wise judiciary could serve the country from.

We elect to the US senate a conscious ignoramus* who cannot

---

*Dobie is referring to Senator W. Lee "Pappy" O'Daniel of Texas, though of course his description fits any number of politicians over the generations.

give a single concrete fact about democracy, who has not the least conception of the constitution, who had never even in imagination guessed at the far-reaching and intricate effects of tariffs, whose sole interest in two world wars has been to avoid service in the first and then to complain about rationing during the second.

It is infantile to go back to Normalcy Harding's motto, "Less government in business and more business in government." The government is going to stay in business because it is the people's business. I had rather fish than think, but if I go fishing anywhere inland in America I'll be fishing for fish planted and controlled by government agencies. Wishing for the simple old days will not bring them back. We had a simple government when we had a simple life. A complex government is required to coordinate and balance the maze of complexities in our increasingly complicated and technical world.

Maybe someday the whole structure of scientifically mechanized civilization will topple over and we will wear fig leaves again in apple orchards instead of electrically heated suits to keep us warm in the stratosphere where the air we breathe comes out of tanks. Until then, the wisdom in government will depend on science—on knowledge.

It is sweet to sing "The Old-Time Religion," but religion by itself cannot manage this tangled world.

Dobie on Civil Rights

It is almost impossible today to fully appreciate Dobie's courage on civil rights. He singlehandedly integrated the Texas Folklore Society in the 1920s and ensured that a promising Mexican American folklorist, Jovita González, became president of the TFS in 1930—a breathtaking accomplishment at the time for a Mexican American woman. He brought aboard the TFS's first African American, J. Mason Brewer, in 1934—some twenty years prior to Brown v. Board.

Throughout the 1940s and much of the 1950s, Dobie was virtually the only major public figure in Texas to openly and fully support civil rights, and he was far ahead of "liberal" politicians of the era.

His public appeals for integration cost him his job at the University of Texas. He lost many readers, fans, and friends as a result of his stands, but he accepted such developments with equanimity. He knew that the rest of humanity would eventually catch up with him.—SD

DOBIE HAS "ABSOLUTELY NO OBJECTION" TO SEEING NEGROES ATTENDING UNIVERSITY
(from the *Austin Statesman*, March 19, 1945)
    "I personally would have absolutely no objection to seeing Negroes attend the University of Texas," J. Frank Dobie, University of Texas professor and author, said Sunday night speaking to a negro audience at the I. M. Terrell negro high school.
DOBIE FLAILED IN HOUSE AND SENATE
(from the *Austin Statesman*, March 20, 1945)
    Representative Jo Ed Winfree, Houston, opened

the attack on Dobie in the House of Representatives in a "personal privilege" denunciation. Representative J. B. Sallas, Crockett, followed with the suggestion that regents release Dobie from his employment at the state university and let him go to the faculty of Samuel Huston negro college in Austin.

Lieutenant Governor John Lee Smith said Dobie's attitude was not surprising. "More than a year ago," Smith said, "I publicly asserted that there was a definite move on foot to bring about social equality with the negro race in the South and that the movement was being encouraged by certain university people.

"This was vehemently denied at the time but Dobie's statement proves my assertion to be based on truth. Should the negro be admitted to the university, of necessity he would be admitted to the various social activities of the school."

"Irresponsible statements of this nature by a university professor do immeasurable harm and can create strife and discord between races."

❖ ◎ ❖

Time to End Injustice (March 18, 1945)
By J. Frank Dobie
It is entirely possible, you know, to refuse to face the future, and to spend one's energies trying to restore the past—as if the living world were a museum of mummies.

About two weeks ago the president of Samuel Huston college in Austin informed me that the institution he represents is sponsoring an open discussion on "America Faces the Future." The president asked me if I would be one of three men, the other two being Raphael Weiner of Austin and Melvin B. Tolson,* professor of Wiley college at Marshall, to lead the "town hall" discussion.

I accepted the invitation and have now experienced two

*Melvin B. Tolson was later immortalized in the 2007 film *The Great Debators*, starring Oscar-winning actor Denzel Washington.

meetings, in San Antonio and Austin. Each was in a Negro church, with a sprinkling of white attendants, among them several soldiers. After each discussion there is a reception with light refreshments at which the men on the program and members of the audience who care to attend get a chance to speak with each other.

What has struck me most forcibly is the serious, decorous, and altogether reasonable way in which Negro citizens, both men and women, are eager to assume responsibilities as well as the privileges of enfranchisement. In working, often in owning property, in paying taxes, in teaching and in learning in their own schools, in military service, where they fight and die like white soldiers.

The word "inspiring" has been so overused and so cheaply used that I seldom use it. However, it has been truly inspiring to me to look into the faces of hundreds of Negroes, and to realize that these people want to help their country as well as themselves by cooperating, by informing themselves, by thinking. I do not see how any fair-minded person who honestly faces the future can be otherwise than glad that the Negroes are coming to have a better chance in this land so boastful of being the home of the free.

Both common decency and self-interest must make all individuals who really prize freedom wish freedom for other individuals.

❖ ◎ ❖

From Dobie's speech at an NAACP-sponsored event in 1946:

To some Texans anybody who advocates Negro education is a "damned Communist." I will say right here that I am not a Communist and that instead of wanting Communism in this country I want democracy.

So long as American citizens in Texas advocate only what Jesus Christ taught and what the constitutions, both state and national, stipulate, our government will never be in danger from Communists.

It is a terrible thing to condemn a human being to ignorance, to deny him opportunities to enlighten himself and his fellow beings. It is terrible not only for him but for those who do the denying.

I am for admitting Negroes qualified for higher education to the University of Texas. And I am for admitting them at once. Such Negroes would find a welcome among a surprisingly large proportion of students.

It is only decent to act justly right now. I am for free minds and free people. I am for democracy.

Evolution is on Our Side

I write from a plot of ground, delightful in itself, at the University of Texas in Austin. Here on this campus, believers in the right as well as the duty to think are combating a gang of fascist-minded regents: oil millionaires, corporation lawyers, a lobbyist, and a politician, who in anachronistic rage against liberal thought malign all liberals as "communists." They try with physical power to wall out ideas and resort to chicanery as sickening as it is cheap.

The Board of Regents at the University of Texas are as much concerned with free intellectual enterprise as a razorback sow would be with Keats' "Ode to a Grecian Urn." —JFD

I CANNOT CONCEIVE of a society hospitable to ideas and intellectual activity that is also at the same time dead set against liberal thought.

A liberal questions; he searches; he studies facts; he tries to interpret these facts. He knows that society is in a constant state of change, that the processes of evolution operate in society just as surely as they operate in the biological world.

People hospitable to liberal ideas will certainly not all agree on any conclusion, but they will not want to annihilate a man who does not agree with them. The man who first demonstrated that the earth is round was very much abused, but that did not keep the earth flat.

This liberal may be constitutionally averse to change; he often is; but he is rational enough to understand that the principle of life is adaptability to change. The American passenger pigeons that once darkened the skies by their flights of millions are now extinct; they could not adapt themselves to the presence of "civilized" man. The coyote once restricted to the plains country west of the Mississippi now catches chickens in Alabama and howls on the Yukon River. He adapted himself.

The liberal perceives changes and tries to think out wise ways by which society can adapt itself to those changes. He is open-minded. When he ceases to question, to examine, he ceases to be a liberal.

His opposite is the reactionary. The reactionary is devoted to the idea of perpetuating petrifaction. He is a theorist, of course. His theory is that somebody away back yonder found the final answer, perfected the final form, and that all questioners of what he regards as final are heretics and ought to be burned.

Often, he is ready to die for his quixotic theory. It is his wisdom, not his sincerity, that concerns us. Hell is paved with good intentions. History has many instances of generations and nations that have perished in the struggle to perpetuate petrifaction.

The mirage of the reactionaries now getting into their saddles all over America, in Texas and the South especially, is that this country can go back to the "normalcy" that flowered in Harding's administration and became chaff in Hoover's. These mirage-led realists think that if they can just get rid of the New Deal, branch and root, then we can have again all the blessings of our often spoken-of forefathers.

The way to kill the Great Dream of the Freedoms is to make the people believe that the Roosevelt administration is nothing but another name for socialism, to blind them to the ideals for the Common Man that have been so eloquently set forth. The mirage they are following is a picture of the golden age of Standard Oil.

Those who oppose progressive change for the good of all are like the old-time fellow who lived by a boghole in an unpaved public road. He got a dollar each time he pulled out an automobile from the boghole with his team of mules. He did not want public funds to be used to pave the road. That, he said, would interfere with his free enterprise. He condemned the idea as socialism.

It takes more power of thought to meet change than to make

it. Eli Whitney's invention of the cotton gin made the Civil War inevitable. Compared with the amplitude and nobility of Lincoln in mastering the Civil War, Eli Whitney's genius measures no higher than a tinker's.

No mechanical propeller of society into a higher standard of physical living—Thomas Edison, Henry Ford, and so on—has evidenced any power of intellect toward the conduct of society amid resulting change.

To make machines, money, wealth, and war successfully entails a trivial exercise of the intellect compared with the wisdom required to meet the problems machines, money, wealth, and war bring to society.

The haters of Franklin Roosevelt have never comprehended that he did not so much make changes as recognize them, to lead peoples to see them more clearly and force governments and worshippers of the status quo to adjust themselves to changes. Roosevelt has been adjusting to modern, industrial, highly complex times in the democracy that took form in America in very simple, agricultural times. His adjustments have meant the extension of democracy.

Spokesmen preaching the gospel of free enterprise cry out that the Tennessee Valley Authority—and also the Lower Colorado River Authority in Texas—are socialistic. A lot of things that used to be regarded as socialistic are now taken for granted as part of American democracy. Name calling will not halt evolution. If government electricity from government dams over the Tennessee River is socialism, very well, let it be socialism.

I have never heard of a man with wide views harming his country. The history of every country is dark with the harm that has come from ingrowing, short-range, provincial views.

The most heartening thought that liberals can enjoy is that evolution is on their side. It would be contrary to the law of life if the mass movements of mankind over the centuries were not toward liberty. People who distrust change, who distrust democracy, who distrust ideas always rely on and worship mediocrity. The cold fact is that they cannot find eager, active minds accepting the theory of petrifaction. Consequently, they put mediocre minds in power. Mediocre leadership may thwart evolution for a time, though they can never direct it when the deluge comes.

It is not so much a duty to be a liberal as it is profitable and a pleasure. A liberal who gives up because the majority is not with him misunderstands existence.

In this time of one-world interdependence and of complexities that relate the price of oil and the wages of drugstore clerks in Houston to affairs in Iran, the best governed country must be that country whose leaders are best informed on vast complexities and who have rare powers of thought to arrive at wise conclusions. In the realm of human relations no leader can approach greatness who does not comprehend the inevitability of change.

The law of life is movement, and movement is motivated by hope. If the hope is blind, then the movement accomplishes nothing. If the hope is guided by powerful intellect and noble character, the movement is toward freedom and justice for all.

On Censorship

Of late, some people seem to consider that the chief reason for advocating libraries and the reading of books is to enable America to catch up with the Russians on sputniks. I consider such reasoning puny and lopsided. Books, and therefore libraries, contain the inherited wit, wisdom, humor, life, cream of all the jests of all the centuries during which humanity has left a record of what it's thought and done. The "immortal residue" of the human race lies in books. The great reason for reading books and for valuing libraries is to live life more abundantly, to think more justly, to be in love more delightfully, and to use the sputniks more wisely when we get them.—JFD

THE BOOK BURNERS are rising again—the John Birchers, the Minute Women, and the other fanatics who fear vitality and intelligence and seek to perpetuate petrification.

Now they've taken twelve books off the shelves at Amarillo. An objector in Houston calls for removing Nathaniel Hawthorne's *The Scarlet Letter* from the school library. Another objector in another school wants Plato's *Republic* seized. At Baylor, Eugene O'Neill's play, "Long Day's Journey into Night," has been suppressed.

It seems that people who like to live at ease in this world—and I'm among them—are not nearly so obstreperous in making objections as the zealots are. An individual can be a patriot and still have an idea of "Americanism" different from the idea of a censor. Any person who imagines he has a corner on patriotism and wants to suppress all conceptions to the contrary is a bigot and an enemy to the people.

Words objected to in modern books abound in many old books. D. H. Lawrence's *Lady Chatterley's Lover* and Henry Miller's *Tropic of Cancer* have the four-letter words, all right, but I did not encounter in them any words that I had not already learned from older boys when I was growing up in a religious country community in the nineteenth century. I've been hearing the words ever since. I probably got more of that language out of Chaucer, who wrote toward 600 years ago, than out of any other writer. I don't believe that either hearing them or reading them has changed my way of looking at life much.

So why all this hocus-pocus, holier-than-thou piety in considering a book that has a four-letter word in it? It's as sad as you can get in this world where we have such a short time to enjoy ourselves. It's not realistic words but realistic ideas that the holy patriots object to. Think of being penned up with a bunch of censors and then having to read what they and their kind would leave in a book!

Ignorance is one of the chief evils of the world; exposure to all sorts of books mitigates it. Censorship is never to let people know but always to keep them in ignorance; never to bring light but to always darken.

School history textbooks are the newest target. The more censoring of textbooks, the weaker they become. Some of the "patriots" want to go back and have textbooks that specialize in battles and elections. Historians understand now that nine-tenths of history is social history—it's about people. I think we are better off with histories about people who change, even change their minds sometimes, than with histories about generals riding white horses.

No use kidding ourselves—schoolchildren aren't fools. They don't live in vacuums. They're not going to be much influenced by dull propaganda, tail-twisting, and flag-raising put into a textbook.

The legislature now wants Texas textbooks to emphasize "our glowing and throbbing history of hearts and souls inspired by wonderful American principles and traditions." If you get so much throbbing and inspiration in textbooks, you're not going to get knowledge. The only safe book with them is one lacking in vitality. To them safety lies in dull minuses, and that's what the schoolchildren of Texas are going to get in textbooks if they are printed to pass the patriotic censors.

I am for textbooks selected on the basis of strength, of vividness, of justice, and the beautiful. I believe that teachers of cultivated minds and tastes should pass on readers and histories with the idea that the books should be readable.

In Jefferson's words, "Error of opinion may be tolerated where reason is left free to combat it." All we're asking is to leave reason free. Nobody can know what all the errors are. Wisdom will not die with us.

PART 9

Life and Literature of the Southwest

While I am in one world it is forever my fate to hear the music of the other: in the university I am a wild man; in the wilds I am a scholar and a poet.—JFD

Professional Educators and the "Unctuous Elaboration of the Obvious"

The average PhD thesis is nothing but a transference of bones from one graveyard to another.—JFD

I CAME TO THE UNIVERSITY OF TEXAS as instructor in English in the fall of 1914. I was twenty-six years old and had just taken an M.A. degree at Columbia University, but the University of Texas seemed as fresh to me, as I look back now, as Southwestern University at Georgetown seemed when I entered it as a freshman in 1906. The enrollment was around twenty-two hundred. It wasn't hard for an instructor to come to know most of the teaching staff.

The head of the English Department was Dr. Morgan Callaway Jr. During a conversation with him not long after I started teaching, he informed me that having thought through a subject he had not yet found himself wrong in an opinion. As head dictator of the department he had found virtually no underling worthy of promotion to full professor—his own rank. He was a genuine scholar and an intellectual disciplinarian, but he didn't believe in a mere instructor having enough free time or enough money to get worldly minded.

I never pleased Dr. Callaway more than one time when I referred to Thomas Nelson Page's essay on the decay of manners. That was a favorite subject with him—the decay of manners.

Dr. Callaway generally carried a parasol and a bag of books and papers. He always tipped his hat to an acquaintance or friend even if it were necessary to deposit a part of his burden on the ground in order to have a free hand. Of course, everybody tipped his hat to Dr. Callaway.

A landmark on the campus at the time was Judge Simpkins, professor of law. He had been in the Confederate Army and wore his white hair and beard long and flowing. I never heard of his saying anything interesting beyond addressing his law students as "My Young Jackasses."

Shortly after Judge Simpkins died, Dr. Callaway told me that he was now bereft of somebody to reverence. He said he had reverenced his father and that Judge Simpkins had been a man to reverence at the university—solely on account of his seniority, I deduced. It was evident that Dr. Callaway thought young instructors could do no better than reverence himself.

Another character on the campus was Judge Townes, dean of the Law School. He also belonged to Civil War times. He was not flamboyant in the way that Judge Simpkins was; he was firm and kind but in thought belonged to the past century. He didn't believe in public schools. In his opinion nobody should be taxed to educate the children of another man. The words "creeping socialism" had not yet come into use, but Judge Townes considered the public school system too socialistic for individual rights.

❖   ◉   ❖

The university in 1914–15 listed forty-seven courses in Education. A state law—promulgated by the Education hoaxers—required credit for nine hours of their pabulum in order to get a teacher's certificate. When I had been in college and decided to become a teacher I signed up for a course in Education. Any moron who slept through the classes could have got the credit. I learned, in nine months, to open the schoolroom windows if it was warm and to close them if it was cold.

E. C. Barker, professor of history at the University of Texas and master of sardonic realism, used to define Education as "the unctuous elaboration of the obvious." He claimed this to be a

quotation from somebody else, but in popularizing the definition got credit for originating it. I have quoted him and in turn
received credit for originality.

The majority of these professional "Educators," their minds
dulled by quackery and prevented by quackery from becoming
cultivated in a civilized way, develop into quacks themselves. I
have never encountered one possessed of a first-class mind,
though I have encountered a few fairly good ones. Many are dull
well-meaners, cunning climbers, and exponents of the paltry.
They take theatricality for humanity and banal moralisms for
thought. Dullness in schoolbooks is not boresome to them; dullness is their trade; it is safer than vitality.

All the public school superintendents and a great many college presidents hold degrees in Education. They are Johnny-on-
the-spot with Rotary Club optimism, football teamwork, Dedica-
tion-to-America Week, and such as that. Nearly all of them are
stuffed with religiosity—which is not a religion. The conception
of education held by too many superintendents is mostly limited
to what can be bought with money—buildings and equipment, to
winning athletic teams, and patriotic palaver. They are as mouthy
on patriotism as on religion. They seem to presume that love of
country can be legislated into effect.

Considering their contribution of flabbiness rather than of
fiber to the minds of tens of millions of Americans during the
twentieth century, I accuse them of having been far more lethal
enemies to society than all the Communists dreamed up by the
late Senator Joe McCarthy along with all the Communists put
down in his books by FBI Hoover.

❖ ◎ ❖

Journalism, as an agent of learning, is on a par with Education
spelled with a capital E. There was no journalism department at
the University of Texas in 1914, and few suffered its absence. Then
as now the best newspaper writers depended on natural intelligence, cultivation of the art of composing words, and knowledge
gained outside of all journalism classes.

Courses in Journalism prevent students, by taking up their

time, from studying economics, history, biology, anthropology, languages, English literature, and other subjects that fortify the mind. What a journalist needs is intelligence, and an educated mind, and mastery of the craft of writing. He can't get any of these from courses in journalism.

A big university has to have big buildings, of course. I doubt that the intellectual content of any journalism instructor has been advanced by moving into a million-dollar building that often makes me think of the old saying about a forty-dollar saddle on a twenty-dollar horse.

❖ ◎ ❖

As the Teutonic Ph.D. system was adopted by American universities—in strong contrast to its disregard by British and French universities—vitality was smothered, strangled, starved out. For the wardens of pure scholarship in the English Department at the University of Texas, the standard resided in the Teutonic Ph.D. system—bent on solidifying the spirit of literature into studies of grammar and form.

These Ph.D. theses and Ph.D.-istic "studies" and other lucubrations make the publications of the Modern Language Association among the dullest ponderosities on earth. For those university presses that took them on they proved to be very expensive— and not much more respected by the able-minded than other vanity printings.

The one thing needful to all scholarship, as to all literature and art, is vitality.

If the choice were necessary—but with all the great literature of the world available it never will be—I guess I'd prefer sterile fact imbedded in Teutonic turgidity over hot air piped out in the form of Professional Educators and other banalities.

Pure history, also Teutonic derived, is a naked collection of documented facts. If the facts are patterned into pictures or directed into conclusions, purity is defiled. Yet I am more appreciative of pure historians than I once was. Most of them are teachers, and while they may not open windows they do not shrink intellects—like political school superintendents and academic flunkies of material power. Pure historians seek truth and discipline minds, and the pure histories they write are profitable to consulters.

Nevertheless, excellence in historical writing comes only when interpretative power, just evaluation, controlled imagination, and craftsmanship are added to mastery of facts.

❖　◎　❖

At the University of Texas, I eventually came among the Doctors of Philosophy on the so-called "Budget Council," responsible for the hiring, firing, and promoting of teachers in the English Department. At those meetings, I never heard any consideration given to a teacher's intellect, wit, love of beauty, urbanity, or any other concomitant of what is generally considered a civilized person. The emphasis was always on what he was "producing in the scholarly field," with little emphasis on the quality of production.

A teacher's power to communicate to his classes ideas and a passion for literature had virtually no weight with the Sanhedrin. I nearly always went away from these meetings, and also from any of the few meetings of the General Faculty that I attended, depressed and remembering Keats's "inhuman dearth of noble natures."

Yet I know plenty of professors whom I like and whose company I enjoy. It is the professors who think like academicians that give me the fantods.

The proper business of English teachers—or teachers of any other literature for that matter—is not to teach pupils to make a living but to lead them to more abundant living even amid the daily round of doings.

This assertion implies no hostility to the teaching of trades, techniques, and professional skills. It is a recognition of the potentiality in most human beings for a fuller life.

Many times the teacher must groan to herself or himself, "I have piped unto you and ye have not danced." But always there are some who had rather see than remain blind. Always there are reachers for the stars and yearners after the high and lovely.

On the Texas
Institute of Letters

The county-mindedness, asinine jingoism, and plutocratic ignorance that the name Texan has come to connote in many quarters will hardly make any writer now living in Texas who takes literature seriously feel complimented at being disposed of as "a Texas writer," any more than Emerson could ever have been labeled as merely a "Massachusetts writer."—JFD

I HAD NO PART in organizing the Texas Institute of Letters. Somehow I once felt averse to writer organizations. Nor have I ever thought writers' colonies strengthening to their colonists. Among good minds iron sharpeneth iron, but in coterie-colonies, rust generally rusteth iron.

On the other hand, after work all through a prolonged morning, a light lunch, maybe a light nap, physical exercise, and tending to odds and ends until "The Hour," and then supper, no writer could live more abundantly than in conversation with genial, mind-playing companions, whether writers or not.

The Texas Institute of Letters has evolved into an institution to which various Texas writers, I among them, feel increasing allegiance and owe increasing debts. We are debtors to any institution or person that raises the level of civilization and enlightenment.

The Texas Institute of Letters has acquired the kind of substantiality that only tradition can give an institution. While sponsoring writing within the realm of Texas, the Texas Institute of

Letters would hardly now advocate a writer or a book solely on geographic accidence—or incidence.

The forces to make Texas idolize physical properties and ignore, even condemn, intellectual properties need no support from the Texas Institute of Letters. The more anti-materialistic, anti-conformistic, and anti-chauvinistic this Institute is, the more nobly Texan it will be.

Along the Devil's River—
and Away from
the Cedar Pollen

Here I am living for a few weeks alone in a cottage furnished with an electric stove overlooking the Devil's River Lake, about twenty-five miles northwest of Del Rio. There are no cedars in these rocky hills. Otherwise I would not be here and away from the pollinating, hay-fever-giving hills of Austin.—JFD

T HIS IS SAID to make one of the best sheep and goat ranges in America. Del Rio calls itself the wool capital of the world. Most of the landowners here are against government interference in business, but all of them are for the government's maintaining a guarantee on wool prices and for putting up the old tariffs to prevent the importation of wool.

There are no coyotes in this country and there are many government trappers employed to keep any from coming in. Coyote eat some sheep, but the sheep in reality are vanquishing not only all coyotes, but all wild cats, all eagles, most of the grass, and nearly everything else but sheep raisers' bank accounts.

The two lakes on the Devil's River are made by government dams built twenty years ago for flood control and the manufacture of electric power. The public is free to fish in the waters, but the fish, in my limited experience, seem determined to stay where they are. The pleasure of fishing, anyhow, consists mostly in the exercise of the faculty of hope.

There are many coots, popularly called mud hens, on the lakes. They nest in the cattails bordering the water wherever the soil has been deposited on the rocks. They add greatly to the interest and charm of the lakes. They are protected by law, but I saw a young man shooting at them with a .22 rifle. He said they eat the feed that ducks like. His interest in ducks lies solely in killing them.

He also shot at a beautiful kingfisher. He said it ate minnows. His sole interest in minnows is using them for bait. Like Davy Crockett, his interest in nature comes altogether from being "wrathy to kill." My definition of a true sportsman is one who never kills anything except game or a proven predator.

Civilized man, so-called, is the most insatiable and pitiless of all predatory animals. It is his lack of a sense of humor and sense of fair play that makes him talk so piously about the virtue of killing the "blood-thirsty killers" of the world.

In truth there is nothing any more repulsive about the remains of a quail killed by a wild cat than there is about the bones of a quail on a plate in front of a lady sitting at a table lighted from silver candlesticks. The appetite of both animals is natural and healthy, and they are equally bloodthirsty. One wants the blood cooked; the other likes it raw.

As I contemplate life from my perch above the Devil's River, I expect to see the government go on protecting sheep against any potential predator, protecting home wool from foreign wool, protecting cattle from the hoof and mouth disease, protecting grapefruit grown in Dallas from whatever it is that those officials on the roads out of the Rio Grande Valley inspect and confiscate grapefruit against.

I don't, however, expect to see the government protect anybody from the deadly male cedars that, for some of us poor mortals, poison the air with their pollen.

Change, Change, Change

King Canute resented change and was ignorant of the processes of evolution. He tried to keep the tide from coming in by having it lashed with whips. I have belonged to a good many King Canute Clubs in my lifetime, none organized and the majority of them containing only one member.—JFD

LONG AFTER THE SAFETY RAZOR had become popular, I continued using an old-time strap and razor blade. Sometimes while strapping my razor and scraping the hair off my face in the dressing room of a Pullman car, I noticed users of electric safety razors regarding me as a curiosity. I was too strong against changing razors to care.

Likewise, I was fiercely opposed to the replacement of oilcloth curtains on automobiles by hard tops and glass windows. If you ask why, my answer is sheer ignorance and mule-headedness. I was used to one way and didn't want another way intruding.

I was as fiercely adamantine against a floor furnace in our house as I was against glass windows in an automobile. Had I been reared in a cave I should certainly have been against a home fire that did not fill the shelter with smoke—and would have used a club on any innovator trying to build a flue.

Until I was gray-haired, I still considered it unmanly to drink tea. Why? Because I grew up with men who drank coffee and did not drink tea. It took me a long time to change to tea on occasion.

My opposition was based on sheer ignorance and prejudice. All prejudices are forms of ignorance. I remember being disgusted with a man guest who sipped a glass of whiskey and water more slowly than a watched pot boils on a half-cold stove. Now I won't drink whiskey any way but slowly, but I was for the old-time way of downing a slug at one gulp. What a barbarity!

Recently my bank in Austin, a most excellent bank and most agreeable to me, printed my name on checks and gave me a number. I'm up in the neighborhood of 36 million. I know there aren't that many accounts in the bank, but I suppose they didn't want to start with anything under 36 million. I told my banker friend that I didn't like this change a bit, that I preferred old Ben Lilly's way of writing a check on a piece of brown paper, on a shingle, or on a piece of aspen bark. He said if I wanted to write a check on a shingle, the bank would cash it. Now I find that signing a check with my name already printed on it and with a number under the signature does not subtract any more from my bank balance than signing a shingle would subtract.

Perhaps my resentment of change in this instance, as in many others, was resentment against the increasing mechanization of life.

Meantime, the great clock ticks on at an increasingly accelerated rate. There have been more changes in farming since the advent of the tractor than there were in centuries preceding. Such changes betoken other changes and cause still more changes. A single man with machinery can now cultivate maybe twenty times as much land as a single man could cultivate in 1860.

Millions of people in America and in other countries go on calling aloud upon God every Sunday to "give us this day our daily bread." Concern over daily bread used to be common. Now for the vast majority of English-speaking people the daily bread is taken for granted along with water and air, though people work for it.

Comparatively few of them are as much worried about the next meal as with the next installment due on an automobile, a television set, or some other machine. I venture that more people in the United States are concerned with dieting than with getting enough to eat. The "daily bread" item in public prayer is obsolete, but the prayer won't be amended.

The fact that tens of millions of well-fed people have ceased to cry out of empty bellies to God for bread means that the farmer is receding as a power in economics and government. Laws in an attempt to keep him dominant will prove as futile as were laws passed earlier in this century to prevent automobiles from frightening horses off the road.

Change, change, change. I hear people constantly talking about how the morals of the country are going to the dogs. The son of an old-time cowman invited me by letter the other day to a meeting at which we good people would drink whiskey, get logged on barbecued meat, roll up our eyes, and lament the passing of those times when "a man's word was as good as his bond."

Living right now, I am confident, are just as many people whose words are as good as their bonds as ever lived. I know several of them.

Numerous young people of both sexes around me are a tonic to life and a golden promise for the future. Anybody familiar with human records must know that from the times when writing began until now, lamenters have moaned over the worsening of society.

Of course, things are terrible, but I doubt very much if they are more terrible than they were when knighthood was in flower and most citizens were serfs, or than they were when the church was so strong that heretics were burned for not being orthodox, or than they were when people were put in prison for debt, or when women scrubbed floors on their hands and knees, or when preachers all over the South used the Bible to "prove" that slavery was ordained by God.

There is a sickening amount of religiosity with us now, but the hypocrites always with us and always thriving on minds made credulous by orthodox theology probably do not comprise a higher percent of the population than they comprised in the last century.

Well, it's wonderful to realize that man is a part of evolving nature and not isolated from it like some imagined God. It's wonderful to reflect that during millenniums of changes the species while losing its tail has gained a little in brain power.

The hope of the humanity lies in evolution.

Two Texas Barbecues,
Sixty Years Apart

It may not seem a long way from a barbecue on the Nueces River in southern Live Oak County in the summer of 1903 to a barbecue on the Pedernales River west of Johnson City in the spring of 1963—but the events are worlds away from each other—and not just because the recent barbecue was hosted by Vice President Lyndon Johnson and his wife Lady Bird Johnson on the LBJ ranch.—JFD

WHEN I WAS A BOY in Live Oak County, ranch people of the region had a picnic every summer under great live oak trees near what used to be Barlow's Ferry on the Nueces. The four main features of the barbecue were: (1) New tubs filled with lemonade around great chunks of ice that sold at 5 cents a glass—a big glass at that—and took whatever nickels I had. (2) The barbecuing of beeves over big pits. (3) Tournament running in which the rider who speared the most rings received a new saddle as a prize. (4) The musicians.

These musicians were two, sometimes three, Mexicanos with a fiddle and guitar. They didn't sing as I recall. They stood and played near the wonderful tubs of ice cold lemonade. They played "La Golondrina," "Over the Waves," and other waltzes. I didn't want to hear anything else. I heard nothing else, and for days and nights after this barbecue the strains of the music would haunt me.

There would also be a few Mexicano workers around the barbecue in addition to the working musicians. At that period nobody thought of calling a Mexicano anything else than a Mexican unless it was some derogatory word. "Latin American" and "Mexican American" was decades away.

Far more Mexican American families than Anglo-American families lived on the ranches, but no Mexicanos except the musicos and the laborers would be at the barbecue. No Mexican American could go into a restaurant or an ice cream parlor at Beeville, twenty miles away, and sit down with what were called white people to refresh himself.

Yet his music and his lore were then accepted as part of the cultural inheritance of the country. The Mexicanos' contributions in music, song, story, history, and labor—especially as vaquero anteceding cowboy—entered into the life of English-speaking Texas people long before the Mexican Americans themselves were allowed to enter into that life. Individuals of Mexican descent now teach at the University of Texas. In 1903 very few indeed attended the University of Texas. In many towns, Mexican American schoolchildren were segregated.

We come now to the barbecue in April 1963 on the LBJ ranch. It honored delegates to the United Nations from twenty-five countries scattered over the two hemispheres. These UN delegates spoke Portuguese, Spanish, English, Norwegian, Romanian, Japanese, Congolese, Arabian, Turkish, and other languages. They were in every color of humanity.

To this cosmopolitan barbecue came as invited guests several civilian Negroes and Mexican Americans of Texas. I met Porfirio Salinas, landscape artist of San Antonio. Mrs. Dobie and I sat at the table with Vice President Johnson and M. J. and Ada Anderson, civil rights leaders from Austin. Henry Gonzales, congressman from San Antonio, and his wife came to the LBJ Ranch before escorting the UN people to a welcome in San Antonio.

I suppose that some of the Texas legislators and senators now passing a law prohibiting the flying of the United Nations flag on any property owned by the state of Texas would not have felt at ease at the LBJ barbecue. Nor would many John Birchers. Some of them might have felt more at ease at a Ku Klux Klan barbecue.

Change is ceaseless; evolution is forward.

Upon reflection, I had a far brighter time at this barbecue on the LBJ Ranch than I had drinking ice cold lemonade when it was an annual treat only at barbecues on the Nueces River in Live Oak County sixty years ago.

The Writer and His Region

Writers will always be listening for the rhythms of their living places.
Whatever the rhythm of our part of the earth is, not one of us will catch
it unless we can sometimes sit in "wise passiveness" and hear "tidings
of invisible things."—JFD

I HAVE HEARD SO MUCH silly bragging by Texans that I now think it would be a blessing to themselves—and a relief to others—if the braggers did not know they lived in Texas.

Good writing about any region is good only to the extent that it has universal appeal. Texans are the only "race of people" known to anthropologists who do not depend on breeding for propagation. Like princes and lords, they can be made by "breath," plus a big white hat—which comparatively few Texans wear. A beef stew by a cook in San Antonio, Texas, may have a different flavor from that of a beef stew cooked in Pittsburgh, Pennsylvania, but the essential substances of potatoes and onions, with some suggestion of beef, are about the same, and geography has no effect on their digestibility.

Regionalism's blanket has been put over a great deal of worthless writing. A writer—a regional writer, if that term means anything—will whenever he matures exercise the critical faculty. Mere glorification is on the same intellectual level as silver tongues and jukebox music.

The hope of regional literature lies in out-growing regionalism itself. Nobody should specialize on provincial writings before he has the perspective that only a good deal of good literature and wide history can give. I think it more important that a dweller in the Southwest read *The Trial and Death of Socrates* than all the books extant on killings by Billy the Kid.

One of the chief impediments to amplitude and intellectual freedom is provincial inbreeding. I am sorry to see writings of the Southwest substituted for noble and beautiful and wise literature to which all people everywhere are inheritors. When I began teaching "Life and Literature of the Southwest" I did not regard these writings as a substitute. To reread most of them would be boresome, though Hamlet, Boswell's Johnson, Lamb's Essays, and other genuine literature remain as quickening as ever.

A true culture, beyond the sociological use of the word, is always informed by intellect. The American populace has been taught to believe that the more intellectual a professor is, the less common sense he has; nevertheless, if American democracy is preserved it will be preserved by thought and not by physics.

Editors of all but a few magazines of the country and publishers of most of the daily newspapers cry out for brightness and vitality and at the same time shut out critical ideas. They want intellect, but want it petrified. Happily, the publishers of books have not yet reached that form of delusion. Unless a writer feels free, things will not come to him, he cannot burgeon on any subject whatsoever.

No sharp line of time or space, like that separating one century from another or the territory of one nation from that of another, can delimit the boundaries of any region to which any regionalist lays claim. Mastership, for instance, of certain locutions peculiar to the Southwest will take their user to the Aztecs, to Spain, and to the border of ballads and Sir Walter Scott's romances. I found that I could not comprehend the coyote as animal hero of Pueblo and Plains Indians apart from the Reynard of Aesop and Chaucer.

Among the qualities that any good regional writer has in common with other good writers of all places and times is intellectual integrity. Having it does not obligate him to speak out on all issues or, indeed, on any issue. He alone is to judge whether he will continue to sport with Amaryllis in the shade or forsake her to write his own Areopagitica.

Intellectual integrity expresses itself in the tune as well as in argument, in choice of words—words honest and precise—as well as in ideas, in fidelity to human nature and the flowers of the fields as well as to principles, in facts reported more than in deductions proposed. Though a writer may write on something as innocuous as the white snails that crawl up broomweed stalks and that roadrunners are wont to carry to certain rocks to crack and eat, his intellectual integrity, if he has it, will infuse the subject.

There is no higher form of art and, therefore, no higher form of patriotism than translating the features of the patria into forms of dignity, beauty, and nobility. Becoming a Philistine will not enable a man to interpret Philistinism, though Philistines who own big presses think so. Sinclair Lewis knew Babbitt as Babbitt could never know either himself or Sinclair Lewis.

Nothing is too trivial for art, but good art treats nothing in a trivial way. Nothing is too provincial for the regional writer, but he cannot be provincial-minded toward it. Luminosity is not stumbled into.

A Corner Forever Texas

Dobie's plea for "A Corner Forever Texas" was never embraced by the University of Texas. Instead, his vision eventually came to life at the Wittliff Collections at Texas State University in San Marcos, founded in 1986 by Bill and Sally Wittliff, who were inspired by Dobie. Housed atop the campus's main library, the Wittliff is a museum and archive that collects and preserves the papers of the Southwest's leading writers. In addition to hosting researchers, it also celebrates the "Spirit of Place" through exhibitions, public events, and books—including the book you are now holding.—SD

E VER SINCE THE University of Texas was established, there has been much talk about making it "a university of the first class." A good deal of the talk has been made by people who seem to think that if the university could get as many books in its library as Harvard has, as high a salary for its professors as Yale pays, as large a percentage of Ph.Ds in its faculty as Johns Hopkins catalogs, as much laboratory equipment as the Massachusetts Institute of Technology possesses, etc., all the "first class" requirements would be satisfied.

A really great university is something more than a successful ape. It has a character and an individuality peculiar to itself. In great universities like Oxford and the Sorbonne, this character is an expression of the civilization that the university both represents and influences.

An outstanding characteristic of a truly great university is that it belongs to its environment, as cypresses belong to the clear streams of Central Texas, as cottonwoods belong to the water courses of the West, as live oaks belong to limestone soil and post oaks to sandy soil.

Any form of civilization that has a distinguishing virtue must be an outgrowth from the native, a development of the inherent. How is it that the great and rich—for it is rich in many ways—University of Texas does not make the Texas Collection the jewel of its bibliographical possessions? The pride of California and of the University of California is the Bancroft Library, so rich in all that pertains to California.

Scholars teaching in the university with the hope of getting a higher bid from some other institution have done their best to make this Texas an imitation of Harvard, Johns Hopkins, or some other university far afield. By negation, neglect, lack of sympathy and knowledge, they have operated to starve out and smother down the native currents of life as they are preserved in Texas chronicles, traditions, and attitudes toward life.

The bent of much of so-called higher education in Texas has been toward Texas life and culture very much what the policy of the Indian Bureau of the United States long was toward Indians—make them cease to be what they are and become imitators of something they could never be.

The library of the University of Texas is probably comparatively richer in the fields of Shakespeare's age and of Alexander Pope's age than in the field of Texas. It is fine that we have these riches of another land. But why cannot the printed material representing the very life blood of Texas, the records of the soil of Texas and the people who have lived on that soil, be housed in a fitting way?

The Texas Collection should be as complete respecting Texas as the British Museum is respecting England. A corner eloquent, beautiful, interesting—a corner belonging to the land and expressive of it—a corner that would through its influence pervade the whole university and the whole state—a corner forever Texas.

When, several years ago now, I proposed to the professors of English in the University of Texas a course in the literature of

Texas and the Southwest, the proposal was refused with the reply that the Southwest had no literature. I then proposed a course in Life and Literature of the Southwest guaranteeing that we at least had life. The course has convinced me that there are thousands of young Texans becoming acutely conscious of their right to know more about their own cultural inheritance.

There might be a combination of rooms furnished in native woods, not forgetting the mesquite so characteristic of much of the land. The rooms would in their amplitude and simplicity express the spirit of Texas. It would be something that belonged to Texas, out of the past and for the delight of the future.

The influence of such a center for the Texas Collection is incalculable. The rooms would by their very nature invite students—and people also not registered as students—to linger and read. The influence would be felt in the nearly related fields of the South and the West.

Most of all, the Texas Collection, thus properly set off, would engender in the minds of the people of Texas, particularly the young people, an awareness of their own land, history, traditions, cultural inheritance. If education does not lead a person to view with interest and intelligence the phenomena of life about him, what function has it? The function of education is to relate people to their own environment.

It seems to me that other people living in the Southwest will lead fuller and richer lives if they become aware of what it holds.

If any great literature expressive of Texas and the Southwest ever evolves, it will—insofar as academic influences are concerned—evolve from one who has savored the backgrounds of Texas that are preserved in the Texas Collection.

Adios. I hope this course has opened some windows for you and has enabled you to relate yourself more harmoniously, intelligently, and pleasurably to your environment.—From Dobie's final exam, Eng. 342, Life and Literature of the Southwest

Acknowledgments

S O MANY GOOD PEOPLE have opened doors to Dobie for me, sharing their experiences and perspectives. I'm also indebted to many friends and colleagues who have offered support and encouragement along the way. The generosity of all of these people helped create this book. Among those I'd like to thank are Bill and Sally Wittliff, who had the vision to save Dobie's remaining literary papers and establish the Wittliff Collections at Texas State University.

Thanks also to Dudley and Saza Dobie, Marcelle Dobie Smith, and other members of the Dobie family who have been so supportive and generous with their time and feedback over the years. This book also benefited from significant Dobie print collections donated to the Wittliff Collections by Al Lowman in 2004 and Patti Clark in 2017–18.

I'm also grateful to my colleagues at the Wittliff Collections for creating such a wonderfully nurturing work environment: David Coleman, Carla Ellard, Lauren Goodley, Lyda Guz, Tabitha Henderson, Ramona Kelly, Elizabeth Moeller, Hector Saldaña, Katie Salzmann, Amanda Scott, Karen Sigler, Mark Willenborg.

Many friends and writers have inspired and guided my thinking on Dobie over the years: Marc Simmons, Mark and Linda Busby, Sam and Rebecca Pfiester, Bill Minutaglio and Holly Williams, Sergio Troncoso, W. K. Stratton, Carmen Tafolla, Cary Clack, Robert Flynn (who broke horses for Dobie's grandfather), Ann and Rob Weisgarber, Becky Duval Reese, Ron and Elaine Querry, Lonn and Dedie Taylor, Wes Ferguson, Michael Adams, Bill Sibley, Mary Margaret Campbell, Judy Alter, Fran Vick, Sarah

Bird, Sandra Cisneros, Chip Dameron, John Phillip Santos, Naomi Shihab Nye, Ben Fountain, Stephen Harrigan, Elizabeth Crook, Connie Todd, Dick Holland, Gwynedd Cannan, Bob Barton, Dot Moore, Michael Barnes, Tom Zigal, Eddie Wilson, David Marion Wilkinson, Christopher Cook, Jesse Sublett, Cathy Supple, Gardner Smith, and Jan Reid.

I'm also thankful to these excellent writers and good friends who made time to read and comment on this book: Stephen Harrigan, Naomi Shihab Nye, John Rechy, and John Phillip Santos.

I'm grateful to Rachel Harris and Charis Wilson for having reached out to me about Charis's and Edward Weston's encounter with Dobie, and for alerting me that Weston, one of America's greatest photographers, had "graphlexed Dobie" at the Dobie home in Austin in 1943. I eventually tracked that photograph down at the Center for Creative Photography at the University of Arizona, where Weston's archive is held. Anyone who marvels at the magnificent Dobie image on the cover of this book needs to know that it is possible only because of the Center for Creative Photography's fine staff, which includes Shandi Wagner, Deidre Thompson, and Alexis Peregoy.

I'd also like to thank the excellent staff at Texas A&M University Press, who were so enthusiastic and supportive of this project from the beginning: Shannon Davies, Thom Lemmons, Gayla Christiansen, Mary Ann Jacob, Kristie Lee, Christine Brown, Kathryn Lloyd, Katie Duelm, Patricia Clabaugh, and everyone else at the press. I'm also deeply grateful to my excellent copyeditor, Dawn Hall.

Finally, with much love and gratitude to my wife, Georgia, daughters Natalie and Lucia, and good dogs Truman and Ralfred.

Story Credits

1. Coyote Wisdom

"This, I Believe"

From "This, I Believe," as cited in the essay. Supplemented by many individual (one-sentence) quotes from across the breadth of Dobie's work.

"How My Life Took Its Turn"

From *Some Part of Myself*. Originally published by Little, Brown, 1967. Reprinted by the University of Texas Press, 1980. Now out of print.

"Voice of the Coyote"

Primarily from *The Voice of the Coyote*. Originally published by Little, Brown, 1949. Reprinted by Bison Books/University of Nebraska Press, 2006. Supplemented with "The Coyote's Charm," *Audubon*, January–February 1963, and "The Humanity of Brother Coyote," *Defenders of Wildlife*, January 1964.

2. On the Trail with a Storyteller

"Across the Bolsón de Mapimí: Echoes of the Comanche War Trail"

From *Tongues of the Monte*. Originally published by Little, Brown, 1947. Reprinted by the University of Texas Press, 1980. Now out of print.

"Charles Goodnight of Amplitude"

From *Cow People*. Originally published by Little, Brown, 1964. Reprinted by the University of Texas Press, 1981. Now a print-on-demand title.

"Searching for Lost Tayopa"

From *Apache Gold and Yaqui Silver*. Originally published by Little, Brown, 1939. Reprinted by the University of Texas Press, 1985. Now a print-on-demand title.

"The Last of the Mountain Men"

Primarily from "On Ben Lilly," in *True West*. November–December 1963. In that account Dobie rewrote and expanded his original account of meeting Ben Lilly. Selections from that piece were combined with additional material from the original book: *The Ben Lilly Legend*, originally published by Little, Brown, 1950. Reprinted by the University of Texas Press, 1982. Now a print-on-demand title.

"On the Trail of the Panther"

Originally published as "Lion Markers" in *Country Gentleman* magazine, May 1928.

3. Open Range Tales

"Snowdrift: The Hunt for Montana's Last Wolf"

Originally published as "Snowdrift: Lonest of All Lone Wolves" in *Outdoor Life*, April 1952.

"The Dream That Saved Wilbarger"

From *Tales of Old-Time Texas*. Originally published by Little, Brown, 1955. Reprinted by the University of Texas Press, 1984. Now a print-on-demand title.

"Sancho, the Tamale-Loving Longhorn"

From *The Longhorns*. Originally published by Little, Brown, 1941. Reprinted by the University of Texas Press, 1982. Now a print-on-demand title. The introduction for this selection comes from two Dobie newspaper columns: *Dallas Morning News*, January 1, 1940, and the *Austin American,* November 6, 1960.

4. The Southwestern Tempo

"Earth Rhythms and the Southwestern Tempo"

From "Cow Country Tempo," *Texas Quarterly*, 1964. Also Dobie newspaper column, *Dallas Morning News*, December 12, 1943, and Dobie's preface for *A Treasury of Western Folk-Lore*, edited by B. A. Botkin. Crown Publishers, 1951.

"The Mesquite"

From *Natural History*, May 1943. Also *Arizona Highways*, November 1941; *Southwestern Sheep and Goat Raiser*, December 1, 1938; *Southern Agriculturalist*, August 1947.

"What Every Curandera Knows"

From unpublished typescript, J. Frank Dobie Papers, Wittliff Collections, Texas State University, Box 11, folder 6. Dated March 26, 1937. The small insertion (on "urine" cures) comes from Dobie's "Piss & Vinegar" file, also unpublished.

"The Madstone Cure"

From "Madstones and Hydrophobia Skunks," *Southwest Review*, Winter 1958.

"Praying for Rain"

From *Cow People.* Originally published by Little, Brown, 1964. Reprinted by the University of Texas Press, 1981. Now a print-on-demand title. Also from *Guide to Life and Literature of the Southwest* (public domain.)

"The Campfire"

From "The Fire," *Texas Game and Fish* magazine, June 1962.

5. The Brush Country

"A Plot of Earth"

Originally published in *Southwest Review*, Spring 1953. Later published in *Some Part of Myself.* Little, Brown, 1967. Reprinted by the University of Texas Press, 1980. Now out of print.

"The Buried Gold at Fort Ramirez"

From *Coronado's Children: Tales of Lost Mines and Buried Treasures of the Southwest.* Originally printed by South West Press, 1930. Reprinted by the University of Texas Press, 1978. Now a print-on-demand title.

"I Remember Buck"

From *The Mustangs.* Originally published by Little, Brown, 1952. Reprinted by Bison Books/University of Nebraska Press, 2005.

6. Wild and Free

"Cedar Fever"

From J. Frank Dobie Papers, Wittliff Collections, as indicated in given dates. Also from the cited article published in the *Austin Statesman*, January 25, 1928, and Dobie's letter to the *Statesman* in that same issue.

"The Beginnings of Big Bend National Park"

From "The Texan Part of Texas," *Nature*, 1930.

"The Longhorn's Dying Bellow"

From *The Cattleman* (official publication of the Texas and Southwestern Cattle Raisers Association), March 1926.

"Stompedes"

From *The Longhorns.* Originally published by Little, Brown, 1941. Reprinted by the University of Texas Press, 1982. Now a print-on-demand title.

"Wild and Free"

From *The Mustangs.* Originally published by Little, Brown, 1952. Reprinted by Bison Books/University of Nebraska Press, 2005.

"The Paisano, Our Fellow Countryman"

From *In the Shadow of History*, the Texas Folk-Lore Society, 1939. *Texas Parade*, October 1953, and *Frontier Times*, Fall 1961.

7. Europe Amid Two World Wars

" . . . From Two Letters to Bertha Dobie during World War I"
J. Frank Dobie Papers, Wittliff Collections, Box 17.
"A Day with the Basques"
From *Southwest Review*, vol. 13, no. 4 (1927).
"Birds under Bombs: In England during World War II"
From *A Texan in England*, Little, Brown, 1945, and "A Texan Teaches American History at Cambridge University," *National Geographic*, April 1946.
"The Tom Paine Fortress over England," *Freethinker*, July 1944, and several Dobie weekly newspaper columns from 1943 to 1945.
"Across the Rhine: Travels in Postwar Germany"
From "What I Saw Across the Rhine," *National Geographic*, January 1947, and several Dobie weekly newspaper columns between March and June 1946.

8. Texas Needs Brains

"Texas Needs Brains"
From *The Texas Ranger*, October 1946, and "Texas," in *Transatlantic*, November 1943.
"True Patriots and Pappy O'Daniel"
From Dobie weekly newspaper columns: November 8, 1942; June 21, 1942; October 11, 1942.
"Only a Man with Eyes in the Back of His Head . . ."
From several Dobie weekly newspaper columns during World War II, including December 31, 1944; May 20, 1945; April 22, 1945; September 3, 1944; and January 31, 1943.
"Dobie on Civil Rights"
From Dobie weekly newspaper columns of March 1945 and newspaper stories, March 18, 1945. Dobie speech to NAACP, *Texas Spectator*, December 1946.
"The Difference between Liberals and Reactionaries"
From several Dobie weekly newspaper columns: June 17, 1951; November 2, 1952; January 10, 1954; April 20, 1952; December 3, 1944; December 29, 1957.
"On Censorship"
From *Southwest Review*, Summer 1962, and Dobie newspaper column, February 24, 1963.

9. Life and Literature of the Southwest

"Professional Educators and the 'Unctuous Elaboration of the Obvious'"
From "No Idea Where I Was Going" and "A Schoolteacher in Alpine," both in *Some Part of Myself*. Originally published by Little, Brown, 1967. Reprinted

by the University of Texas Press, 1980. Now out of print. Additional material from "Out of Regionalism, a Larger View," *Saturday Review*, May 21, 1960.

"On the Texas Institute of Letters"

From *A Brief History and Directory, the Texas Institute of Letters, 1936–1956* (privately printed).

"Along the Devil's River—and Away from the Cedar Pollen"

Newspaper column, February 16, 1947.

"Change, Change, Change"

Texas Observer, January 8, 1959.

"Two Texas Barbecues, Sixty Years Apart"

Newspaper column, May 12, 1963.

"The Writer and His Region"

From *Guide to Life and Literature of the Southwest* (public domain) and "The Writer and His Region," *Southwest Review*, Spring 1950.

"A Corner Forever Texas"

From "The Alcade," *University of Texas Alumni* magazine, April 1938.